MAKE A CHRISTMAS WISH

Julia Williams has always made up stories in her head, and until recently she thought everyone else did too. She grew up in London, one of eight children, including a twin sister. She was a children's editor at Scholastic for several years before going freelance after the birth of her second child. It was then she decided to try her hand at writing. The result, her debut novel, *Pastures New*, was a bestseller and has sold across Europe.

To find out more about Julia go to her website at www.juliawilliamsauthor.com or follow Julia on Twitter @JCCWilliams.

By the same author:

Pastures New
Strictly Love
Last Christmas
The Bridesmaid Pact
The Summer Season
A Merry Little Christmas
Midsummer Magic
Coming Home for Christmas
A Hope Christmas Love Story

Make a Christmas Wish

JULIA WILLIAMS

AVON

AVON

A division of HarperCollins*Publishers*
1 London Bridge Street,
London SE1 9GF

www.harpercollins.co.uk

A Paperback Original 2015

1

Copyright © Julia Williams 2015

Julia Williams asserts the moral right to
be identified as the author of this work

A catalogue record for this book is
available from the British Library

ISBN-13: 978-1-84756-359-0

Set in Minion by Palimpsest Book Production Limited,
Falkirk, Stirlingshire

Printed and bound in Great Britain by
Clays Ltd, St Ives plc

To my fabulous twin, Virginia Moffatt,
my first reader and greatest cheerleader.
About time too xxx

Two Weeks till Christmas

Joe's Notebook

- *What makes a mother?*
- *A mother cooks*
- *A mother picks me up from college*
- *A mother falls asleep in the afternoon*
- *A mother is always there.*

When I was little my mum always told me to look at the brightest star in the sky and make a Christmas wish, and it would come true.

The brightest star in the sky is Polaris: the North Star, the star that guides travellers home.

Tonight I looked through my telescope and made my Christmas wish.

Maybe Polaris can guide my mum and bring her back home.

Then we can be a family again.

Part One

Christmas Past

Christmas Past

Livvy

I come to in the car park, sitting on the ground, feeling very confused. I remember the car, the kid, and an incredibly painful bang on the head, and lots of people flapping around me, but nothing else. But that must have been hours ago. It's dark now, and I am alone and I can't quite remember why I am still here. Did they leave me behind? Why didn't they take me to hospital? That's weird. I feel in my pockets for my mobile. I must ring Adam, my husband. He and our son Joe will be so worried. That reminds me, I'm cross with Adam for some reason, but I can't think why. I can't find my phone. I must have dropped it when the car hit me.

The. Car. Hit. Me.

I stop for a moment and try and absorb the logic of this. If the car hit me, why am I not hurt? And why am I still here? And why is it dark? – Oh no . . .

Adam

When I hear my wife is critically ill in hospital I'm standing out at the front of our office having a surreptitious conversation with Emily – I don't want everyone at work knowing

5

what's gone on. It doesn't make me proud to know how secretive I've become in the last few months.

'How did she find out?' asks Emily in a tense whisper.

'I don't know,' I say. 'That's not really the point any more.'

'This changes everything,' says Emily.

I sigh. 'I know. Still, it had to come out some time, but I wish I'd been the one to tell her.' I don't know. I've wanted to, so many times in the last few months, as my home life has been deteriorating to beyond even what I could possibly have imagined. During that time Emily had become the one beacon of light in my life. But would I have ever found the courage? And then there's our son Joe of course. What on earth is this going to do to Joe? Guilt and misery lodge uncomfortably in my stomach. We've had some rotten Christmases in the past, but this one could be shaping up to be a humdinger.

'Adam, there you are! I've been looking for you everywhere.' It's my PA, Marigold. She looks really upset. The words come tumbling out of her so fast I can't quite take them in. 'I'm so sorry, Adam, but you have to go to the hospital. There's been an accident. Livvy's been badly hurt.'

'What?' I'm not sure I've heard correctly. 'Emily, I've got to go, Livvy crisis.'

'You have to go,' Marigold says frantically. '*Now*. She's in the hospital.'

I'm ashamed to say that my first thought is that Livvy's pulling a stunt – her way of getting back at me. But when I finally speak to someone at the hospital, it seems she really has had a bad accident. 'I'm sorry to tell you she's in a critical condition, Mr Carmichael,' says the doctor. 'I suggest you come immediately.'

I dither about whether to pick Joe up or not. How will

he react? But if things are as bad as they say, will Joe forgive me for leaving him behind? So, in the end, I grab him from his sixth-form college, and we get to the hospital to discover that Livvy is in Resus. We're shown into a family room, which feels ominous. My heart is pounding and I feel really sick. Nobody will tell us anything, but everyone speaks in hushed tones, and I am beginning to fear the worst.

Livvy

I start to remember. It was two weeks until Christmas Day and I was on my way to Lidl to get some Christmas shopping, still staggering from the news I'd just heard. Adam, my lovely husband Adam, had been unfaithful to me. I mean, I knew we had our problems, and I'd felt for a while that he'd been quite distant, but Adam, having an affair? I was reeling with shock, and mad as hell. There I'd been, sorting out a lovely Christmas for us, and he'd been playing away.

As I got out of the car, a part of my brain was still calmly planning our Christmas dinner, while the other part was concentrating on angrily texting Adam: *You bastard, how could you?* Talk about multitasking. I knew how and why he could of course – I'd given him enough cause over the years.

I was so angry I wasn't paying attention, so I foolishly stepped into the road in front of a car driven by a 17-year-old learner driver whose dad had taken him to Lidl's car park to practise safely. The poor lad panicked when he saw me, and accelerated instead of braking. I could see his terrified face staring frantically from the dashboard, as to my horror I realized the car was speeding towards me, and I could do nothing to stop it.

I didn't feel any pain on impact, but the car hit me side

on, spun out of control and crashed into the recycling bins. I flew through the air and landed head first into the trolley man who was collecting stray trolleys abandoned by lazy shoppers. I'd have got away with a few breaks and nothing more if it hadn't been for the damned trolleys. Unfortunately for me, I received a glancing blow to the head, which resulted in a haematoma.

Just my luck.

I felt a moment of excruciating pain, and then people gathered excitedly around me, and the boy driving the car was wailing loudly, 'What have I done?'

I could just make out the sounds of sirens in the background before everything faded to darkness. The last sound I heard was the music blaring from the store: 'Simply Having a Wonderful Christmas Time'. Just peachy.

The next thing I knew I was lying on a stretcher and the lights were hurting my eyes. I seemed to be in a vehicle of some kind and we were going at a hell of a lick. I heard a voice saying, 'Livvy, stay with me,' before everything faded again.

When I came to I felt as though I was floating in a dream-like state. I couldn't quite work out where I was, until I looked down and saw lots of people dressed in blue overalls, wearing face masks and looking grave. They were standing over a body. I was beyond spooked: what the hell was going on?

'And clear!' someone said, and a charge went through the body, but nothing happened.

The man holding the defibrillator shook his head and someone said, 'Time of death: two fifteen p.m.'

Gradually they moved away from the body, unclipping monitors and drips, and suddenly I realized I was looking down at myself.

What just happened? I was thinking. *I can't be . . . can I?*

I must be having some kind of strange dream. In a moment Adam and Joe are going to be by my side and I will wake up and everything will be OK.

Adam

Telling Joe I'm off to fetch us a hot drink I go out to the A & E reception desk to ask if there's any news, but no one can tell me anything. When I'm coming back with a weak hot chocolate for Joe and a tepid coffee for me, I overhear one of the nurses say something about how long they've been working on her, and my alarm rises. Oh God, what is happening? One moment I'd been thinking the worst of my problems was facing up to leaving Livvy and now – I seem to be caught in a terrible, unbelievable nightmare. However unhappy we've been together, I don't want anything to happen to Livvy. I feel I am standing on the edge of a swirling abyss, unsure where my future lies.

Guilt, remorse and an overpowering sorrow threaten to overwhelm me but I am trying to hold it together for Joe's sake. Yet, when he eventually asks, 'Mum is going to be all right isn't she?' I have nothing to offer.

'I don't know, Joe,' I say, sipping my insipid coffee and feeling sick with fear and anxiety. This can't be happening to Livvy. It just can't.

But it is. As soon as the nurse comes into the room, I know, without her saying.

I make out the words 'I'm so sorry,' but I don't really hear them, and I'm aware that Joe is rocking back and forth. I try to hug him, but he pushes me away, and then I hear a terrible howl.

It is some moments before I realize it's coming from me.

There is a shout from somewhere, and suddenly I feel as though I have been yanked from the room I am in, and now I am floating in another, smaller white room, where a nurse is sitting down with a shocked-looking Adam and Joe, saying, 'I am so so sorry.'

Joe is rocking backwards and forwards and I can feel his distress. I try to go to him, but I can't reach him. I can feel the pain coming from him in waves, pain beyond anything that I have ever felt before, and I find myself howling with him. And then I hear Adam break down and I can see into his jumbled thoughts. One thing stands out very clearly: he is very very sorry and he loves me very much. Whatever else he has done to me, losing me has cost him dear.

Suddenly I am dragged into a long dark tunnel. I am screaming and shouting, 'Bring me back! I need to go back!' but to no avail. The darkness overtakes me, and after that there is nothing.

And here, now, in the car park in the dark, I hear a voice pipe up beside me: 'And the penny drops . . .'

I would have jumped out of my skin if I'd had any to jump out of. I look around suspiciously in the dark, but I can't see anything.

'Oh my God, I'm—'

''Fraid so,' says the voice cheerily.

'Dead?'

'Very,' says the voice.

This is getting extremely weird.

'Who are you?' I say.

'A friend,' purrs the voice, which doesn't exactly reassure me.

I look around me at the empty car park. I can't quite believe it: I'm still here. I'm still standing. I feel the same. How can I be *dead*?

'Common reaction,' is the response. 'But sorry, you've definitely shuffled off your mortal coil.'

'Aren't there supposed to be choirs of angels or something?' I say. If I have really died, shouldn't I be entitled to a fanfare of sorts?

'That's not quite how it works,' says the voice smugly.

I'm beginning to dislike its owner intensely.

'Why am I here, then?' I ask.

'Where do I start? You're still here, because you're not ready to pass over yet.'

'What do you mean?' I am instantly on edge. 'Why do I get to hang about? If I'm dead, why can't I just go on to wherever I'm supposed to go in peace?'

'In the words of the trade, you have unfinished business.'

'Damn right I have unfinished business,' I say. 'This is ridiculous. I have to get back to my husband and son. They need me. I want to talk to someone in charge.'

'Afraid you're stuck with me,' says the voice patiently. 'And your attitude ought to give you a clue.'

'What's wrong with my attitude?' I say. 'I'm a nice person. There's nothing wrong with me.'

'Well, for a start, why are you so angry all the time?'

I bristle again. I've been carrying my anger around for so long, I can barely remember sometimes what I'm so furious about. It's the sort of thing Adam has been saying to me for years, and I've always thought he was exaggerating. But now I'm here alone in this car park, apparently dead, with a disembodied voice for company, I think perhaps he has a point. There's a dark pool of fury inside me, something I've suppressed for years and one of a

11

number of places I don't want to go. But I am not going to tell the voice *that*.

'Who are you?' I say instead and, to my astonishment, a mangy-looking black cat wanders up and perches on a bin.

'Call me Malachi,' says the cat, stretching out its paws. 'I'm your spirit guide.' This is not in the slightest bit reassuring.

I must be delusional. It's the bang on the head. I've fabricated that I'm dead and in a car park talking to a cat. In a moment I'll wake up in hospital and see Adam and Joe peering worriedly at me and everything will be normal again.

'Right, this has gone beyond a joke,' I say. 'I am going to leave now.'

'You can try,' says Malachi, 'but you won't get very far. You need to listen to what I say. Just because you're dead doesn't mean you can ignore the rules.'

'I can't be dead,' I wail again. 'This isn't happening.'

'Sorry to disappoint, but you're very very dead. Anyway, in the situation you find yourself in, what's so odd about talking to a cat? This isn't who I really am. Just a convenient shape I take on in moments like this. I could be a tramp, but the police would probably move me on. A cat's more convenient. No one pays much attention to a cat scavenging through the bins at midnight. More to the point, I'm here to help you.'

'Why?' I say suspiciously.

'Because it's my job,' says the cat wearily. 'Though, quite frankly, I've had easier material to work with.'

'What do you mean by that?' I say, furious again.

'Well, let's start with untangling the mess you've made of your life.'

12

'I haven't made a mess of my life,' I protest. 'I liked my life. I'd really like it back please.'

'Too late for that,' says Malachi. 'But we can put a few things right if you like. We can start with your past.'

'Suppose I don't want to,' I object. I make a point of never looking back and wondering if I could have done things differently. That way madness lies, if you ask me.

'Fair enough,' says the cat. 'But I can't help you till you want to be helped. If you're not prepared to listen to me, you'll be stuck here until you're ready to move on.'

'I refuse to listen to this,' I say. 'Any minute now I'm going to wake up and this will have been a horrible nightmare.'

'Your choice,' he purrs. 'You stay here guarding the bins then. Let me know when you're ready. *I've* got better things to do with my time.'

With a flick of his tail he is gone. And I am left here alone, floating around Lidl's car park, trapped on the very spot where I died.

Emily

Emily Harris hadn't been sure whether to go to Livvy Carmichael's funeral or not. She knew Adam wouldn't be able to talk to her, but she wanted to support him anyway. She'd tentatively texted him to let him know she'd be there, but he hadn't texted back. She had no idea what that meant. They'd barely spoken since the awful night when he'd rung her to tell her what had happened. She had no place in this. Adam had to be there for Joe, and Emily knew in her heart that might mean whatever they'd had together could be finished forever. She felt desperately sad that Livvy was dead – no one deserved such an end, not even her rival who had caused Adam untold pain for years. But now Livvy was gone she didn't know where it left her and Adam. Maybe he was only with her because everything had been so hard for him. Their love might fade away in the fallout from this terrible tragedy. It was shitty and miserable but there was nothing she could do.

Emily crept into the back of the packed church. The mood was sombre, and she felt blacker than she'd ever felt in her life. Poor Livvy. What a godawful thing to have happened. Poor Joe. Poor Adam. Poor bloody everybody.

The organ started to play 'The Lord's my Shepherd', and everyone rose. In a blur, Emily watched Adam, his fair head bowed, looking blankly ahead escorting Joe, his skinny frame hunched and miserable, and a small fair-haired woman, who must be Livvy's mum, Felicity, as they followed the coffin down the aisle. The three of them clung to each other, for support, and Emily felt more than ever that she had no right to be here. She nearly turned and fled, but Adam glanced up at her as he walked past and gave her a quick and grateful smile. He looked so sombre and sad. Emily wished beyond anything she could be by his side.

The funeral passed in a blur. Felicity got up and read something about Death not being the end in such a dignified manner, Emily felt a lump rise in her throat. She had a sudden terrible memory of her own mother's funeral, and marvelled at Felicity's courage. Emily couldn't do anything but sob that day; to be able to read for your own daughter and not break down took some doing.

Adam also read a passage about love. He didn't look at the congregation, focusing his attention on getting every word out. Emily could see what it cost him, and longed to be with him to comfort him. And then Joe got up, and said simply. 'My mum was the best. She looked after me, and now she's gone. And I miss her.'

There wasn't a dry eye in the church after that, and the rest of the service was punctuated with people sobbing. After it was over, Emily escaped as quickly as she could. The family were going on to a private burial, and she had no intention of attending the wake.

A crowd of people clustered around Joe, Adam and Felicity, so Emily walked down the path to the road where her car was parked. She'd done what she came to do. Although Emily had thought what she and Adam had was special, Livvy being dead altered things. Her rival was gone, but not in a way anyone would have wanted. Was Adam's love for her enough to withstand his grief? All Emily could do was wait and see if Adam would come back to her.

As she was unlocking the car door, she heard a shout, 'Emily, wait.'

It was Adam. The temptation to hug him was immense, but Emily hung back.

'I just wanted to say thanks,' he said. 'It meant a lot that you came.'

'Of course I came,' said Emily. 'How are you bearing up?'

'Not well,' said Adam. He looked tired and strained.

'You'd better get back,' said Emily uneasily. 'People might talk.'

'I'm not sure that matters any more.'

'You have Joe to think of,' she pointed out.

'I know,' said Adam. 'Emily, you do understand, don't you? Joe has to be my priority right now. And – well – the next few months, I might not be able to see you, and I wanted to say it won't be because I don't want to.'

'Oh Adam,' said Emily. 'Of course I understand.'

15

They were both a bit weepy now.

She could see the funeral party breaking up.

'You have to go, Adam,' she said. 'But if you ever need me, you know where I am.'

'I'll be in touch,' he said.

'When you're ready,' said Emily. Who knew how easy that would be?

'I mean it,' he said. 'I know this is a big ask, but please – can you wait for me?'

With that he was gone, and Emily got in her car and drove home, wondering if she'd ever see him again, but hoping more than she'd ever hoped before that she would.

Livvy

I spend a long time in a foggy blur, not entirely sure where the days, nights and months go to, but unable to reach out to anyone I love, to at least see if they're doing OK. I get the odd vague impulse – round the time of my funeral, I can feel Joe's distress, and occasionally I sense that Adam is trying to talk to me from somewhere, but it's like a broken radio wave, it comes to me from such a distance, I am not even sure it is *him*. In the midst of the fog I feel a terrible pain and sense of loss. There's something I should be doing, but I don't know what it is.

And then . . .

On a winter's night when a storm is raging in my car park, suddenly I can hear Joe in my head. I can feel his confusion clamouring in my brain.

'So is Emily my new mum, Dad?' he asks.

Who the hell is Emily? And why is Adam looking for a new mum for Joe?

'Over my dead body,' I snarl, and suddenly it's as if a whirlwind has torn me from the car park.

What the—? I'm standing in my front room, with no clue how I got there. I am stunned but delighted. Finally I'm out of that damned car park. Then I look around me and see Adam, Joe, and a pretty dark-haired woman I don't know, but vaguely recognize, decorating the Christmas tree.

A strange woman in my house. With Adam. And Joe. What on earth is going on?

Christmas Past

Livid doesn't cover it. I hurl myself at the dark-haired woman in MY front room in a fury.

'Who the hell are you?' I yell. 'What are you doing here? In my house, in my life?'

I want her to be terrified. I want her to react. But all that happens is the woman shivers, and says, 'That's odd. I just felt someone walking over my grave.'

Crap, I can't even haunt people properly. All I want is for Adam and Joe to see me, to know I'm there, to want me back, the way I want them back.

'Oh quit feeling sorry for yourself.' Malachi hasn't gone away. Oh good. 'If you'd not turned your back on me a year ago all this would be sorted by now. They do need you and you need them, but possibly not in the way you think.'

'What do you mean?' Why does Malachi have to talk in riddles?

'You have things to sort out, things to put right.'

'What are you talking about?' I'd blush with fury if I could.

'You really don't know?' says Malachi. 'Here, let me show you . . .'

With a jolt, I'm awake. With a living breathing human body. I'd forgotten how good it is, to feel and see and taste and smell. Wait. I remember this. I look around me. I'm sitting in a hospital bed, watching my newborn baby asleep in his cot. A sudden rush of love – hormones? – flows through me. Here is my baby at last, after all the false starts. My miracle baby.

But where is Adam? We've waited so long for this baby, been through so much, and he's not here.

Then I remember. I've gone into early labour and Adam's abroad. He thought we had time. We both did, but I've ended up giving birth alone, among strangers, in this unforgiving place. The midwives have been kind, but overworked, and Mum is away visiting friends, and can't get here till tomorrow. I have never felt so lonely. And now I'm lying on a hospital bed, and my baby is waking up and I can't reach him. Because of my epidural I can't get out of bed. I'm tired and hungry and sad and overwhelmed. This is not how it was meant to be. How can I be sad on the happiest day of my life?

When the baby starts to cry, I don't know what to do. I ring the buzzer but no one comes. I'm here on my own with a crying baby, and I feel like crying too. And I know it's unfair of me, but I'm very angry with Adam. But then, miraculously, Adam is here. He's dropped everything and flown home as soon as he could, just to be by my side. He's so happy about the baby, and so pleased to see me, I forget my anger, and bury it deep. Nothing matters now but us and our new son.

And then I'm back in the future, where I'm dead, and talking to a mangy black cat. I can still feel the anger burning in the back of my throat. I've been angry with Adam so long, I'd forgotten when and where it began. Was it really then? The day that Joe was born?

I stare disconsolately at Adam and Joe and their new friend.

'So what do I do now?' I say.

'First,' says Malachi, 'you need to get their attention.'

This Year

Two Weeks before Christmas

Adam

A year ago? How can it be a year since my world imploded so spectacularly? As if it wasn't fucked up enough.

Before Livvy died, everything was going to be so different. I wasn't proud of myself for doing it, but I had met and fallen in love with Emily. I'd been planning to tell her, but then Livvy found out anyway: *You bastard. How could you?* The very last words my wife said to me. In the circumstances, they were no more than I deserved, though Emily tells me I'm too hard on myself. But if . . . if I'd supported her more in the beginning, if I'd understood the toll of looking after Joe had exacted on her . . . My world is full of ifs.

I can remember the day I first met Livvy as clearly as if it was yesterday. It was our first term at uni in Manchester, and there was this bright, vivid, red-headed girl standing in the student bar, downing shots in a competition and drinking all the boys under the table. I was too shy to talk to her that first night, but gradually I found myself more and more drawn to her, and to my surprise my interest was reciprocated. It was Livvy who took the initiative from the first, kissing me suddenly and fiercely one night when we'd sat out all evening staring at the stars together. She was so unlike anyone I'd met: a free spirit, spontaneous in a way I wasn't. She breathed life into me, showing me there was more than the staid and rather restrictive outlook my parents had given me. It was a magical, wonderful time. Since she's died, I often think of those days and wonder how it could have gone so badly wrong.

But it did, and instead I've spent the last year picking up the pieces of my life. Even though our marriage was a sham by the end, I was devastated when Livvy died. I never got to say sorry that a love that had started out with such hope and promise had disintegrated in the way it did, and now there was no possibility of ever putting it right.

And now here we are and it's coming up for Christmas again, and I owe it to Joe to try and make things cheerful even though it's the last thing I feel like doing. I'm never sure how much of what's happened he's taken in, and wonder what is going on inside his head. He says things like, 'My mum is dead,' deadpan to complete strangers, showing no emotion. Emily says we just have to support him the best we can. So today, though I'm not sure I have the stomach for Christmas decorations (last year the lights seemed to twinkle malevolently at me as if proof of my guilt), Emily and I are putting up the Christmas tree. We always put the tree up a fortnight before Christmas, and Joe with his obsessive need for order has had it written on the calendar for weeks.

Actually, it turns out to be fun. It's been a really blowy day, and after Joe and I put flowers on Livvy's grave first thing, we went for a wet walk down by the canal. We get back home and make hot chocolate and sit by the fire drinking it, feeling cosy and warm, till Joe starts insisting it's time to decorate the tree. I'd thought he might not want to do it today, on the anniversary, but he is insistent. 'We always decorate the tree two weeks before Christmas,' he says. 'Mum won't like it if we don't.'

It makes my heart ache to hear him speak about her in such a matter-of-fact way. He must be grieving for Livvy, but it's hard for him to articulate it.

'Five thirty,' Joe says now, pointing at his watch – time is very important to him – 'if we don't do it soon, it will be dinner time and too late.'

'OK, Joe,' I say, 'let's get on with it.'

The wind is howling down the chimney now, and the kitchen door rattles. This is an old house, with ill-fitting doors and windows. We've always meant to get double glazing, but I like the old sash windows, and wooden frames. They give the place character, though on a night like tonight I'm not grateful for the draughts blowing through the house.

Joe in his methodical way is sorting out how to decorate the tree. After the lights go up, he insists that certain decorations, like the Santa he made for us when he was five, and the reindeer Livvy once bought him at a Christmas market, take pride of place. Then he organizes the baubles according to a colour scheme: gold, red, silver hung in serried rows round the tree. This is something Livvy used to do with him, and I had no idea he had it down to such a fine art. Emily and I are there to do things the way Joe likes them, and I am finding it quite soothing.

After the baubles, Joe makes us wrap the tree in tinsel – he won't let us use red because 'it doesn't look right' – and I mean literally wrap it. It is starting to look overloaded, but he won't hear of us taking any off.

We've just put the last bit of tinsel on the tree, when Joe suddenly looks at Emily in that disconcerting way he has and asks, 'Are you my mother now?'

Oh God. I'm not ready for this.

I have tried really hard to introduce Emily into our lives slowly. Luckily Joe already knows her from the swimming club we go to on a Monday evening. Joe was always so full of energy in the evenings, I started taking him as a way to tire him out before he went to bed. Being Joe he takes it very seriously, and won't leave the pool till he's completed a hundred lengths.

It was there that I first met Emily. After a messy divorce, she took up swimming, not only to get fit, but, she told me later, to do something positive for her. I swam to disperse my demons. The pool was the one place where I forgot about everything, and it relaxed me. And every week there was this pretty petite brunette in a red cap and black costume, swimming in the same lane as me. Somehow we bonded at the deep end, and though we never intended it to, one thing led to another.

A huge gust of wind howls down the chimney, making the flames flare up, and I feel a whoosh of cold furious negative energy hit me right in the solar plexus. At the same time the lights on the Christmas tree flicker on and off. The other two don't seem to notice, as they're engrossed in putting the rest of the decs away. I go and fiddle with the plug and the lights come back on.

Emily stands back and looks at the tree, 'There, doesn't that look lovely?' she says.

Joe smiles.

'Now we can start Christmas,' he says.

Livvy

'How do I do that?' I say.

'You're a ghost,' explains Malachi. 'You have powers, try them out.'

'What, like this?' I say, and I let out a huge scream that

24

gratifyingly causes the Christmas tree lights to flicker and go out.

'What the–?' Adam says, going to the plug and switching them back on.

Now I've got their attention. I run through the house screaming at the top of my voice, causing lights to go on and off, but all that happens is that Emily jokes about power surges and Adam says, 'Maybe there's a problem with the wiring. I'll call an electrician in the morning. We must get it sorted before Christmas.'

I've run out of steam. Defeated, I go out into the garden, and stare disconsolately at the moon.

'Well, that was a waste of time,' I say as Malachi lopes up next to me again.

'You're not a very patient person are you?' he says. 'It will take time.'

'Why can't they see me?' I say. I so want Adam and Joe to know I'm here. I've turned away from the moon and am staring in at the lounge, where Joe looks happy to be with Adam and his new woman. I feel shut out and cold and sorry for myself. Why am I still here, if none of them need me? Joe clearly likes the new woman otherwise he wouldn't be decorating the tree with her. He's particular like that. I thought maybe I'd hung around for Joe. But it turns out he is even less like other people than I thought, and doing quite well without me. It reminds me of all the times I felt so useless as a mum even though I tried so hard to get it right; now I'm dead, I'm worse than useless. I stare through the window and the memories come crowding in.

I think it was that first Christmas with Joe when I finally realized something was wrong with him. Always a difficult baby, at nearly a year old he still wasn't sleeping through the night, and I found it difficult to bond with him. He

25

was often fractious when he was awake and I was exhausted with the effort of looking after him. I felt guilty – after the miscarriages I should have been thrilled with my new baby – but when I mentioned it to Adam, he told me I was imagining things.

'All babies cry,' he said. Like *he* knew anything about it. He was working really hard to pay off our crippling mortgage, spending long hours away from home, frequently away on business. It wasn't his fault; he just couldn't see how hard it was for me.

'Yes, but not like this,' I said.

Adam didn't listen. No one listened. My nearly retired doctor, who was kind, but overworked, had I think dismissed me as a neurotic mother. Not difficult after those early weeks when I cried all the time and was eventually diagnosed with postnatal depression. My mother always thought I looked at the cup half empty. My friends thought I just had a difficult baby.

But that Christmas it all changed, at which point even Adam had to believe me.

That Christmas was when Joe started banging his head every night. We'd put bumpers round his cot as we were told to do, but it didn't seem to make a difference. I'd put him in bed every night and, thump-thump-thump, it would start. It was distressing to watch, but if I tried to cuddle him or take him away he cried. I sometimes felt as though my touch was toxic to him.

Then there was the way he didn't seem to respond to his name, or smile very much. I felt so sure it wasn't the way he should be developing, I started looking things up, though Adam told me I was looking to find something that wasn't there. But he had to admit things weren't right when we were unwrapping presents after Christmas dinner and

Joe completely freaked and threw himself on the floor, screaming. Nothing would console him. Not Adam, who could normally calm him down, nor my mum, who prided herself on her perfect touch with babies. And certainly not me. How could I not feel useless?

At first no one could say what was wrong, though I stuck to my guns and kept asking. All anyone could tell us was that Joe wasn't developing the way he should. He had only just learned to crawl, and wasn't making any attempt to stand up. As he grew towards toddlerhood, he reacted even more badly to my touching him. It broke my heart to hear him scream when I went to hug him, and I was covered in bruises where he lashed out at me. It was as though he were locked in his own little world.

I began to avoid mother and baby groups, unable to be sure that Joe would play nicely or kick off by throwing toys, hitting the other children or banging his head on the ground. As the babies in my antenatal group grew, it was becoming more obvious that Joe was different. I'd lost my first two babies, and now this. Maybe I wasn't cut out to be a mother.

It wasn't until Joe was nearly three, after months of consultations and meetings with experts, that we found out why.

'Asperger's? What's that?' Adam asked, looking pale.

So they explained as kindly as they could. How Joe found it difficult to interact socially, how he wouldn't have the emotional and social cues that other people did, which could make him appear unsympathetic and different to the other kids. How it was likely he wouldn't last in the state system at school.

'Oh shit, shit,' said Adam.

'But how? Why?' I wanted to know.

And then Adam told me about his brother. The one no one ever discussed and who I didn't know existed till then. He lived locked away in a home because Adam's parents couldn't cope with their secret shame.

I was flabbergasted. I should have known this sooner.

'I'm sorry,' Adam said over and over again, his face pale with distress, 'I should have told you, but – Mum and Dad, they never want to talk about it. And I've never felt able to either.'

What did it matter either way? Would it have made anything different? I'd have still chosen to have Joe; after all Adam's turned out OK. It's a lottery. And we just lost.

Malachi jumps up next to me. 'Don't give up so soon,' he says with an unexpected kindness in his voice. 'Listen to me and everything will work out.'

'Listen to you, how?' I say, unconvinced.

'Let me take you on a journey,' he says. 'There's a lot you need to learn.'

Chapter One

Adam

Suddenly all the lights in the house begin flickering on and off, as if someone is maniacally flipping switches. I have a vague sense of unease about it and go to check the circuit breaker, but none of the fuses have blown and all the light switches seem to be working.

'Must be a power surge,' jokes Emily. 'Everyone's probably turned their lights on at once.'

I'm not so convinced.

'Maybe there's a problem with the wiring,' I say. 'I'll call an electrician in the morning. We must get it sorted before Christmas.'

The lights seem to settle down, and the wind too, so I dismiss my unease as the product of an overactive imagination. But later when I go into the kitchen to start dinner, the back door blows open. I go to shut it and stare out at the night. It's stormy and cold, and the wind is howling in the trees. I shiver. It's not a night to be out in, and yet I could swear there's someone there, in the back garden, who is exuding menace and anger.

'Is anyone there?' I call, but no one answers; all I see is a mangy black cat which runs in front of my path.

It must be the stress, I think. What with stress and guilt, I'm losing it. With one last glance at the garden, I shut the door and go back inside. But my sense of unease lingers on.

Emily

'OK, Joe, how do you think that looks?' Emily smiled at Joe as they surveyed their – well mainly Joe's – work decorating the Christmas tree. Over the past few months she and Adam had been spending more time together and slowly letting Joe get to know her, but she still fretted that they were taking it too fast. Joe was such an enigma, and Emily found it hard to know what he was thinking. Apparently Livvy was the only person who understood him intuitively. Whatever her faults, Joe had been very close to his mum. Adam was still finding little notes he'd written to her around the house.

'Joe needs a routine,' Adam kept telling Emily, 'and at least he knows you from swimming. That helps a lot. Besides, he likes you.'

That was a huge relief. It was so hard to tell.

Funnily enough it was Joe who led Emily to Adam two Christmases ago. When Emily had lost her husband, Graham, to a girl in the marketing department, she had been devastated. At her friend Lucy's insistence, she'd moved from North to South West London to start a new life, part of which had involved Emily taking up swimming, and it was at the Monday swimming club where she first spotted Joe.

Up and down. Up and down. He swam decisively with certain strokes, driven by some inner compulsion that Emily recognized. In her own way she swam just as obsessively as he did.

Adam came later. Emily was vaguely aware of a man who swam in her lane. Occasionally they'd bump into one another and mumble watery apologies. That moved to quick smiles as they lowered themselves into the water, and the occasional comment about how cold it was. They'd just moved to a shared joke of how much better it was when you got out when Emily ran into him in a café in town, having coffee with Joe. It had been late December two years ago and Emily had been mooching disconsolately around the shops, feeling her single status acutely. She was going to Lucy's annual Christmas bash that night and knew she'd be one of the few unpartnered people there; while she was glad to be shot of Graham, she sometimes wished someone new would come into her life.

She had noticed Adam immediately because he looked as lost and bereft as she did. Although she didn't recognize Joe straight away, there was something about the still way he sat which seemed familiar. And Emily's eye was also caught by the fact that he was repeatedly arranging his cutlery in order.

'Hi,' Adam said, with a smile that lit up his face and dispelled the look of gloom that had settled over him.

'Hi,' Emily said a bit dubiously, wondering why a complete stranger was accosting her in a coffee shop.

'It's Adam,' he said. 'From swimming.'

'Ah,' Emily said, recognition dawning, 'always better when we get out.'

'That's right,' Adam said, with a disarming smile.

An unfamiliar warm tingle spread over her. Apart from her best friend Lucy, Emily didn't know anyone locally, and it was lovely to have someone recognize her for a change. And Adam was far more handsome than she had so far noticed, with fair hair, just turning to grey, and bright

31

blue eyes that sparkled when he smiled a crinkly smile. Emily took in his smart jeans and casual attire. She'd already clocked his lean body in the pool, but not the rest. Funny how you didn't appreciate how good-looking someone is when they're practically naked.

'I didn't recognize you with your clothes on,' Emily blurted out, then blushed profusely. He'd think she was a complete idiot. But Adam laughed and invited her to join them.

'Who are you?' Joe looked suspicious.

'You know this lady,' said Adam. 'She goes swimming. This is . . . actually, I don't know your name.'

'It's Emily.'

'Adam,' he said, and again that lovely smile, which made Emily melt a little at the edges. He seemed kind and friendly, and it was nice to interact with someone other than the girlfriends she saw occasionally.

'Hello Emily from swimming,' said Joe, rearranging his cutlery once more.

'You're a good swimmer,' Emily said cautiously.

'I swim a hundred lengths,' said Joe proudly.

'That's amazing,' Emily said. 'I can usually swim sixty.'

'I swim a hundred lengths,' said Joe again. 'Every week.' Then he retreated into folding and refolding his napkin.

'Joe's got Asperger's,' whispered Adam.

'Oh,' Emily didn't quite know how to respond to that; she'd never met anyone with Asperger's, but Joe seemed very sweet if a little insular, so she smiled encouragingly at him, and hoped she'd got it right.

They sat in the café for ages, drinking coffee after coffee and chatting away as if they'd always known each other. Joe sometimes joined in, sometimes not. It was a magical couple of hours and Emily felt the warm glow deepen as the minutes ticked past. Here she was, spending time with a lovely man who seemed genuinely kind, friendly and interested in her. It was Christmas – maybe things were looking up.

All too soon for Emily, Joe started tugging at Adam's sleeve.

'Eleven forty-eight, Dad,' he said. 'We have to meet Mum at twelve thirty. And have lunch. Lunch is at one p.m.'

Oh. Mum. Stupidly, the fact that Adam and Joe were always alone had prompted Emily to begin to hope Mum might be out of the picture.

'Yes,' said Adam. 'We'd better go.' And a little of the sparkle went out of him. 'Lovely chatting to you, Emily. See you next week.'

They left and Emily felt bereft, firmly back in the land of singledom. Just her luck the nicest man she'd met since the Graham debacle would be married; they usually were. After what Emily had been through, she had no intention of destroying a marriage.

But as it turned out that was exactly what she'd done. Emily never set out to seduce Adam, nor he her. It had been a gradual process: of chats in the changing room before or after swimming; of the occasional drink with the swimming club and making sure she always sought him out; and then eventually of running into him one night when she came home from work. He was frantic. Joe had gone walkabout and Adam had no idea where. Emily automatically offered to help, and they tracked him down to a school friend's house, where Joe was sitting rocking back and forth, saying, 'Mum wouldn't talk to me.' That was Emily's first glimpse of the hell Adam and Livvy were living in.

'It's as much my fault as hers,' Adam had explained to

Emily later. 'I've always tried to support Livvy and Joe, but she seemed to cope so well with Joe when he was little, sometimes I felt she didn't need me. Joe came first, which was natural, but it seemed that he was all she wanted. Somewhere along the line we stopped communicating, and I don't think I quite appreciated the toll looking after Joe took on her.'

It wasn't long after that they had kissed for the first time and from that point onwards, Emily's relationship with Adam had changed and deepened, and then they were in too deep to get out without hurting people. It wasn't what either of them had intended.

And then, a year ago, Livvy had died and everything had changed. Adam had been in a state of profound shock and Emily couldn't help him. She had had to sit on the sidelines wondering whether she'd ever see him again. For a while she'd wondered if that was going to be it; whether the love affair which had made her heart sing would be snuffed out just as surely as Livvy's life had been.

But a few weeks after Christmas, Adam had started to call her.

'I'm sorry,' he said, 'I'm going mad here. I have to talk to someone. And you're the only person who understands.'

At first Emily was wary, not sure if Adam even knew what he wanted; not sure if the love she felt for him was reciprocated. She had deliberately avoided going to swimming, because seeing him there was just too painful, but one blustery February day she'd taken herself off for a walk down by the river, and suddenly there was Adam, standing before her. The weeks of frustration and anguish melted away and they were in each other's arms before they knew it.

'I'm so sorry for not seeing you,' Adam had said when

they went to a bar to sit and chat. 'I made a mess of every-thing with Livvy, and I really don't want to make a mess of it with you. I have to think about Joe. You do understand that, don't you?'

'Of course I do,' said Emily. 'What happened has happened, and we have to deal with that. Let's just see where this goes.'

It was clear that whatever they had begun just wasn't going to go away, and so they started things up again. Slowly at first, and gradually. They had a few dates while Joe was at his grandma's. One Saturday they managed a whole wonderful day in town, visiting the Millennium Wheel, and ending up with a show and a meal, and a night in a hotel. It was like starting all over again, like a proper couple. Emily began to feel that they were on surer ground, that this might settle into something permanent after all, just like she'd always hoped. After a few months, Adam began to invite Emily round to the house for short periods, letting Joe get used to her being there. They'd tried not to rush things for the sake of Joe, who though he barely mentioned Livvy clearly still missed his mum, but he seemed to tolerate Emily, so much so that Adam had recently dared to start asking Emily to stay over occasionally.

If anyone had asked Emily she wouldn't have chosen it this way. Adam still had a lot to deal with, and she worried about the responsibility of Joe, and how she would cope if she ever became his stepmother properly. Joe was lovely, and she was very fond of him, but frequently felt out of her depth. If she were to be with Adam permanently she'd have to take that on. It was a big ask, but Adam made her happy. And she made him happy. That had to be worth something, didn't it? If only things didn't have to be quite so complicated . . .

And then, today, Joe had dropped his casual bombshell. He had looked at her so calmly and said, 'Will you be my new mother?' and Emily had felt floored. His old one had found it so difficult it crucified her marriage. She wanted Adam for always, but Joe? How could she possibly be up to the task?

Livvy

I am really confused about why I'm still here. Malachi seems to think that by showing me what went wrong with me and Adam, I'll be able to pass over sooner; at least I think that's what he intends. He's a cat of very few words. But can that really be it? I know we had our problems, but I'm sure we could have sorted them out. Is Malachi trying to make me let go? Well, I can't do that. If I'm not here, how will Joe manage? Adam does his best, he always has, but Joe *needs* me. I want to be there, to see him through college, to know that he's going to be all right. It doesn't seem fair that I cannot.

And I want to make Adam see me; to hear me; to feel *my* pain. I loved him – still love him – and he seems to have forgotten about me, instead intent on playing happy families with this new woman. Yet I know from his reaction after I died, and the pain that I could feel emanating from him at my funeral, that deep down, Adam hasn't forgotten me. Emily is clearly just a blip, someone to help him through the bad times.

Adam and I, what we had was special. I knew it from the first moment we got together properly, after a night in a club in Manchester. I'd clocked him before; a gorgeous fair-haired boy, always on the fringes of our group, who seemed too shy to talk. So I made the first move that night. We got chatting and never stopped. He walked me back to my halls of residence, and as it was a beautiful summer's evening we ended up talking all night on the little patch of green outside my room. We lay flat on our backs looking at the stars, picking out star constellations for one another. His was Perseus and mine was Cassiopeia. It's something we introduced to Joe when he was little. It was a wondrous evening, and I knew that I was destined to be with this man for the rest of my life. We were meant to be together: two halves of the same whole.

True, things didn't turn out the way we planned. Life ended up tougher than either of us could ever have imagined on that halcyon perfect evening. But we loved each other, and we were together for twenty years; how can this Emily compete with that? And yet looking in on them, it's as if I've never been. The thing I can't bear is that now Joe seems to want a new mum. That's a bitter pill to swallow. Somehow I have to get back so they both know that what they need and want is me. Malachi is wrong. I'm not ready to pass over yet because my life is unfinished. I have to make sure my boys are all right.

I'm determined to get them to notice me. Adam can't be moving on with someone else already, he can't.

At least I'm free of that damned car park. It's immensely liberating to be able to go places now, although according to Malachi there are rules about everything. I can pass through doors and windows; I have learned about switches and banging doors shut, but I'm still having trouble levitating stuff. It's pretty damned exhausting if I'm honest. Making people notice you when you're dead turns out to be very hard, but Malachi says that's because most people aren't susceptible to listening to spirits, so they tend to ignore them. All I know is I wish right now that Adam wasn't the sceptical type.

The day after my ineffectual attempts to haunt the house, I follow Joe to the shops. I'm glad to see Adam's letting him have some independence, now he's 17. It was something we argued about a lot. Adam was worried about how Joe was going to cope when he grew older. I was too, but I saw it as my job to make sure Joe could lead an independent life. He's awkward round people, sure, but he's clever, and the college I got him into has expertise in dealing with kids with his problems. Because Joe struggles with exams, he's doing BTechs in Astronomy, Physics and Maths. My dearest wish was that he could get into college and do a degree. I know he dreams of being the next Brian Cox. 'Who knows, Joe,' I used to say to him. 'Reach for the stars. Everything's possible if you believe it to be.'

I follow Joe to a cheerful cosy little café on the high street, my heart sick with longing. I wish he could see or hear me. It kills me that he can't. I love this café; the people here know him, and automatically produce a cup of hot chocolate the way he likes it, with cream and marshmallows on top. We used to go there together, and I'm pleased the staff still look after him. Joe always gets agitated if things don't follow a certain order, and though he's better at managing the anxiety he feels now he's older, he still finds it difficult.

He sits down by the window, and I sit opposite him, not sure if he's aware of me, but feeling happy to be near him. He looks well, and, for Joe, reasonably content, though it's always hard to tell.

I can't help myself. I lean over and touch his hand – Joe still doesn't like a lot of physical contact, but as he's got older he's got better about the odd touch here and there, which is something I've always been grateful for – but he moves it away and rubs it as if something is itching him, and he stares right through me.

'Joe,' I want to say, 'can you hear me?' but can't bring myself to. The disappointment of him not answering would be too crushing.

Joe's looking a bit agitated now, constantly scanning the crowds of Christmas shoppers marching past outside and looking at his watch. It's a cold wintry day, and the café is packed, the windows steamed up.

'Eleven thirty-two and ten seconds, oh dear,' he's muttering. 'Eleven thirty-three point 0 five.'

He looks at his watch again – it's a chunky ugly thing I bought him a couple of Christmases back, but he likes it because it has second hands on it. Time is vital to Joe. He hates people being late. I can feel his distress as the time slips to 11.35 and fifteen seconds. He's clearly waiting for someone and they are late.

I can feel his panic rising, and without thinking about it I slip into the seat next to him and say, 'It's all right Joe. Deep breaths.' I whisper, as I would if I were still alive and he could hear me. Though the episodes are rarer these days, when Joe's distressed he can get a bit agitated and restless if things don't work out the way he wants. Sometimes he just paces about muttering to himself, but occasionally he throws things. I don't want him to do that here with no one to fight his corner. I can remember too many times when he has in the past. 'Remember, Joe,' I say, 'not everyone is as clever with time as you are. Be patient.'

'Patient,' Joe repeats.

What? Can he hear me? I feel a deep surge of joy.

'Joe, it's Mum,' I say. 'Can you hear me?'

But there's no reply as he's distracted by someone flying

through the door, saying, 'Joe, I'm so sorry I got held up.'

I withdraw in disappointment. I was so sure I'd made a connection.

'You're five minutes and thirteen seconds late,' he says accusingly, and a pretty girl of around 17 with long fair hair slides into a seat opposite us. She's dressed warmly in a thick hoody, scarf, gloves, leggings and boots.

Wait a minute.

A *girl*?

When did Joe start meeting girls? What else have I missed in the last year? I'm cursing my stupidity for not having listened to Malachi at the beginning, and escaped the car park. I shouldn't have let all that time go by.

'I should have synchronized my watch,' says the girl, taking off her gloves and smiling. She has a nice reassuring smile, and it seems to be enough to diffuse his tension.

'You should have,' he agrees. He leans over awkwardly and pecks her on the cheek.

The girl smiles, and says, 'What's the plan?'

'I have to buy presents,' says Joe with the lopsided grin I have always adored. It makes me feel happy just seeing it. 'Look. I have a list.' He proudly presents a scrap of paper with an intense and detailed-looking list on it: *Dad, Emily, Caroline, Granny*.

'I don't need to see my present, remember?' says the girl – Caroline? – 'It's a surprise.'

'Yes, a surprise,' says Joe and smiles again. 'Only the best for my best friend.'

The girl blushes.

'Oh Joe, thank you,' she says, and takes his hand tentatively. I think he's going to flinch, but he doesn't.

'Yes,' says Joe happily. 'I like having a best friend.'

My son has a best friend who's a girl? Where on earth did they meet?

They sit and drink coffee, and talk about Christmas. I watch them together and want to hug her. She seems lovely and I am so pleased Joe has met a friend who treats him normally. And then Joe says, 'I need to buy a present for my mum.'

'Joe,' Caroline says, 'remember . . .'

'I know, Mum's dead,' says Joe conversationally. 'But I can put it on her grave. It's Christmas. My mum has to have a present at Christmas.'

And then, unable to contain myself, I let out a howl of pain. I can't stand to be here. In my distress I knock Joe's drink over.

'Oh no!' says Joe, agitated by the mess, but Caroline quickly calms him down, and wipes everything up.

'What was that?' Caroline says.

'My mum,' says Joe serenely. 'She needs a present for Christmas.'

I hurl myself through the glass, and out on to the street. I am trapped in a nightmare where my son senses but can't see me. How am I ever going to sort this out?

Chapter Two

Livvy

I plough headlong through the present-laden shoppers, vaguely aware that I am causing reactions as people stop and look puzzled as I push past them. And I am very much in distress. One old lady drops her bag of apples, and a small child says, 'Who is that lady, Mummy?' but I race on heedless, oblivious to anything but the pain I feel at losing my son, until I reach a bench down by the river, and collapse on to it, sobbing.

'What do you think you are playing at?' Malachi emerges from behind a bin. 'You're being far too noticeable.'

'I thought it was only people who were susceptible who could see me?' I say.

'Usually that's true,' says Malachi, flicking his nose up in disgust. 'But you were making quite a scene, which is hard for most people to ignore. And that child definitely saw you – it's because she's young and still has an open mind. You should be more careful.'

I stare moodily at the flowing river. If I wasn't dead already, I might be tempted to throw myself in.

'So?' I say. 'I'm upset. Wouldn't you be?'

Malachi doesn't get it. Here I am, dead, watching my

42

husband and son blithely getting on with their lives without me. I don't mind about Joe, I'm glad he's happy, but I miss him dreadfully, and it hurts that I can't seem to get near him. And it hurts even more to think that Adam doesn't need me. Isn't that enough to justify a tantrum?

'Well stop feeling so sorry for yourself, and start thinking,' says Malachi. 'You need to put things right, not make them worse. That's what I'm trying to tell you. And having a hissy fit and disturbing everyone in the vicinity is not helping.'

'How am I possibly making anything worse?' I say. 'I'm dead. How much worse does it get?'

'Oh, I don't know,' says Malachi. 'Your old life wasn't all that wonderful.'

'What do you mean?' I say. 'My life was great. We were a family. We were happy. I've only been dead a year and my husband's got a girlfriend and my son's talking about a new mum, and buying a present to put on my grave. Wouldn't you be upset?'

'Hmm,' says Malachi, 'I think it's time you stopped feeling quite so sorry for yourself and started looking at your life properly. Was it really that brilliant?'

Stop feeling sorry for myself? The cheek.

'Whose side are you on?' I snarl at him. 'I thought you were supposed to be helping me.'

'I am,' says Malachi, 'you just need to pay attention. Now think about it, really think.'

So reluctantly I start remembering things, and I have to acknowledge that sometimes it was less than perfect. In the weeks leading up to my death, Adam and I had been rowing a lot – I think he was upset with me about something, but I'm not sure why. And Joe – I have a sudden flashback to Joe being quiet and retreating in on himself, as if I'd made

43

him sad. I have a nagging feeling I might have done something wrong, but I can't remember what. Perhaps Malachi is right and my old life wasn't that perfect. Still, it was better than being dead.

'You can sort things out,' says Malachi encouragingly. 'You just need to remember how. You have to find a way of reaching out to them, so you can say sorry. Only then will you be able to move on.'

'But none of them can see me,' I say. 'Even Joe can only hear me sometimes.'

'Which is a good start.'

'I suppose so,' I say.

Since I've been back, I've been counting on being able to get through to Joe. He at least can hear me; that had to be grounds for hope.

'There are other ways of getting heard,' says Malachi. 'You aren't required to throw things and freak people out by switching lights on and off you know. Go back to the house. Watch them, and learn.'

'OK,' I say reluctantly. Honestly, it's come to something when the only person I can talk to is a mangy old black cat.

'Oi, I heard that,' says Malachi.

Great, a mangy old mindreading black cat is my sole companion. Maybe he's right though. Maybe I need to make Adam listen to my side of the story, so we can be a family again.

Adam

It's Monday morning, and I'm yawning as I stare at spreadsheets that don't seem to be making much sense. I didn't sleep well last night. I kept dreaming about Livvy, about our early days together which began with such hope and joy. Sometimes it's hard to imagine how it went so wrong. When I met Livvy she was fun, beautiful, intoxicating to be around. We spent a wonderful summer together at the end of our first year at university, and by the end of it we were deeply in love. We took an utterly magical trip round Europe together and I knew very early on I was going to get married to her, so when she got pregnant in our final year it seemed like the obvious thing to do. When she lost that first baby, we were both heartbroken, but we bounced back and it was fine. More than fine, it was wonderful. I loved her even more, knowing how vulnerable she was. Our shared heartache made us much stronger.

I kept grasping something of that in my dreams but then they kept changing. One minute I would be holding her hand, laughing, and the next she would be dying, alone on the tarmac, without me there. In reality she had been declared dead soon after I got to the hospital, but in my dreams I am always trying to reach her. Last night's one is particularly vivid, and this time I nearly get there. I am racing to the car park, and I see her, beautiful and sad, bathed in light as she walks into the car. Her last words break my heart and are still ringing in my ears as I wake up. 'Why, Adam, why?'

After that, I can't sleep. I get up early and go downstairs to turn on the kettle and make a start on the mountains of work waiting for me. The marketing company where I work as a financial director helpfully has its year end in December, so while everyone else is on the downward run to Christmas, I am working pretty much to the bitter end. By the time Emily and Joe get up I'm feeling shattered, but there's no rest for the wicked, so after Emily makes pancakes for us all we pile out of the house together. Emily, who works in IT for a hip design company in London, heads to the station, while Joe goes off to college. I walk part of the way with Joe and, just as I say goodbye, he says, 'Where do you think Mum will be this Christmas?'

Although I am used to Joe asking questions like this since Livvy died, it never fails to get me. I don't believe in an afterlife, but I can hardly tell Joe that I think Livvy is gone for good.

I mutter something about her always being with us, and Joe brightens up and says, 'I think she's a star in the sky watching over us. Just like Grandad.'

When Joe was eight, Livvy's dad died. They were very close, and it hit him hard. After that he used to worry terribly that something would happen to me or Livvy, and, tapping into his love of astronomy, Livvy came up with the idea that when we died we'd watch over him as stars in the sky, which seemed to comfort him. He hadn't mentioned it for years, but it was as good an explanation as any.

'Grandad's star is Orion,' explains Joe. 'Because he liked hunting and Orion is the Hunter. Mostly it's too cloudy to see him properly, and all you can see is the three stars on his belt. But sometimes you can see the whole thing, and it's so cool, Dad, he looks like a hunter, with a bow and arrow and everything. And Mum's star is Venus. Although technically Venus is a planet – but anyway – Venus is the morning and evening star because she's the first thing you see in the morning and the last thing at night. Just like Mum used to get me up in the morning and put me to bed at night when I was little. If I look at Venus, that's Mum watching me.'

'I'm sure she is, Joe,' I say in relief. I pat him on the shoulder, and he goes on to college, while I make my way to work.

By 11 a.m. I have had three cups of coffee, and am flagging badly. I seem to have been looking at the screen forever, not getting anything done, when I get the distinct impression there is someone standing behind me. I look round. Nothing. Why would there be? Everyone else is gossiping about the office Christmas party this afternoon, not even bothering to focus on work. There's an air of jollity about the place which I'm not sharing. I've got so much to do that I don't want to go to the party. A year on and celebrating Christmas somehow feels all wrong. It's been a year, but still my sadness about what happened to Livvy hangs over me. Emily and I are going through the motions for Joe. He needs the order, the stability; at least that's what Livvy always said. And his routine and order have been spectacularly shot to pieces this last year.

If it hadn't been for Livvy managing to get him into that college, I'm sure he'd be in a much worse state. That was one thing she always got spectacularly right. From the moment of Joe's diagnosis, she worked hard to make sure he always had the best support at school. She gave up the job she loved in advertising so she could stay at home with Joe and fought every bit of red tape, and unhelpful officialdom, to make sure Joe got everything he needed. Without her, Joe would never have come this far. I used to worry terribly that she was making Joe such a focus that she didn't have much time for herself, and tried to get her to go away on the odd girlie weekend. But she always found it hard leaving Joe, and said she didn't mind about work, Joe needed her. Perhaps I should have pressed her on that. Sometimes she did seem sad and overburdened but, try as I might, I could never get her to share her thoughts with me. Looking back I can see I failed her there. She made Joe her world, and sometimes I think that was a mistake.

She left friendships slide, and didn't develop any outside interests the way I had. I should have seen that, I should have helped more. But to my deep regret I didn't.

A familiar mixture of grief, guilt and self-disgust washes over me. I want to put my head in my hands and wake up. But these spreadsheets need doing, and at least they'll distract me. So I plough on. And then . . .

. . . my computer freezes.

Suddenly it's as though someone has taken over the keyboard. A new window opens up. It's Livvy's Facebook page. I'm reminded I should have closed it down after she died, but I don't have the password. Besides so many people have left tributes there over the last year, I can't bring myself to. And secretly I go on it sometimes, and look at pictures of us in younger, happier times. Emily says I'm being morbid. Maybe I am.

The screen seems to have frozen on one particular picture. It was from our first trip abroad, when we went Interrailing round Europe. There Livvy is in a café in Venice, sunkissed, her auburn hair flowing in the breeze, laughing in delight. I remember that day well. We'd overdosed on sightseeing and spent the day wandering the streets, buying knick-knacks in shops, stopping for ice cream in tiny little piazzas; we ended the day sitting in this café, watching the gondolas plying their trade on the canals. It had been perfect, glorious; and there she is captured on my screen; a record of our happiness frozen in time.

I sit and stare at the picture, and have a moment of brief joy, thinking that not all my memories are tainted, followed swiftly by a familiar stab of pain that Livvy isn't here and I can't tell her. I stare for a long time feeling immensely sad, and then shake myself out of it. This isn't going to get my spreadsheets done.

The screen still seems to be frozen, so I press alt, control, delete. Nothing happens. And then an instant message pops up.

It says: *I'm sorry.*

What? I go cold all over. Is this some kind of sick joke? Maybe one of my colleagues is playing a prank on me. I look around but everyone seems to be chatting cheerfully about the party. Besides, why would anyone do something like this?

Who is this? I reply cautiously. But there's no answer, just a cold breath on my neck and a chill up my spine.

Emily

Emily was working late. Being in IT meant she had to be flexible, and tonight she was needed to help sort out the office mainframe, which had overheated. Adam had invited her to his company's work do, and she was still in two minds as to whether to go. Emily had met a couple of Adam's workmates, but she knew that Livvy had been a popular figure in the office, in and out of there since Joe was tiny. It made Emily nervous to think that people might be judging her, though Adam told her she had nothing to worry about. Emily would much rather go out somewhere just with Adam, particularly as Joe was spending the evening with his new friend, Caroline, a girl he'd met at college. Adam hadn't been all that keen on going either, but his work colleagues had been a great support to him after Livvy had died, and he felt he had to show his face, so Emily thought the least she could do was keep him company.

'Come on, Ems, it will be fine now,' said her boss, a skinny bearded twenty-something called Daniel, who ran Digit AL, the small company she'd found herself temping at for the last few months. 'Some of us are going for a drink – do you want to join us?'

'Thanks Dan, but I've got plans.' Emily liked the atmosphere of the place, which was run by geeky lads, most of whom looked barely out of their teens. They were a lot of fun though, and on another occasion she might have been tempted to join them; she found their company energizing. But she was already late for Adam's party, so she closed down her computer and set off across a chilly, frosty London, squashed on busy trains full of people in cheery Christmas mode. Emily wasn't quite feeling the Christmas vibe this year – there seemed to be a lot of tricky moments to get through before the day itself, and she still wasn't sure she and Adam were getting it right with Joe.

Emily's heart was in her mouth as she entered the room. She'd never been big on work parties – Graham had always made it spectacularly clear that she wasn't terribly welcome at his. And Adam's office was small and closely knit and everyone knew each other's families. She felt that people were curious about this new woman in Adam's life.

Adam had kept his problems at home very much to himself so nobody at work had known what really went on, and now Livvy was dead she had attained martyr status. Emily was the new woman, suspiciously new to some, and she knew that she was viewed with distrust in some quarters. People wanted him to be happy, but clearly felt he should have left a decent period of mourning. But how long was a decent period? None of them knew Adam was on the verge of leaving Livvy when she died. Emily hadn't meant to fall in love with Adam; hadn't meant to be a home wrecker, and yet that's what had happened, although to be fair she had come along after the wrecking had been done: Adam and Livvy had done that all by themselves. Even so, she couldn't help feeling the anxious tug of guilt.

Emily scanned the crowds, relieved to find Adam in the corner with his mates Phil and Dave. That was good. She'd met Phil and Dave several times before and they were fun, and had seemed to accept her readily.

'Hi,' she said, shyly. 'I made it then.'

'So you did,' said Adam, giving her a massive hug, which made her feel warm all over. 'We don't have to hang around too long if you don't want to.'

Adam knew she had been feeling nervous about tonight. Maybe she'd get her wish and they could sneak out for a quiet dinner later.

'What do you want to drink?' he said. 'There's a free bar for the next hour or so.'

'Double vodka and Coke, thanks,' Emily said and Adam raised an eyebrow. It wasn't like her to drink spirits, let alone doubles, but she was feeling stupidly nervous and she needed some Dutch courage.

'Party's going well, I see,' she said, nodding at a group of the sales team who were singing lustily and out of tune in a corner by the fire, while some of the younger staff looked like they might be up for some extracurricular activities in dark nooks and crannies. The mood was light and fun, and Emily tried to relax into it.

She sipped her drink and let the boys' idle chatter flow over her. The boys were taking the mickey out of the MD, who was currently ogling his secretary, who though young enough to be his daughter was clearly loving the attention.

'You jealous, Dave?' Adam laughed. 'I thought you were in there.'

Dave, according to Adam, was the office lothario.

'I wish,' said Dave. 'She's the one that got away.'

'Glad someone's immune to your charms,' Adam laughed, ordering another round.

One drink led to another, and Emily's mood started to shift. To her surprise she found she was having fun and wondering what she had worried about. Another couple of vodkas later, she was even flirting outrageously with Phil and Dave, who were great company. Even Marigold, Adam's dragonlike PA – a brassy forty-something who acted about sixty – who had always been sniffy with Emily, had grudgingly wished her a merry Christmas.

Adam introduced Emily to the sales team, and before long, with a 'Come on, Emily, be a sport,' she found herself roped into a very raucous singalong of 'Last Christmas'. It suddenly pulled her up short. Last Christmas things had been very different. Adam had been about to leave Livvy and then she'd died. Was it too soon for Emily to be taking her place? The thought made her feel anxious and sad. Deciding that the vodka wasn't helping, next time she was at the bar Emily switched to red wine.

As she was returning from the bar to rejoin Adam and the boys, Emily felt a weird sensation, as though someone had punched her in the gut. Her glass of wine flew out of her hand, and spilled all over her, Phil and Dave. Bugger bugger bugger. Why on earth had she chosen to wear a cream dress?

'What the —?' Emily said, feeling very flustered. 'I'm so sorry, I don't know how that happened.'

Fortunately Phil and Dave laughed it off, but Emily went to the toilet to clean herself up feeling very unsettled. It had really felt as if someone had pushed her. Deliberately. Which was ridiculous.

'You're imagining things,' she said sternly to herself, as she reapplied lipstick. 'You've had too much to drink.'

Pulling herself together, she went back to the party, running the gauntlet past Marigold and her group of cronies. They all turned to look at Emily as she walked by, and this time she knew she wasn't being paranoid.

She just caught Marigold mutter something like, 'Look at her, bold as brass,' and another woman say something about stepping in a dead woman's shoes. Emily would normally have chosen to ignore them – what did she care what they thought of her? But she was still rattled about the spilled drink and she was tired of Marigold's insinuations, and fed up of being judged by someone she barely knew.

So she turned round and stopped squarely in front of them, and said, 'If you've got something to say, say it.'

They all looked embarrassed apart from Marigold, who said defiantly, 'You didn't take long to get your feet under the table. That poor woman has only been dead a year, and just look at you cosying up to Adam, when he's vulnerable.'

'That is none of your business,' Emily said, furious with Marigold for prying where she had no right to, 'and as for cosying up to Adam, we were good friends before Livvy died.'

'*Just* good friends?' Marigold cast a sly aside to her friends.

'Oh go on, why don't you come out and say it?' Emily burst out, knowing exactly what Marigold was getting at. They had always been careful, but Adam had worried that Marigold suspected something. 'You know you want to.'

'Say what?' Marigold looked innocent, which made Emily even more sure that she had known all along.

'That you think Adam and I had an affair.'

There was a slightly stunned silence. Even Marigold looked awkward.

53

'I didn't say that,' she protested.

'But you bloody well thought it,' Emily said. 'And for your information, it's true.'

There was a huge gasp, and her words came out louder than Emily intended. 'For all you nasty-minded gossip mongers out there, yes, Adam and I had an affair last year. For your information he was about to leave Livvy. And then she died. Put that in your pipe and smoke it.'

At that moment there was a lull in the chatter at the bar, and Emily's words carried across the cavernous silence which suddenly fell in the room.

She looked across to Adam, who was standing holding his pint, horrified. Dear God, what on earth had she done?

Chapter Three

Adam

The blood drains from my face as I hear Emily's declaration. Phil and Dave look shocked. They knew little bits of my life, and that things weren't always happy with Livvy, but they didn't know about Emily. I hadn't told anyone. Years of treading a fine line at home had left me unable to communicate with even good mates about what was really going on. Besides, how do you admit to anyone your marriage isn't working any more? That you dread going home for fear of what you will find? That you are watching your wife drinking herself into an early grave and are powerless to stop it? That you're sleeping in separate beds and barely talking? I had kept my problems to myself for so long, it was difficult to know where to begin. Besides, there was always the hope that things would get better, and we could go back to the way it was. And then I met Emily, and she blew me away. Suddenly I had found someone who made me happy again, someone I could laugh with, someone who wasn't permanently angry with me. I didn't know how to tell anyone all that, so I had told nobody. But now everyone I work with is staring at me and they all know I cheated on my wife. My now *dead* wife.

After a few stunned moments, someone behind the bar puts the jukebox on, and everyone goes back to chatting as if nothing has happened. I guess, as this is a Christmas party, there are already other more scandalous things happening in the corners of the room.

'You kept that quiet,' Phil says accusingly.

'Sorry,' I say, 'it wasn't an easy thing to confess. Things at home weren't exactly brilliant.'

'Blimey,' says Phil. 'I really hadn't had you figured for the playing-away-from-home type, that's more Dave's style.'

Dave grinned ruefully; as the survivor of two failed marriages and innumerable affairs himself, he struggles to deal with commitment.

'I'm not,' I say, 'really I'm not. It's just – things were difficult, really difficult, and Emily just came along . . .'

'You don't have to explain to us,' says Dave, patting me on the back. 'Good for you, mate. Emily's great. Don't listen to the gossips. What do they know?'

'Thanks,' I say, 'I appreciate it.'

I can see Emily is standing looking slightly dazed by what has happened. I have to get her out of here.

'Time to go I think,' I say firmly, grabbing her by the arm, and steering her towards the cloakroom. Emily is staggering all over the place. Shit, what's got into her? She never normally drinks this much. She knows I hate it.

'Adam, I'm so sorry,' she says. She looks a little shocked, as if she's not quite sure what happened.

Neither am I, but if I wanted to stay here any longer, I've changed my mind. It was a bad idea to come. A bad idea to bring Emily. For whatever reason, Livvy had a strong support team in my office, and still has. None of them know what she was really like. They just saw the happy family, admired how together we were despite the problems with Joe, and were shocked and stunned by what had happened to her. Everyone was great after Livvy died, but I know they all think Emily's on the scene suspiciously soon. I wish they'd leave their suspicions and nastiness to themselves.

And now I'm cross with Emily for coming. For getting drunk. For ruining the evening. It's unfair of me I know, but for the first time I feel a prickle of anger that Emily isn't Livvy. Despite everything that went wrong between us, what happened to Livvy wasn't fair. I didn't want to be married to her any more, but neither did I want this. Since she died I've been in limbo: missing her, grieving for her, trying to be strong for Joe, treading water with Emily, feeling guilty that she makes me so happy, not sure I deserve this second chance. It's not Emily's fault, or anyone else's. It just is.

The fresh air seems to sober Emily up a little. Immediately she's remorseful in the way that drunks always are, and for a moment I'm so reminded of Livvy I feel sick. She says, 'I'm sorry, Adam. I drank far too much. I hope I haven't made a fool of you at work. I was just so nervous, and then I spilled my drink and I heard Marigold gossiping about me and . . .' She looks at me with genuine regret, and I realize, of course, she's not Livvy. This is the first time I've ever seen Emily get drunk. She likes to enjoy herself, certainly, and one of the great things about her is we can have a good time without alcohol being involved – when I think of Livvy, even in our early days our nights out always included drink. I probably shouldn't have taken Emily to the party. It was too soon. That's the problem: everything's too damned soon.

I take her into my arms and hold her tight.

'Nah, it's all right,' I say. 'Everyone at work's been really great to me this year, but to be honest, I'm fed up of people talking about me behind my back. You're the one good thing to happen to me in the last few years. I don't care what anyone else thinks. At least the truth's out in the open now. Come on, let's get dinner.'

'I promise to drink water,' says Emily, and we wander down the high street looking for somewhere to eat. As we approach an Italian we like, which doesn't look too busy, I see a black cat walk across our path.

'Ooh, hope that's lucky,' says Emily, squeezing me close.

'Yeah, me too,' I say vaguely.

'Are you sure you're not angry with me?' Emily is so contrite, I can't possibly be cross any more. I just look at her and know that whatever happened in the past I want her in my future.

'I'm really not,' I say and give her a hug. Christmas is coming. Life is very different, but I've got Emily beside me, and at the moment, I feel as if I can take over the world.

Livvy

I am in shock. My memories of the day I died have become mired in fog thanks to all that time spent in the car park. I knew I was texting Adam angrily about something, but – maybe I didn't want to remember? – the exact words of my text had been banished to the back of my mind. Now I realize I must have known from the minute Emily was in the house that she was the Other Woman, but I didn't want to admit that Adam could possibly have carried it on after I'd gone. I felt his anguish when I died. I know he still has feelings for me. I just know it. It makes me more determined than ever to win him back. Malachi's right: we

58

have unfinished business. I need to show Adam what he's missing. I lost him to Emily once; I'm not going to let it happen again. Especially where my son is involved.

I hadn't really had a plan when I went to the party. But hearing Marigold and her mates gossiping, it seemed a good idea to see if I could nudge them in the right direction. I remember vaguely that Marigold has always been keen on psychics, so she's very susceptible, which meant it was quite easy for me to get into her thoughts. Sadly, Adam and Emily seem to be far too sceptical, which is making it much harder to get them to listen to me. But with Marigold it was easy. All I had to do was sit down beside her, and drop the idea that Emily and Adam hadn't wasted much time and hear her repeat it to her neighbour.

'You'd think he might have waited a bit longer, don't you?' said one of the girls from the sales team.

'It's indecent,' snorted another.

'If you ask me, it's been going on longer than any of us think,' was Marigold's contribution to a collective gasp from the rest of the table, including one from me. It didn't take long for the rumours to fly. Marigold can always be relied on to pass on a bit of gossip. I think she's probably half in love with Adam. Maybe she thought he'd find comfort in her arms. Emily must have come as a hell of a shock. I could feel the hatred positively bristling off her. I wasn't really expecting Emily to confess to a full-blown affair, though. How could Adam have done that to me? What had I done to deserve it? I am reeling from the shock. I am going to split them up, and she will keep her claws off Adam. He's mine.

Not that I appear to have succeeded in that endeavour. Having thought that Adam would be angry with Emily, he seems to have got over it annoyingly quickly. If I had the tiniest drink at an office party, Adam was always tediously on my case about it. I remember one spectacular row when he accused me of showing him up because I'd danced on a table with the managing director.

'I was only having a laugh,' I'd protested. 'You have no sense of fun any more.'

He'd looked at me in incomprehension, then said, 'Maybe my idea of fun is different from yours.'

We'd gone to bed that night in separate rooms, and he never referred to it again. But now, look at him, forgiving Emily so easily, when she'd embarrassed him far more than I ever had. It doesn't seem fair.

I follow them as far as an Italian restaurant and watch them go inside. They're sitting at a table looking totally loved up, and it makes me feel sick to my stomach just to watch them. This won't do at all.

'And what did you think you were going to achieve with that stunt?' Malachi appears on the street, looking very pissed off.

'I had hoped that it would make Adam see the error of his ways and remember it's me that he loves, not Emily.'

'In case you'd forgotten, there's a bit of a flaw in your plan.'

'Yes, yes, I know I'm dead and I can't have him back,' I say impatiently. 'But it's as if Adam has forgotten all about me, as if I never even existed. I want him to remember it's *me* that he loves. Not this – this Emily person. I want him to *mourn* me!'

'Well, good luck with that,' says Malachi, nodding at the couple in the window, 'because quite frankly, this is not the reason you're back. I keep telling you, you need to put things right.'

I am not in the mood to listen. This is my life – well it was – not Malachi's.

'Yeah yeah, I know,' I say. 'But as it goes I think you're wrong. And I'm going to prove it.'

'On your own head be it,' says Malachi, with a shrug. And with that he vanishes, leaving me with my nose pressed up against the glass, looking in, like a child outside a sweet shop.

Emily

'This is better,' said Emily as they squeezed into a table by the window of Carlo's, a family-owned restaurant she and Adam were rather fond of.

The restaurant was busy and over-adorned with tinsel and gaudy Christmas decorations, according to Carlo's quirky style. There was a small plastic tree on the bar, its lights flashing on and off intermittently. It even had a drunken-looking fairy on the top. Emily knew how she felt. The effects of the alcohol, combined with the cold walk, had made her feel decidedly woozy.

'Water, lots of it,' she said when the waiter came to their table.

'Good idea,' said Adam, though he ordered a beer as well.

Now they were here, Emily was starting to feel a little less out of it. Remorse poured through her as she kept running over the cringe-inducing moment in the bar.

'I hope I haven't caused you loads of grief at work,' she said, reaching over to take Adam's hand.

'I doubt it,' said Adam. 'We'll be a one-hit wonder. After tonight, there's bound to be more juicy gossip for people to mull over. Like I say, you've probably done me a favour. Anyway, let's not talk about that now. It's done.'

Emily breathed a sigh of relief. One of the nicest things about Adam was that never dwelt on stuff too long. On the whole, Adam was a pretty calm person. He must have been to put up with Livvy so long. His anger when it came was fast, furious and over quickly. Graham would have eked that one out for weeks, whereas Adam's favourite phrase was 'never let the sun go down on your anger'. And he never did – at least not with her, which was one of the many reasons Emily had fallen in love with this kind, funny man. He always tried to do the right thing. He always tried to be even-handed about Livvy too, refusing to bad-mouth her.

'She was sick, Emily,' he'd say, 'she wasn't always like that. Maybe I could have done more . . .'

He always looked so sad then, Emily felt there was a place – a Livvy place – where she couldn't reach him. Sometimes she wondered what would have happened if Livvy had lived. Would Adam have still been trying to help her? Emily rather suspected he would.

'How did I get so lucky to find you?' Emily said, lacing her fingers through his, still feeling the thrill of his touch.

'Ditto,' Adam said, and they stared at each other, soppily happy.

There was a sudden bang on the window, which made them both jump, but then they laughed for jumping, and Emily squeezed Adam's hand tightly.

'I've been thinking,' Adam said, 'about what Joe said the other day.'

'About me being his mum?' Emily said. 'I don't want to replace Livvy.'

'That's not what he meant. That's Joe being very literal. He hasn't got a mum. You can be his new mum. It makes sense in his head.'

'I suppose,' said Emily, 'but . . .'

'It's daunting, I know,' said Adam, 'but we have something here. Something special. I'd forgotten till you came along that I could be happy, and you make me so happy. I know it didn't come about in the best of circumstances, and we didn't plan it like this. But what I've learned from what happened to Livvy is that life's too short. We can't put constraints on how we feel or what we do, just because of what other people think. After what we've both been through, we deserve some happiness; that's if you're prepared to take Joe on.'

Emily's heart did a double flip and her mouth went dry.

'Adam, what are you saying?' He couldn't be about to propose, could he?

Adam looked at her. 'Well, in the short term, will you move in with us?'

'Oh Adam.' Emily was awash with conflicting emotions. 'I'd love to, you must know that. But . . .'

'You're worried it's too soon?'

'A little,' said Emily. 'And then there's Joe – I want to do the right thing by him.'

'I know,' said Adam. 'It won't be easy. But we love each other; I think we can make it work.'

Emily gulped. She'd fought hard for her independence after Graham left, and always sworn she'd take her time settling down with someone else. But Adam wasn't Graham and, as he had said, life was short.

'You think?'

'I know,' said Adam firmly. The windows rattled again, making them both start. It was clearly getting very windy out there. 'I thought I'd had my shot at happiness. But then you came into my life. And we could waste our time worrying about what's happened or grab the moment and be happy. That's all I want now.'

'Me too,' Emily said, feeling a little tearful. It wasn't quite a proposal, but then Emily hadn't expected one so soon. She squeezed Adam's hand. 'Yes,' she said. 'Yes, I'd love to.'

Outside in the street the wind blew rubbish down the road, and people braced themselves against the wind. But Emily sat in a warm bubble of happiness. Whatever happened next, she had Adam at her side, and that was all that counted.

Joe's Notebook

My mum is dead.

I saw her in the hospital.

I went to her funeral.

That is very bad.

Sometimes my eyes feel wet and I don't know why.

But then I look through my telescope at Venus and I feel better. I know Mum is watching me.

Emily is going to be my new mum.

I like Emily.

If she had a star, I think she would be a star in Libra. She is a very balanced person.

It is good she wants to be my mum.

But . . . I made a Christmas wish. I asked for my mum to come back. And I think it might have come true.

You can only have one mum.

I don't need two mums.

That wouldn't be right.

Christmas Past

Livvy

Nooo!!! I howl at the restaurant window and the cold sleet seems to come down harder. I am so frustrated. How will I ever get Adam to notice me again when he's so loved up with Emily? Emily is going to get my life. Raging, I blow through the streets, nudging the Christmas revellers, making more than one of them mutter about someone walking over their grave. How could this be happening, how? Why has Adam forgotten me?

'You know how.' Malachi appears as I finally settle down on a park bench where I watch the sleet coming down in sheets, and the ducks shivering in the bushes.

'No, I really don't,' I say.

'You've got to stop with the blame game,' he says.

'Why?' I say bolshily. 'What's it to you?'

'I am trying to explain to you,' says Malachi patiently. 'You have unfinished business with Adam and Joe. You need to set things right. And you can start by taking responsibility for what you've done.'

What have I done that's so bad? I've done nothing wrong, or not that I can recall. Malachi is winding me up.

* * *

With a start I find myself back in my house again. But it's around fourteen years ago, I think. It's Christmas Day. We've had a lovely cosy Christmas Eve sorting three-year-old Joe's stocking, giggling in hushed whispers while we creep into his room and hang it by his bed and then curling up together with a bottle of wine in front of the fire. It feels perfect, like we're a proper family at last. Gradually the shock of Joe's diagnosis has faded and now we're in coping mode. I've decided not to go back to work. Joe needs me too much. And fighting for him takes up all my time. It was a wrench leaving my job as a copywriter for a big advertising firm. I'd worked hard to get where I had, and to be honest I hated being at home at first, but what else could I do?

The upside though, is that Joe is much calmer now I'm around. He's still not great about being touched or hugging me, but at least he longer screams when I hold him. And now he's getting older, I can reason with him more. Things are coming together in a much better way, and I'm thrilled that he was chosen to be a wise man in the nursery nativity. I had a lump in my throat when he lisped 'Frankincense,' when asked what he was giving the baby Jesus. Although it's hard, there are moments like this of pure unadulterated joy, which I treasure.

Adam has taken a job closer to home, which means he's around a lot more. It's less money, but we're both grateful that he is so close. Joe and I frequently pop into the office to see him and Adam's colleagues are brilliantly supportive. I feel like Adam and I are a team now. He insists I have a break at the weekend and has started taking Joe to swimming lessons on a Saturday, giving me some precious time to myself. I am lucky to have such a wonderful husband. So many of the women I meet in the Asperger's support group I go to occasionally have been left to struggle on alone. I know Adam would never do that to me. He adores Joe, and I couldn't have asked for a better dad for my son. We're dealing with this, and it will be OK. Finally, after three tough years, I think we've turned a corner – so much so, that when Adam brings up the perennial topic of a brother or sister for Joe – something I've been resisting because it scares me – I don't give him an outright no.

Today, Adam's parents, Mary and Anthony, and my mum and dad are coming for Christmas lunch. It's the first time we've hosted. We moved into this house when we first got married. It was all we could afford at the time, and desperately run down, but we didn't care, because we were just so happy to be together planning our future. I fell pregnant with Joe quite soon after we moved in, and although it was an anxious time, it was also thrilling the first moment we heard Joe's heartbeat, and I started to feel I might get all the way through this pregnancy.

The house was still in chaos when we brought Joe home, and Adam worked really hard to make it habitable for us. It still needs loads of work; the back door always rattles, and we could do with a new kitchen, but I absolutely love it. Prices round here are so expensive, we can only afford a smallish three-bedroom cottage, but it's a step up from the flat we lived in before. I feel we've finally graduated into the world of adulthood (something my mother has always seemed to feel is lacking in me). This is our family home, where we are making a success of bringing up our son, despite all the difficulties involved, and I'm determined to show our parents how well we're doing. Today is going to be a wonderful day.

To begin with everything goes swimmingly. Joe is well behaved and quiet, though I notice him flinching from

Mary's hug. My mum at least has the sense not to touch him unless invited to.

The turkey, which I've been cooking since 6.30 a.m., because our oven is so temperamental, is cooked to perfection. The wine is flowing, the conversation is relaxed, and even the Christmas pudding lights first time. Adam and I have been working together seamlessly to make sure everyone has what they want. I couldn't have asked for more. I pour myself an extra-large glass of wine after lunch, something I reckon I deserve.

And then it's time for presents. We gather round the tree, complete with decorations that Joe has made at nursery, as well as the more traditional sort Adam went out and bought to mark our first Christmas in our new home. The lights are sparkling and bright, and presents are spilling over themselves.

Joe's the only grandchild in both our families so I suppose it makes sense that he gets spoiled. But it's when we start unwrapping presents that all hell breaks loose.

In their wisdom, and without consulting me, Mary and Anthony have decided that Joe needs one of those sound-light jobbies that helps kids learn their alphabet, as Adam has told them he's behind on a lot of the skills other kids his age have. For a normal kid, it was probably a great idea. For Joe, it's a disaster.

'Ah,' I say, foreseeing trouble, 'I think I might take that for later.' (I make a mental note to take it to the charity shop at the first available opportunity.) Joe can be sensitive to noise and light, and coupled with a busy day that has slightly broken his routine, I'm not sure it will go down too well.

But Mary is too quick for me. She is clearly proud of her gift, and wants to share it.

'Look, Joe,' she says, 'look what it does.'

She starts the machine and it emits light, and beeps and whistles. I can see Joe is getting agitated.

'Wait,' I say, 'it's too much, Joe doesn't like it.'

'Nonsense,' says Mary, who always knows best, 'of course Joe likes it, don't you, Joe?'

She's trying so hard, but she's got it all wrong.

Then Joe puts his hands over his ears and lets out a high-pitched scream, before throwing himself on the floor and kicking wildly.

'I'm so sorry,' I say as I dodge Joe's flailing limbs to calm him down. 'He's sensitive to noise.'

'Sensitive to noise? Never heard such rubbish,' says Anthony. 'Nothing wrong with him, he needs a firm hand.'

'No. He doesn't,' I say as patiently as I can. 'Joe's condition means that he needs the opposite. He needs care and consideration.'

'Well, of course you will insist on spoiling him.'

I look at both my in-laws with increasing dislike. How dare they judge me, when they couldn't even cope with their own son? Suddenly I feel deeply resentful of them. Adam and I are doing our best to care for ours. We might not be getting it right, but it's a damn sight better than the way they have behaved. Joe might be hard work, but we both love him. I cannot imagine how any parent could make the decision to hide their child away the way Mary and Anthony have.

'At least he's not hidden away, out of sight,' I burst out. The words are out of my mouth before I've registered. Maybe I shouldn't have had that last glass of wine.

'Livvy!' says Adam, shocked.

'I beg your pardon.' Anthony's face goes purple. 'How dare you?'

'Sorry, sorry,' I say backtracking wildly, conscious that Adam is looking at me in horror. 'I shouldn't have said that. I don't know why I did.'

'You have no idea what we've been through,' Mary has gone pink with anger. 'You have no right to judge us.'

But you feel the right to judge me, I think bitterly.

'I'm sure Livvy didn't intend any upset,' Dad steps in smoothly, and I feel like hugging him. 'Did you, Livvy?'

'No, no I didn't,' I say. 'I'm sorry, it was an unforgivable thing to say.'

'Yes it was,' says Anthony tightly, making me angry again. If he and Mary hadn't been so damned critical I'd never have said anything.

Dad pats me warningly on the arm; I think he can tell I'm boiling up again, and there's an awkward silence before Mum says brightly, 'Mary, could you give me a hand in the kitchen? I think we could all do with some tea and Christmas cake.' Dad meanwhile gets Anthony going about the inadequacies of Tony Blair's leadership, which distracts him beautifully – it's a subject close to his heart. It's such a British reaction. No one is prepared to acknowledge the elephant in the room. Part of me thinks it's ridiculous and we should talk about this, but that's just not Adam's family's style.

Eventually my in-laws are mollified, I calm Joe down, and an uneasy peace settles over the afternoon. But Anthony and Mary make their excuses early and Mum and Dad aren't far behind, so I know that the day hasn't been a success.

Adam is furious when I've shut the door. 'Thanks for that. Didn't you see how upset Mum was?'

'What about how upset I am?' I say. 'I'm livid. Your dad more or less accused me of being too soft on Joe, when if they hadn't given him that sodding toy none of this would have happened.'

'I know,' says Adam looking uncomfortable. 'But you know what Dad's like, he doesn't really understand.'

'How can he, when he got rid of your brother as soon as he could,' I say bitterly.

'Livvy, it wasn't like that,' says Adam. 'Harry lived with them for a long while before they couldn't manage any more. Things were different then.'

Harry: the unspoken secret in Adam's family. I'm not sure Adam even knows where he lives, though I've tried to get him to find out. I think they should have a relationship, particularly because of Joe, but he doesn't want to upset his parents.

'Not that different,' I say. 'If they loved your brother, they'd never have sent him away. I could never do that to Joe.'

'And I would never ask you to,' says Adam. 'I'm sorry about what Dad said, but please don't be so hard on him. He didn't mean to upset you.'

I'm not so sure about this, but I can see Adam is trying to make up. Still, I can't forgive him for taking his parents' side. Adam should have supported me, and he hasn't.

'I'm putting Joe to bed,' I say, a process that can take some time on his best days. 'He needs to stay calm after what happened today.'

'Whatever.' Adam looks defeated, and I nearly go to him then, and tell him it's all right. But it's not all right. My illusion of a happy family has been well and truly shattered today.

When I come back downstairs, I sit down next to Adam and give him a hug, and say, 'The new baby thing? Let's leave it for a while longer, yeah? I think we've both got enough to deal with right now, don't you?'

'I suppose,' says Adam.

I pour us both a glass of wine, and we sit in front of festive TV as the fire burns out in the grate, and we don't talk for the rest of the evening.

Chapter Four

Twelve Days to Christmas . . .

Emily

Emily woke up with a stinking hangover, relieved she'd decided to take the day off to finish her Christmas shopping.

Adam presented her with a cup of tea and a kiss before heading off to work.

'What did I do to deserve you?' she said, kissing him back.

Adam hugged her again and left, leaving Emily to doze until later, when, feeling a little less grim after a shower, she got dressed and went to the shops.

Despite the hangover, she was enjoying herself. Emily loved Christmas shopping. She revelled in the excited bustle of the shoppers, the cheesy Christmas music, and the festive lights. It made her feel nostalgic for her childhood, when Mum had always taken her to their local shopping centre to see Father Christmas. One day she hoped she'd be doing that for children of her own, although there was a lot to get through with Adam first. She'd never imagined getting to her mid-thirties and not being settled down with kids.

But then she'd never imagined inheriting a 17-year-old stepson either, let alone one with Asperger's who'd just lost his mother. To her relief, Joe seemed to accept Emily and like her, but despite him asking if she was his new mum Emily worried about how he would really take it if she did move in with him and Adam. Then she decided she couldn't worry about it now. She would spend today focusing on the good stuff.

Emily loved the expectation and the thrill of finding something you knew the person you were buying for would like. She'd already bought her dad a new set of gardening gloves and a mat to kneel on for when he was tending his allotment. Despite being the youngest-behaving 65-year-old Emily knew, Dad had recently started to complain about backache when he was digging, so she hoped he'd appreciate the present. She was also on the lookout for some military history books for him, as he was an obsessive history buff.

Emily had agreed to cook Christmas dinner for Adam, Joe and Felicity this year, which neatly avoided the annual how-to-cope-with-the-latest-new-woman-in-Dad's-life dilemma. Although Emily didn't begrudge her dad his girl-friends – he had been on his own for a long time and she knew he got lonely – his tendency to entertain a different woman every year could get a bit exhausting. And it was often excruciating for both of them watching him behave like a lovesick teen, particularly as Emily knew, but his lady friends tended not to, that it wasn't going to last.

So instead of Emily going to visit her dad, he was coming to them for an early Christmas the following weekend. Adam had suggested inviting Felicity too, to break the ice between her and Emily before Christmas Day. He seemed to think having a third party around would mean Felicity would have to be polite to Emily. Emily wasn't totally convinced by the wisdom of this idea, particularly if Dad turned his silver-fox charm on Felicity, but at least it would give her a chance to get to know Felicity with an ally by her side.

She wandered into Waterstone's where a group of small children was sitting around on bean bags entranced by a storyteller reading *'Twas the Night Before Christmas*, and found what she was looking for. She also picked up a book on astronomy for Joe, who was obsessed with stars. Emily had never met him without having a long conversation about dark matter, the big bang theory and whether alien life existed. Adam had also set him up a little observatory in their loft, and it was not uncommon for Joe to drag one or other of them up there to see some obscure star Emily had never heard of and could barely make out. But it made Joe happy, and she loved Adam for going out of his way to do that for his son.

Emily mooched around for a bit, picking up a thriller for Adam, and a couple of picture books for her friend Lucy's little girls, an adorable five and three. Lucy had been Emily's best friend since their teens, so it seemed like a no-brainer to move near her when Graham had ditched her. Thanks to meeting Adam, despite all they'd faced in the last year, it had been one of the best decisions of Emily's life. Particularly in the long lonely months after Livvy's death, when Emily wasn't sure that she and Adam even had a future any more, it had been great to have Lucy on hand offering support and wise advice.

Emily had arranged to meet Lucy for coffee today in Marks, as she was getting some last-minute bits while the children were at school and nursery. It had been a while since they'd seen each other, and Emily was looking forward to catching up on the gossip, and letting her know the latest with Adam. Lucy was one of the few people Emily had entrusted with the truth of her relationship.

Her friend came from a hugely dysfunctional family where people seemed to swap partners like it was going out of fashion – her mother was already on her third husband. Lucy's mantra was: do no harm (although Emily felt guiltily that she hadn't stuck to that one) and secondly: you can't help who you fall in love with. This was very true. Emily had never intended to fall in love with Adam and, realizing the danger she was in early on, had tried to avoid him as much as possible. But then one night they'd met accidentally in a bar, and the goodnight kiss Adam had given her had turned into something more. They had both leapt back, apologetic, promising each other it couldn't happen again, and Emily had deliberately avoided swimming for a few weeks. But they lived in a small town, and it was inevitable that they would run into one another occasionally. Despite their best efforts, Emily and Adam found themselves drawn together; they were both swept up in an emotion they could neither deny nor control, and Emily couldn't be sorry. Adam was simply the best thing that had ever happened to her. Even though Livvy's death had made their relationship more complicated, she was hoping that now with the anniversary out of the way, and Joe beginning to accept that Emily was part of Adam's life, they could finally begin to build a future for themselves. Adam asking her to move in was a good start.

Emily found Lucy already sitting down at the table. Her 8-month-old baby, Amy, was asleep in the buggy. Lucy looked trim and energetic as ever, her dark hair tied in a neat ponytail, her smart jeans, jumper and jacket showing no evidence that she was dealing with a small baby twenty-four/seven. Emily had no idea how her friend managed three of them, but Lucy always made it look like a breeze.

'How are things in the love nest?' Lucy greeted Emily. It was a running joke.

'Fine,' Emily said, sitting down with her Americano. 'Actually, more than fine. Adam's asked me to move in.'

'That's brilliant.' Lucy gave Emily a hug. 'I'm so happy for you.'

'Me too,' said Emily. 'Except that I made a bit of a tit of myself last night.' She then proceeded to fill Lucy in on the events of the previous evening.

Lucy hooted with laughter. 'You eejit,' she said.

'I know,' said Emily. 'Anyway, that's not what I wanted to talk to you about. This thing with Adam . . .'

. . .'is very simple,' said Lucy. 'You love him, and he loves you. End of story.'

Emily grinned, Lucy always had the knack of making her feel better about life.

'So you're moving in, that's exciting. How's Joe about it?' Lucy knew all about Joe. In her old life she had been a social worker, and was really helpful with advice about Joe's condition.

'Well, he did ask if I was going to be his new mum,' said Emily.

'Which is great, but . . . ?'

'But . . . it's such a lot to take on. Sorry, I didn't mean it like that, I don't want to sound selfish. But how can I be a mother to Joe? I haven't the experience and, from what Adam tells me, Livvy was amazing with him. He's had to go through such a lot, and I don't want to make things harder for him.'

'That is perfectly understandable,' said Lucy. 'It's a massive thing you're doing. I'd take it one step at a time if I were you. And never try to be Joe's best mate.' She shuddered. 'God, do you remember that awful woman my dad dated when I was fifteen? Kerry, I think her name was. She was constantly trying to take me out shopping and having girlie chats with me. It was excruciating.'

Emily grinned. 'I can't see me doing that any time with Joe.'

'There you are then,' said Lucy. 'So long as you show sensitivity and understanding it will all work out in the long run. And in the meantime you can use this Christmas as a testing ground. If you have a great time together, Joe is bound to be more relaxed with you.'

'Oh yes, Christmas,' said Emily with a grimace. 'I'm really looking forward to being with Adam, but how on earth am I supposed to deal with the ex-mother-in-law?'

Emily was torn about Christmas. In the two years she and Adam had been seeing each other, she'd understood she couldn't be with him at Christmas, particularly last year, but she'd longed for them to have time together. And now they had, but it came with Felicity attached. Much as she wanted to cuddle up to Adam under the mistletoe or next to the Christmas tree in the evening, she was dreading getting through the day itself.

'It'll be fine,' Lucy said, a veteran of awkward family Christmases. 'Just make sure everyone has enough to drink that they're happy, but not too much to be emotional, and you'll be OK.'

'We've got Dad coming over this weekend, so we're all meeting up then,' Emily said. 'With Dad there everyone has to at least be polite to each other.'

'You'll have to warn him off trying it on with Felicity,' Lucy said, knowing Emily's dad of old.

'Oh he probably will,' said Emily, 'but at least it will take the heat off me.'

'Goodness, is that the time?' Lucy looked at her watch. 'I've got to get Chloe from nursery. You won't forget my Christmas drinks party will you?'

'Wouldn't miss it for the world,' Emily said. Lucy's Christmas drinks parties were legendary, but Graham had always been reluctant to go to them. One of many benefits of not being married to him any more was that Emily now could. She hugged Lucy goodbye, and watched her dash down the high street at breakneck speed, slightly envying her her chaotic family life and wondering wistfully how soon she and Adam would be in a position to have children of their own.

Emily carried on mooching around the shops, and then headed home. It was starting to sleet slightly and she hurried to get out of the cold. As she turned the corner to her street, Emily felt a sudden rush of cold air, and the weird unsettling feeling that someone was behind her, and then she slid slightly on the slippery pavement, tripping over and tumbling to the floor. She sat up slightly winded, but otherwise unhurt. The vague uneasy feeling that someone was there remained, and she had the distinct impression that something or someone had tripped her up. But when she looked down the street there was no one and nothing there.

Adam

Joe is sitting in the lounge watching TV when I come in from work a couple of days later. There is a delicious smell coming from the kitchen. Felicity, Livvy's mum, is clearly cooking for us again. She comes over twice a week, to keep Joe company, she says, though I sometimes wonder if that's true. I think she's been lonely since her husband James died, and losing Livvy has been a further massive blow to her. I get the feeling it helps her to keep an eye on us, and make sure we eat. And heaven knows I'm grateful, particularly on nights like this evening when I have to work late.

'Hi Dad,' says Joe, then turns back to the screen. 'I'm watching a programme about black holes. It's awesome.' Then he's off explaining enthusiastically about supernovas and the expanding universe, and other things I don't understand. I listen to him fondly. I love his space obsession. It's been something that's kept him focused and calm since he was a small kid. There's something about the stars being both mutable and yet fixed in a pattern that he can relate to in a way that he can't to a lot of other things in the world. He finds comfort in the darkness and vastness of space, which has been a great boon. 'You should watch this, Dad, it's great,' says Joe, finishing his monologue.

'I will, Joe, I promise,' I say, as he switches back to what really interests him.

'Is Granny here?' I ask.

'Yes,' says Joe, barely looking up.

I go into the kitchen and brace myself for a lecture. I've only recently broken it to her that I am seeing someone else, and she's been a bit sniffy about it, though she did agree that meeting up with Emily and her dad before Christmas was a good idea. Of course, it must be hard for her thinking I've found someone to replace her daughter, so I accept her negativity about it with good grace. Felicity has been great to us, and I love her very dearly. I would feel lousy if I've upset her – and even lousier if she ever found out the truth about when Emily and I got together.

'Hi,' I say and lightly peck her on the cheek. 'That smells good.'

'My special chicken stew,' she says, smiling. She always looks so at home in the kitchen, and she's an exceptionally good cook. 'You boys need building up.'

Her favourite saying since Livvy died. She often used to do this when Livvy was alive, while never acknowledging the reason she needed to be here. The closest she ever came to speaking of it was to refer once or twice to 'Livvy's little problem'. Sometimes I used to wish we could talk about it honestly, rather than skirting around the issue with euphemisms. We both knew what Livvy's 'little problem' was, but somehow it was easier to bury it under the carpet. I realize now that was wrong. If I had been more insistent about getting Livvy help, perhaps things would have been different. But on the few occasions I'd suggested it Livvy's reaction had been explosive and I hadn't pursued it. I did persuade her to go to counselling for a while, but she said it was a waste of time, and refused to discuss it further. And so I'd left it, drifting along, hoping things might somehow miraculously get better.

So much left unsaid and undone. It kills me that I can never change that.

Felicity turns to me, and says, 'Tea? Or beer?'

'Tea, please,' I say. My head has been pounding all day from last night. I'm getting too old for drinking in the week.

'Good,' she says, 'because I think we need to chat.'

I feel I know what is coming.

'It's about Joe,' she says firmly, which is something of a surprise. I thought I was going to get a lecture. She shuts the kitchen door, which leads into the lounge, makes the tea and we both sit down. Outside a cold wind is rattling at the door. I really need to insulate this house properly.

'He keeps saying he's seen his mum,' Felicity says. She

betrays no emotion. In fact, as far as I know she's barely cried since losing Livvy. She was like a rock at the funeral, when Joe and I were total messes. Felicity is such a stoical character, she would probably hate me to see her weakened by emotion. But she must feel it with her husband also gone. Joe and I are all she has left.

'What? What do you mean, *seen* her?'

'He says he was having coffee with Caroline, and she sat next to him and talked to him.'

This was new. I hadn't known Joe had the capacity for that sort of imaginative leap.

'I think it must be the fact it was the anniversary,' says Felicity. 'Maybe we ought to visit Livvy's grave again. Help him find some closure. He also says he's bought her a present. It's lovely, of course, but I'm worried he hasn't taken on board the fact she's gone and isn't coming back.'

'What do you think we should do?' I say. Felicity, much like her daughter was, is good at practical solutions.

'More counselling, perhaps?' Felicity says. She looks anxious and unsettled, not like herself at all. She always exudes such calm and confidence to the world. 'It might help.'

'It might,' I say cautiously. Joe did have counselling after Livvy died, but I wasn't convinced it helped him much. 'It might be better if I tried talking to him first.'

Really, I'm freaked out. I hadn't anticipated this reaction. I wish I knew an easy way to help my son.

'There is something else.' Felicity pulls a face. 'And it's a bit delicate.'

Ah, here we go.

'It's about your young lady,' begins Felicity.

'Emily, yes?'

'Joe told me he's asked her to be his mum.'

'I know, and you probably feel it's far too soon,' I say, 'and that with Joe still missing Livvy so much, it might complicate things for him, but we'll take it slowly, I promise—'

'I think you should go for it with Emily,' says Felicity, to my surprise. 'It might help him accept what's happened. Emily being around won't bring Livvy back. And I know how difficult it's been for you.'

Her expression softens.

'Livvy was my daughter, but she had her problems, and you were more understanding than most husbands would have been. And yes, I'd love to have the chance to meet Emily and her dad, thank you for inviting me.'

'Felicity, I don't know what to say.' Whatever I've been expecting, it wasn't this. I give her a huge hug. My relationship with my parents isn't exactly brilliant – they've hardly been in contact since Livvy died, and have gone off on a cruise this Christmas. In many ways Felicity has been more of a mum to me than my own mum. My voice cracks slightly as I say, 'Thanks for being so generous. I know this can't be easy for you.'

'Don't say anything,' Felicity says, her own voice choking slightly. 'It's not what I would have wanted, but it's what it is. I can't promise to like this Emily. And if Joe is upset by any of this, I'll never forgive you, but let's take it a day at a time.'

At that moment there is a huge gust of wind, and the back door blows open, gusting in the sleet. I get up to shut the door, and the lights go out.

Joe comes into the kitchen from the lounge.

'Hello, Mum,' he says.

'Joe,' I say, 'can you see me?' He is staring right at me, and I feel like I might explode from the sudden wave of joy that hits me. It's the happiest I've felt since I came to in the car park.

'What do you mean?' Adam says. 'Joe, you know Mum's not here. She died. You understand what that means, don't you?'

He's so gentle with Joe. I would have hugged him if I could. I go to Adam, but he stares right through me. I so want him to notice me; to feel his touch, yet he doesn't even know I'm here.

'Mum's turned the lights off,' says Joe in a matter-of-fact way, 'but it's OK, she'll turn them back on again.'

I feel totally stupid then, and focus on the mains switch, which I've just worked out I seem to be able to turn on and off at will. Within seconds the lights are back on and Mum and Adam are standing looking aghast at Joe.

'See, I told you,' says Joe, but he carries on looking right through me. 'It's OK, she just wants to be with us.'

'If she is here, I'm sure she'd only be thinking of us,' says Adam cautiously.

'Of course I am!' I snap pettishly. 'What on earth would you expect?'

I am dismayed. Why can't they see me? What does a girl have to do to get noticed around here?

'That's right,' says Joe happily. 'She just wants to say hello.'

I feel totally rubbish then. I'd been so angry when I came in, furious with Mum for saying Emily should move in. Whose side was she on, anyway? Clearly not *mine*. But Joe's response has taken the wind out of my sails. I only want to talk to him properly, to tell him I love him.

'I'm going to watch TV now,' says Joe, "Bye, Mum.' And with that he's gone.

Adam and Mum look at one another.

'Now do you see what I mean?' says Mum. 'I think you really ought to get him to see a counsellor again.'

'OK,' says Adam reluctantly. 'I hope we can find someone who understands Joe this time though. Joe looked at the last one as if he had two heads. I'll get on to the GP in the morning, see what she advises.' Our GP has known Joe his whole life. It's a reasonable thought.

'He's not grieving,' I say, though of course no one hears. 'Because he knows I'm here. He's the only one who does.'

Every moment I've had since I arrived back to the house, I've been sitting with Joe when he's on his own. He knows I'm there because he talks to me about his astronomy projects at college, and about Caroline, who he's thinking of asking out. He doesn't appear to hear all my responses, but I know he's happy I'm around. If only everyone else could see it too.

How was I ever going to get through to them? I need to speak to Adam and Joe to tell them how sorry I am, to tell them I love them. The thing is, for all Malachi tells me I've got to sort my shit out, now I'm here, in my house, seeing my husband and son, all I want is to be with them again, I can't let Evil Emily become Joe's new mum, I just can't. That is going to happen over my dead body.

And as for Mum, I'm furious with her for accepting Emily into the family so readily. 'You wouldn't if you knew what I know!' I yell furiously, but of course she can't hear me.

Malachi has shown me how to channel my powers to

move objects, but I still haven't mastered it very well. But it's time I step up Campaign Haunt My Husband a notch, to make him take notice of me once and for all. So I concentrate really hard on tipping the fruit bowl off the table, although it seems to require more effort than switching the power on and off, and it's a struggle to push it over the edge.

It lands with a satisfying crash on the floor, with the apples and satsumas rolling everywhere.

'What was that?' says Adam, nearly jumping out of his skin.

'That, dear husband,' I say, 'is only the beginning . . .'

Chapter Five

Emily

Emily was shopping in Tesco's for Christmas. It was the first time Emily had ever cooked a Christmas lunch – Dad, bless him, had managed to get his friendly women to cook for him after Mum died, and when Emily was married, they'd always gone to Graham's for a dull family Christmas dinner, the implication being that she wasn't really up to the task. Emily loved the way that Adam pulled his weight in their relationship.

'You're doing Christmas Day,' he'd said, knowing how much it meant to her, 'so I'll cook for your dad and Felicity.'

Despite her anxiety about how they were all going to get through the day, Emily couldn't help feeling excited as she wandered down the aisles filling her trolley. Their first Christmas together: she had to pinch herself to believe it could be happening, particularly after last year when she thought she might never see Adam again. On reaching the turkey aisle she was surprised by the choice. How on earth did she work out what she wanted? She enjoyed spending time in the kitchen but her cooking hitherto had been of the spag bol, pasta-bake type. Graham hadn't often been in for dinner, and when he was home they'd tended to live on takeaways and ready meals, so the thought of cooking a full Christmas dinner was giving Emily palpitations. She didn't have a clue what kind of turkey to buy. Regretting her rather independent decision not to consult Adam about it, Emily stood looking at the turkeys feeling ridiculously incompetent. She wondered whether she'd bitten off more than she could chew. She so wanted to prove to Adam that she could step into his family and make Christmas special for all of them, but she was beginning to appreciate that it might not be as easy as that.

This was ridiculous. Independent cooking didn't mean Emily couldn't consult an expert, so she rang Lucy, who had years of experience of cooking Christmas dinner.

'As it's your first time, I'd be tempted to go with a turkey crown,' Lucy advised.

'I'd rather do it properly, if I can,' Emily said.

'OK. It's too late to order a turkey from the butcher's, so get yourself a frozen turkey and make sure you defrost it in plenty of time.'

Apparently Lucy had forgotten to do this the first year she cooked turkey and they had to have chipolatas for lunch.

'If you want to play it really risky you can panic-buy on Christmas Eve, but I've been there, and believe you me, you don't want to do that.'

Even with Lucy's helpful advice, Emily still found herself gawking like an idiot at the huge selection of turkeys.

After some deliberation, she settled on a ten-pound bird. Better to have leftovers, right? And the boys had huge appetites.

Then she raided the Christmas pudding section. Having accepted her limitations, Emily wasn't quite brave enough to make one of them. The selection was vast: orange-flavoured, fruit-filled, boozy. So many varieties. Who knew? She chose two, in case everyone hated the marmalade one, which she herself quite fancied, and heaped packets of mince pies on top. Then she couldn't resist lots of treats and booze. By the time Emily got to the till, her trolley was piled high.

Tesco's was crammed full of grumpy people buying food like it was going out of fashion, and the tills were manic. Eventually it was Emily's turn and she started loading her purchases on to the belt. As she picked the turkey up, she felt a slight frisson of unease, as a familiar sensation of cold menace came over her, and then the turkey slipped out of her hands and landed with a thump on her foot.

Emily screamed out loud, and started hopping on her good foot. She couldn't believe how much it hurt.

'Are you all right?' The girl on the till came rushing round, and made her sit down at a chair behind the till. She called over a supervisor, who insisted that Emily fill in an accident form. 'I'm fine, really,' said Emily, squirming with embarrassment as she watched the queue behind her go into meltdown. She tried to stand up, but the pain was horrific so she had to sit down again.

After twenty minutes the pain had receded a little bit but Emily was still hobbling, so the supervisor accompanied her to the car with her trolley. Mortified by the incident, Emily's earlier good mood had vanished.

It was sleeting again as she loaded the food in the car. A possible white Christmas was forecast, though Emily wasn't convinced. She felt sure the nearest they'd get to snow would be this miserable grey slush.

As Emily shut the boot, she felt a trickle of unease. She had the weird sensation that someone was watching her; someone very angry and spiteful. Which was ridiculous.

The car park was full of tired, hungry shoppers, none of them interested in what Emily was doing. She was imagining things.

Adam

'Joe,' I say, poking my head round the doorway, after Felicity has gone home. 'Can I have a word?'

'A word? What word?' Joe looks blank for a moment, and then I say, 'Can I talk to you?' and he relaxes and motions me to sit down on his bed. He's constructing a model of the latest space shuttle. He is absorbed in its intricate lines, and I usually love watching him work. But I have to interrupt him now.

'Joe,' I begin cautiously, 'would you like to talk about Mum?'

'Mum died,' says Joe cheerfully. It's disconcerting the way he does that, as if he hasn't quite taken in the enormity of what has happened. Yet at other times he can seem sad, like he's really missing her.

'Yes,' I say. 'So yesterday – you understand that she has gone and won't ever come back, don't you? You know you can't have seen her.'

'I didn't see her,' says Joe, 'but she's here. I feel her in my head.'

This is worse than I thought. My heart contracts with pain for my lovely vulnerable son. What a godawful thing to have happened to him so young. I've tried my best, but I clearly haven't picked up on how much he is missing his mum.

'The thing is, Joe, you know that can't be right, don't you?' I say. 'I know it's a nice thought to imagine Mum is talking to you, but it's not true.'

'Yes it is,' says Joe, 'because Mum hasn't gone yet. She wants to see us still. She misses us.'

'Joe,' I say, a chill going down my spine. 'What are you saying exactly?'

'Mum's a ghost,' says Joe, 'and she's pretty pissed off with you.'

As well she might be.

This is madness, though. Joe seemed to cope very well after Livvy died, but then his reactions aren't like other people's. Though we both howled together at the graveside, and he even let me hug him, since then he's retreated into himself, while appearing to be perfectly happy. He always says he is when I ask. Now I feel terrible. I've let both him and Livvy down. I know Livvy would have handled this much better than I am doing. I miss her suddenly with a terrible aching pang.

'Look, Joe, I think maybe we should go and see Dr Clarkson, have a chat about some of the things you're feeling.'

'OK,' says Joe, shrugging his shoulders, 'but I'm not mad, you know.'

'I never said you were,' I begin.

'You thought it, though,' says Joe dispassionately. 'But, honestly, I'm not mad. Mum's here and I think she's planning to stay.'

Livvy

I've been quite pleased with myself since I made Emily drop the turkey on her toe. Small and petty I know, but it made me feel better, even though I know Malachi will tell me off.

But now, listening to Adam and Joe's conversation,

93

I'm pretty put out. Adam will have Joe seeing a shrink before I know it, and I hadn't planned for that at all. He doesn't need to see a shrink, he needs me, and for Adam not to ruin his life by bringing that conniving cow into it.

I mull over my (limited) options, and decide I'll just have to stick with the plan of upping the haunting, so they all realize I'm there, and that Joe isn't making it up. I decide I've been way too tame so far, and I need to create the maximum chaos. So I start moving stuff around. I'm getting better at it now, and I have to confess it's tremendous fun; particularly seeing the puzzled look on Adam's face when he finds something somewhere unexpected.

I hide Adam's phone under the sofa. I unplug his iPod and put the charger in a saucepan at the back of a cupboard. He only discovers it when he's cooking dinner the next night.

I deliberately don't take anything of Joe's, until I hear Adam talking about it worriedly with Mum.

'I'm worried Joe is taking things,' he said. 'But if I ask him he looks at me blankly. I'm not sure what on earth I should do.'

'It doesn't seem like Joe,' Mum said. Because it's not Joe, I try and scream at them. Honestly! The pair of them are being so dense it's driving me nuts.

So I up it a notch, and put Mum's purse in Adam's briefcase, and Joe's wallet in Mum's handbag. It takes a lot of effort – the poltergeist aspect of haunting your family is a lot more tiring than I imagined it would be, and I am exhausted at the end of it all. Malachi tells me even though we're dead ghosts need space to replenish their energy levels.

'I feel like I'm losing my mind,' says Adam to Evil Emily, next time she's round. (I'm pathetically pleased to see she's still limping.) 'I just can't work out what's going on. I can't seem to find anything any more. If I believed in such things, I'd say we had a poltergeist.'

'We do,' says Joe, who's calmly colouring in the corner of the kitchen. 'It's Mum, she's trying to get our attention.'

'OK, Joe, even if that were true,' says Adam cautiously, 'I don't see why she should be hiding our things.'

'Because you're not listening to her of course,' says Joe. 'She just wants you to listen.'

'That's right,' I say, standing between Adam and Emily, 'please listen to me.'

I knock a cup on the floor.

But Adam looks right through me and says, 'Careful, Joe,' and shrugs his shoulders at Emily, and that hurts more than anything else could. What do I have to do to get him to see me?

Emily touches Adam's hand and it goes right through me. I feel sick, trapped in the middle like this, feeling the love that flows between them. 'Did you get an appointment?' she says.

'Yes, we're seeing Dr Clarkson tomorrow.'

'It will be fine,' says Emily. 'It's only natural that Joe's been upset by everything.'

'I'm not upset,' says Joe chattily, getting up to make himself a drink. 'But Mum is.'

And I am. Suddenly I feel as if my heart will burst out of my chest – well, if I still had a chest, or a heart for that matter.

I let out a wail and the Christmas cards that Adam has been opening slightly lift off the table. Hang on, *that's* new.

I didn't know I could levitate stuff. I try wailing again to no avail. And then I get down by the table and let out an ear-splitting scream, and the cards blow off, scattering in all directions.

'You have to admit,' says Emily, '*that* is odd.'

Chapter Six

Adam

Today I've taken time off work I can ill afford, to take Joe to the doctor's, trying to find out proper answers to his behaviour. I feel anxious. Livvy always dealt with the medical stuff, and I am completely out of my depth. What if there's something seriously wrong with him? Joe has enough problems. I can't stand the thought of him suffering any more because of losing his mum. Emily has agreed to come with us, more for my moral support than his. I don't think Joe cares one way or another. In fact, he seems quite indifferent about the whole thing.

When Dr Clarkson calls us in, I have no idea what I'm going to say to her. I like Dr Clarkson, she's kind and friendly, with a no-nonsense air about her. I saw her for a bit in the first awful weeks after Livvy died, when I was completely poleaxed and wasn't sleeping. She prescribed me tablets, which I still don't take because they made me feel so spaced out, it was as if I wasn't functioning. Terrible as it was feeling the way I did, I preferred that to the effects of the medication.

'Hi. What can I do for you?' she says, a mixture of professionalism and ready sympathy.

'Erm,' I clear my throat.

And then Joe interjects, 'Dad thinks I'm mad.'

'Joe,' I protest. 'That's not why we're here.'

'And do you think you're mad, Joe?' Dr Clarkson asks kindly.

'No,' says Joe. 'I have Asperger's. *That's* different.'

'Yes, it is,' says Dr Clarkson, smiling. 'So can you tell me what's been happening?'

'Mum's come back,' says Joe.

'Right,' says Dr Clarkson. To her credit she doesn't bat an eyelid. I suppose she hears all sorts in here. 'And what makes you think that?'

'Because she came to visit me in the café and calmed me down,' says Joe. 'No one but Mum can do that. And she sits with me in my room and I tell her about physics and my friend, Caroline.'

I start. I wonder if Caroline has become his girlfriend? I suppose it makes sense that he can't tell *me*. Maybe that's why he's pretending Livvy's here. Dr Clarkson is clearly thinking on similar lines.

'And you don't think you're imagining that to help you?' she says gently. 'You've been through a rough time. It's only natural.'

'It's Mum,' says Joe stubbornly. 'She's upset about Dad and Emily, only no one else is *listening*.'

Emily and I exchange nervous glances. We'd discussed the events of the previous evening when we went to bed last night. Emily still thinks the cards blowing off the table was strange, but I am doggedly determined it must have been a gust of wind.

Emily didn't agree. 'I know it sounds bonkers,' she said, 'but I've been having the strangest feeling that someone is watching me. And I swear something tripped me up in the street the other day. Then there was the turkey incident and what happened in the bar at your party. I didn't spill that drink by accident.'

'This is nonsense. So you've suddenly developed a clumsy streak,' I snapped, because the thought of that made me feel too anxious. I refuse to believe that Livvy has come back. Dead is dead. I saw her body. I watched her coffin go in the ground. I don't believe in ghosts.

'What if you're wrong and Joe and I are right?' Emily was still persisting this morning before we came here, much to my annoyance.

'There are no such things as ghosts,' I said. 'I'm sure there's a rational explanation for everything that's happened to you, and as for Joe I'm worried about him. Maybe Dr Clarkson can help.'

Now we're here and Joe is saying stuff that sounds completely mad, I am feeling more anxious than ever.

Dr Clarkson looks at us now. She knows about the affair. I was in such a state after Livvy died, I took time off work for stress, and the whole story came out then.

'And how do you feel about your dad and Emily?' Dr Clarkson says carefully.

Joe looks at us both.

'Emily's nice,' he offers, 'but she's not Mum.' Ouch.

'I see,' says Dr Clarkson. 'Joe. Please can you go and sit on one of the brown chairs near the reception desk? You can choose which one. I need to have a quick chat with your dad.'

'OK,' says Joe. He seems totally unfazed and dutifully leaves the room.

'How long has this been going on?' Dr Clarkson asks.

'A few days,' I say. 'I guess with the anniversary last week everything has suddenly become very raw again.'

'Has anything unusual happened apart from that?'

Where do I begin? I think. But I'm not sure I should share that, otherwise Dr Clarkson will think I'm mad too.

'Joe did ask if Emily was going to be his new mum,' I say. 'We were both shocked.'

'Hmm,' says Dr Clarkson. 'Joe seems fine in himself, but it might be the stress of the anniversary and thinking you're going to replace his mum has triggered some kind of psychotic episode. I think I probably need another opinion.'

'I'm not sure another counsellor would help,' I say. 'Joe didn't do too well with the last one.'

'No, not that,' she says. 'I think he needs some quite specialist advice. In the meantime I'm going to write down a prescription for Joe, which might help to calm him down if he gets upset again.'

Medication? She wants to medicate my son? Livvy would kill me if she were here.

'Are you sure that's necessary, Dr Clarkson? Can't we solve this another way?'

'Well, it might help in the short term,' she said. 'I can understand your concerns, but what I'm prescribing isn't addictive at all, and it's a very low dose. You could always see how thing go, and wait a while longer. But it might be helpful knowing you've got it in the house to prevent him becoming agitated and upset.'

She puts her glasses on, and taps away on her computer, but when she goes to print out the prescription, she frowns.

'Oh,' she says. 'Sorry, the printer seems to be on the blink.'

She tapped some more and still nothing happens. I look at my watch surreptitiously; I need to get to work.

After five minutes Dr Clarkson says, 'I'm so sorry about this. I'll leave it in reception for you to pick up later.'

I feel I've been given a reprieve.

'In the meantime, I'll refer Joe to Dr Sabah, at the teenage health clinic, but I'm afraid it will be the other side of Christmas now.'

The other side of Christmas seems an age away, but it doesn't look like we have a choice.

'Thanks for your help, Dr Clarkson,' I say.

We get up to go and then I spot a trailing cable.

'Think I might have found your problem,' I say. 'The printer's unplugged.'

'Really?' Dr Clarkson frowns. 'I could have sworn I'd plugged it in.'

Emily

Poor Adam, thought Emily as he went to work after the appointment. He looked so miserable and worried, Emily offered to take Joe for a hot chocolate and see if she could get him to open up a bit.

Adam looked hugely relieved when she suggested it.

She gave him a kiss and then said brightly to Joe, 'Shall we go to the café by the river?'

Joe's eyes lit up. 'Yes please,' he said. 'Can I have a large hot chocolate with cream and marshmallows, please?'

'Your wish is my command,' said Emily.

It was a grey miserable day, and a bitter east wind blew in their faces as they approached the river. Despite the festive cheer in the café, Emily had been left disturbed by what the doctor had said. What if Joe was seriously unwell? Although Adam had tried to be upbeat for Joe's sake, Emily knew he was worried sick.

Joe in the meantime seemed quite unconcerned. He sat cheerfully drinking his chocolate, wittering on about the technical specifications of the telescope he'd asked for for Christmas. Emily didn't understand a word, but was enjoying listening. He was keeping up a constant chatter about the constellations, and his enthusiasm was infectious. On a good day Emily could just about tell where the Plough was but Joe was a veritable encyclopaedia. He didn't chat to her very often, and it was lovely listening to him talking about it, even though Emily couldn't help herself from slightly drifting off when he went into a long description about stars she'd never heard of, and from there into a rambling monologue assessing the evidence about whether or not aliens existed.

'They must,' he said. 'There are so many other planets out there. I can't see why some of them don't support life. It's illogical to think anything else.'

Emily laughed.

'I suppose you could be right,' she said, thinking how relieved she was to be having a conversation about the possibility of alien life, instead of about his dead mother coming back from the grave.

'And if you think about it,' he continued, 'it's not so unreasonable to think that ghosts exist. If there's life on other planets, why shouldn't there be an astral plane which none of us can see?'

Oh good, they were back on ghosts again.

'I suppose it's possible,' Emily said.

'I know it is now,' said Joe happily, 'otherwise Mum wouldn't have come back.'

'Joe,' Emily began cautiously, 'will you tell me why you're so certain it is your mum? All the things happening at home could be coincidence. Your dad's been saying for ages he needs to fix the wiring at home. Things get lost all the time. You and your dad are so untidy I'm not surprised you can't find anything. And it's so draughty in your house, it's no wonder the cards blew off the table.'

She said this with rather more conviction than she felt, because despite Adam's insistence that nothing untoward was happening, she'd been seriously rattled by the events of the last few days, especially when she was on her own. And Adam was so worried about Joe, she hadn't wanted to push him into talking about it further. What was more, despite her own misgivings, Emily didn't really want to encourage Joe into believing his mum had come back to haunt them. The creeping fear which she was tamping down, because it was utterly ridiculous, was that if Livvy had reappeared, she might be about to exact some terrible revenge on her and Adam. Why else would she be here now, of all times?

'That is a logical explanation,' admitted Joe, 'but I know it's Mum. I hear her thoughts in my head.' He tapped his head and smiled. 'I've told you before. She just wants to talk to us, and Dad isn't paying attention. That's why she's doing all the stuff with the lights and everything.'

'But if she's so determined to talk to your dad,' Emily argued, 'why doesn't she appear in front of us?'

Joe frowned.

'I don't think she can,' he said. 'I think she needs us to let her in.'

He sounded so certain, Emily felt a chill up her spine. What if Joe was right? What then?

Livvy

I am steaming mad when we leave the GP's surgery. I cannot believe that Dr Clarkson has suggested medication for Joe, or that Adam's even considering it. There's nothing at all wrong with him, only none of them can see it. I have to

103

find a way of communicating with Adam, and soon, or Joe will be sectioned before I know it.

It was satisfying to pull the plug out of the printer, so Dr Clarkson couldn't print the prescription. I must skip back later and make sure it gets lost in the system. If Adam remembers to go back, he'll be sent away again, and this close to Christmas he might not have time to go and get it. That will give me the opportunity to make my presence properly felt, and there'll be no need to feed mind-altering chemicals to my son.

I drift through the ranks of Christmas shoppers, so happy and excited about the coming season, and wander in and out of pubs and restaurants in the evening, full of shiny happy people. I feel discontented and alone. It would be nice to meet some other ghosts to share this misery with. Who knew being dead could be so lonely? The only person who remotely acknowledges my existence so far is Joe, and I've not managed to talk to him. In fact, I've only made matters worse.

Maybe I should try Mum. She'll be a tough nut to crack. As a renowned sceptic – she wasn't even very convincing about Father Christmas when I was little – I know she'll resist me. But it's worth a try, even if I get a lecture for my pains, which I probably will. Mum never stinted from putting me right when she thought I'd gone wrong, and I suspect, like Malachi, she'd think I'm handling things badly.

Mum lives in a two-up two-down off the local village green. It's small, but pretty, and she keeps it spick and span. She downsized after Dad died, and I'm glad she's in a position to be comfortable. Now I'm gone there's only Adam to look after her in her old age, and it might be tough for him to manage that. Adam and Emily. I feel angry all over again. How can Mum be on their side? What about me?

It makes me feel sad to think that even Mum seems to have moved on, and is getting by without me. She's my mum and though our relationship was prickly when I was alive, I miss her badly. No one tells you that the dead get to grieve for the living as much as the other way round. But it's true. I miss Mum, Joe and Adam with a fierce ache, and it feels like Mum has forgotten all about me. She's my mum; surely she must still think of me sometimes?

Mum is sitting at the piano practising Christmas carols when I arrive. She's playing 'O Little Town of Bethlehem', and I sit and listen for a minute; it's lovely to hear her play and sing again.

She'll be getting ready for the Christmas services. I feel a pang. Christmas carols were such a huge part of my life growing up; such a feature of Christmas. I miss that too. It's been years since we sat down and sang together. Mum's not particularly religious, but she loves the music and, to be fair, so do I. It's an absolute joy listening to her sing. The sound takes me back to being little, when, Father Christmas issues notwithstanding, Christmas seemed a magical and simple time. In my memory it's always snowing and we're all smiling, and I make snowmen with my dad. Though I know that probably only happened once, the perception is still strong. Amazing how memories, particularly good ones, cast such long shadows.

I sit listening to Mum sing, and my heart feels peaceful and content for the first time since I died. My earlier rage has dissipated. Tentatively I approach the piano.

'Mum?' I say. 'Can you hear me?'

Mum stops, frowns, adjusts her glasses, and begins to play 'Silent Night'. We used to sing this together when I was young. Mum would provide the descant to my alto. I always envied her the purity of her soprano voice. Dad sometimes joined in, though in the main he preferred to listen. We were so happy then, the three of us, a secure and tight little unit. Somehow, though I retained that closeness with Dad, I lost it with Mum, particularly after he died. I feel utterly bereft. My mum is standing right by me and I can't reach her, or talk to her, any more than I could when I was alive. It makes me feel very lonely.

I go and stand behind Mum and sing with her. I realize she can't hear me, but it comforts me to be this close to her. Sure, Mum drove me mad when I was alive, but she's my mum, and sometimes I was really horrid to her. Hang on, where did that thought come from? I had never considered it before. Mum was often on my case with Joe, and always seemed to be there, under my feet. I got very fed up with what I saw as her interfering. But she was only trying to help. It's only just occurred to me that maybe I should have listened harder.

Joe's Notebook

Do ghosts exist? Logic says they don't. When you're dead you're dead.

Is logic wrong?

There might be life on other worlds for all we know, so why not think there is life after death?

Dad and Emily think I am mad because I've heard Mum talking to me.

I know I'm not mad.

Mum was there in the café with me and Caroline. She's been moving things round the house. She's been switching the lights on and off and making it cold.

She sits in my room and listens while I talk to her.

I know it's her.

I'm not mad.

Therefore ghosts must exist.

My mum is still here.

Christmas Past

'Ah-ha, we have progress.' Malachi finds me sitting on the green by Mum's house, watching people struggling home in the cold. 'You're beginning to see the impact of your behaviour on other people. That's what you need to understand before you can move on.' I feel disconsolate and miserable, and in no mood for Malachi. Did I really treat Mum badly? It makes me feel horrible to think that I might have.

'Maybe not all the time,' says Malachi, 'but I'd say you tried her patience quite a bit.'

'Well she tried mine,' I snap defensively. 'You have no idea what it was like for me always having her around.'

'Oh I think I do,' says Malachi remorselessly. 'And I'd say you were damned lucky to have had her there.'

Suddenly I'm back in the house again, and sitting with a 5-year-old Joe. He is carefully building pieces of Lego, one on top of the other, crafting some fantastic building, as he does. Mum is there too, sitting watching him, and helping him when he needs it.

I have a jolt. I remember this moment so clearly. It was

a difficult time and I was at the end of my tether. The feelings of panic and nausea return to me.

I am on the phone to Claire, Joe's key worker. Joe is now at school and it's not going well. They've tried their best, sending home a letter to the other children about how Joe has a special brain and doesn't understand things the way they do, but it's not working. The class teacher is stressed and hasn't been trained for this. Joe is one headache too many.

Joe does have a one to one helper: a local mum who's come back to work to fit in with the family. She's getting training on the job. It's not ideal. Besides, I get told by the other mums that she often gets hiked off to help the other kids, and at break time Joe is left to his own devices. The reception kids get it, and leave him alone, little enough not to notice the differences between them. They understand when Joe sits in the corner rearranging his pencils, or stands up occasionally muttering things to himself; that's just what Joe does. But the bigger kids tease him. Today there's been an incident, and Joe has hit another boy. His mum has complained. I might have done too, if I were her and didn't have an Asperger's son.

My arms and legs are proof of Joe's violence, when he doesn't understand what is happening. But I know he doesn't mean it. He lashes out because he is lost in a world of his own, and our world seems alien and frightening to him. Now he's sitting here with his Lego, he's calm and happy as Larry. If you manage him right, he is a sweet boy.

'Which they're not,' I explain to Claire. It's not the first time we've had this conversation. 'And he was provoked.'

'I do sympathize,' says Claire, 'but I think we might need to reassess his situation. A mainstream school might not suit long term.'

'So you mean he has to go to special school?' I say flatly.

Ever since I found out about Adam's brother, I have dreaded this.

'It might be the best way,' says Claire gently. 'Certainly, when he leaves infant school. You need to plan a strategy. I can help you.'

She carries on talking but I don't listen any more. I don't want to hide Joe away in a special school like Adam's parents did with Harry. It started there, and then they sent him away permanently. Though Adam has shown no signs of wanting to do the same there's a bit of me that's really afraid he might think this is what we should do too. He never sees his brother and barely ever talks about him. It terrifies me history might repeat itself, and Adam's parents will persuade him we should send Joe away. That was why I was so desperate to keep Joe in mainstream school, but it's clearly not working.

I am utterly miserable when I get off the phone. Mum says, 'Everything OK?' though it obviously isn't. I wish she wasn't here, putting her oar in. I wish I could go and hide and be alone somewhere and someone else could take this burden off my shoulders. Because though Mum is here and I can take a couple of hours out, it's not enough. I need weeks or months away from this. And I am never ever going to get that. There are some days it's just too hard, and today is one of them.

I don't answer her, but I go to the kitchen and do what I sometimes do on days when it gets too much. It's only 4.30 p.m. but it's dark already, and the sun is well over the yardarm. I pour myself a large drink and stare out at a mouldering sky.

Mum follows me in. 'That's not an answer you know.'

'Don't you start,' I say savagely. Mum has been telling me I drink too much since my teens. 'It's only one. And I've had a shitty day.'

'You know best,' says Mum, with pursed lips, though that's obviously not what she thinks. She goes back to Joe, while I continue to stare out at the garden. Before I know it, I seem to have downed the glass. So I pour myself another one. One more can't hurt.

Chapter Seven

Ten Days to Christmas

Emily

'I feel like I'm a prize sow in a pig judging competition,' wailed Emily as she and Dad set off to walk to Adam's house. She was beyond nervous about meeting Felicity and deeply grateful that Dad had driven down earlier in the day for their pre-Christmas get-together.

'She's bound to be curious,' Dad said.

'But what if she hates me?'

'How can she hate you?' That was her dad all over: always good at knocking down his daughter's insecurities. 'She'll probably be pleased that Adam's found a lovely girlfriend. Try to concentrate on the fact it's Adam you want to be with, not Felicity. Don't worry too much about it.'

But Emily couldn't be soothed.

'What if I hate *her*? I mean Livvy sounds like a total nightmare, and she must have got that from somewhere,' Emily said.

'And the sky might fall in,' said Dad. 'You worry too much. Now come on, let's get going or we'll be late, and you do want to make a good impression, don't you?'

'Thanks for coming, Dad, I appreciate it,' said Emily, as she took his arm and they walked down her street. 'And I hope you don't mind we're not coming to you on Christmas Day.'

'Mind, of course I don't mind,' said Dad. 'You know me, I like to have fun at Christmas. If you're there I'd have to be fussing about looking after you.'

Dad still hadn't quite worked out which worthy village lady was going to host him this Christmas, but 'I've had three offers,' he had said with a twinkle. Emily had laughed, 'And I'm guessing they don't know about each other? I've a good mind to ring them up.'

'Don't you dare, young lady. I never interfere with your love life.'

This was perfectly true. After Graham he hadn't asked questions, and just offered support. And last Christmas, in between being hand-fed strawberries at inappropriate times by the then squeeze, he'd offered sympathetic and helpful advice about how Emily should cope with the situation she'd found herself in. Still, grateful as she was to him, Emily was relieved not to have to be playing third wheel to her dad this Christmas. It was going to be much better all round seeing him on her own territory.

Dad was clearly not all that desperate to spend time with his daughter either. The action in Little Bisset was likely to be much more interesting than anything he'd find visiting her. If she could only get over the hurdle of meeting Felicity for the first time with no major hiccups, Emily might even start to get excited about her first Christmas with Adam, despite her nerves.

Emily had already warned Adam to tell Felicity that her dad was a notorious flirt, but he'd assured her Felicity hadn't so much as looked at a man since her husband died.

Maybe she would turn out to be that rare thing; a woman who didn't succumb to her dad's charms.

'How are you feeling, Pumpkin?' Dad said as they walked arm in arm down the high street.

Emily squeezed his arm with gratitude. Despite his frequent emotional dalliances, Dad could often show surprising empathy.

'Quite frankly I'm terrified. I understand why Felicity wants to check out the woman who's replacing her daughter, and I suppose I have to do this sometime. But bloody hell, I wish it were over.'

'Don't worry so much,' Dad said again. 'If it all gets too tricky I can always turn my charm on her.'

'Don't you dare,' laughed Emily, but she did feel a bit better.

Adam had told her she was fretting too much as well, but Emily couldn't quite believe him. However he clearly loved Felicity, and she'd been very good to Adam and Joe. In the first awful months after Livvy died, Emily, of course, stayed away, wanting to keep a low profile. Felicity had been a great support for Adam and Joe, even though she knew that things hadn't been good between him and her daughter.

'I'll never forget that,' he'd told Emily. 'She was like a rock and she'll always be part of my family.'

From that moment Emily had resolved to do her best to like Felicity too.

Emily's nerves hadn't calmed down by the time they arrived with her bottle of Pinot Noir, and port provided by Dad. She felt as if she were about to attend the worst kind of job interview.

It was another windy evening, though thankfully not raining. A mangy black cat ran across their path as they got up to the front door.

Since she'd talked to Joe, Emily was beginning to have weird fantasies about Livvy returning from beyond the grave, to punish her. She wasn't normally fanciful, but then again it wasn't like her to imagine someone had pushed her so she spilled her wine, or tripped her over or dropped things on her toes. Her foot still felt dodgy.

And even though Emily knew it was so utterly barking she couldn't admit it to anyone – not even Adam – she kept feeling as if there was a malicious presence around her. It was probably only her anxiety about whether Joe and Felicity could ever accept her, and her guilt at the fact that the person standing in the way of her and Adam's happiness wasn't around any more. If it were her she'd sure as hell come back and haunt the other woman.

Adam opened the door and gave Emily a cautious peck on the cheek, and shook Dad's hand. He looked nervous too, and Emily could see someone hovering in the background.

'This is Felicity,' Adam introduced her to a smiling neat fair-haired woman in her late sixties. She was thin as a pin, and very elegant. She didn't look very scary.

'Emily, welcome,' she said. 'It's lovely to meet you.'

And she gave Emily a hug. The woman whose daughter she'd replaced; the woman whose daughter was dead. Emily, choked by her generosity, wasn't sure she deserved it.

'Adam, you never said your mother-in-law was so young and pretty,' said Dad. Oh God, he was off. He had that smooth patter down to a fine art.

'And Adam never told me that Emily's father was such a charmer,' said Felicity with asperity. But she blushed. 'I'm Felicity, you must be Kenneth.'

'At your service,' Dad said, taking her hand and kissing it.

'Please make him stop, someone,' Emily laughed. 'I don't want to have to vomit into my dinner.'

'Adam's doing the cooking tonight, would you believe?' Felicity said.

'I'm not that incapable,' protested Adam.

'No of course you're not, dear.' Felicity patted him on the arm, and gave Emily a knowing look. 'Which is why you and Joe survive on takeaways when I'm not around.'

Emily suppressed a snort. That was *exactly* what Adam did when she wasn't in the house. She liked the fact that Felicity had the measure of him. They exchanged conspiratorial glances.

'You have to forgive us poor pathetic men,' said Dad. 'We all miss a woman's fine cooking.'

'I'm surprised you can keep a straight face,' Emily retorted. 'I swear you never cook for yourself, but there's always some mug in the village who'll bring you round some dinner.'

Felicity raised an eyebrow. 'You look quite well fed to me,' she said, and Emily had to laugh. None of the adoring village women ever called Dad up on anything. Felicity might do him some good. In that moment, Emily knew that she liked Felicity. Maybe Christmas was going to be OK after all.

Livvy

I'm fuming, and stamp around the house knocking over Christmas cards and rattling the Christmas tree, for all the good it does me. Everyone's getting on so famously they pay no attention. What is Mum playing at, being so welcoming to Emily and her dad, having shared jokes about Adam? That's what she and I used to do. Am I so unimportant to her?

117

She misses you, the thought pops into my head. It sounds like Malachi's thought, not mine. Maybe. She's doing a good job of pretending otherwise. She takes everyone into the lounge, and is pretty soon cosying up to Emily's dad. He keeps complimenting her, and though she bats it back, she's acting all coy. Since when has Mum started flirting with men? And if she's got to choose one, she'd better bloody well not choose *him*!

I'm determined they're not going to get to the end of the evening without acknowledging my presence.

First things first; I decide to make the sauce boil over. Adam's actually quite a good cook, but he's done an over-complicated recipe involving lamb noisettes. Typical Adam, when he does cook, he tends to do it in style. While he's busy bringing in drinks, I turn the gas up on what's supposed to be a slow-cooking redcurrant sauce. I've discovered over the last few days I can properly touch things now, so it's pretty easy to get the sauce to start bubbling, and sticking to the bottom of the saucepan.

'Shit!' Adam runs into the kitchen just in time to see half his beloved sauce boiling over on the cooker.

'Everything OK in there?' Felicity calls.

Adam has not very subtly left her, Emily and Kenneth to bond. Jeez. I might be dead, but I can still read my husband like a book.

'Fine,' calls Adam, though I can see him panicking. He rushes round trying to scrape congealed sauce off the top of the cooker and back into the pan. It's quite comical watching him, and I am laughing until, woof! It hits me. A strong burst of emotion. Adam is really suffering. Suddenly I want to reach out and comfort him, tell him it will be all right.

I can feel his panic and near despair. He stares at his

reflection in the kitchen window and I get a strong sudden sense of his sadness and guilt. He's not sure about what he's doing. He misses me. There's still love for me there. I can feel it. It makes me more determined. If *only* he could see or hear me, I know he'd realize he's making a big mistake.

Adam

I stare out into the darkness, wondering if I'm doing the right thing. It matters so much to me that my mother-in-law and my girlfriend can get along. I'm glad that Kenneth is here to act as a buffer. Judging by the roars of laughter coming from Felicity, he at least is a huge success. I know Felicity is trying very hard to make this work for all of us, but I worry that it's all so fragile still, it could go disastrously wrong.

The thing is, though, even if Emily hadn't come on the scene when Livvy died, would I be a mourning widower right now? My relationship with Livvy got so complicated, so rotten, I'm not sure there was anything left of the love we once shared. It makes me sad that we lost that. We were so young when we met, and she was so gorgeous and fun to begin with. We got married far too soon, after Livvy fell pregnant, and I wanted to do the right thing. Looking back, perhaps that was our first mistake. Because we lost that first baby, and then the next, and suddenly my bright vivid wife was full of a sadness and pain that I couldn't take away from her. I think a lot of the joy went out of our relationship back then, only I couldn't quite see it at the time. And after that the drinking started. Livvy had always enjoyed alcohol, but she began to drink in an unhealthy compulsive way, and I'd felt powerless to stop her.

We were so happy though, when we finally had Joe; we

moved into this house and Livvy even stopped drinking for a while. I really thought we'd turned a corner. We both had visions of filling it with Joe's brothers and sisters. Of course, that never happened.

Somehow over the years we lost each other, and that early heartache resurfaced and ate away at Livvy in the most destructive way. I tried to help, but she wouldn't let me in. She was locked in a world of pain and I couldn't help her. It killed me to see her like this, but in the end she rebuffed me so often, I found myself focusing on work, and spending as much time with Joe as I could to give her a break. In the end all we had in common was Joe. I'd still be sad about that now, and about the way Livvy died, without Emily, but would I feel any different today? I suspect not.

The temperature drops suddenly, and I feel a whoosh of something – cold air? – go through me, and am overwhelmed with grief, for what we had and what we lost, and for what Joe doesn't have any more. Livvy was a good mum to him. Left to me he'd never have come as far as he has. I admired her for that, even in the worst times. I'm not sure I'm up to being his champion the way she was, though I'm going to try my hardest. She got him his place at college, and had already started planning for him to live an independent life. 'Oh Livvy,' I whisper, 'I'm not sure I can look after Joe well enough without you.'

That sense of grief overtakes me again, almost like a physical pain. And what's weird is, though I'm bent double over the sink, howling like an animal, but silently, I have the strangest feeling that this isn't my pain. I pull myself up straight and stare at my reflection in the window.

'You're losing it,' I say to myself, and then for a fleeting second I could swear I see Livvy standing behind me.

'Get a grip, Adam, get a grip,' I tell myself. This is ridiculous. Joe's recent oddness is beginning to take its toll. There's nothing wrong here. Just not enough sleep and being overwrought with everything that has happened. Still, I do wish desperately I could see Livvy again so I can ask for her forgiveness. That way Emily and I can face our future together with a fresh start.

Chapter Eight

Livvy

I can feel Adam's pain washing over me in waves. For a fleeting hopeful moment, I think he sees me, and then the connection is gone and he pulls himself together. Joe comes in to help lay the table and I watch them fondly as they potter about together. Adam's patient with Joe, always prepared to give him space and time. It's one of the many things I love about him. My two boys: how I miss them.

Kenneth comes to join them, to ask for another beer, and the three of them start on a good-natured chat about the football. Joe seems to have decided Kenneth is all right, because he's joining in. Sometimes when he meets new people he can appear totally standoffish, as he doesn't engage straight away, but Kenneth has clearly passed muster.

'Do you want to see my astronomy lab?' Joe asks, a clear sign that Kenneth is accepted.

'Maybe later, Joe,' Adam says automatically. Joe often wants to do things straight away, when it's not totally convenient, but Kenneth replies, 'I'd be honoured to,' and I wish I could hug him before remembering that he's the enemy.

I don't linger long in the kitchen. I can't risk Joe starting on about me being there again. So I go and see what Evil Emily and Mum are up to, and immediately wish I hadn't.

'So you and Adam,' Mum's saying. 'Tell me about when you met.'

Emily blushes. As well she might.

'I hope this isn't too difficult for you, Felicity,' she says.

'Difficult?' Mum sighs. 'Difficult is never seeing Livvy again despite the differences we had. Difficult is worrying about Joe. It's not what I would have chosen, but it's what's happened. I don't want to see Adam unhappy, which he has been for a long time,' – that gives me a jolt, I hadn't realized Mum was so perceptive, and I feel a moment of gratitude that she *does* seem to be missing me – 'and I can see how happy you make him. To be quite honest, over the last few years with Livvy, I didn't often see him with a smile on his face. You've brought that to him, Emily. Maybe it's meant to be.'

Huh! Happy with Emily and not with me? Mother, whose side are you on? My earlier feeling of gratitude evaporates into anger. I fan the fire in the lounge with fury. A log flares up and tumbles down into the grate, sparks flying everywhere.

'Tsk, tsk.' Mum gets up to sort it out.

Traitor! I snarl at her, but she's looking through me as usual. I had no idea it was so bloody hard to haunt people.

'Anyway,' Mum comes back and sits down next to Emily and pats her hand, 'I'm pleased Adam has someone. And I think you're good for Joe. Just be careful you know what you're taking on.'

'I think I know,' says Emily.

Do you? Do you, really? I think bitterly. You've no idea how hard it's been. No one has. I put in all the groundwork and you reap the benefit of my labours. Once again, it doesn't seem at all fair.

Joe, Adam and Kenneth return from the kitchen bearing plates of steaming food, so I settle back in and wait. I want them to notice me. But I need to bide my time.

Adam

I'm relieved to see that Emily and Felicity are getting on like a house on fire when Joe, Kenneth and I come back in. They're bonding over Benedict Cumberbatch ('Such a sweet boy,' says Felicity) and George Clooney ('How lucky is Amal?' sighs Emily), till I cough to remind them we're here.

'Dad gets compared to George Clooney a lot, don't you Dad?' says Emily, with a sly grin.

Kenneth has been widowed a few years now. Emily is always saying how lonely he is.

'It has been known,' Kenneth demurs, till Emily teases him with, 'Or at least that's what your fan club in the village tell me.'

'Oh do they now?' Felicity actually twinkles. I've never seen her twinkle. She looks a little pink, and hot under the collar. Good God, is she actually flirting with Kenneth?

'It might have been mentioned,' Kenneth says modestly, 'but Felicity, has anyone told you you resemble a young Helen Mirren?'

'Not this week,' says Felicity. 'You were doing quite well up until then.'

Emily and I exchange glances. This is super-weird, but if it helps the evening go off without a hitch, then I for one am all for it.

The first course passes without incident. If anyone

notices my burnt sauce they're far too polite to mention it. Kenneth is good company, regaling us with tales of the village women who pursue him constantly, as if it's some kind of hardship.

'Come on, Dad, you can't have your cake and eat it,' laughs Emily. 'Either accept their very generous attention or be single again.'

'You have no idea what it's like to be so much in demand,' says Kenneth mournfully.

'Yes, well that's quite enough of that,' says Felicity with another twinkle. She seems to be enjoying putting him in his place and it's very entertaining, so the atmosphere is quite jolly. I am feeling relaxed by the time Joe and I clear the plates away and bring in dessert.

'Shop-bought, I'm afraid,' I say. 'But it's triple chocolate pudding. Joe's favourite.'

'And yours,' says Joe.

'OK, and mine,' I concede.

'Just as well you do all that swimming,' says Felicity. 'Otherwise you'd both get really fat!'

Some things don't change. Felicity's always been one to call a spade a spade.

At the mention of swimming, I could have sworn I felt the table tilt. I grabbed several glasses before they fell on the floor.

Felicity looks troubled.

'Mum knocked the table,' says Joe placidly. Kenneth looks puzzled but is too polite to say anything. I ignore Joe, not wanting to encourage him.

'More wine?' I say to Kenneth, and pour myself another drink.

This is a great evening, and I am going to enjoy myself.

The evening had gone far better than Emily could have imagined. Felicity was great company, and while it was slightly weird seeing her flirt with her dad, it also took some of the pressure off Emily, who was occasionally able to sneak an odd sideways thumbs-up to Adam. Felicity was giving Dad as good as she got, which was something no one had done to him for a long time. Even so by the time pudding came, he had her wrapped round his little finger. Emily's mum used to call it his Midas touch, and normally it made Emily cringe. But tonight she was glad of it, and Felicity was clearly enjoying having some male company, so no harm seemed to be done.

Emily had decided she liked Felicity and felt incredibly sorry for what she had been through. It must be tough to lose your only daughter. Emily could relate to that. She had been coming up for her thirtieth birthday when her mum died, just at the point when they were getting to be friends. Emily still missed her wisdom and good advice – particularly so in the last year. Maybe she and Felicity could give each other something they were both lacking. Emily really hoped so.

Adam was a bit twitchy, which Emily put down to him being as nervous about this evening as she was. He nearly knocked all the glasses off the table at one point, but by the time Emily made coffee he seemed to have relaxed a bit. Joe appeared to be happy too, and so far had only mentioned his mum once.

And breathe, Emily said to herself. The evening had exceeded her expectations. Perhaps if they could get through this honeymoon period she and Adam could build the life together that she dreamed about.

Emily brought the coffee in, and was just pouring it out

when the fire suddenly went out and a bone-chilling cold descended on the room. Emily shivered. That feeling of unease had returned very strongly. What was going on?

Adam got up to try and relight the fire, and there was a sudden blast of air as the kitchen door blew open and something jerked Emily's arm. She was freezing cold and could feel prickles on the back of her neck. Suddenly she felt very scared.

The cups on the table started to rattle, and then the table began to move, seemingly of its own accord. Then it wasn't just moving, but rising into the air, till it was hovering above them, close to the ceiling. Everyone stood open-mouthed, unable to take it in.

'Is this some kind of trick?' her dad said, looking fascinated but a little unnerved. Emily hadn't told him about what had been happening. It sounded too mad. Now she rather wished she had.

'No trick,' said Adam, and Emily could detect an edge of panic in his voice. 'Joe, are you doing this?'

'No,' said Joe, 'I keep telling you. Mum is.'

Felicity looked ashen. Like everyone else, she couldn't quite believe what was happening.

'Livvy?' she whispered, tears in her eyes. 'Is that you?'

And with that the table dropped to the floor with a sudden clatter, coffee cups spilling everywhere. The fire roared in the grate, and the lights that had dimmed lit up again properly. Then the kitchen door closed itself gently.

Nobody said anything for a few moments and then everyone started talking at once.

'What the—?'

'Did you—?'

'Did that actually happen?'

Till Joe said, 'Now do you believe me?'

Chapter Nine

Emily

'I wish Mum would stay,' Joe said sadly, as everyone continued to sit in shocked silence. 'I really want to see her.'

'Joe, we don't really know what happened tonight,' said Adam. 'There has to be a rational explanation. You know the wiring's dodgy, and it's so windy, that might have blown the fire out.'

'The wind didn't lift the table,' said Joe stubbornly. 'That was Mum.'

'What's going on?' Dad said, who with good reason was looking confused.

'Do you want to tell him or shall I?' said Adam, and with that they launched into a litany of the odd things that had happened.

'Your dad's right, Joe,' said Dad. 'Even if it is a ghost, which I doubt, it might not be your mum.'

Emily wished she could be so certain. Something weird was happening, and if they did have a ghost, who else could it be? She wasn't imagining the presence she could feel, full of spite and bile. Despite her initial scepticism, Emily was becoming convinced that Livvy had come back to get her revenge. Should she be frightened? What could Livvy do to them? To her?

The evening ended in rather subdued fashion. Dad kept trying to find rational explanations for things, but Felicity had gone very quiet and sombre. Even Adam hadn't been able to come up with any satisfactory explanations.

Emily walked back to her flat arm in arm with her dad. It was a wild night, with gale-force winds which nearly blew them down. Winds which were enough to levitate a table? It seemed unlikely, but there was no denying *something* had.

'Do you think the dead really come back and speak to us?' Emily said when they eventually arrived back home, windswept and soaked through. She poured them both a bedtime brandy, and they sat down in front of the fire.

'I have no idea,' Dad said, 'but I've often wished I could chat to your mum. I mean properly chat. I talk to her all the time on the allotment.'

He'd never said that before. Dad and Mum had both loved that allotment; it was their pride and joy. Emily felt a little thrill of pleasure that her dad still thought about Mum. Sometimes it felt as though he'd forgotten all about her.

'I do too,' Emily said and Dad gave her an awkward hug.

What Emily had most wished for after Mum died was to see her again. Thirty was too young to be motherless. There was so much Emily had needed to ask her, so much she wished she'd said. In the depths of her misery, in the months following her mum's death Emily had even visited a medium; anything to get near her mum once more. All the medium had said had been vague things about the afterlife and Mum being happy and always with Emily,

129

which hadn't been desperately convincing. If anything it made Emily think that when you die that's it, and there was no afterlife. But after tonight, Emily's certainties had been severely shaken.

When she came down the next morning after a restless night's sleep, she found her dad making pancakes. He looked chipper and cheerful, unlike Emily who'd been tossing and turning all night and felt like death warmed up.

'Won't you stay a bit longer?' she said. It was rare she got her dad to stay at hers, and after the oddity of last night she felt she needed some of his common sense and down-to-earth chatter to help her feel grounded.

'No, I should head home,' he said. 'I think there might be something on tonight.'

'You mean you've got a better invitation?' Emily laughed. 'Who's the lucky lady this time?'

'No one you know,' muttered Dad, having the grace to look slightly embarrassed. 'I really must be off, I promised to pay my respects to Felicity on the way home.'

'That was fast work even for you,' said Emily. 'When on earth did you get her address?'

'Oh she mentioned a book I might be interested in last night,' Dad said vaguely – as if. He gave Emily a huge hug and said, 'Try not to worry about all this nonsense about Livvy. Everyone's bound to be uptight because of the anniversary and Christmas. Grief does funny things to people. There'll be a sensible explanation.'

'I'm sure you're right,' said Emily, though she wasn't convinced. She waved him goodbye and tried to settle down to watch some TV, but she was feeling so unsettled within half an hour, she felt the need to get out of the house and go for a walk. It was still windy, and as she bent her face against the cold a gust blew several leaflets in her path, just as a black cat ran in front of her. She bent to pick them up, intending to put them in the bin, but was stopped in her tracks when she saw what they were advertising.

Psychic Zandra As Seen On TV!!! the leaflet said. *Coming to your local theatre for one night only!!!*

One night only. Tomorrow night in fact. It felt like a sign. Emily kept one of the leaflets and thoughtfully put it in her pocket. Under normal circumstances it would seem a bit extreme to consult a medium, and after her previous experience Emily had become very cynical about spiritualism. But if Livvy really was out there, and they could communicate with her, maybe she could have her say and they could give her the peace she needed to leave them alone. Maybe. Emily didn't really hold out much hope for that. If Livvy was a ghost, she was an angry and bitter one, and probably the last thing she wanted was to lose her husband to Emily. But it was worth a try.

As Emily turned back to head home another black cat walked between her legs and purred. It looked just like the one she'd seen earlier. Then it wandered away, but turned back to look at Emily. If she hadn't known any better, she could have sworn it *winked.*

Adam

'A medium? Are you crazy?' Emily has rung me up at work on Monday to tell me her plan. I've still got mountains of work to do before Christmas. A lot of people have only got a week left but, thanks to the year end, I'm working up to the last minute. Before all this happened, I'd been looking forward to Christmas – despite all the stress of the anniversary. This is the first year I get to spend it properly with

131

Emily. I just can't wait to have time off, and flop around at home, maybe going out for the occasional walk or run. Now with Joe still maintaining his mum is a ghost, Emily being convinced he's right and the weird evening we've just had, I'm getting a nervous feeling in the pit of my stomach. I don't believe in ghosts or the afterlife, but something very very strange is happening in my house and it makes me feel out of control – not a feeling I like.

'No,' says Emily, 'I wouldn't even think about it normally, but even you, Mr Super Rational, have to admit the last few days have been odd. I know it's probably all nonsense, but it can't hurt to at least try.'

I'm not really convinced, but I've never seen Emily so anxious, and I end up agreeing to go along with it to pacify her. We decide not to take Joe, as we think it might wind him up more. As it happens, he's arranged to see Caroline tonight. 'She's cooking me Christmas dinner,' he says happily, which surprises me somewhat. Caroline is a new friend Joe has made since he started college in September. She seems like a lovely kid, and I'm really pleased that she accepts Joe for who he is. I wonder sometimes if there's something romantic going on, but if there is Joe hasn't said. They seem to have bonded mostly over physics.

I'd have expected Joe to say that Caroline has to cook something else, as you can only have Christmas dinner on Christmas Day, but she appears to have the knack of gently introducing him to new things. She's good at understanding Joe's quirks while at the same time treating him like a normal human being. Very few of his peers seem to be able to do that, so I'm grateful to her.

When I go out at lunchtime, I take a walk to the theatre to see what all the fuss is about. There's a big poster on the wall showing a smiling Zandra, all teeth and sympathy, with the words: *Putting YOU in touch with your loved ones.*

There are some leaflets in the foyer of the theatre, and a gaggle of excited elderly ladies buying tickets. I pick up one of the leaflets. There's a lot of bumf about how Zandra can help resolve your issues with the Dearly Departed, or Those Who Have Gone Before. I notice that Zandra never actually uses the word *dead*. That would be far too brutal. Instead she makes it sound like your loved ones have just gone on a little holiday, as if they've popped over to Spain and can Skype you at any moment.

The Dearly Departed are apparently on the other side of a door, just waiting to talk to us. And of course Zandra is the conduit through which they can communicate. Yeah, right. I'm sure if there are a bunch of dead people *really* waiting on the other side, they'd be knocking the damned door down and trying to get in. Livvy certainly would be. Although ... with all the strange things happening, perhaps that's just what she has been doing, and Joe's right, we've not been listening. No. I refuse to believe that. This is mad, there has to be some other explanation.

I take a leaflet anyway, and wander down the street towards my office. A gentle snow shower has just started, and I shiver slightly as I make my way back to work. I'm still not sure about this, but as I get to the entrance a mangy black cat is sitting on a wall staring at me. It feels like an omen. I'm going to give it a go.

Livvy

'Everything going well then?' Malachi finds me sitting outside a café watching Joe and Caroline together. I've been watching them for ages, not getting too close in case Joe feels I'm intruding. He looks so happy to be with her, it makes me really glad. I'm pleased he seems to have found a friend who understands him.

Actually, I'm exhausted. This levitating business has really taken it out of me. But I don't tell Malachi that.

'It's fine,' I say. 'They're finally beginning to notice I'm there.'

'Right,' says Malachi, 'but what have you actually achieved apart from freaking Emily out?'

Dammit, he's right as usual. Why do I get saddled with such a smart arse for a spirit guide?

'Not much yet,' I say, 'but I'm working on it.'

'Well get yourself down to the theatre tonight.' Malachi nods at me and a leaflet blows on to my lap.

'Psychic Zandra?' I say. 'Isn't that a) rather humiliating and b) aren't all these people frauds?'

'Zandra's a fake. But unbeknownst to her, she has a modicum of talent which occasionally allows her to get in touch with a very superior spirit guide. Ghosts flock up to see him to get through to the other side.' There are other ghosts? Lots of them? Why hasn't Malachi told me before? It would have been nice to have someone to talk to.

'He has a gift for linking the dead with their living friends,' Malachi continues. 'Zandra has just enough of an open mind to allow him to let people come through.'

'There's a psychic for ghosts?' I say. 'You're having a laugh.'

'Straight up,' Malachi assures me solemnly. 'Go and see for yourself. You'll find him in the Underworld basement bar. It's where all those who haven't been able to pass on hang out. You never know, you might meet some like-minded people.'

'Like-minded people? What, you mean others like me?' I'm staggered. I've got so used to being on my own, it hasn't occurred to me that there might be somewhere the dead meet up.

'Yup,' says Malachi. 'Did you think *you* were the only one?'

'Well, yes, actually, I did,' I say indignantly. 'I've spent pretty much a year on my own, and now you're telling me I could have had some ghostly pals for company.'

'You weren't ready to meet them,' says Malachi.

'Are you this much of a bastard to all the spirits you guide?' I mutter in disgruntlement.

'Probably,' says Malachi. 'But remember, it was you who elected to stay in that car park all that time, by refusing to listen to me in the beginning. If you hadn't been so stubborn, we could have got through all this months ago.'

I go to protest, but he has a point.

'So don't forget. Underworld tonight,' says Malachi. 'I think you'll find it illuminating. But be careful, some of the people who go there have a . . . different way of looking at things. Don't be taken in by them.'

Oh great, another enigmatic warning. Why doesn't Malachi ever tell me anything straight? I'm tempted by his suggestion, but I refuse to be bullied into it, so I say, 'Perhaps,' and Malachi yawns and stretches, and says, 'Your choice.'

He wanders off down the street, and then pauses and says, 'Of course, Adam and Emily are going to be in the audience.'

Now I have to go.

Joe's Notebook

I have a new girlfriend.

Her name is Caroline.

She is very pretty.

I have never had a girlfriend before.

I like having a girlfriend.

If she were a star, she would be in the constellation of Virgo, because she is pure and perfect and right.

Caroline understands about Mum. She knows I am not mad.

I don't think Dad does.

I am not sure Dad wants Mum to come back.

This makes me sad.

I hope he changes his mind.

I wish Mum would come back for Christmas.

That would be good.

Christmas Past

I follow Malachi to the theatre feeling intensely irritated with him. He has an air of superiority about him, as if he knows something I don't.

When we get there, he says, 'Now remember why you're here. You need to seek closure, and you're not going to find it if you go off on a rant. When you get through to Adam, try and listen to what he has to say too.'

What on earth does he know about it? Adam betrayed me. End of. And there were so many times when I felt let down by him when Joe was very small. It got better as Joe got older when Adam used to help me out by taking over at the weekends, but by the end we never did anything together as a family and that still makes me sad. I think I have every right to be angry.

'Do you?' says Malachi. 'Then remember *this*.'

I'm about to snarl at him to stop reading my mind, when he's done it again, and I'm standing at the school gates on a wintry November day, in absolute despair.

Clouds are scudding across the sky, and a cold wind whistles across the playground. I have just come out of a meeting with the school. A place cannot be found for Joe in the juniors next year, and I have to look elsewhere. I've been given a pile of forms to fill in for specialist schools in the area – 'special school' – the very term makes me shudder, but I know they're right. Joe is falling so far behind here, and the bullying has got worse. His peer group is picking up on his differences, and one or two of them are exploiting them. There are sly kicks in the playground, and whispers when he does something the other kids perceive as odd. The school is trying its best, but they can't cope, and if I'm honest I don't want Joe here any longer. But the thought of the battle ahead fills me with horror. The school that Claire has suggested for him is a long way away and hideously oversubscribed. What if he doesn't get in there? What then?

'You look like you've got the world on your shoulders.' One of the mums I know, Miranda, has just come from her weekly volunteering session listening to the Year 2s read. We're on reasonably friendly terms, and she's been sympathetic about Joe's problems, which is more than some of them have.

I tell her all about it, and to my horror I begin to cry, big racking sobbing tears. I am mortified; normally I am stronger than this, but today the battle feels too hard, and I am defeated.

'What you need', she says, linking arms, 'is cheering up. How about we play hooky and try that new gastropub in town?'

As a rule I never socialize with the other mums during the daytime, since there always seems to be so much to do at home. However much I try to I never seem to get on top of the housework, and though Adam never says anything, I can sometimes feel a slight impatient, 'What do you *do* all day?' tone in his voice. He works so hard, and he always pulls his weight when he comes home, so I can't blame him for not wanting to walk into chaos every day. I want him to come home to a comfortable tidy house, but somehow everything overwhelms me. I know I should go back and sort the washing out and clean the kitchen, which is a tip, but for once I think, what the hell. I'm touched by Miranda's kindness, and it's good to have someone to talk to.

Which is how we find ourselves at lunchtime squeezed in a corner with the other ladies who lunch at a trendy bar, where we order burger and chips at astronomical prices, and to my surprise Miranda orders a glass of Sauvignon Blanc. I never drink during the day. It's my cardinal rule. And recently I feel that I've been drinking more than I should in the evenings, so I've been trying to cut back.

'You're not having Coke,' says Miranda firmly when I try and order one. 'After the morning you've had you deserve something stronger.'

Instead of a glass of wine she changes her order to a bottle.

'It's a bit early,' I protest.

'First rule of motherhood,' says Miranda with a wink, 'it's *never* too early.'

A bottle later, I'm feeling quite a lot better; the wine has certainly helped. I belatedly order some water, not wanting to be plastered at the school gate.

By the time we've had coffee and cake – at Miranda's insistence, cake in her view is the very thing I need to cheer me up – I am feeling a little bit unsteady on my feet. I think I've covered it up until I trip over when we leave, and Miranda giggles at me. She doesn't seem tipsy at all. I suspect I may have had more wine than she has. Oh well. This is a treat.

'Goodness, look at the time,' says Miranda, 'I really have to go, chores to do before the school run.'

'Me too,' I say. I give her a big hug. 'Thank so much, Miranda, I feel much better. You're right, I should do this more often.'

When I get home, I look at the state of the house, and decide I'm taking the rest of the day off. I've played hooky already today – why not continue? I grab myself another glass of wine, and sit down to watch some mindless daytime TV. It's cosy and warm in the house, and I feel sleepy, so I curl up on the sofa, and nod off.

Two hours later, I wake up to the key turning in the lock. It's cold and dark, and I don't feel warm and cosy any more. I have a blinding headache, and my throat feels dry as dust.

Adam is suddenly in the lounge, Joe at his side, looking confused. I sit bolt upright.

Shit. Joe. The school run.

I've slept through it.

'Where were you?' Adam says. 'The school rang me, and you've not been answering your phone. I've been worried sick.'

Feelings of guilt and humiliation wash over me as I'm catapulted back into the present.

I don't look at Malachi, I am too ashamed to face his gaze, but I say reluctantly, 'OK, I'll listen.'

Chapter Ten

Christmas Present

Eight Days till Christmas

Livvy

Because I am unsettled and miserable after what Malachi has shown me I leave him at the theatre and go for a moody ramble down to the river. I feel better down here. We used to love the river, Adam and I. It was one of the reasons we moved to the area. As I mooch about gazing at the fast-flowing water where freezing-looking ducks bob about unhappily on the surface, I try to remember happier times. We did have some happy times, I know we did. But they're buried in a welter of the misery and discord that character-ized the last few years of my life.

Then I think, so, I forgot to pick Joe up from school. So what? It was *one* time. I was there for him every other day. And from the force of the memory I can see now I must have been badly depressed. I felt responsible for getting things right for Joe, and it was hard. Though Adam tried to help, I mostly felt on my own. I don't think he ever quite understood how exhausting the toll of fighting Joe's corner was though he always came with me to meetings with the endless streams of teachers, ed psychs, doctors and social workers. He had work to take his mind off it; I had nothing, and I found it exhausting. No wonder I had the occasional drink, who wouldn't have? And there was no harm done. I fell asleep on the sofa, and forgot the school run, but Adam was there to pick Joe up. What was the big deal? Malachi's making far too much of it.

I nearly decide I'm not going to bother with Underworld, or go to the show. This whole communing-with-the-dead thing is probably not going to work anyway. Psychic Zandra sounds like a total fraud, the sort of person I'd have ridiculed when I was alive. But I'm fed up of being alone with no one to talk to apart from a nagging cat. If there are ghosts out there, I'd love to meet them. I can't believe I couldn't have met them before now. What's Malachi's game anyway? I'd love to know if anyone is having as many problems being dead as I do.

In the end, I find myself drifting into the theatre at about 7 p.m. At first I can't work out where Underworld is. The bar in the foyer looks the same as all these places do; it doesn't look as if it is peopled by spirits. This is just a normal theatre where normal people go. I used to take Joe here to the pantomime when he was little. There's no underground bar. This is ridiculous.

'Psst!' A voice comes from behind me.

'Sorry?' I turn to see a strange little egg-headed man with round-lens glasses, peering at me. He's wearing tartan pyjamas, a scruffy brown dressing gown, tattered slippers and is smoking a pipe.

'Don't judge me,' he says, clearly seeing my surprise. 'This is what I was wearing when I died.'

'I wasn't,' I lie. I'm intrigued. He's the first ghost I've met since I've been dead. 'Do you mind my asking how you died?'

'Had a heart attack on my front doorstep, collecting the milk,' he says, 'and you?'

'Hit by a car.' Is this the form when you meet other ghosts? Discussing how you died? I suppose it's a common point of contact.

'Your first time?' he says. 'It takes a while to work it out, but the entrance to Underworld is here.'

He vanishes through a door, which I thought led into an ordinary cupboard. I follow him feeling like I'm going into Narnia. There's a slight glow on the back wall against which mops and buckets are stacked. I go towards it and realize that the wall isn't solid, but a shimmering moving mass. I tentatively put my hand through the wall, and then withdraw it, marvelling. This is so cool. Boldly, I follow the man through it. At first it feels like walking through water, and then I'm catapulted down some stairs into a noisy lively bar. This is most definitely *not* Narnia. There are literally hundreds of people here. Bass music is pumping really loudly, and purple lights flash on and off. A wag has decorated it with pictures of skeletons and floating spirits.

WELCOME TO UNDERWORLD WHERE THE DEAD PARTY LIKE THERE'S NO TOMORROW

Someone clearly has a sick sense of humour.

'What do you think?' my friend in the dressing gown asks.

I'm staggered. I had no idea this was here, and wish I'd known earlier. Why didn't Malachi *tell* me? Hidden among these heaving crowds, there might be another ghost I can befriend.

'Come on, let's get you a drink,' says my friend, who introduces himself as Robert.

144

'What, we can drink here?' I am confused. I can't do normal things like eat and drink. How does that work?

'This is a spirits pub,' says Robert. He digs me in the ribs. 'Geddit?'

I'm beginning to find Robert just a teensy bit irritating, but I let that pass.

'We can all drink in here,' says Robert. 'We're the same in this room. It's a kind of halfway house to where we go next.' He looks a little wistful. 'If we ever get there.'

I'm intrigued despite myself.

'Why, how long have you been here?'

'Too long,' says Robert mournfully. 'My problem is I fell out very badly with my son. I was always going to make it up to him, but then I died. I've tried haunting him, but he's horribly resistant.'

Great. Now I feel guilty about having mean thoughts about him.

'Doesn't your spirit guide have any advice for you?'

'Um, we sort of fell out too,' says Robert, adjusting the glasses on the end of his nose awkwardly.

'Is there nothing else you can do?' I say. 'I'm having a few problems passing over myself.' This sounds terrible. If Adam continues resisting me, will this be my fate?

Robert looks shifty all of a sudden.

'I did try something else,' he says, 'but I wouldn't recommend it.'

'Which was?' but he's clammed up. He takes me to the bar and disappears, muttering something about having to go and see Letitia, whoever she is.

Although Robert isn't ideal company, I feel lonely as I approach the bar, but the barman, a gorgeous tall black guy, welcomes me with a big grin, and says, 'Your first time?'

I nod, feeling ever so slightly surreal. I'm in a bar, with

145

other people. It seems so very normal except that apparently we are all dead.

'I'm Lenny,' says the barman, pouring me a drink. Hell, how am I supposed to pay for that? I don't have any money. Seeing my discomfort, Lenny winks. 'It's on the house,' he says, giving a huge belly laugh. 'After all you're not going anywhere.'

I take a sip. I can drink it. I can actually drink it. And it tastes like vodka. I get that same burning rush I used to love, and a heady feeling as I have alcohol for the first time in a year.

'You need to meet Psychic Steve,' says Lenny, though I haven't asked a question.

'I do?' I say.

'You've got that first-timer what-the-fuck-am-I-doing-here? look on your face. I'm guessing you're here to try and connect with someone?'

'I am.'

'Then Psychic Steve can help,' says Lenny.

'Psychic Steve?' *This* is the name of Malachi's spirit guide. Oh dear God, the afterlife clearly has con artists too.

'Don't look like that,' says Lenny. 'He helps a lot of people talk to their loved ones. He's very popular. There's a queue, so you'll have to take your turn.'

I turn to see a tall rangy man, with long ratty dreadlocks, wearing a T-shirt saying Proud to be Dead and skinny black jeans, surrounded by people of all ages, sizes and nationalities, all clamouring for his attention. He clearly thrives on it. Feeling absurdly nervous, I go and join them.

Emily

The Christmas lights in the high street were twinkling brightly as Emily and Adam approached the theatre.

146

Normally Emily loved the lights and the warm fuzzy feeling as Christmas approached, but this year, with all the mayhem in her life, they failed to work their magic. The restaurants and pubs were thronging with cheerful people putting aside their woes as they geared up for the festive season. Emily longed to be like them, longed to have nothing to worry about apart from entertaining on Christmas Day, and wished she was going anywhere but to see Psychic Zandra.

'I'm not sure we should be doing this after all,' she said as they approached the theatre.

'Now she tells me!' Adam was exasperated. 'Come on, Emily, it was your idea.'

'I know, I know,' said Emily. 'But there has to be an explanation for what happened. Maybe we're just suffering from some form of mass hysteria.'

Emily had gone over and over the events of the other night in her mind, trying to make sense of it but still drawing a blank.

'Do you really think that?' said Adam.

'No,' admitted Emily. 'It's just . . . I'm scared, Adam. What if Livvy is haunting us? What then?'

'And what if she's not?' Adam hugged her. 'This is probably going to turn out to be a waste of time, anyway, but now we're here we may as well give it a whirl.'

'There will probably be three old ladies and a dog there,' Emily said.

'I wouldn't be sure of that,' said Adam. He stopped and whistled as they approached the theatre. The queue was spilling out on to the street.

'Christ, there are a lot of poor saps out there.'

'And we're two of them,' said Emily. 'Still, nothing ventured and all that.'

As they entered the foyer they were immediately accosted by Zandra's sidekicks who made them fill out a questionnaire about their loved ones.

'Don't give anything away,' hissed Adam. 'This is how these charlatans work.'

The questions seemed quite straightforward: details about your background and family life, who you wanted to talk to from the Other Side, but Emily tried very hard not to reveal anything they could use. When it came to the question about who she wanted to talk to, she suddenly realized, that if there was an afterlife, the only person she really wanted to choose was her mum. Not wanting to give Zandra more ammunition than she had to, however, she wrote down Livvy's name instead.

Once the forms were filled in they were ushered into the bar and given a complimentary glass of mediocre wine. The bar was full of people of all types and ages chatting about seeing Great-Aunt Jessie or Grandad again; one lady insisting very loudly her late husband had selfishly not told her where his share certificates were.

'I can't move on,' she was saying to her friend. 'Not till I know what the old bugger's done with them. So typical of him to have left me potless.'

She was very well dressed, and dripping in jewellery. The conversation swiftly moved on to shopping at Liberty's.

'She doesn't look potless to me,' Emily whispered to Adam.

Adam grinned, but whispered back, 'Be careful. I bet they've got spies everywhere. Don't say anything revealing at all.'

'I think that's a bit paranoid,' Emily laughed, but did as Adam asked, keeping the conversation light, telling him all about her day mining the IT coalfield instead.

After ten minutes a gong sounded and a disembodied voice called, 'All ticket holders are now kindly invited to take their seats and meet Zandra, who hopes to connect as many of you as possible with your loved ones.'

Emily and Adam followed the crowd through to the theatre and took their seats. The lights dimmed, and the overture from *Phantom of the Opera* started to play – 'Jeez how corny,' muttered Adam. People started clapping and cheering as the tension began to build.

'God, what on earth have we come to?' Emily grimaced at Adam. 'It's like some kind of nutty religious rally.'

But, judging by the rapturous applause, they were the only ones to think so. The lights dimmed and a solemn silence came over the crowd, and then as if by magic Zandra was there. Where on earth had she come from? One minute there was no one and then to a standing ovation she was suddenly on stage. There must have been some kind of clever stage business going on.

'Wonder how they did that?' Emily whispered, but Adam shushed her.

A silence fell once more as Zandra stood quietly waiting, and a sudden prickle of unease went up Emily's spine. They were trying to reach Adam's dead wife? Perhaps they should have left well alone.

And then Zandra began to speak.

Adam

I blink as Psychic Zandra appears on stage. She looks nothing like her photograph. A mousy little woman, with bouffant brown hair, who wouldn't say boo to a goose. She's dressed in a tight shiny pink suit and plastic pink heels. She speaks in a Southern American accent which sounds made up to me.

149

'How y'all doing?' she cries, and the audience treat her to another round of applause. I get the feeling Emily and I are the only people here not acting as if she's some kind of visionary saint.

'Any first timers here?'

Emily and I look at each other. If we're really serious about getting through to Livvy, we're going to have to own up. Slowly we raise our hands, and I am at least relieved to see that half the audience are in the same boat. No reason for her to pick on us then.

Zandra runs through a few tips about what to expect from the show, and of course comes out with the greatest get-out clause ever – her spirit guide, inevitably a Native American called Flying Spirit, can't always communicate with the dead so the messages don't always come through. Apparently his filter is off sometimes.

'Oh yeah?' I whisper to Emily. 'I knew this was a con.'

But nonetheless there's a strange ripple of anticipation running through the audience, and I can't help getting swept up in the atmosphere though my scepticism is rewarded by Zandra's first attempt.

'I'm getting a J – Jamie? John? Someone wants to talk to John,' Zandra says with confidence.

No one responds.

'I'm sure it begins with J,' Zandra says, looking puzzled.

A young woman in the front leaps up.

'I'm Jane,' she says.

'Jane! Of course!' Zandra snaps her fingers. 'I could feel something wasn't quite right. I have your brother here.'

Jane swallows and looks a little pale.

'I'm getting . . . he died, violently . . . in a bike accident, am I right?' She looks triumphant, but Jane shakes her head.

'No, he committed suicide,' she whispers.

'On a motorbike,' Zandra persists.

'By swallowing pills,' says Jane, looking fed up.

Zandra can feel she's losing her audience, so she waves her hands and says, 'The way of his passing isn't important, it's the message I'm getting.' She shuts her eyes as if concentrating hard.

'Jane, your brother is sorry. For all the hurt he caused you. He never meant to do it. He loves you very much.'

Jane starts to sniffle a bit.

'I love him too,' she says. 'And I forgive him.'

This is greeted with more rapturous applause, and by the time Jane sits down, apparently satisfied that her brother Jimmy's spirit is finally at rest and he's now passed on to a better place, the audience seem to have forgotten the dodgy bit at the beginning.

Her next attempt is a little more convincing. She gets a man called Andy to stand up and after a couple of false starts we learn that Andy's mum is happy and well and he isn't to worry about her.

After that it's a constant litany of people apparently being put in touch with their loved ones, but there's a sameness about the conversations which makes me suspicious.

By the time the first half is over, I'm convinced we've made a mistake coming. There is nothing for us here. Zandra is pandering to desperate people who only hear what they want to. Emily and I spend most of the interval in the bar, trying to work out how she managed to know just enough about the people who stood up to make it sound half convincing.

I hear a voice, which I think I recognize, and turn to see a woman who is spectacularly drunk stagger behind me knocking glasses over.

'She knew, she knew my dad,' the woman is slurring.

I am so reminded of Livvy, it's painful. Oh God, the times she did that to me in public. The times I had to cover up for her: 'Livvy's unwell; Livvy's feeling under the weather' – the euphemisms I used. I feel a punch in the gut, and then I get the distinct impression that Livvy is right here, standing next to me. I shiver, but the moment passes, and the interval is over and we return to our seats.

To begin with, the second half of the show proceeds very much like the first half. I'm amused to notice Mrs He-Hid-The-Share-Certificates is given short shrift by her supposed husband, but generally people seem happy with what they are told. Most of the audience seem to have fallen for it, hook, line and sinker, and I imagine I must be the only cynic here.

The show appears to be winding up, and then something very different happens. The curtains seem to blow a little, though there isn't a breeze in the theatre, and Zandra's whole body starts to shake. I think she's having some kind of fit, but suddenly she stands bolt upright, and stares ahead, speaking in a male voice which doesn't sound like hers. It must be some kind of projection. The audience, which had been getting a bit rowdy, hushes down again.

Then Zandra turns and looks in our direction.

'I'm getting a name. A female name, beginning with E. Someone wants to talk to, is it Emma? No, not Emma, *Emily*.'

Emily goes pale, and stands up.

'I'm Emily,' she says.

'I've got someone who wants to talk to you,' says Zandra in her spirit voice. 'And she seems a bit cross.'

Emily gasps, and I bite back a sudden presentiment of fear. Could Livvy really be coming through?

Zandra's voice subtly changes, and then she speaks as a female again, but it's not a voice I recognize.

I breathe again. This is part of the act, it's not Livvy. But then Zandra says, 'Hello Emily. It's Mum.'

Chapter Eleven

Emily

Emily stood up in stunned disbelief when Zandra said her name. Surely there must be another Emily in the audience? She couldn't take in that Livvy might actually be there, wanting to talk to her, and that this wasn't some huge trick. Heart racing, Emily tried to tell herself that nothing was going to happen when the spotlight focused on her. But then, the voice she heard wasn't Livvy's: it was her mum's. Emily gasped. It couldn't be. After all this time, she was actually going to speak to her mum? She grasped hold of the seat in front of her to steady herself.

'Mum?' she said, willing herself not to faint.

Five years of missing the chief cheerleader in her life. Emily had so often wanted to be able to reach out, speak to her, ask her advice. And now, apparently, here Mum was, wanting to talk to her only daughter.

'Is that really you?' Emily asked hesitantly.

'Of course it is,' said Mum, sounding a bit grumpy. 'Who were you expecting?'

Thousands of questions flooded through Emily's brain. Was she OK? Where was she? Did she miss them? But she found herself paralysed, unable to speak. Then Mum – if it really was Mum – said, 'I don't have much time. I'm just passing through. I've just come from having a nice cup of tea on the allotments, and I need to get back to my friends. I'm only here to let you know you've got stuff to deal with.'

'Erm—' First conversation with her dead mother in five years, and Emily was getting a telling-off. That wasn't the way it was meant to go. She felt 13 again, caught out sneaking behind the bushes in the local park having a crafty fag.

'I can't help telling you. I'm a little disappointed. I thought you'd know better than to mix yourself up with a married man. Even though I do understand the circumstances.'

Despite getting a scolding in front of hundreds of people, Emily couldn't help smiling at that. Typical Mum. Never short of an opinion about Emily's love life, never afraid to pull her punches if she thought Emily was making a mistake on the boyfriend front. She hadn't been that sold on Graham.

Then Mum's tone softened. 'But love, I'm worried about you. This isn't the way to start a happy new relationship. You've done someone else a great wrong.'

'I know,' whispered Emily. 'So how do we put it right?'

'You have to listen to Livvy,' said Mum. 'Or face the consequences.'

Which was so exactly what Emily had been thinking all this time, it was all she could do not to run on the stage and hug Zandra then and there.

'Livvy,' Emily said, feeling cold all over. Livvy had the power to hurt her and Adam, she could feel it.

'Yes her,' said Mum. 'She's got some issues of her own to sort out. But you need to help her. So don't ignore her when she does come through.'

'Why isn't she here now?' Emily asked.

'She's a bit – erm – indisposed.' Mum sounded almost embarrassed. 'Sorry, I have to go. I want to get back to the allotment. You take care, love.'

'Mum, wait,' Emily said, desperate to keep the connection for longer, but then she was gone, leaving Zandra blinking in the spotlight. Zandra looked a trifle confused, as if she didn't quite know what had happened, but she recovered quickly and moved on to the next person in the crowd.

'I'm getting a – yes, a message is coming through for is it Imelda?'

'That's me!' a woman shouted from the back of the auditorium, but Emily wasn't listening. She sat down trembling and turned to Adam.

'What was all that about?' she said.

Adam

Emily looks white as a sheet when she sits down. She doesn't talk about her mum much, but I know how Emily misses her still and I can tell she's shaken up.

'How?' she whispers. 'How can Zandra know all that?'

'It's some clever trick,' I say. 'Maybe it was something in the form you filled in.'

But I'm not sure any more. That was horribly convincing.

'I just don't buy that,' says Emily. 'She knew about Livvy. And she always used to say she was going to the allotment. It was like her calling card. How on earth could Zandra possibly know that?'

It is odd, I have to agree. And it makes me feel pretty uncomfortable. I'd thought this would all be nonsense and had mainly gone along to placate Emily. But I'd noticed that the temperature had dropped when Emily was talking to her 'mum'. Granted that might be some special effect arranged by the theatre, but it hadn't happened when anyone else had spoken to Zandra, so why did it for Emily? And Zandra had appeared completely out of it and not a little disorientated when she came round. That hadn't happened earlier either. If she was faking it, she was extraordinarily good.

There's a bit of me that's disappointed too. If there really are dead people out there, who Zandra is somehow able to channel, and Livvy is one of them, why hasn't she come through? I'm not sure if I want to believe that she's a ghost and she's haunting us, but if she is, I want to be able to tell her how sorry I am for the way things ended. There have been many times over the last year when I've taken myself alone to her graveside, and told her as much. It's my private way of trying to atone for what happened. But dead is dead, and if it's forgiveness I'm seeking, I'm not going to get it talking to a headstone. Now for the first time the possibility hits me that Livvy might actually still somehow be around. And if she *is* still here, it would be good to be able to communicate properly, the way we never could when she was still alive. Talking to a gravestone doesn't have quite the same effect.

The rest of the show passes in the same vein as before, and I've more or less gone back to my position that it's all made up, and Emily's been tricked somehow into handing out personal information, when just as Zandra is winding up the show she goes suddenly limp and starts shaking violently. And then a male voice calls out, 'Hey guys, it's DJ Steve here, come to show you how the dead party!'

The theatre fills with the sound of rap music, the lights start flickering on and off, and I get the distinct impression that Zandra isn't alone on the stage . . .

Party, party, party. I'd forgotten how much fun it was. And it turns out that spirit drinks do the business just as much as their earthly counterparts do. Vodka never tasted this good when I was alive. I'm fired up with all the people here. All having the best time. God, I wish I'd known about this place earlier. I wouldn't have spent the last year moping around.

My new best friends introduced to me by Lenny, Sanjay and Keona, two troubled twenty-somethings who apparently had a suicide pact, keep tempting me to more shots, and then we're on the dance floor rocking our moves.

From time to time Psychic Steve, or DJ Steve as he also likes to be known, stops and says, 'We have a call for Albert. You're wanted upstairs. Your wife wants to know where you left your share certificates.' And Albert staggers up to the mike and says 'Silly cow, as if I'd tell her that,' before vanishing. Or he stops still and actually channels through to someone in the theatre upstairs. We can only hear one side of the conversation. One little old lady in a sari, who barely speaks a word of English, is crying with happiness because she's talked to her long-lost daughter and another is shouting, 'I'm free,' now she's given her ex what for. Everyone hugs her delightedly as she says her goodbyes, and then she turns to face a light, pausing and smiling at everyone before fading beatifically away.

With so many shots under my belt, I can't remember the reason why I'm here. I decide to take a break from dancing and wander up to DJ Steve, who gives me a wink and says, 'Hey babe, how's it hanging?'

'Great,' I say. 'In fact, it's better than great. I can't believe Malachi never told me about this place before.'

'Yeah, well Malachi isn't the partying type.' He shrugs.

'Too right he isn't,' I say. 'All he ever does is nag me.'

Steve looks at me thoughtfully.

'If you ever get sick of dull old Malachi, come and find me,' he says. 'You don't have to follow the rules, you know, and you look like the kind of girl who can handle it.'

He winks at me again and then gets distracted as someone is badgering him about getting through to their uncle.

I wander off to find Keona and Sanjay, but they seem to have got lost in the crowd. So I decide to sit down for a bit. Meeting all these new people has me ridiculously tired . . .

It turns out it's quite easy to doze off in a nightclub for ghosts when you've had a few. I deserve a nap, I think. I've hardly slept since I died.

There's a tap on my shoulder, and I jerk away. A dark-haired middle-aged woman with a kind smile is standing before me. She reminds me of someone, but I can't think who.

'You missed your slot,' she's saying to me, through a fog. 'I had to go through for you, and now I must go back.'

She fades before my eyes.

Lost my slot? What does she mean? And then I remember. *Damn.* Emily and Adam. I was supposed to prove to them I'm still here. Not get pissed. Oh bugger. Malachi is so going to have something to say about this.

The party is still in full swing, people are dancing energetically, and DJ Steve is ramping up the volume. Just as well the living are so deaf and blind to what's all around them, otherwise someone might call the police.

I go up to him and say, 'I know I missed my turn, but is there a way we can give them a taste of all of this, so the sceptics in the audience can be converted too?'

'Sorry, doll, it's not part of my remit,' he says, turning back to his decks.

Then he sees the look of disappointment on my face.

'Although . . . technically I'm not supposed to, but I could do with a laugh,' Steve says. 'And for a babe like you, I'd happily do anything.'

I blush and feel quite overcome. He really is rather good-looking.

'Can you do that?' I say. 'It's not against any rules or anything?'

Steve gives me a crooked grin. 'I've never been one for playing by the rules, me.' He looks a little the worse for wear. I wish he was my spirit guide. He's a whole lot more fun than Malachi.

He holds up his hands. 'People. Listen up. Who fancies bringing the house down?'

Chapter Twelve

Livvy

And bring the house down we do. There are people swinging from the chandeliers, climbing the curtains, and an intrepid crew get hold of the spotlights and start shining them on the audience, who are caught somewhere between a laugh and a scream. I hear several gasps as the stage lights up like a disco on acid.

Meanwhile, stage hands rush on the stage, to try and hustle Zandra off it, but Zandra – or rather Steve – who is now controlling her, lands a right hook on one of their faces and the rest back off. People started to throw things around, and hundreds of us pour off the stage and into the audience who are belatedly waking up to the realization this is not part of the show, and are now screaming for dear life. The lighting crew dim the lights as we go among the audience blowing on their necks, and tapping them on the shoulders. It's the most fun I've had since I died; I had no idea that being dead could be such a blast.

And then I see Adam and Emily, in the middle of the crowd, and I stop short. They are both looking stunned and clutching hold of one another. Nice one, Livvy, you've just brought them even closer together. I feel ashamed of what I'm doing. I came here with a purpose, and I've got distracted and nearly let the best opportunity of talking to Adam since I died slip through my fingers.

I run to Steve, who's still busy fending off the stage hands, and shout over the chaos, 'Please! Can I go through? There's someone I need to talk to.'

Steve shrugs his shoulders, as he knocks another of the stage crew back into the wings. 'Sure, why not,' he says.

'Are you going to get into trouble for this?' I ask, thinking how Malachi is going to respond.

'Maybe,' he says, 'but hasn't it been fun? You should come to Underworld more often. You've really livened things up.'

And then he winks at me, and I can't help winking back. I feel a blast of energy between us before I am tugged forwards, and with a jolt I realize I am standing on the stage in Zandra's body, scanning the crowd once more for Adam. It feels odd having a body again. I stare in awe at Zandra's hands – hands, how strange they seem. Then I remember why I'm here.

'Adam!' I shout desperately above the din. Steve is trying to calm people down but it's pandemonium as people are climbing over seats in a desperate and futile attempt to get out.

'Adam!' I scream with all my strength. Shit, he'll never hear me over this racket. The mayhem is continuing apace, and the flashing lights are getting wilder and wilder, so I run to the front of the stage and yell, 'Adam!' one last time. This time he hears me and stands up, white as a sheet.

'Livvy?' he says incredulously. 'What the hell is happening here?'

I can't believe after all this time, I finally have a connection; he knows I'm really here. I feel a moment of over-powering joy. At last we can talk to each other. I want to say something, but I'm so choked I can't quite find the words. There he is, my lovely Adam, scarcely looking a day older than the day we met twenty years ago. I am so over-whelmed by his presence I don't know what to do. I know I should be saying sorry, but I stand there speechless. I am so focused on Adam, I haven't noticed Emily straight away, but when she gasps I see Adam is clutching tight on to her. There is a sharp stabbing pain in my gut, and all my bitter-ness and anger about Emily rises to the surface. I had only planned as far as talking to Adam, but all I can see is Emily standing in my way, and I am overcome. Adam left me for her. He left *me*. How could he?

'Adam, you bastard,' I gasp out. And then I can't do it any more. I pull myself out of Zandra's body, and stumble away from the stage, fleeing the theatre among a teeming crowd of ghosts who've got bored and given up, heading back down to Underworld.

Tonight has been an unmitigated disaster, and it's all my fault.

Adam

'Adam, you bastard.'

For the first time I am convinced Livvy is back. It certainly sounds like her, and after her final text to me I shouldn't be surprised she's angry. I'm in a state of shock like the rest of the audience. I have no idea what has gone on here tonight, but it's been terrifying. If this has all been put on by Zandra and her crew, it feels horribly horribly real.

'Livvy,' I manage to say, 'I'm so sorry,' but there's no response. And then Zandra seems to shudder and take

163

control again, saying, in her normal voice, 'All of you, out! Show's over.'

There's a ripple and the sound of hissing, and then the curtains stop swaying, the lights go back on and there's silence. During a nervous pause I can see Zandra is trying to compose herself, and then the audience is clapping wildly. It's as if none of them want to believe what they've just witnessed, they're all pretending it's part of the show.

Zandra is lapping it up, wandering about the stage, taking in the applause.

'I'm sorry about the interruptions,' she says. 'We've had some very naughty spirits in tonight. But after all, it is Christmas, and even on the Other Side people can still enjoy themselves.'

There is a roar of approval from the crowd at this. They seem to be swallowing Zandra's version of events, hook, line and sinker. Emily and I look at one another.

'Are they all blind?' said Emily. 'Are we the only ones who think something strange happened here tonight?'

'Looks like it,' I say as the audience gradually calms down while Zandra is thanking us all for coming and telling us where her road show will be going after Christmas.

'Like anyone in their right mind would want to go through that again,' I mutter. I certainly don't. I have never been so spooked by anything in my life before.

We file out with the crowds, people chatting excitedly about what they've seen tonight. As if it were a laugh, a joke. In contrast I feel wrung out and exhausted. If that was Livvy, her anger has hit me hard. What have I done to her? She's dead, and the thought of her still suffering because of me is horrendous, despite everything that went wrong between us.

'I don't know about you,' Emily said as they left the theatre, 'but I could use a drink.'

Adam nodded silently. He had been very quiet since the show finished, and Emily could feel he had gone distant on her. She wished she knew what he was thinking. All she did know was that she'd gone into the theatre a sceptic and come out a believer. First Mum, then Livvy. It was too much of a coincidence. Moreover whatever people were now convincing themselves that they'd just experienced, the flashing lights, the lights dimming, the music playing and the cold breaths on the backs of their necks felt all too real, and from what Emily had read about Zandra her shows were never that gimmicky.

If this was real, where did that leave them? Joe was right: Livvy clearly wanted to get in touch, but judging by what she had said to Adam, she was pretty angry. Emily knew that Livvy had a right to feel hurt, but a part of her also thought Livvy was being unfair. She had rejected Adam long before Emily had met him. And why couldn't they have this shot at happiness just because Livvy had died?

'So . . .' Emily said cautiously, as Adam knocked back a vodka and tonic really fast (which was worrying in itself, Adam never normally touched spirits), 'I think we might have to face the fact that we're actually being haunted. If that wasn't Livvy I don't know who else it could have been.'

Adam didn't reply. He looked ashen, every bit as bad as he did in those first terrible weeks after Livvy had died. It made Emily angry.

'I know Livvy's dead and I should feel sorry for her,' Emily said. 'But hasn't she done enough? She caused you so much heartache when she was alive, and now she's still delivering it in spades from beyond the grave. Why can't she just let it go?'

'I think', said Adam, 'I need another drink.'

'OK.' Emily touched his hand. 'It's not the answer though.'

'Don't you know that I of all people understand that?' Adam said, his voice bitter.

'I know, I know.' Emily kissed him on the cheek and went to the bar, where she ordered two more shots. She was waiting for the drinks when someone jostled her.

'Oh it's you,' she said in surprise. 'What the hell happened in there?'

Zandra was standing in front of Emily, with her crew, who all looked like they'd had a heavy night of it already. She turned and paled slightly.

'I need – give me a moment,' she said. 'Where are you sitting?'

'Over there.' Emily pointed to where Adam was staring sadly into space.

'Flying Spirit came through to me after the show. I need to speak to you both,' said Zandra. 'I'll be over in a jiffy.'

Emily took the drinks back to Adam, who accepted his gratefully.

'I needed that,' he said. 'Bloody hell. What an evening.'

'You can say that again.' Zandra was gliding into the seat next to them. Emily noted with amusement that she'd lost her Atlantic twang, and reverted to an Essex drawl. 'Your wife certainly stirs up trouble.'

'But—' protested Adam as if part of him still couldn't quite believe what had happened.

'That wasn't me tonight,' said Zandra. 'Whatever you may think of me, I do have a connection with the Other Side, and no one has caused that much mayhem before. My guide has told me all about your wife.'

'You really think it was Livvy?'

'I do,' said Zandra. 'And I sense a soul in more trouble than most. She wants to pass over but can't. She clearly has unfinished business.'

Emily glanced at Adam, wondering how well he'd take that.

'It's true,' he mumbled. 'There was – stuff – unresolved when she died.'

Emily tried not to flinch at that. It would never have been easy for Adam to tell Livvy that he'd wanted to leave her. Then she'd found out and sent Adam a furious text, and then – boom! – a car had hit her and the next thing they knew she was dead. Though he never said as much, Emily knew Adam still blamed himself. If they hadn't been having an affair, if Livvy hadn't been upset and been paying more attention, they might eventually have been able to sort everything out in a kinder, more humane way and one that protected Joe. But they had and she wasn't. No one's fault; just appalling sodding luck.

'So here you are,' said Zandra. 'I have a suggestion. I don't do this very often, but your Livvy gave me a big headache tonight. I can't have her disrupting my show again. So I am willing to do a private seance for you, for a small fee, so you can make peace with your wife. What do you think?'

'I think it's a terrible idea,' Emily blurted out. Who knew what madness Livvy would inflict on them if she had Adam's undivided attention? Although . . . maybe there'd be another opportunity to talk to Mum again.

'What do you think, Adam?' she asked tentatively.

Adam looked up bleakly.

'Yes,' he said, 'I owe her that. Let's do it.'

167

Joe's Notebook

Dad and Emily are out tonight, which is why I am at Caroline's.

It's good to have a girlfriend.

Maybe that's why Dad is with Emily.

Mum died and he needed a girlfriend.

I think Mum made Dad sad sometimes.

He is often sad.

I don't like Dad being sad.

Emily makes him happy.

This is good.

If Dad were a star, I think he'd be Polaris. That's the star that leads you home.

And now Mum's not here, Dad leads me home.

I wonder if he can lead her home too?

Christmas Past

'Well, well, well.' Malachi appears by my side as I sit on a bench with a thumping headache. You get hangovers when you're dead? How does *that* work? Do you also get fat from eating too many cakes?

'Has someone got a guilty conscience?' says Malachi, leaping up next to me. I swear he's purring.

'Go away,' I say grumpily; my head is pounding too much to face this conversation.

'You're proud of your little display, are you?' he says.

'It got a bit . . . out of hand.'

Malachi snorts.

'Mind you,' he adds, 'when DJ Steve gets involved in anything, there's always trouble.'

'I thought he was one of you lot,' I say.

'Freelance,' says Malachi, looking disgusted. 'He thinks the rules don't apply to him.'

'So why did you send me to him?' I say, exasperated.

'Because I thought you at least might behave responsibly,' says Malachi. 'Despite the fact you're not easy material, I do have high hopes that one day you'll come good.'

Gee, thanks for that endorsement.

'And who sets the rules anyway?' I want to know. 'How do I know you're right and Steve isn't?'

'Steve isn't exactly wrong,' says Malachi, 'but his methods are unorthodox and I don't approve. Everyone needs order, especially when you're dead. If you'd only listen to me, we'd get this over and done with much sooner.'

Yawn. Yawn. Yawn.

'At least Adam knows I'm here now,' I offer.

'There is that,' says Malachi, 'but I still don't think you're getting it.'

'Getting what?' I say, frustrated. I'm sick of Malachi talking in riddles.

'You still haven't faced up to where things went wrong. And it's no good blaming Adam for everything.'

'He was the one who had an affair,' I say snappily.

'You really don't remember, do you?' Malachi says. 'Here, let me remind you.'

It's Christmas Eve and 8-year-old Joe is in bed. We've got Adam's parents again this year. Adam has begged me to be on my best behaviour. And I'm trying, I really am, but they're constantly on my case about Joe, like they're experts or something. Them. The parents who can't bear to be in the same room as their autistic son.

I've been drinking mulled wine like it's going out of fashion and have managed to keep a lid on my tongue so far, but I'm relieved when they decide to go to bed early. Somehow although I thought I was completely organized for Christmas, I've still got presents to wrap.

'Do you want me to help?' says Adam. Yeah, right. That's always been my job. And actually, I can see he's knackered. Now his parents are in bed, I'm feeling quite jolly, looking forward to sitting by the fire on my own wrapping things up.

'No, no, you go on,' I say. I settle myself down with a glass of wine and *Home Alone*. It always puts me in the Christmas mood.

'And you'll do Joe's stocking, right?' says Adam.

'Of course.' I wave him away, feeling a sudden surge of resentment. When have I ever not done Joe's stocking?

The wrapping takes longer than I'd thought it would. The Sellotape is fiddly and I keep tearing the paper. Adam's mum's present – a foot spa, all the rage this year – looks like it's been dragged here by Santa, but it can't be helped. And Joe won't care if some of his presents are a bit of an odd shape.

By 2 a.m. I'm done. I gather the presents up and put them by the tree, but forget I'm still carrying my glass, and accidentally tip red wine on the damned foot spa. Sod. Have to do it again.

Now I'm having difficulty with Joe's presents. Which ones were for the stocking again? I can't remember. I'm sure it will come back to me . . .

'Livvy, Livvy,' Adam is shaking me awake. 'Joe's up and wondering where Santa is.'

Oh shit! It's 5 a.m. and I must have fallen asleep.

I think I'm still drunk, because I've got the giggles, and Adam seems quite cross, which is making me laugh even more.

'Oh go to bed,' he says in disgust. 'I'll sort it.'

I stagger upstairs, and the next thing I know it's daylight. Blearily I look at the clock. It's 10 a.m., and I'm completely alone. I'm also still dressed. Why? Where's Adam with my Christmas breakfast? *Oh*.

The turkey. I sit bolt upright. At this rate Christmas is going to be a disaster.

I throw some clothes on and fly downstairs to find Adam,

his parents and Joe sitting in the kitchen. I can smell the turkey.

Adam looks exhausted.

'I am so sorry,' I say. 'I must have overslept.'

'Yes, you must,' says Adam, and there's a strange look in his eye. 'It's OK, Mum helped me with the turkey.'

'Thank you.' I'm gabbling. I never intended this to happen. Adam's parents aren't fond of me and I want so hard to impress them.

We exchange Christmas greetings, and Joe proudly shows me his stocking presents, and then I breezily take over, as if that was the plan all along.

'You entertain your mum and dad,' I say brightly, when Adam offers to help. 'You don't see them very often.'

But as soon as I'm alone in the kitchen, I feel a slump coming on. There's a black hole in my memory about last night. Somehow I feel Adam is cross with me, but I can't think why. I only had one or two drinks, and it *is* Christmas. That's what everyone does. Why can't I have a drink now?

Suddenly, I feel an overwhelming desire for bubbly. That's supposed to be good for hangovers. Hair of the dog is what I need. As I chop vegetables and listen to *Carols from King's*, soothing though it is, I feel rattled and slightly on edge. It's not the end of the world that I overslept on Christmas Day, is it? I pour myself a wine glass full of champagne to make myself feel better. It's never too early to drink on Christmas Day.

'What's going on?' Adam comes into the kitchen. He seems furious for some reason. What is wrong with him today?

I raise my eyes blearily from the kitchen table, where I appear to have been having a little doze. The kitchen is in chaos. Apparently I was cutting crosses in sprouts when I fell asleep. There's a smell of burning coming from the hob. It must be the potatoes that have boiled dry.

'If you insist on ruining Christmas for me,' Adam hisses, 'can you at least think about your son.'

I have never seen him so angry.

I try and laugh it off, but suddenly I find I can't. Instead I start sobbing. It's Christmas Day and Adam is angry with me, and I just can't figure out why.

'Christ, Livvy, you're a disgrace,' says Adam. 'Go upstairs and sober up. I'll call you when lunch is ready.'

I stumble out of the kitchen, and run into Joe.

'Mum?' he says uncertainly, and he looks so lost I feel worse than ever.

'I'm sorry, darling. Mummy's not feeling very well,' I slur. I'm a poor excuse for a mother and a wife. Somewhere in my drunken state I realize I've behaved very badly this time, and there's no coming back from this.

I'm catapulted back into the present, in shock at what I have seen. Was that how I behaved? I seemed to have blanked it from my memory.

'Oh,' I say to Malachi in a small voice.

I had no idea how hideous I could be when I was drunk.

'Oh indeed,' says Malachi. 'Now do you see? Your life was a mess before you died, and deep down I know you feel bad about that. You can't pass over till you've put things right with the people you love. *That's* why you're still here.'

Part Two

Christmas Present

Joe's Notebook

What is a mum?

A mum has a drink in the afternoon, but ssh, it's a secret.

A mum forgets me sometimes.

A mum sleeps in the afternoon.

A mum isn't always here.

I remember the notebooks Joe used to leave lying about the place, with his thoughts laid bare. How could I have forgotten them? Each was a knife in the heart, to remind me of how much I'd failed him. No wonder Adam turned to Emily. I wasn't there for him either.

If there was only a way back. If only I hadn't died in that crappy car park. I could show them how truly sorry I am.

'That's what I've been trying to tell you,' says Malachi. 'You have to go to Adam and Joe and say you're truly sorry. I know it's rough you died before you were ready but it's time to let go and accept Adam is with Emily and move on.'

'I just can't do that,' I say. 'Adam still cheated on me. It wasn't all my fault. Besides, I don't want Emily to have him, I want him for myself.'

Malachi raises an eyebrow.

'Livvy,' he says patiently. 'That's not the way it works. You're dead. You don't get to pick up your old life again. You have to accept it's over.'

'Isn't there some way I can do it?' I ask. 'David Niven did it in *A Matter of Life or Death*.'

'That's a film,' says Malachi, rolling his eyes.

'But don't you see?' I say. 'This is my second chance. If there was only a way I could start again with Adam, I'd make it work this time.'

'No,' says Malachi very firmly. 'That's never going to happen.'

I get the feeling there's something he's not telling me, but he refuses to be drawn.

'But say I hadn't died,' I say. 'What then? I just can't believe that this is it, that I don't get any more chances.'

'OK,' says Malachi. 'Maybe this will make you change your mind. Let's see how things would have worked out if you *hadn't* died.'

And then I'm back in the car park. Frantically texting Adam. I'm so angry with him, I am not paying any attention to my surroundings. How could he do this to me and Joe? How could he? I step out in the road without looking, and too late I see the car coming towards me. This time I feel every bruising inch of impact as I fly through the air, screaming, and hit the shopping trolley. Oh God, it hurts.

And now I'm lying on the ground, surrounded by anxious faces, and the driver standing stunned, saying tearfully to his dad, 'I didn't see her, I didn't see her.'

I'm in so much pain, at first I don't appreciate that the voice I hear screaming is me. Everything hurts and throbs, and all I can think about is Adam and Joe. What will become of them? I have to survive this, I *have* to.

'Call nine nine nine,' I hear a voice shout.

'They're on their way,' another responds.

I'm drifting in and out of consciousness, but I hear the sirens, and realize in a detached kind of way they are coming for me. If I can just hang on a bit longer. I feel like darkness wants to envelop me though, and it's very tempting. In an odd moment of lucidity I wonder if I am on the brink of death, till I hear a calm, kind voice saying, 'Stay with me, Livvy, stay with me,' and I am being prodded and poked from all angles. It hurts, and I scream out in pain, but I am going to stay with them. And then I'm on a stretcher, and being transferred to an ambulance. Someone has put a mask on my face, and given me an injection, and the pain is starting to recede. I am vaguely aware of the blue light going, and having the absurd thought that Joe will be cross to have missed a ride in an ambulance, before everything fades into blackness.

Then I'm awake in a hospital bed with lights shining in my eyes. I don't appear to be in any pain, but there's a drip attached to my arm, and I feel as I have just been through a pummelling. A friendly black face swims into view and a cheerful voice says, 'Well you gave us a fright and no mistake. There are two people here who are very glad to see you.'

I open my eyes properly and see the welcoming sight of Adam and Joe. Adam is crying and holding my hand tight, and saying, 'Sorry, sorry,' and Joe is saying loudly, 'Is Mum going to die?'

'No, she's not,' says Adam firmly, and I look into his eyes and see the love that I've been missing. He takes my hand,

'Oh Livvy,' he says, a catch in his voice. 'I nearly lost you, and I'm so sorry.'

No, I'm not dying. I'm not dead. And though I know we still have to face up to what Adam's done, I don't care. I have my two boys back with me. Where they belong.

Chapter Thirteen

Christmas Present

One Week to Go

Adam

Emily and I are busy getting things ready for the seance. It feels surreal. I am about to have a seance to try and talk to my *dead* wife. Two weeks ago, the idea of such a thing would have been crazy, but now? Emily and I have been going over and over the events at the theatre, yet we cannot find any rational explanation for what has happened. I remain sceptical about Zandra's ability either to reach Livvy if she really is there, or whether I'll be able to talk to Livvy the way I want to. If she does come through, if she is prepared to listen, I need to apologize for what happened; I need her forgiveness.

If . . . Livvy alive had an appalling ability to hold on to grudges. God knows what she'll be like now she's been dead a year. But if this is the only way we can stop her causing trouble, so be it. Besides, despite everything that's happened, I genuinely want her to be happy. It used to tear me up inside seeing how unhappy she was. I tried to help her, but she would never admit to us or herself that she had a problem, and in the end I was too hurt by her constant rejections to try any more. How do you keep on coping day in and day out, watching someone you love pressing the self-destruct button, knowing they won't listen to you? That's how I justified it to myself, but now I wonder if I could have, *should* have, tried harder.

We've moved the table to the centre of the room.

'Do you think we need candles?' asks Emily.

I think about all the films I've ever watched in which a ghost arrives and blows out the candles. If that happened we'd both be freaked out.

'Best not,' I say.

I've also sent Joe to Felicity's for the night. I haven't told either of them what we're up to, and Emily hasn't told Kenneth. I can't risk Joe going off on one, and neither of us wants Felicity or Kenneth to think we're going mad. Despite what they've both witnessed, they've been rationalizing the event ever since, Felicity convincing herself that she never saw the table move, and Kenneth that we had all imagined it. Luckily, Joe is happy at Felicity's, where the atmosphere is always calm and ordered. He generally visits once a fortnight anyway.

'This is insane,' says Emily as she reorganizes the chairs.

'I know,' I say, kissing her on top of the head. 'But we have to try it.'

The doorbell rings and in sweeps Zandra, and a plump little twittering man wearing an ill-fitting suit, who I assume is her manager before discovering he's actually her husband.

'Sandy, are you sure about this?' he is saying. 'I think you might be biting off a bit more than you can chew here. You were exhausted after the incident at the theatre.'

'I'll be the judge of that, Norman,' says Zandra, putting

him in his place, which I suspect is where he spends a lot of his time.

She comes into the lounge, and looks approvingly at the way we've set things up.

'Let's dim the lights, shall we?' she says. She refuses a drink. I sense she's nervous and wants to get on with it.

First of all she insists on a tarot reading.

'I need to get a feel for what's going on here,' she says. 'Livvy seems an unhappy soul, and there must be something stopping her passing over. The tarot cards may offer us a clue.'

I look at Emily. I can just about swallow a seance, but tarot cards – really? I try hard to tamp down my cynicism.

We sit down opposite Zandra, who asks me about Livvy, and I give her an edited version. I'm not comfortable telling her all my secrets.

'Let's see,' she says, and shuffles the deck. She lays down three cards, then turns them over one by one.

The first is called the Lovers.

'Aah,' she says, 'there are difficult decisions to be made here. There's a struggle going on.'

I grimace at Emily. She could have worked that out from what I have told her.

The next card is the Wheel of Fortune, which she explains signifies good luck, but then she turns the card over and says, 'But in this instance it might mean bad things are going to happen.'

Too late, they seem to be happening already.

When she gets to the third card, she blanches and hurriedly reshuffles the cards.

'Something's not quite right,' she mutters, and deals again. This time she gets the Empress first time around, signifying marriage and fertility. She breathes a sigh of relief and turns over the second card. It's Death, which makes me wince, but Zandra smiles and says, 'Death doesn't have to be bad, it can mean change.' She turns over the third card, and gasps.

'What is it?' I say.

'The Hangman,' she says. 'It turned up before, but I thought it must be wrong.'

'Why?' Emily wants to know. Zandra is looking quite agitated, and it's a little unnerving.

'Because it can mean sacrifice,' she says. 'You may have to lose one thing to obtain another.'

I shiver. I am trying to convince myself this is nonsense, but there's something about the way she says it that puts the wind up me. Zandra meanwhile is focusing on reshuffling.

'The tarot isn't clear today,' she says, 'it's as if I'm getting interference.'

She has another go with Emily, and gets the Lovers, the Wheel of Fortune and the Empress, which seems to make her happier, and she gives a more confident prediction that Emily and I will have a happy future, if we can resolve the issues of our pasts.

'That's a very big if,' I mutter.

Zandra seems more fake here, in my living room, than she did on stage. If I were a ghost, I'm not sure I'd choose to come through her, but her alarm about what she has seen in the tarot cards feels genuine, and makes me uneasy.

She puts the cards away, and then says, 'Are you two ready for this?'

I look at Emily, who smiles, and say, 'Ready.'

'We need to hold hands, and shut our eyes,' she says, 'and if we are open enough, the spirit of Livvy will come through.'

Feeling utterly ridiculous and desperate to get this over

with, I join hands with Emily and Norman, while Zandra says in sepulchral tones, 'Livvy, are you there? Adam wants to talk to you.'

Emily

Emily didn't know what she'd been expecting. But the first ten minutes of the seance were, well, *boring*. They sat in silence in the semi-darkness, with their eyes shut. Any minute now Zandra was going to start saying, 'Om . . .'

Emily glanced surreptitiously around the room. Zandra seemed to have gone into some kind of trance. She sat leaning slightly backwards, and although her eyes were open, they stared out unblinking. She was barely breathing, and her face had turned a slightly greenish hue. It was mildly unnerving, and Emily found herself having to look away. She glanced at Norman, who managed to look nervous and pious at the same time, while Adam had a look of rigid intensity on his face. The room was silent except for the sound of Norman's heavy breathing. Nothing was going to happen. This was utterly ridiculous.

Emily stifled the urge to giggle. What were they even doing here? Her earlier scepticism returned. Did they really think Livvy was going to speak to them?

'Livvy are you there?' Zandra intoned.

But there was only silence, and the sound of the wind coming down the chimney.

Norman's hand gripped Emily's tightly. It was horribly sweaty and slippery, and Emily wished she wasn't holding it. Hysteria rose in her gullet. They'd simply got carried away by the odd things that had been happening, and started to believe in ghosts, when of course there were no such things. Zandra and Norman had fed on that weakness, and were going along with this to make money out of them both. They must be laughing all the way to the bank. This was arrant nonsense.

Then she heard it. A voice whispering vehemently in her ear: 'I'll show you nonsense!' The next thing Emily knew, she could feel it again: that horrible sensation of cold and the nasty spiteful presence. Oh God. It *was* real, Livvy was actually here. All Emily's rational thoughts flew away as she was overcome with cold blind panic.

A hard sharp slap on her cheek made her yelp. She leaped out of her chair at the exact moment when a bulb in the chandelier light above the table exploded and shattered, just where she'd been sitting.

'What the—?'Ashen-faced, Emily turned to look at Zandra, whose voice had suddenly changed. She stood up and looked at Emily with those ghastly staring blank eyes. To Emily's fevered brain she didn't look human any more.

'Get out of my house!' Zandra said, and then collapsed back in the chair.

Now it was official. Emily wasn't just scared. She was *terrified*.

Livvy

Zandra is one big fat disappointment. I thought she had a connection with the dead. She can barely hear me, though I've been shouting in her ear for ten minutes. Maybe she needs Psychic Steve by her side, but I have it on reliable authority from Malachi that Steve is recovering from an all-nighter and is not currently available. I think Malachi wants me to manage this alone. I know he wants me to try and find some common ground with Adam. But honestly?

I got here long before Zandra did, and the sight of Evil Emily making up to Adam, asking if he's OK, touching his arm in a way that is obviously false, makes me sick. Why can't he see what she's like? It's so obvious she's a woman on the shelf, who wanted to take someone else's man because she couldn't get one of her own. Before he knows it, she'll be presenting him with squalling brats and poor Joe will be pushed out of the equation.

Malachi has shown me a different version of the present, and hinted that there might be a way back, but doesn't seem keen I should take it. But what if he's wrong, and rather than accepting my lot, I've actually returned to chase Emily out of Adam's life? I feel I've been given another chance to make things better for me, Adam and Joe. This time I won't drink. This time I'll get help, and Adam will fall in love with me again. I know he still has feelings for me. The way he held my hand in the hospital in the vision Malachi showed me wasn't a lie. He loves me still, deep down; I just need to remind him of the fact.

And so I slap Emily and make a lightbulb explode above her head. I don't want to *hurt* her, just scare her a bit. Make her *see* being with Adam is too much, so she can leave him for me.

I thought I might be able to come through properly if Zandra opened her mind enough. But for all her 'I can speak to the dead' business, she is fantastically small-minded about the whole spiritualism thing, and seems to only half believe it herself. So, after a huge effort, all I can do is shout at Emily through her before collapsing in a small heap. Zandra seems equally worn out with the effort, and comes to several minutes later, looking confused.

'Did Livvy come through?' she asks.

'Not exactly,' says Adam, grim-faced, 'but she did send us a message.'

He points to the lightbulb, smashed on the table, and Zandra goes pale.

'Oh dear,' she says. 'Oh dear, oh dear.'

'What?' says Adam.

'You have one angry spirit there,' says Zandra. 'I don't think I can help you any more.'

'So what do you suggest?' says Adam. 'Do we just have to put up with this?'

Zandra looks at him intently.

'I don't think Livvy wants to listen to reason,' she says. 'I wouldn't normally suggest this, but if I were you, I'd seriously consider an exorcism.'

Chapter Fourteen

Emily

An exorcism? That sounded a bit drastic.

'I really don't think that will be necessary,' Emily said. 'I'm sure Livvy didn't mean any harm. She was probably trying to frighten me.' Which, to be fair, she'd more than succeeded in doing.

'She's very angry,' said Zandra. 'And it's only going to get worse. I'd really think about it, if I were you.'

She and Norman gathered up their things and beat a hasty retreat. Emily got the impression they couldn't wait to be out of the house. Zandra even waived her fee.

'I couldn't possibly charge you. It wouldn't be right, not in the circumstances,' she explained.

They dashed off leaving Adam and Emily staring at one another in disbelief.

'Are you OK?' said Adam. 'I can't believe that just happened.'

He pulled Emily close to him and kissed her. She felt warmed and comforted by his embrace. It felt normal and right in circumstances that were anything but.

'Me neither, but I'm fine,' Emily lied. In truth, she was

scared witless, but it wouldn't help Adam to know that. 'A bit shaken, but fine.'

'I couldn't bear it if something bad happened to you,' said Adam. 'If Livvy hurt you . . .'

'Nothing's going to happen to me,' Emily said, with more conviction than she felt. 'Livvy was probably just making a point.'

In reality Emily wasn't at all sure. At the moments when she'd imagined she could feel Livvy close by, Emily had felt her exuding waves of malicious energy. And she had exploded a lightbulb on Emily's head, which was drastic by anyone's standards. The fire flared in the grate as if to prove her point. Was Livvy still there, watching? The thought made her shiver.

Adam was clearly shaken up by the lightbulb too.

'This is a nightmare,' he said. 'I didn't know what was going to happen there, but at the very least I was hoping we could talk to Livvy. But now I don't know what we're going to do. Livvy seems determined to get rid of you.'

Emily noted wryly that Adam was no longer trying to find excuses for what was going on and, like her, she could see he was genuinely scared.

Taking a deep breath, she pulled herself together.

'She can try,' she said, kissing Adam, 'but bad luck for you, I'm not going anywhere.'

'Please don't,' says Adam, and kissed her back with such enthusiasm, Emily remembered that she was alive, Livvy was not, and Adam had chosen her not Livvy. She was damned if she was going to be pushed around by a jealous ghost.

'Come on, the night's still young, Joe's out for the evening, it's nearly Christmas,' Emily said. 'Let's do something normal, and go to the pub.'

So Emily wants to play hardball does she? I know I'm here to get Adam and Joe back, but I feel like a gauntlet's being laid down. I need to teach Emily a lesson before I go any further. We're fighting over Adam now, and I'm determined I'm going to win this particular battle. And as to me not wanting to hurt her, Emily is clearly more naïve than I thought. If I had real fingers that could actually throttle, I'd have *no* compunction about putting them around Emily's perfect little neck. Well, maybe that's a little extreme, but it's cathartic to fantasize.

I follow Emily and Adam to the pub at a discreet distance. It's sleeting, and there's a cold wind blowing, and they're huddling together for warmth. It makes me so angry to see them together, I am more determined than ever to split them up. I wonder what my next move should be. Perhaps if I'm with them all the time, if Emily gets the idea that nowhere is safe from my presence, maybe she'll do the decent thing and let him go.

Maybe.

I think I see Malachi in the distance. I really don't need a lecture from him about bad behaviour so I move closer to Emily and Adam, who are standing outside the Fox and Grapes. It was a favourite of mine and Adam's in the old days. Please don't bring her in here, I think. Can't you find somewhere new?

'Oh look, there's a band on,' I hear Emily say. 'Come on, it could be fun.'

'Anything to take our mind off things,' says Adam. I am getting the feeling he isn't quite as keen as Emily on trying to behave as though none of this is happening. Good. I might be able to work on that. I need to exploit any division opening up between them.

I follow them into the pub. It's rammed, heaving with people who are enjoying themselves in that slightly desperate, pre-Christmas we're-all-out-to-have-fun kind of way. The band are great, playing a whole series of covers I like, and they're good at it, the guitarist in particular. For a while I just stand there and listen, taking it all in. They have a fabulous mix of blues, rock and Christmas favourites. I allow myself to get lost in the music and forget all about Adam and Emily for a while, remembering instead happier days with Adam when we were younger, coming here for Sunday lunch with Joe in a pram, before we knew there was anything wrong with him. We had many good times together, and we were so much in love with one another back then, I can't believe it's gone away; it's just got buried under all the things that came between us over the years. I need to remind Adam why we fell in love in the first place. Then I know everything will be all right.

I'm perfectly happy until the band begin to play 'Fairytale of New York', and Emily and Adam start dancing.

No!!! How can he? Doesn't he remember anything? That was *our* Christmas song. I am so not having that.

Adam

To my surprise, Emily and I are having a brilliant time. It's wonderful to forget for the moment that I am being haunted by my dead wife, and remember that it's nearly Christmas and I am with Emily who I love very much. I think I fell in love with her that very first time we met in the café and she was so kind to Joe. There's just something about Emily. Not only is she gorgeous, but she's kind and funny and sweet, and it wasn't long before I was completely obsessed. I tried to ignore it, and pretend it wasn't happening. I'm not a natural-born adulterer, but then one day, after a particularly bad run in with Livvy, I found myself in the bar alone on a Friday night. Emily had been going to meet her friend Lucy, but at the last minute one of the children was ill, and she was also alone. We got chatting and by the end of the evening I was pouring my heart out to her. Emily listened and didn't judge, and I loved her a little bit more. When it was time to go, I leaned in for a peck on the cheek, and suddenly I was swept up in a feeling I could neither control nor prevent, and began to kiss her with a passion I had forgotten I was capable of. But it was replaced all too soon with feelings of guilt and mortification, which Emily shared. We agreed then and there it couldn't happen again. God knows we tried to resist the temptation, but we couldn't keep away from one another. Life at home was so intolerable, I was desperate for the slice of happiness Emily gave me. And still does.

I'm a little drunk, so when 'Fairytale of New York' comes on I grab Emily for a dance, which is unusual for me. Livvy always complained that I needed a bomb under me to do so.

Emily is singing along, as are the rest of the pub. The mood is merry and festive, just as it should be. I begin to relax a little; the stress of the last few days finally receding.

And then it happens.

There's a bang and a flash from the Christmas tree lights, and they go out, followed by the lights in the pub, one by one. The band stop playing and we hear a sudden explosion from the electric guitar as the fuse pops; the room goes horribly cold.

There are a few yells and a general air of disquiet, but the landlord yells, 'Don't worry, everyone, I'll get the lights back on in a jiffy.'

He disappears to the cellar to turn the circuit generator

back on, while I give Emily a worried glance. Oh no . . . I squeeze her hand and try to banish dark thoughts. The landlord is soon back with a load of tea lights. 'The switches all look OK,' he says, baffled. I'm not. It's Livvy, it has to be. He swiftly lights candles, creating a mellow festive mood, and the band start to play again, the guitarist swapping his electric guitar for an acoustic one. They switch to more folksy music, which fits the mood, and people begin to relax again, enjoying the change of pace.

The band are halfway through a Corrs song when the door at one end of the bar gusts open and all the candles blow out. This happens several times before the landlord gives up and gets a torch instead. Mutters of unease ripple round the pub, and several people get up to go.

Desperate to keep his crowd together, the barman shouts 'Drinks on the house till the lights come back on!' which is effective. There's an immediate stampede to the bar, and the waverers are persuaded to stay.

Emily and I both know what's happening.

'Bloody Livvy,' says Emily, 'what's she up to?' and then – oof! – falls straight into me.

'What?'

'She pushed me,' says Emily in indignation. 'Livvy pushed me.'

I look around, nervously wondering where Livvy could be. I wish I could see her.

'Livvy, if you're there, give it a rest, will you? We just wanted a night out.'

The fire flares up, and there's another 'Ow!' from Emily, and an indignant, 'She pinched me! I am getting so hacked off with this!' Then the lights go back up and the band resume playing.

'What the hell are we going to do with her?' I say.

194

Chapter Fifteen

A Week before Christmas

Adam

I'm still mulling over what to do on Sunday when Felicity rings me to remind me Joe and I have promised to come to the Festival of Carols at the church where she sings. It's not really my thing, but Livvy always used to take Joe and he likes going. Now she's not here, it's my job. It's hard being both mum and dad to him, but I am doing my best.

Joe and I arrive at church in plenty of time. St Mary's is a large Victorian church, hidden away down a dark alley, surrounded by its graveyard. I used to like walking among the tombstones wondering who all the people were buried there. That's lost its appeal in the last year.

The bells are ringing and there's a brightly lit Christmas tree outside the church, which lifts my spirits. The light flowing from the church porch seems to banish dark thoughts.

Father Matthew is standing outside in his surplice, greeting people. An avuncular figure, with greying hair, I recognize him from Livvy's funeral. I don't know him well, but he was kind to us last year. How kind people are has become my barometer for judging them. So many of them were awkward and didn't know what to say. I've lost touch with a fair few in the last year who hadn't even bothered to send a card. At times like that you learn who your friends really are.

'Adam, Joe.' He shakes our hands enthusiastically. 'Welcome, welcome. Great to see you both.'

I feel sorry for him if he believes the welcome will make us come back. He knows I'm a dyed-in-the-wool atheist, who doesn't believe in all that life after death claptrap, as I told him in no uncertain terms last year. But bless him, he tries. I don't plan on telling him I might be having a bit of a change of heart on that one.

We go near to the front at Joe's suggestion, 'So we can see Granny properly,' and sit down. 'Leave a space for Mum,' he adds.

'What do you mean?' I say, thinking, please, not here too. Joe still doesn't know we've been to the seance or had Zandra round to ours. I haven't quite found the words to tell him.

'Mum will come,' says Joe, with a beatific smile on his face. 'She always comes. She likes the carols.'

I'm not sure that ghosts who haven't yet mastered the art of passing over as they should are able to enter churches – something to do with hallowed ground perhaps? – but I let it pass. If it comforts Joe to think that Livvy is here, who am I to disillusion him? And if she's got it in for Emily, I know she'd never ever hurt or upset Joe.

I forget about it as the service starts. For a non-believer, it's a bit of an ordeal. It's very long, with endless Bible readings, from the Angel Gabriel visiting Mary to the final visit from the three Wise Men. The quality of the readers is patchy. The woman who reads the story of the Virgin

Birth has such a beautiful voice, I get a lump in my throat. Even for an atheist like me, there's something touching about the story of the baby born in a stable. But the elderly chap reading the story of the visitation of the shepherds has me nearly nodding off, and I have to fight hard to stop myself giggling when one overdramatic lady reading the bit about Joseph and Mary looking for shelter feels the need to act it out. I like the carols though, and Joe is singing along so lustily (albeit out of tune) that it's hard not to feel a little Christmassy.

And then as we get up to sing 'Silent Night', Joe says, 'Hi Mum,' and I suddenly feel as if Livvy is standing right next to me. The hairs on the back of my neck rise – can she really be here? It's weird but I feel as if she is leaning against me, and she's not angry, but peaceful, and it comforts me – for a moment, it feels like we are a family again. Together at Christmas, just as it should be. Just as we were so many years ago. I am hit by an overwhelming sense of anguish. By the time we get to the end of 'Silent Night', I find that I am crying, for loss and love and things that can't be regained.

'Livvy,' I whisper, 'I'm so sorry.'

Livvy

I wasn't sure if I'd be able to get into church. I thought I might be held up at the door. But as I walk through the hordes of worshippers pouring in, I see that Reverend Matt is not alone. There's another older vicar, dressed in old-fashioned garments, standing next to him, who's just as dead as I am.

'Welcome, welcome,' he says.

'You mean, I'm allowed in?' I say dubiously.

I am desperate to enter the church, but thought I would be stopped at the door. Aren't there rules about it? Joe and I always went to this service together to hear Mum singing. I love the carols, and I simply want to be near them both.

'Of course you're allowed in,' says the vicar. 'This is the house of God. All are welcome, see?' He motions to a group of ghosts who are milling around at the back. It's nice to know I'm not the only one.

'But no trouble, eh?' he adds, as I go inside.

I have no intention of causing trouble. This isn't the place for it. Besides I've spotted that Adam and Joe are together without Emily, which is perfect. And Mum is there processing down the aisle in her choir gown, like always. For a moment I feel a pang. Mum has done so well, carving a life out for herself since Dad died, and I never told her how proud I was of her. Now that I'm dead, I am beginning to see I took her for granted. Why did I do that? When she was always there, in the background, helping? It's not just my life I've lost, it's the people in it, and I feel sad and lonely, trapped on the other side, looking in.

Before I go to sit with Adam and Joe, I cross over to the choir stalls and stand beside Mum. I don't know whether she's aware of me, but I draw enormous comfort from her singing 'Once in Royal David's City'. I've always loved that carol, and listening to Mum makes me feel very peaceful. I tell her she sounds lovely.

Then I look over to Adam and Joe. They are my everything, and I need to be with them. So I go to take my place next to them, right where I belong.

I know Joe can feel me, because he grins and says, 'Hello Mum,' but Adam I'm not so sure of.

I lean into him, resting my head on his shoulder. It may

mean nothing to him, but there's a warmth and tenderness coming from him, and I feel comforted by his nearness. And when I hear him whisper how sorry he is, I know he's felt me too.

This is what my life was, and still should be. I can't bear the thought of Emily taking my place. I sit up. I am damned if I am going to let her. I hadn't meant to hurt her with that stupid lightbulb. But maybe I can scare her into thinking I want to.

Emily

Emily was sitting in her flat wrapping Christmas presents, with a glass of wine in hand and cheesy Christmas music playing, talking on the phone to her dad, who had been down to his local for a port and Stilton tasting.

'I've had a lovely evening, Emily,' he was hiccupping. 'And you'll never guess who's invited me to dinner?'

'No idea,' laughed Emily. 'It could be one of any number of mad fools.'

'It's Sherry Matthews if you must know,' said Dad. 'And she's not mad, but rather lovely.'

'I really don't want to know, Dad,' said Emily as she grappled with the Sellotape.

'Mind you,' he continued, 'she's not as lovely as the divine Felicity. You will tell her I was asking after her, won't you?'

'She's out of your league, Dad. And I think she can see through your wiles.'

'A man can try,' sighed Dad, and then added, 'How's everything else? No more funny stuff?'

Emily had been giving him a very edited version of events, partly so as not to worry him, partly so that he didn't think she'd completely lost it. To her surprise, Dad had been remarkably accepting of the idea that his daughter might be being haunted by her boyfriend's dead wife.

'There's more to this world than we know,' he said wisely. Emily had had no idea her rational dad even thought like that, but he told her he changed his opinion when Mum had died.

'It was like she was trying to get through to me,' he said. 'I'd go in our bedroom and smell her favourite scent, and then the first rose came out on her birthday, and I knew it was her saying everything was OK. So now, I think, who knows what goes on? I certainly don't. Anyway, I hope nothing untoward is occurring.'

Emily wished he was there so she could have hugged him. It made her feel better, knowing she could talk to someone else about it. She hadn't dared mention any of this to Lucy, who despite being a good friend would either laugh or tell her she should see a shrink.

'Dad, there's nothing to worry about really,' said Emily, omitting to mention what had happened in the pub; there was no point making him fret. 'I'll give you a ring before Christmas, if I'm ever lucky enough to catch you in.'

'Love you, sweetheart,' said Dad and hung up, leaving Emily alone with her pile of presents.

It was quite restful being away from Adam's house for a bit. Although Adam had asked Emily to go to carols with him and Joe, she had made her excuses. It was something they probably needed to do together anyway. The last thing she wanted was for Joe to think she was trying to muscle in on Livvy's place.

The last few days had been intense to say the least, and Emily was enjoying sitting here belting out the words to 'Do They Know It's Christmas' at the top of her voice without interruption. Her flat felt cosy and warm, and she was having a serious think about whether she was quite ready to leave it yet. Even without all the Livvy nonsense, she might have had second thoughts. After Graham had left her, Emily had fought hard for her independence. It had been a slog selling the joint house they'd shared in North London and getting a mortgage on this little flat, but Emily had been very happy here. She'd enjoyed living a life beholden to no one but herself. Should she give that freedom up and take on a stepson so soon? Even for Adam? Maybe they should wait a bit longer.

She was just sticking down the Sellotape on Felicity's present – a gardening trug and clippers, as Emily knew from Adam she loved her roses – when she heard a bang, making her nearly jump out of her skin. Emily went to the hall, and discovered the front door had blown open. Had she left it on the latch?

Oh no, surely Livvy wouldn't come here? Emily was overcome with rage; how dare Livvy enter her private sanctuary?

There was another bang on the bathroom door and the sound of taps running. Emily flew into the bathroom to turn them off. The mirror was steamed up and to her horror she could see words forming on it. Livvy was writing a message.

LEAVE HIM ALONE. HE'S MINE.

'Oh grow up, Livvy,' Emily said. 'He can't be yours, you're dead, remember?'

The door banged behind her, making her start once more. She wiped the message off and then heard yet more banging coming from her bedroom. There was another message in lipstick on her mirror:

FIND YOUR OWN MAN!

Emily felt her anger leach away into fear. What was Livvy planning to do? What did she want?

There were notes now, blowing from the notepad she kept by the phone across the floor, saying:

LEAVE . . . HIM . . . ALONE

Emily grabbed them and crumpled them in the bin.

'Livvy, you don't scare me!' Emily said with a confidence she didn't feel. She could almost hear Livvy saying, 'Oh, yeah?' in her head, because the reality was she was scaring Emily half to death. She was alone in the flat with a very angry ghost who hated her. She could hardly ring 999.

And then she found another message on the mirror in the lounge.

I'M NOT LEAVING UNTIL YOU DO.

Shaking with fear, Emily sank to her knees in dismay.

Oh God. Livvy really wasn't intending to go away. What was she planning to do?

Joe's Notebook

We went to church with Granny.

I like to hear the carols.

Mum likes the carols too.

That's why she came to church with us.

There we were, Mum, Dad and I.

I think even Dad felt her this time.

And maybe Granny did too.

I hope so.

Granny is often sad about Mum.

I don't want Granny to be sad.

Maybe the carols made her happy tonight.

I know they made Mum happy.

That's good.

Christmas Present

'That was both unkind and unnecessary,' Malachi hisses at me from a bush behind the front door to Emily's flat. The hackles on his back are rising. Oops, I think I've really pissed him off this time.

'I'm feeling quite pleased with myself actually,' I say. 'That was enormous fun.'

'To scare Emily half to death?' snorts Malachi. 'That is not what you're meant to be doing.'

'I don't care what you think I should be doing,' I say. I'm fed up with him hassling me. 'I want Emily out of Adam's life, and I'm not going to let you stop me.'

'OK, you asked for it,' says Malachi. 'Here's another little peek into that wonderful life you're after. Enjoy,' and he strolls off with his nose in the air.

I am back again in Malachi's idea of the present, but not how I imagined it. The car pulls up outside the house. A few months seem to have passed and it's a cold April day, with a vicious wind. I start to get out of the car, and Adam says, 'Steady! I know you're keen to get home, but you're not ready to do it on your own.'

I try to laugh, but I'm puzzled. What's going on? It seems I must have been in hospital a long time, and I look on in horror as Adam takes out a wheelchair from the back of the car, and manoeuvres it into position by the passenger door.

'I'm not getting in that,' I say flatly.

'Livvy.' Adam's voice is gentle. 'You have to accept the situation. At the moment, you need it. Come on, please don't cause a scene.'

He looks desperate, and I notice rings around his eyes. I'm being a bitch, it's not his fault. But I'm in a wheelchair? Is this permanent?

I allow Adam to help me into the chair and say nothing as he pushes me up the new ramp to our house. There's a banner saying *Welcome Home, Mum* above the door, which Joe has made.

'Do you like it, Mum?' he says, and I smile and say, 'Of course I do.'

Adam is clearly on tenterhooks as he shows me round the house to see how I will react to the changes that have been made. There are grab rails everywhere and our down-stairs cupboard has been converted to a wet room. I want to explode with rage. I survived the accident only to end up in a wheelchair? It can't end like this. I want to let out all the things in my head, but one look at Adam tells me I mustn't. My heart bleeds for him. He's is trying so hard. Everyone is.

'It won't be forever,' says Mum with that fake cheerful smile on her face, trying to make this seem better than it is. 'We'll soon have you up and walking again.'

Even Adam's parents are here as part of the welcoming committee and being kind to me. And that spooks me the most.

Only Joe is guaranteed to be straight with me.

'Will you ever walk again?' he says as Adam pushes me into the lounge, and I ooh and aah at the cards and flowers that people have left, and the cake that Mum has made. Everyone's made such an effort, and it is rotten to feel so ungrateful.

'Joe!' says Adam. 'Of course Mum will walk again.'

I glare at Adam. Lying to Joe is so not helpful.

'I don't know, sweetie,' I say. 'Apparently I was pretty smashed up in the accident. It'll take time to find out how much better I'm going to be.'

'Livvy!'

Now I've shocked Adam. I'm clearly supposed to be putting a brave face on this, but it's impossible when I've come home in a wheelchair, to a house fitted with disabled aids.

'Now that's not the attitude, young lady,' says Mary. 'You're lucky to be here. It could have been very different.'

Oh good, from her lofty perspective of being both alive and not in a wheelchair Mary is about to launch into a little homily of why I should be grateful for the things I have. I am going to enjoy this.

Fortunately, Adam butts in with, 'Mum's got a point, Livvy. A fraction higher and you might not have been here. It doesn't bear thinking about.'

For his sake and not for Mary's I say, 'I know, I know I've been lucky, it just feels overwhelming, that's all.' I squeeze his hand and try to be cheerful, but as I look around at my home, and my family surrounding me with love and concern, I'm not sure that I feel very lucky right now. And just as I'm thinking this, I'm suddenly back at Malachi's side, feeling shaken to the core.

Chapter Sixteen

Six Days till Christmas

Emily

Emily grabbed her things and raced round to Adam's house, too scared to stay in her flat for a moment longer. Although what if Livvy was waiting for her there? The thought terrified her, but anything was better than being on her own.

Adam was back from church, and Joe was round at Caroline's, so Emily was able to pour out the story without worrying about Joe overhearing. She was so hysterical she could hardly get the words out.

'Adam, she hates me. She wants to get rid of me. I can't stand it any more. We have to do something.'

Adam held Emily tight. 'I am so sorry for this,' he said. 'I'm so sorry that Livvy is putting you through it. It should be me she's punishing, not you.'

'It's not your fault,' Emily said, with a watery smile. 'You can't help having a psychopathic dead wife.'

'This is getting serious,' said Adam. He looked thoughtful, and then went to a drawer in the kitchen, and rooted around in it.

'What are you looking for?' Emily was puzzled.

'Hang on a minute, ah, yes here it is, Zandra left this, in case we needed it. I think we might now.' He handed Emily a card which bore the legend:

> *Fr Dave, Exorcist Extraordinaire*
> *Troubled by spooks, disturbed by noises in the attic?*
> *Consult Fr Dave. Your Expert in Exorcism.*

'How about it?' he said. 'It's got to be worth a shot, surely?'

'Doesn't that sound a bit vindictive?' Emily said, although really, if it worked, it would certainly solve their problems.

'We can't go on like this,' said Adam. 'Look at you, you're terrified. What if Livvy really hurt you?'

It was true, Emily had never been so scared in her life. Livvy had rattled her badly.

'Maybe Livvy just wants to scare me off,' she said.

'It's a bit of a risk to take,' said Adam.

'What about Joe? He'll be so upset. You have to think about Joe.'

'I know,' Adam sighed, 'I really don't know what to do. But I don't think Livvy's left us much choice. Maybe if I explain to him . . .'

They looked at each other helplessly.

'Seems like we're between a rock and a hard place,' said Emily eventually. 'OK, let's give it a go.'

Livvy

They want to exorcize me? Huh. I was only trying to *scare* Emily. And I still need to talk to Adam. Some people take things way too seriously. I don't really want to hurt her, I just want her out of my family's life. I feel like Dolly Parton.

Please don't take my man, just because you can, thanks to the inconvenient fact that you're alive and I'm not.

Emily's young and pretty enough to find anyone. Why did she have to choose my Adam?

Because you let him down. That's a sneaky thought, worthy of Malachi. I squash it immediately. I don't want to think about any of this being my fault. Adam cheated on *me* and I'm the dead one. I'm the victim here.

There's no point going to ask Malachi how I avoid an exorcism. He'll probably tell me I deserve it, but someone at Underworld must have an idea about what to do.

So I head straight there, knowing I'll at least get a sympathetic hearing. From what I observed from the night of the seance, they're a pretty tight-knit community. The dead look after their own. I need help and fast, because the last thing I want right now is to be shut out of Adam's life permanently. Besides, I'm not quite sure what happens when you're exorcized, particularly when you haven't finished whatever your unfinished business is. Do you get sent to hell? It doesn't sound like it would be very pleasant.

There aren't many people at the bar. DJ Steve is lolling around looking like he's had a big night. His eyes are red-rimmed, and he's puffing on a cigarette.

'Now you're a sight for sore eyes,' he says. 'And after the night I've just had my eyes are really sore. Fancy a drink?'

'Sounds tempting,' I say, laughing. DJ Steve has a way of cheering me up.

'Are you allowed to do that in here?'

He looks, flicking his dreadlocks over his shoulder. 'Who's going to stop me? Nobody here can get secondary lung cancer.'

That is a point I hadn't considered.

'How's it hanging?' he asks. 'Do you fancy a drink?'

'Not tonight,' I say. 'I'm here for some advice. My husband wants me exorcized.'

'Now that's a bad rap,' he says. 'What a fool. If you were mine, I'd be dying to have you back if I wasn't dead already.'

'Well you're not, sadly,' I say. 'And my husband wants rid of me.'

God, that sounds terrible. He's so keen to have me out of his life, he wants to cut me away. For the first time since I started all this haunting malarkey, I wonder if I'm taking the right approach. Rather than driving a wedge between Adam and Emily, I seem to have succeeded into pushing him into her arms.

'Steve,' I say, 'is there a way to get back properly, so I'm visible to them? Malachi skated over it when I asked him. If my husband could actually *see* me, I'm sure he'd think differently.'

'Well,' says Steve, 'it's tricky, and not without – um – complications, but I do know someone who might be able to help – though you might not like the end result.'

'And that person is?' I say. I refuse to be fobbed off by Steve, like I have been by Malachi. 'Come on, you must know.'

'Name of Letitia,' says Steve, 'but you gotta be careful round her. She talks the talk, but she can be . . . tricksy.'

'Tricksy, how?' I say. Is this some kind of conspiracy? Even the rebellious spirit guide is trying to put me off.

'Well, you'll see,' says Steve. 'Just be careful what you wish for, Letitia's wishes can come true in ways you don't expect. And there are people here who could tell you a tale or two.'

I'm not interested in what anyone else can tell me, I'm impatient to meet this Letitia.

'But she can help?' I persist. What is it with these

underworld types and their doom-mongering. We're all dead, how much worse can it get?

'I never said she couldn't help,' says Steve. 'Just that things might not turn out exactly as you hoped.'

'I don't care,' I say, 'I can't go on like this.'

'Well, I'll see what I can do,' says Steve, and for now I have to be content with that.

Adam

I'm sitting at work fingering Father Dave's card: *Exorcism my speciality*. It sounds incredibly stupid and naff. Do priests normally advertise their powers of exorcism? Reports are piling up on my desk. Everyone wants to push things through before they go away by the end of the week. I know I should be getting on with them, but I can't concentrate.

This is such a huge decision. I told Emily I'd give Father Dave a call and arrange for him to come round. I don't want anything to happen to her, and it seems like the logical thing to do. But I'm torn. Do I really want to take this path? Get rid of Livvy completely? It strikes me we might have been given a second chance here, Livvy and I. If only I could reach out to her, get her to talk to me, try and sort out what went wrong with our marriage and make her accept what's happened is for the best. If we could make our peace with one another, maybe she can go to – wherever the dead go, and Emily and I can really get on with our lives.

And then there's Joe. I am worried about him. He's been spending a lot of time in the attic looking through his telescope in the last few days, and seems to have become even more withdrawn. He says Livvy is sitting with him. Ever since this started he's been fixated on the idea of seeing his mum again. How will he take it if I send her away for good? If I don't explain this to him in the right way he'll be really angry with me and he'll have lost her once more. But if I don't try the exorcism, maybe Emily and I won't get the chance to be together happily and instead we'll be stuck in this limbo forever, my guilt about Livvy and Livvy's actions poisoning our future.

But it's *already poisoned*. Another thought comes to me. Livvy hasn't shown any signs of being anything other than bitter and angry. She hasn't tried to talk to me any more than she did when she was alive. She doesn't want to stop being seen as the victim. She doesn't want to put things right. I have to face it: it didn't work with Livvy when she was alive, why should it work now she's dead?

I pick up the card again. Father Dave, exorcism. Cutting out. Getting rid. Time to move on.

I dial his number.

Chapter Seventeen

Livvy

DJ Steve leads me to a back bar where a beautiful, sleek-looking black woman is sitting holding court to a group of what I can only call acolytes. She's stunning, dressed in a slinky black dress, her only adornments a silver necklace and some plain pearl studs; her long legs are encased in satin tights, and she is wearing leopardskin kitten heels.

'Let me introduce you to Letitia,' says DJ Steve. 'She can help you get what you want. But be warned, it might not be what you need.'

Letitia – I'm sure Robert mentioned her name the first time I came to Underworld. She seems important, as even DJ Steve is deferential around her, and as she flashes her brown eyes I sense an undercurrent of danger. Everyone around her seems overwhelmingly respectful. I swallow hard. What am I doing? I feel sure that Letitia comes under the term unsuitable in Malachi's terminology. But then I decide I don't have a choice and I have to act fast.

Letitia smiles at me. It seems a friendly smile, but there's a dash of menace in it. I wouldn't like to get on the wrong side of her.

'So I've been hearing you're having some trouble, hon,' she says.

'You could say that,' I say. 'My husband wants to exorcize me.'

'Now that's just vicious!' says Letitia. 'These Lifers just don't understand sometimes.' Her voice drips like honey, it's utterly mesmerizing, and soon I find myself telling her everything.

'I didn't make much of my life,' I tell her, 'but I seem to be making a total cock-up of my death. I never get anything right.'

'Never say never,' says Letitia with a surprisingly infectious grin. 'You just gotta think positive, girl.'

'So what can I do?' I say. 'If I go back to the house, they're going to try and get rid of me.'

'You leave that to me, honey,' says Letitia. 'I can help you, if that's what you want.'

'I do,' I say, 'so long as – you know – it's legit.'

She laughs again, a deep rolling laugh. 'Ain't no laws when you're dead, honey,' she says, which seems to contradict everything Malachi has told me. 'Or not like any you'd recognize. We're going to fool your husband into thinking he's got rid of you, and then we'll come right back, and knock him – kapow – between the eyes.'

That sounds more like it. I was clearly right to come to her for advice. At last someone on this side of the life/death divide who seems to know what they're talking about.

'Between the eyes,' agrees Steve.

Letitia looks at him pityingly and says, 'Now shush, Steve, you have no idea what you're talking about. Livvy and I are going to have a bit of a chat. There are some secrets which are for her ears only.'

215

Letitia takes me into a little room at the back end of the bar. It's simply decorated but chic, rather like her.

'Drink, honey?' she says, pouring a glass of wine.

Why not? I think. While it's not ideal, it's better than where I might soon be going. I may as well drink while I still can.

'So, now, tell me everything,' she says. 'Why does that husband of yours want to get rid of you?'

I pour out the whole story, about how Adam and I fell out of love – 'Partly my fault,' I find myself admitting to Letitia in a way I haven't been able to to Malachi, about Emily, and about Joe. Most of all about Joe.

'Well that's too bad,' she says. 'A boy needs his mother.'

Yes, I think, this particular boy really really does.

'So can you help me?' I say when I get to the end.

'Let me ask you a question?' she says. 'What do you want – deep down in your heart?'

'To be back at home with Adam and Joe,' I say in a heartbeat. 'To have a chance to put things right.'

'That should be doable,' said Letitia. 'But you have to understand, these things are unpredictable. People don't always behave . . . the way you want them to. Are you prepared for that?'

'Adam and Joe will,' I say with utter confidence. I know it's a question of reaching out to Adam again. I *can* make him come back to me.

'Well in that case,' she says with a grin, 'what are we waiting for? First off, we have to stop this exorcism working properly, and I have just the thing for that.'

She goes to a cupboard in the back of the room, and roots around in the drawer until she finds what she is looking for. Then she produces a phial of an amber-green liquid. I swear it fizzes when she lifts the lid.

'What's that?' I ask. 'Is it some kind of drug?'

'Oh no, honey,' she says, holding the phial between her elegantly manicured fingers. 'I just prefer to fight fire with fire. Your friendly exorcist will try to cast a spell to get rid of you; this is its antidote. It's not strong enough to entirely negate the spell, but it will stop you from being cast out completely.'

'And you're sure it will work?'

'Oh yes,' says Leititia, with that dazzling smile and those flashing brown eyes. 'Trust me. I've done this before.'

Adam

Felicity is looking dubiously at me as I'm arranging the lounge the way that Dave suggested to me. I hadn't wanted to tell her what was happening, but she'd got wind via Kenneth that things were getting a bit out of hand. After her hysterics on me, Emily hadn't been able to stop confessing all to him, and Felicity had been on the phone straight away to check we were all right.

'I'm still not sure if I understand what's going on,' she had said, 'but if Livvy is causing all this trouble, I've a good mind to give her a talking to, dead or not. She shouldn't be behaving like this to Emily. It's unkind.'

Which is pretty decent considering Livvy is her daughter. Felicity is a great listener; I ended by confiding what Livvy had been up to, and found her surprisingly sympathetic. Now she is looking at me questioningly.

'Do you think this will actually do the trick?'

'I have no idea,' I say. 'But I feel we have to try everything. Are you sure you're OK with me doing this?'

Felicity sighed. 'Not really,' she said. 'But I think if it is Livvy causing all this grief she's left us with very little choice. I'd love to be able to talk to her, but she doesn't seem to want that. Sadly she's always been stubborn. I want her to be at peace, and if this is the only way . . .'

The doorbell rings and Father Dave is standing on the doorstep. He doesn't look much like a vicar. He's arrived on a motorbike, so is clad from head to foot in leather, but when he takes his gear off he's wearing what looks like a pair of velvet pyjamas, which is incongruous to say the least. There's not a sign of a dog collar.

'Hi,' he says, 'call me Dave.'

Of course he does. Anyone less likely to perform an exorcism I can't imagine.

'I'm Adam,' I say.

'So tell me a bit about your wife,' says Dave. 'Why do you think she's come back? What's preventing her from letting go?'

Where to begin?

'It's my fault she's angry,' I say. 'Mine and Emily's. That's my new girlfriend. But we had problems for a long time before that. We have a son called Joe, who has Asperger's. It was tough on both of us but particularly on Livvy.' I pause, I've been so used to not telling people about Livvy's drinking, it's still quite hard to break the habit. 'Anyway, Livvy and I – it became quite destructive. She started to drink, and I found that – difficult.'

Difficult is putting it mildly. The times I came home to chaos, and Livvy slumped on the sofa with Joe upstairs on his computer, the tea not ready, and nothing to eat in the house; or when she promised me she'd stopped drinking and then I'd find the empty bottles stashed away in the bottom of cupboards; the awful day when she nearly lost her licence . . . After that she had consented to seek help, but she gave up quickly saying they couldn't do anything for her. It was impossible. And I felt bad for not being able to help, and bad for resenting her, and hating what she was doing to all three of us.

'So it's you she's angry with mostly then?' says Dave.

'I think so,' I say, 'but she hasn't taken too kindly to Emily being here.'

'And you feel that Emily is threatened by her?' says Dave.

'Yes,' I say, 'Livvy tried to smash a lightbulb on her head. Emily was lucky it missed her. And then she went round to Emily's flat and left threatening messages everywhere. We're worried it's getting out of hand.'

'OK,' says Dave, opening a little box, and getting out a crucifix, candle and holy water. And a prayer book. I'm tickled, despite myself. With his long woolly beard and strange purple pyjamas he looks more like Gandalf than an exorcist.

'Does Joe know about this?' Felicity asks suddenly.

I deliberately haven't mentioned it. And Joe is at Caroline's. I don't know how he'll take it.

'Not exactly,' I say.

'Adam,' warns Felicity.

'I know, I know,' I say, 'but how can I tell him? Better if he thinks that Livvy has just left us alone.'

'And you can really count on that being the case?' says Felicity.

I know I can't, so I shrug and say nothing, and Felicity says, 'Don't say I didn't warn you.'

I know she's right, but I have no idea what to say to Joe. I'm being an ostrich about it, just like I was about telling Livvy I was leaving.

The doorbell rings again.

'That'll be Emily,' I say, glad of the interruption.

Emily is very agitated.

'Any sign of Livvy today?' she says.

219

'None whatsoever. And when Father Dave has finished, with any luck she'll be gone for good.'

I know doing this may mean I never get the chance to properly make amends, but I also know we can't go on like this.

Emily

The priest recommended by Zandra didn't look much like any priest Emily had ever met before. He was a bit hippyish, with a long raggedy beard. But he seemed competent enough, setting up his crucifix and candle, and then saying very seriously, 'Are you sure this is what you want?'

'I am,' said Emily quickly, but Adam was slower to respond. She wondered whether he really was ready to do this to Livvy. His relationship with her was so complicated, even he didn't know what he wanted, but he nodded anyway, and squeezed Emily's hand.

'OK,' said Dave, in hushed tones, 'let's proceed. First let's turn the lights out.'

He looked very solemn as in sepulchral tones he began to read out a prayer about banishing Satan. Emily had to stifle her giggles. This was crazy. What on earth did they think they were doing? Then he paused and looked round.

'Livvy, are you there?'

There was a rattle and the room went cold, and everyone could feel her. Felicity, who had been looking as sceptical as Emily, grabbed her arm tightly.

'Livvy?' she said uncertainly, but there was no response.

The cold deepened, and Emily could feel Livvy's malice all around her. Hairs prickled the back of her neck. She didn't feel like giggling now.

'You know your time has passed,' said Dave. 'You need to move on and leave the living behind.'

Livvy clearly didn't like this as the fire flared in the grate and the lights flickered on and off. Emily felt more terrified than ever. Livvy evidently wasn't planning to go without a fight.

Dave waved some incense which was so strong it nearly made Emily cough, and he threw some holy water round the room for good measure.

'Livvy, I exorcize you in the name of the Father, the Son and the Holy Ghost,' said Dave, holding his crucifix aloft. Despite her fear, Emily's feeling of the absurdity of it all returned. She almost expected him to say, 'Expelliarmus!' There was no way this was going to work.

There was a sudden flaring of the lights and what sounded like a shriek, and suddenly a whirlwind was blowing through the room, lifting cups, books, papers, and throwing them on the ground. They were all blasted back from the strength of it. Emily could feel Livvy's fury at what was happening.

To his credit, Father Dave held his ground, and lifted his crucifix once more.

'Livvy, I banish thee from this house,' he intoned, his hair and robes blowing behind him, making look more like Gandalf than ever.

The whirlwind blew even fiercer; Emily found herself gripping hold of the sofa so as not to be blown over. Livvy was so strong. And she could see Father Dave almost bending into the wind as if to push her back.

'Livvy!' he shouted above the noise. 'Begone!'

The fire guttered and died, the front door blew open, and with that the whirlwind vanished.

There was a moment of stunned silence before Adam

went to pick up the fallen papers and cups.

'Is that it?' he said nervously.

'I think so,' said Father Dave. 'I can't feel a presence any more.'

Everyone breathed slightly easier.

'That almost seemed too easy,' said Emily, relief pouring over her in waves. And then she jumped as the front door banged again, and Joe came marching into the lounge looking livid.

'What have you done to Mum?' he said.

Chapter Eighteen

Emily

Emily stood with her mouth open, utterly horrified. How on earth were they going to explain this?

'Joe!' said Adam looking shell-shocked. 'What are you doing here?'

'Caroline had to study, so I came home,' said Joe. 'What have you done with Mum?'

'Nothing,' said Adam feebly.

'Don't lie,' said Joe, 'you're not very good at it. Mum's gone, I felt her go through me. She was angry. Why did you make her so upset?'

Emily wanted to say something, but what? Instead she watched Adam miserably trying to justify what had happened.

'Oh Joe,' said Adam, 'I didn't want to upset Mum, but what you have to understand is that she's been causing us a lot of grief.'

'Because you haven't been listening,' said Joe angrily. 'And now you've sent her away.'

He was implacable: cold; angry. This was worse than anything Emily could have imagined.

'Joe,' she tried to intercede. 'Your mum tried to hurt me. She smashed a chandelier on my head.'

223

'She was cross,' said Joe. 'She wasn't going to do anything to you.'

He was speaking as if Emily was a very small and stupid child.

'Yes but then she came to my flat and left nasty messages,' Emily said. 'She frightened me, Joe. What should we have done?'

'*You* should have done nothing,' said Joe. 'You're not my mum.' He turned to Adam. 'You should have listened! I want my mum back.'

It was true, it had always been true, but Emily still felt Joe's bitterness cut through her like a knife.

Joe was very agitated now and kept pacing around the room. Emily looked helplessly at Adam, not knowing what to do.

'Perhaps I should leave,' she said.

'Yes, you should,' said Joe. Emily had no idea he could be that icy.

'Joe!' said Adam.

'I don't want her here,' said Joe. 'I want Mum.'

'Joe,' Adam said again, but Emily shushed him.

And with that Joe went ballistic. Lashing out, sweeping the cups Adam had picked up and throwing them to the floor, pulling the bookcase down so the books came tumbling everywhere, and smashing the lampstand on the table.

Father Dave was cowering in the corner, clearly thinking he'd entered a madhouse, while Felicity and Adam attempted to calm Joe down.

Emily hovered on the outside, not daring to enter the fray. She had never seen Joe like this. She didn't even know he could behave this way, and she had no idea how to deal with it. Besides she felt her presence was making everything worse.

'I'll just leave then,' Dave mouthed at her, nervously gathering his things and dodging a book that Joe had chucked randomly in his direction.

A ridiculous sense of politeness meant Emily felt obliged to show him out.

'Do you really think Livvy's gone?' she said.

'I can't feel any presence in the house any more,' Father Dave said again, 'so certainly for the time being, I'd say so.'

'What?' She was alarmed. 'You mean she might be able to come back?'

'No, no, nothing like that.' Dave was backtracking wildly. 'This normally works, but Livvy seems a very strong character. I've never encountered a spirit so strong.' He nodded towards the lounge, and said, 'I think she has a very good reason for what she's trying to do. You know where I am, if you need me again.'

Thinking it might even be better to have Livvy in the house again than go through another meltdown with Joe, Emily shut the door, and reluctantly returned to the lounge, where Joe was a sobbing mess. Felicity had managed to calm him down, and was promising him hot chocolate, but to Emily's dismay he wouldn't look at either her or Adam.

'I think I'd better go too,' she said. 'I can't think my presence here is going to help.'

'Good idea,' Adam said. He barely seemed to notice her, and Emily tried not to feel a pang. She was no good in this situation. Joe, quite rightly, was the focus of all his attention. As Emily let herself out it struck her that though it looked like they'd got rid of Livvy, perhaps she had won after all.

225

Oomph! The force of the exorcism is far greater than I imagined it would be. I fought it as much as I could but in the end the spell Father Dave cast pushed me out. It actually hurt – as if someone had punched me in the solar plexus, and I may even have screamed. What I do know is that I went flying through Joe, who'd chosen that minute to come home. I felt his distress and anguish when I went through him, but I couldn't reach him to calm him down. I can see I could use that to my advantage eventually, but for now I am lying winded in the street, feeling much weaker than I've done since I came back to haunt Adam. I get up slowly and gingerly, walk up to the house, and bam! I'm on the floor again. There's an invisible barrier that acts like glass, and stops me getting in. I go around the whole house, but only the back garden is accessible to me. Whatever Father Dave has done, he has shut me out of my house pretty effectively.

Bugger. Bugger. Bugger. That has set plan Get Emily Out of My Husband's Life back a bit. Still at least I am still here. I hate to think where I would be if the exorcism had worked properly. Letitia had warned me that her potion wouldn't be totally effective, but I suppose I had hoped for more.

'So what happens then?' I had asked.

'You just wait, sugar cakes,' she told me. 'We'll make them think you're gone for good, and then you come and see me again, yeah? That's if you really want to live again.'

'Of course I do,' I said. Who wouldn't? Does anyone who dies really want to go to the other side? 'Otherwise Underworld wouldn't be packed with lost souls, would it?'

Letitia looked at me strangely. 'That's not the way it is for most,' she said. 'They know their time's up and they need to sort their shit out before moving on. But then there's the ones like you . . .'

'What do you mean, like me?'

'Well you, honey, ain't happy with that, you want more,' said Letitia. 'And I can give it to you. But what I'm offering ain't a quick fix. Them that want Letitia to work her magic have some difficult choices to make.'

I had wanted to ask her what she meant, but she'd vanished into the heart of Underworld, and I didn't see her again for the rest of the night. I wonder if she's totally trustworthy, remembering Malachi's hint that this isn't the way forward. I brush the thought off impatiently. All Malachi has done since he found me in that car park is tell me what to do. At least with Letitia I've got a plan and if Joe is now as cross as I think he'll be, then it's already working.

Adam

It's been two days since the exorcism, and there's no sign of Livvy. This is something to be grateful for, because Joe is refusing to speak to me or Emily. He's locked himself in his room and keeps muttering about traitors. I've never seen him like this, even after Livvy died, and I don't know what to do. Each day I come home from work, and try to talk to him, and each day he refuses to acknowledge me. He is eating his meals in his room, and spends more time than ever in the loft, looking up at the stars. I am at my wits' end.

Felicity is the only one he'll talk to, though he's even called her Judas. She keeps saying, give it time, but I'm not sure she's right. As far as Joe's concerned I sent his mum packing. Can he ever forgive me?

And where does that leave me and Emily? I thought we were doing the right thing, but maybe it's still too soon. It's only been a year. Perhaps bringing Emily into the house this Christmas was a mistake.

Christmas: what are we to do about it? With Joe not speaking to half of us, it's going to be a nightmare. I so wanted to make it right for him this year, and all I seem to have done is make things much worse.

After work I can't bear the thought of going home, so I take myself off for a walk. Emily is coming over later with food for the big day, and I'm not sure I'm up to it just yet.

I find myself wandering down to the towpath where we used to go on family walks when Joe was little. He always liked looking at the houseboats, for some reason. Before he was born, Livvy and I had often joked about buying one.

'It will be cosy, and cute,' Livvy used to say.

'Nice in summer, probably perishing in winter,' I would point out.

'Ooh, but so romantic,' Livvy would reply, 'just think of the fun we could have.'

And then we would cuddle together and walk home, to a meal, or a drink, or a slow lovemaking by the fire. The world had seemed full of possibilities then, no thought that our dreams would perish in the sand.

It being Christmas, the houseboats are looking festive, decorated with sparkling lights, wreaths, and the odd Christmas tree. There are signs saying: *Santa please stop here,* and even a large inflatable Santa in the doorway of one. I envy the people in those houseboats. Unlike mine, their lives look normal and bland.

I watch a couple negotiate a buggy on to one. They are laughing and joking – the toddler between them bonding them in love. Looking at them reminds me of how things used to be. Livvy and I were so happy once. I feel unspeakably sad. We've really messed things up between us, and now I can never put that right.

You need to tell her.

A voice enters my head, and I look around. Weird. There's no one there, apart from a mangy old black cat staring at me balefully. I swear I've seen him before.

Yes you, he seems to say, before giving me a disdainful look and disappearing. Great, now I'm imagining I'm getting advice from a cat. Too bad it's no good. It's too late now. Livvy's gone, and I got rid of her. No wonder Joe hates me.

Joe's Notebook

I am very angry.

Adam and Emily have got rid of Mum.

They said it was because Mum wanted to hurt Emily.

I don't think Mum would hurt anyone.

She just wants us.

And I want her.

I don't want to speak to Dad ever.

He has done a bad thing.

Tonight I looked up at the stars, and there was cloud. I couldn't see Venus.

Where has Mum gone?

I thought she was coming back to us, but thanks to Dad we've lost her again.

I am very angry with Dad.

This is not a good thing.

I wish there was a way to get Mum back again.

Christmas Present

'So everything going according to plan then?' Malachi has found me mooching about the shops, as I've nowhere particularly to go.

'Yes,' I say, 'this was part of the plan. They think I've gone for good, and I'll come back to surprise them.'

'Hmmph!' Malachi twitches his tail in disgust. 'And I suppose this is Letitia's idea, is it?'

'It might be.' I'm not quite sure why I am so defensive when he mentions Letitia, but I get the feeling Malachi isn't too impressed with her. He confirms this when he says, 'Just be careful around Letitia, what she offers isn't always the way it seems.'

'What's that supposed to mean?' I ask. I'm sick of him being enigmatic.

'Just that, Letitia's style is unorthodox, and you've made a big mistake going there. She may promise you the world, but that's not necessarily what you'll get. And quite frankly you'll deserve it. You should have listened to me.'

'At least she's prepared to help me get what I want,' I say.

'But is that what you need?' says Malachi. 'Getting what you want isn't always the answer, you know.'

* * *

And with that, I'm back in Malachi's cheery notion of what the present might look like. Months have gone by, and we're in late summer. We're having a barbecue at home, and Adam seems to have invited all his work crew. I am walking, but slowly. My right leg is still giving me gyp, but this is an improvement on my homecoming.

'It's so lovely to see you up and about at last,' gushes Marigold. 'I have to say I think you've been so brave.'

She's all over me like a rash, and it's a bit much, so I mumble an excuse and head for the kitchen. Adam is by the barbecue joking with his mates Dave and Phil, and for some reason I feel out of things. The last few months while I've been recovering have been tough, and I am aware that I've perhaps not always been fair on Adam. It's a baking hot day, and Adam has made a big jug of Pimm's, which looks inviting. I haven't really been drinking much, I've been on so much medication, but finally I am turning a corner. What the hell – that deserves a celebration.

I am on my third glass of Pimm's and in an animated conversation with one of the marketing guys at Adam's work when Adam comes in.

'Liv, shouldn't you be taking it a bit easy?' he says warningly.

'Don't be a spoilsport,' I laugh. 'It's got more lemonade in it than alcohol.'

'Yeah, while that depends on the quantities, doesn't it?' Adam's tone is a bit sharp, and I look at him surprised.

'Just remember what happened last time,' he whispers in my ear, and with a jolt, I do. I'd decided having a drink on my birthday was a must, even though I was heavily medicated. As a result, the evening was a blur, I'd thrown up and Adam and I had a row.

'I'll be careful, I promise,' I say, kissing him on the lips.

Is it my imagination, or does he flinch a little? Adam was amazing when I first had my accident, but lately I get the feeling he's withdrawing from me slightly. I'm probably being paranoid, but it makes me uneasy.

I pour another glass of Pimm's but put some extra lemonade in it just to appease him. I do that a couple more times, and then decide I need something a bit stronger, so switch to wine. By now the music is blaring, and people are beginning to dance.

'Come on, Adam,' I say, 'let's dance.'

'Livvy,' says Adam. 'I'm not sure this is a good idea.'

'Don't be daft,' I say, 'I nearly died. I might never have walked again, I just want to live a little.'

So we dance for a bit, but the effort is quite exhausting, and my leg seems to be hurting quite a lot. I am determined to ignore it though, and top up my wine and keep going till the pain goes away. But it doesn't, in fact it's hurting like hell, and I have to sit it out for a bit, much to Adam's relief.

I can't think of anything else but the throbbing pain in my leg, and go upstairs to get some paracetamol. I look at them dubiously; from past experience, I know they'll only just scratch the surface. So I go to the bathroom cabinet and dig out the really strong stuff I came back with from the hospital. I know technically you're not supposed to take them with alcohol, but I'm sure one will be OK.

To my relief it works, and by the time I'm back downstairs, the pain is receding to a distant memory. I help myself to another glass of wine, and go out to join everyone in the garden. Except now I am feeling a little woozy. Adam is coming over to me with a concerned look in his eye that I know all too well. My chest is hammering, I feel sick as a dog, and the next thing I know the ground is rushing towards me.

I wake up to find a paramedic staring down at me. 'What have you been taking?' he says.

'I only had one painkiller,' I try to say but my words are slurring and I feel really terrible.

And then Joe is there looking really frightened, and Adam is looking at me so sadly it's like a shot to the heart.

'Oh Livvy,' he says, 'why do you keep doing this to yourself?'

Chapter Nineteen

Five Days till Christmas

Emily

'This is it then?' Emily walked gingerly into the house for the first time since the exorcism, carrying bags of Christmas presents. 'She's really gone?'

'Seems to have,' Adam said. 'Come on, let's get these under the tree, and start planning Christmas properly.'

'Oh thank God,' said Emily. She hugged Adam tightly, feeling the relief pouring off him. 'There doesn't seem any sign of her in my flat either. It was awful her being there. Like I was being spied on.'

Emily started taking presents out of the bags and arranging them round the tree. One of her favourite bits of Christmas, from when she was tiny, was seeing all the presents piled up – even now it gave her a happy thrill of expectation. The tree looked so lovely with the lights sparkling and the presents underneath. For the first time Emily allowed herself to feel a little bit Christmassy. She hadn't dared before, although of course there was still one big hurdle to overcome.

'How's Joe?' she said.

'Still angry,' sighed Adam. 'But I'm sure he'll come round.'

'No, I won't,' said Joe from the door.

'Hi Joe,' Emily said brightly, hoping that his innate sense of politeness would win through, and Joe would at least acknowledge her, but to no avail.

'I don't talk to traitors,' Joe said and walked past Emily into the kitchen. It would have been comical if it weren't so upsetting.

'Joe,' Emily followed him into the kitchen, 'this isn't your dad's fault.'

'He sent Mum away,' said Joe, glowering. 'You both did. She only wanted to talk to us.'

'I know.' Emily sat down at the table. 'And if there was another way, I wish we could have found it.'

'She wants to be with me and Dad,' said Joe.

Emily sighed.

'I realize that, but Joe, she wasn't behaving in a very nice way.'

Joe just shrugged his shoulders and said nothing. Emily was about to give up and then Joe said, 'I miss Mum. I wish she could come back.'

He looked so sad Emily's heart bled for him. Joe was so self-contained it was hard to remember sometimes that he was only 17 and now he'd lost his mother twice.

'I know,' Emily said, and touched his hand lightly. Knowing how he hated physical contact it was a relief Joe didn't push her away. 'This has been very difficult for you, Joe, I understand that. I wish there was some way I could make it up to you.'

'You can't,' said Joe bleakly, 'no one can.'

'I know you're angry with us,' Emily said carefully, 'but please, Joe, blame me, if you have to blame someone. Don't be too hard on your dad. It is Christmas, and he's trying his best.'

Joe looked up then.

'I don't blame you, Emily,' he said. 'Are you still coming for Christmas?'

'If that's OK with you?'

'Yeah,' said Joe. 'It's OK with me.'

And then he took his coffee upstairs and went to play some video game.

It wasn't much, but it was a start.

Adam

From the design studio, Paul McCartney is blaring out that he's having a wonderful Christmas time. Only the weekend to go, and then Christmas will be upon us. The office is beginning to thin out as people start taking their holiday. And there's a distinct feeling of everyone downing tools and not taking anything at all seriously. People are chatting about their Christmas plans, and stressing about everything from present buying to whether they should leave it to Christmas Eve to buy a half-price turkey in Marks. I envy them the normality of their lives. I would do anything for the sole stress in my life to be whether or not I was going to get my turkey on time.

I'm working up to the day before Christmas Eve, and have still got a lot to get through. Normally I'd be chafing at the bit to leave the office as soon as I can. But this year, being at work is a great distraction from the craziness at home.

Things are no better between me and Joe, and he's still not talking to me. The atmosphere at home is tense and difficult; I don't know how to get through to him. All he does is grunt at me. He has at least forgiven Emily, which is something. I think Joe's rationale is that it wasn't Emily's choice to exorcize Livvy, but mine; therefore, I am to blame.

Maybe he's right. I am not sure I made the right choice. Seeing Emily so upset after Livvy had left her those messages was what swung the decision for me. It seemed like whatever we did, Livvy was going to make things harder for us. But now Livvy's gone, I feel an emptiness inside, worse than when she first died. At least when she was haunting us, there was a chance that I could make things right with her. Now she is beyond my reach, and I'll never properly get the chance to say I'm sorry. Joe's right to be angry with me.

I'm working on some spreadsheets in a desultory fashion when the computer freezes. I tap alt control delete to no avail. Surely not? A cold chill goes down my spine. How can she be back?

A message appears on the screen.

You didn't think you'd get rid of me that *easily did you?*

Followed by:

Too right you should be sorry.

Livvy

The look on Adam's face when I take over his computer again is priceless. The colour drains from him and he starts frantically tapping keys as if to expunge me from his system. I helpfully turn the computer off, just so he can be sure it's me. And then, assured he's freaked out, I head back to Underworld feeling gleeful. I could have been a bit kinder I suppose, but he *did* try to exorcize me, and I'm still pretty miffed about it.

I go and seek out DJ Steve and Letitia. I'm feeling triumphant that it was so easy to rattle Adam again. Little does he know what Letitia has planned for him. Despite Malachi's obscure warnings, I'm glad I went to her for help. It's thanks to Letitia I've not been permanently consigned to my grave before I'm ready. The potion she gave me certainly did the trick. There's a whiff of danger about her that worries me a little, but I don't want to question her methods too deeply. Whatever she did, it worked, and I'm still here, something I'm not sure Malachi would have achieved, though it is extremely annoying that I can't get in the house any more, nor can I get to Emily. I'm even crosser with her than I was. I mean, did she have to go all wussy on me? Without that, Adam would never have suggested the exorcism. I still feel like I've been kicked around the playground. Letitia's potion might have worked, but Dave's spell didn't half pack a punch.

The point is that Emily is supposed to be the one beating a hasty retreat, not me. She's meant to be giving Adam up so I can have him, not going round with Christmas presents so they can get all loved up (I watched her from the road, I'd have tripped her up if I could, but all my powers have been reduced after the exorcism).

I know it's a bit of an inconvenience, what with me being dead and all, and the alternative timeline Malachi's been showing me isn't exactly optimistic, but I still think there's a chance for me to sort things out with Adam. Otherwise what has been the point of me hanging around here for a year? I know I haven't been able to get through to Adam as a ghost, but Letitia's offering me the chance to come back properly. I really don't want to screw it up.

'So, lady, you ready to up the ante?' asks Letitia in that strong Southern drawl.

'I certainly am,' I say. 'Adam knows I'm still around now, so it's time to show him what he's missing.'

'And you're sure you're ready for the next step?'

Letitia regards me rather as a snake assesses its prey. There's a hint of menace in her voice and the sense of unease returns. What do I know about her really? Perhaps I should think about this some more. Then I picture Adam curled up in front of the fire with Emily, in my house, playing happy families, and I think however risky it is to do what Letitia suggests, it will be worth it.

'I'm sure,' I say. I feel confident now. Adam is missing me. I felt it when I stood by his computer. He's regretting casting me out. I can work on that, and remind him of what we had. I pushed him into Emily's arms once, now it's time to pull him back out of them.

'But just to warn you,' says Letitia, 'my power only extends so far.'

'Meaning?'

'There's a time limit. This is a special time of year, so you get longer than most, but you can't hang around indefinitely. You have until Christmas Eve to win Adam back or you've lost him forever.'

That sounds a bit extreme.

'And then what happens?'

'Why, you stay here,' says Letitia.

I look around Underworld. I suppose if the worst comes to the worst that wouldn't be too bad. At least I'd have DJ Steve to talk to.

'That's about the size of it,' says Letitia. 'Are you still prepared to take the risk?'

I swallow hard. Am I risking too much to be with Adam and Joe? But then my resolve hardens. I can do this, I know I can.

'Sure as I'll ever be,' I say with a confidence I don't entirely feel.

'There may be unintended consequences,' warns Letitia.

'Consequences be damned,' I say.

Chapter Twenty

Adam

'So she hasn't gone?' Emily looks at me incredulously. 'After all that.'

I came straight round to Emily's flat after work to talk to her about the computer incident, and now we're sitting in her kitchen over a cup of coffee trying to take on board what has happened. I still can't get my head around it. Father Dave sent Livvy packing from the house, we all saw it, so how can she still be here?

'Apparently not,' I sigh. 'I suppose it was too good to be true.'

Emily stares gloomily at her coffee.

'Trust me to get the boyfriend with the dead haunty wife,' she says.

'It's not my fault!' I find myself snapping at her. Lack of sleep for the last week, combined with stress, are getting to me. I am exhausted and wrung out with all of this. Now what does Livvy want?

'I know,' says Emily, reaching for my hand, 'and I was only joking.'

'Perhaps the exorcism has partially worked; Livvy hasn't

243

been at home or at your place. Maybe she's limited in her access to us now.'

'Could be,' says Emily. 'Who knows how things on the Other Side work? Christ . . . how mad does that sound? I didn't even believe there was an Other Side till recently.'

'There are a lot of things I've changed my mind about recently too,' I say. 'But you know what, if Livvy can't get to us at home, why don't we just assume she's not going to ruin Christmas and carry on as normal.'

'Good luck with that,' says Emily, raising an eyebrow.

'Do you have to be so negative?' I say, irritated. 'I'm clutching at straws here. We could at least try to hope for the best.'

'And do you have to be so stupid?' snaps Emily. 'Livvy is not going to let go till she's got rid of me. She hates me. You saw those messages.'

'I'm sure that's not true,' I protest, though I know it sounds a bit weak. 'It's me she's angriest with. Knowing Livvy, she's probably even crosser now I've tried to exorcize her. Like Joe said, I should have listened to her.'

'Listen to what?' says Emily. 'Her poisoning you against me?'

'Emily, don't be ridiculous,' I say. This is getting us nowhere. 'You can't be jealous of a ghost.'

'I'm not being ridiculous,' says Emily. 'Livvy wants me out of your life.'

'To be fair, I can understand why,' I say.

'Great,' says Emily. 'Now you're not going to take responsibility for this, I suppose. We did this to her, Adam. *We* did. And Livvy hates us for it, and wants to punish us. Particularly me. Don't you see?'

'No,' I say angrily. 'I just see you're being paranoid, and Livvy has a point.'

'Oh there's no talking sense to you!'

We stare at each other in hostility.

'I don't want to discuss this any further,' I say. 'I'm going home.'

And with that I walk out of the flat. It's sleeting slightly as I storm off down the road, and I'm cold and damp by the time I'm halfway home. I feel churned up and miserable. It's the first proper row Emily and I have ever had and I was rotten to her. I shouldn't have taken my frustrations out like that.

As I walk along, a soft whoosh of energy hits me. I feel as if someone is standing right next to me, but I am the only person on the street. I stop and look around.

'Livvy?' I say cautiously, but there's no reply.

Livvy

Oh fantastic! I can barely contain my glee. I follow Adam from work to Emily's flat. Presumably he's gone to tell her that I'm still here. It's frustrating being shut out of Emily's flat. I have no idea what they have been saying to each other. Adam doesn't stay long though, and I can tell they've had a row, as he storms off down the road with Emily shouting, 'Adam, don't go!' after him. Good. I've created some cracks in their relationship.

I follow Adam down the street, feeling the misery pour from him. The effects of the exorcism mean I can't get as close to him as I'd like, but I can just brush past him, and get a glimpse of the turmoil in his head. He's beginning to see things from my perspective at last.

I fly over to Underworld to tell Letitia the good news.

'Time for action,' I say. I am so excited. Finally, finally I am going to get what I want.

245

'You're absolutely certain about the path you're choosing?' asks Letitia. 'Because I have to warn you, there is no coming back from here.'

'I know,' I say impatiently. I want to get on with it. 'You've told me all this before. And I understand that it may not work.'

'And you realize this is deep dark stuff you're meddling with,' warns Letitia. 'I don't give this shit out just to anyone. It's the ones like you, who are brave enough not to leave their lives behind, that I can work with.'

I am flattered that she thinks I'm brave and it makes me feel slightly reckless.

'And remember,' says Letitia, 'you have until midnight on Christmas Eve, to win him around.'

'Yeah, yeah, you told me,' I say. 'If I don't succeed, I get stuck here.' I don't have any worries on that score now. I'm confident I can do it. Adam is weakening, I can tell.

'And I own your ass,' says Letitia, smiling knowingly. Despite my confidence, somehow I don't find this reassuring.

'Meaning?'

'Is he worth the risk?' she says.

'He's worth it,' I say, and he is. Making this choice has made me see just how much I love Adam, and Joe needs me. It wasn't fair that I died before we had a chance to sort our marriage out. I deserve this second chance. Besides, I think Letitia is overegging the dire warnings as part of her I-am-the-Big-I-Am-of-Underworld schtick.

'And you're still sure you want to go ahead?'

'Certain,' I say. All I can think about is seeing Adam properly again, and having the chance to remind him of how good we are together.

'I will be normal, right?' I say. 'No funny bumps on the head or deformities?'

'None,' says Letitia.

'Great,' I say. 'Let's do it.'

Emily

Emily felt utterly miserable after Adam left, the argument running through her head like the worst kind of earworm. She knew she was right and Livvy wanted to get rid of her. Why did Adam have to be so stubborn? And why was he suddenly taking Livvy's part?

A sudden clutch of fear gripped her. What if Adam was changing his mind? Perhaps he regretted not having the chance to get back together with Livvy after all.

The more she thought about it, the more Emily worried about what her and Adam's relationship was based on. They had been thrown into such turmoil when Livvy died, perhaps it had only been natural that Adam clung to her afterwards. Maybe he didn't really love Emily at all, had just thought he did? What if Livvy coming back to haunt them had thrown things into sharp relief? They were married a long time. Perhaps that counted for more than an affair that was born out of misery and frustration. How on earth could Emily compete with a dead spurned wife? Livvy had all the moral high ground.

'Hell, Adam is right,' Emily said aloud. 'I am *totally* jealous of a ghost.'

This was ridiculous. Livvy was dead. Emily was the one with a real live breathing body. But however Livvy had done it, she was definitely driving a wedge between Emily and Adam. Maybe it was time for him to be clear about what he really wanted. Emily's presence meant he hadn't had a chance to grieve for Livvy properly. Perhaps they needed to talk about that.

Emily found him at home. He looked as miserable as she felt when he opened the door. Within seconds they were in each other's arms, frantically apologizing to one another.

'I'm so sorry,' Emily said, tears in her eyes, 'I didn't mean to upset you.'

'Me neither,' said Adam.

He pulled Emily into the hallway and they stood holding each other for a very long time. She felt secure in his arms; she'd been wrong, Livvy couldn't touch them. How could she ever have doubted him?

'Adam,' Emily said, pulling away. 'We need to talk.'

'I know,' he sighed. She followed him into the lounge.

Joe was sitting watching *Elf* on the TV. It was his favourite Christmas film. Emily felt sure he'd watched it every week since about October.

Joe looked at her.

'Dad says Mum hasn't gone.'

'No, I don't think she has,' Emily said.

'Good,' said Joe. 'Maybe you can talk to her, if Dad won't.'

Right. Just what Emily wanted to do.

'Maybe,' she said, 'but right now I need to talk to your dad.'

They went into the kitchen and sat down. Adam poured them each a glass of wine.

'Well?' he said.

'Well,' Emily said. 'I think there's an elephant in the room that needs addressing.'

'Oh?' said Adam. 'And that is?'

'Livvy,' Emily said firmly, though she felt on shaky ground. 'I have to know: are you really over her?'

Chapter Twenty-One

Adam

'What?'

Emily had never said anything like this to me before and I look at her in disbelief.

'Of course I'm over Livvy, what on earth makes you think I'm not?'

Although is this strictly true? I know I'm not in love with Livvy any more. I do love her, though; part of me always will, and I hate the fact that I've hurt her. But I'm hating the fact that Emily is sitting in front of me looking so miserable even more.

'Ever since Livvy's turned up, you haven't been the same,' she says. 'I get that you feel bad about what happened. I get that you want to sort things out with her, but since the exorcism, I'm feeling that maybe you think we've – you've – made a mistake.'

Oh crap. Why does everything have to be so complicated? If only life could be black and white, neat and tidy, and you could turn off unwanted emotions like a tap.

Emily takes a deep breath and continues, 'You need to choose, Adam. It's her or me.'

'Emily, don't be daft,' I say, going to hug her. She clings

to me and I can tell she's trying not to cry. I kiss her softly on the top of the head. I feel that I need to be honest, but I choose my words carefully.

'I fell out of love with Livvy a long time ago, whatever we once had it's gone . . .'

'But?'

'But,' how to say this without sounding like an utter bastard, 'I hate the fact that Livvy died, that Joe lost his mum, that I didn't get to sort things out. I do still love her, and I am still grieving for her. Does that make any kind of sense?'

Emily nodded.

'But, Emily, it's you I want, of course it is. Even if Livvy were to turn up here, alive and well, it would still be you.'

'Really?'

'Really,' I say firmly. 'From the very first moment I met you in that coffee shop, you got right under my skin. Livvy and I were over long before you appeared on the scene. I'm not saying I don't feel quite confused right now. I was married to Livvy for a long time and I wish I'd had the chance to tell her properly that I was leaving. But it's you I want and love and need.'

'Oh Adam,' says Emily. She kisses me on the lips and we stand there for a long time just holding one another.

'Now come on, let's stop rowing,' I say. 'I know this situation is crazy, but let's pretend everything is normal, and shall we at least try and have the best Christmas we can?'

'So even if she were here in the flesh, you'd still choose me?' Emily seems to need the reassurance.

'Always,' I say. 'Anyway, that's not going to happen, so don't even think about it.'

'I wouldn't put it past her to find a way,' says Emily.

'How can she?' I say. 'She's a ghost. And if she won't leave us alone we can always get Father Dave to come back. It will be fine, you'll see.'

Emily

Emily sat down to watch TV with Adam and Joe, feeling a lot better. She'd been becoming far too paranoid; Livvy had really got under her skin. But now knowing that she and Adam were strong enough to stick together, Emily was confident that whatever happened next they wouldn't let Livvy wear them down.

The rest of the evening passed peacefully enough. They laughed with Joe – who was thawing enough to talk to Adam again – at some rubbish Christmas quiz shows on TV, and it felt cosy and normal. Knowing Livvy didn't seem able to come into the house any more meant that Emily dared to hope they might be able to actually enjoy Christmas. However much she might want to, Livvy wasn't going to ruin their Christmas Day. Joe also seemed happier, knowing that Livvy was still around.

'You will speak to her, won't you?' he asked, at one point. 'I think it would make Mum happy if you talked to her.'

'If there's a way that I can, Joe,' said Adam. 'I don't want your mum being sad.'

'That's good,' said Joe, 'she'd like that.'

Joe seemed content with that answer and took himself off to bed. Adam and Emily finished the remains of the wine and dozed together by the fire, feeling more relaxed and content than they had since Livvy had showed up. They were together, and nothing else mattered.

'Oh Adam, look, it's snowing,' Emily said, as they cleared up in the kitchen before going to bed.

'Maybe we'll actually get a white Christmas after all,' said Adam.

They stood by the back door, looking out as the snow fell on the lawn, swiftly covering it in a white blanket. It felt like a perfect ending to a shitty day.

'It's so magical,' said Emily. 'I'm going to take that as a good sign.'

'Me too,' said Adam, 'now come on, let's get to bed.'

So they went to bed and made long slow languorous love before falling asleep in one another's arms. Emily had the best night's sleep she'd had in weeks.

By morning the snow was about six inches deep, and the snow ploughs were out and about.

Joe was so excited, he came racing in in the morning to tell them.

'There are angels in the garden,' he said.

'Sorry?' Adam looked confused, until Emily got up to look out of the window.

'Oh I get it,' she said, 'there are snow angels in the garden.'

'Did you make them, Joe?' asked Adam, puzzled for a moment.

'It wasn't me,' said Joe with a shrug.

And then, when they went downstairs to have breakfast, everything became clear. The window had misted up with condensation and Emily went cold all over as she saw a message written on the window.

Oh no.

Did you miss me? it said.

Livvy

Letitia's plan is very simple. She has access to something she refers to as 'old power', which I have a feeling Malachi

252

won't approve of. We're sitting in Adam's back garden, and it's time to take action.

'I'm not making a deal with the devil or anything like that, am I?' I ask. I've no desire to get what I want in this life, only to discover I've made some kind of Faustian pact for the next.

'No you are not, girl,' she replies. 'You need to have more faith in me.'

'OK,' I say, 'so what do I have to do?'

'All you need is some of Letitia's special potion,' she says, 'and you'll have a window of opportunity to go back.'

Special potion? This is sounding a bit like *Death Becomes Her.* I swallow hard; if I remember rightly, things didn't end too well for Goldie Hawn and Meryl Streep in that film. I hope Letitia's potion doesn't have any nasty side effects.

'And I'll be able to go into the house again?'

'Better than that,' says Letitia. 'Once you drink this, you get your body back too. You can walk through that door, like you did when you were alive. That'll stir things up.'

Won't it just.

'Bring it on!' I say.

'But like I said before,' she warns, 'you only have till Christmas Eve to get what you want.'

'Fine,' I say, 'let's do it.'

She hands me a phial of clear liquid. I'm a little disappointed, shouldn't it steam or something like the other one did? But I'm so excited about the thought of actually being near Adam and Joe, I take it from her anyway.

'Now you go, girl,' she says, 'you go and get your man.'

And then, before my eyes, she fades away.

So now I'm back in Adam's garden, sitting outside, looking at the snow. I've attracted their attention with the snow angels and my message on the kitchen window. Time to take things further.

I undo the phial, and look at it. Is it worth the risk? I look up at the house, where I can see Adam, Emily and Joe looking out at the snow angels I made. Of course it is.

I open the phial and go to tip it in my mouth.

Joe's Notebook

I woke up to snow angels in the garden.

It was like magic.

Mum used to tell me a story about a magic snow angel when I was little.

She was a Christmas miracle and came to life on Christmas Day.

I have had my Christmas Miracle.

I am sure the angels are from Mum.

The exorcism didn't work.

This is good.

Dad and Emily don't seem happy.

This is bad.

But I think Mum is back.

This is very good.

My Christmas wish has come early.

Christmas Present

'It's not going to make things better, you know,' Malachi is here again, having a go.

Great. He's come back to try and stop me.

'You're wrong,' I say. I don't care about Malachi's lectures now. 'This is my one chance to get Adam to see the truth.'

'You haven't made his life miserable enough already?' asks Malachi.

'We were happy once,' I say defensively. 'We can be again. I have to at least try.'

'It'll end in tears,' says Malachi, 'but on your own head be it. And remember there are other ways this story can end.' And with a whisk of his tail, I am back in that damned miserable parallel universe he keeps insisting on showing me.

It's nearly the end of October in my alternative present. Christmas is coming, and I should be looking forward to it, considering I could so easily not have seen it. Adam has become quite distant since the barbecue incident. He hasn't gone on about it, for which I'm grateful, but I can feel his disappointment, and he never brings alcohol into the house any more. It makes me frustrated. I made one stupid mistake, it's not like I have a problem now. And now I'm so much better I don't need painkillers, so that's not going to happen again. But Adam watches me like a hawk, making me feel guilty if I so much as look at a bottle of wine. So I'm ending up drinking in secret, when he's out of the house.

Joe on the other hand seems chipper and cheerful, but I hardly see him now. He seems to have acquired a girlfriend from somewhere. She's called Caroline and seems nice, but she's taking up a lot of his time. I should be pleased for him, I never thought that would happen for Joe, but somehow I'm not. I feel like I'm being supplanted; and if Joe doesn't need me, why am I here?

'Maybe you should go back to work,' Adam suggests one day, when I am having a moan about how dull my day has been. I would love to, but after so long I feel deskilled and useless. I am not up to date with new technology, I haven't worked in fourteen years; who on earth is going to employ me? It wouldn't matter so much if I didn't have the nagging sensation that I am losing Adam again. He is vague about his movements after work, and after a lapse of some months has taken up swimming again with a vengeance. I am vaguely uneasy about it – could he be cheating on me? Would he still, after what has happened?

My worst fears are confirmed when I am having a restless mooch into town and I run into Marigold, who insists on going for a coffee. I always got on with her before, but since my accident she's taken to treating me like a small child who needs protection. It drives me insane. She spent months 'dropping by' to help out, which I might have welcomed in anyone else. Most of my so-called friends dropped me like a brick when I was in hospital, even

Miranda hasn't been round. I suggested going for a drink once, but she made her excuses, so I haven't seen her in ages.

And now, here I am having a coffee with Marigold, who won't take no for an answer. When we are sitting down, I understand why.

'I feel I just have to tell you, Livvy,' she says, in a patronizing manner which grates hugely. 'I won't be able to live with my conscience if I don't.'

Can't you, I think, can't you really? But she's unstoppable.

'I'm sorry to be the bearer of bad news' – she's really not, there's a gleeful air about her – 'but I think you ought to know.'

'I think I probably don't need to,' I say. I can tell I'm not going to like whatever it is.

'You've been so brave, Livvy,' Marigold reaches over and grabs my arm, 'and you don't deserve this.'

'Marigold—' I say warningly but she ploughs on.

'The thing is, Livvy,' she says, 'Adam's having an affair.'

'If you're trying to prove to me that it's inevitable that Adam and Emily are going to end up together, it's not going to work,' I say defiantly. 'All you've done is shown me how much I need to do this.'

'Your time here is up,' says Malachi patiently. 'That's what I keep trying to tell you. Don't do this, Livvy, please.'

I pause for a minute. It's almost as if Malachi is begging me. But then I think about the alternative.

'Sorry, Malachi,' I say. 'It's my life and it's what I want.'

Defiantly I tip the phial's contents into my mouth and I swallow Letitia's potion.

Chapter Twenty-Two

Three Days till Christmas

Livvy

The potion is fiery and makes me fizzle with delight – much better than the vodka they serve in Underworld. I feel a weird buzzing sensation go through me. The world shifts slightly on its axis, and for a moment I feel woozy, as if I am about to faint. And then there's . . . nothing. Absolutely nothing has happened. I am standing here, just the same as ever. I am crushed with disappointment.

I march out of the garden, determined to go back to Underworld and demand answers, when I hit the fence. What? Why can't I go through?

And then I realize – I can feel my feet. I can *actually* feel my feet, which are cold and damp from the snow. I look at my hands, and gasp. They're real and solid again.

Letitia's potion has worked.

I'm back.

It is damned cold out here though. I had forgotten what cold felt like when I no longer had a body, but now it's seeping into my bones from having made the snow angels. I'm still dressed in the clothes I died in. Unlike this winter, last winter was very mild. So though I'm wearing a fleece and jeans, I've only got a thin top underneath it. And my fleece is very damp.

'Time to see who's right,' I say to Malachi with a determination I don't totally feel. Maybe Adam won't be quite so delighted to see me as I am hoping he will. But faint heart never won fair prince. Or something. Ignoring Malachi's tut of disapproval, I march up to the back door and bang loudly on it.

There's no reply. Maybe they went back to bed after they saw my message. Tentatively I try the handle and the door opens.

I go into the kitchen, and to my disappointment find no one there. But I'm actually properly in my kitchen. I stop for a moment to marvel that I can touch the rough wooden surfaces of our vintage kitchen; run my finger along the top of the new Belling cooker we bought a year before I died; sit down at the old rickety table where I have had so many family meals. This is the house of our dreams; the house we brought Joe into as a baby. I am really back. And I know that I can make things right and we can be happy again.

'Hello?' I call. 'Anyone there?'

And then it's as if an electric shock has gone through me. Adam is standing in the doorway, looking as he always did. It's as though I'm seeing him for the first time. I take in the fair hair with the slightest hint of grey, the piercing blue eyes, and the ready smile. He is wearing black jeans and a hoody. He's even lovelier in the flesh than I remember. I had forgotten how much he made my heart sing. He takes my breath away, and I have to resist the urge to throw myself into his arms. Because much as it goes against the grain to say so, Adam doesn't look all that pleased to see me.

261

He's gone white as a sheet, as if he can't quite believe what he's seeing.

Oh my gorgeous Adam. How I've missed you. Please, I plead with him silently, please remember how it was.

'Adam,' I say tentatively.

'Christ!' He looks at me in horror, which is not quite the response I'm after. 'Livvy, is that really you?'

Adam

Shock doesn't cover it.

Of all the strange things that have happened in the last few weeks this has to be the strangest. Far from having got rid of Livvy, she seems to be standing in my kitchen, looking very much alive.

I can barely take it in . . . but she looks amazing. Her auburn hair is damp and curly from the snow. Her green eyes light up mischievously as she takes in my shock. It's definitely Livvy, and she looks so stunning I am reminded for a moment of how she was when we first met.

How can she even be here though? I am at a loss for words.

'Livvy,' I manage to stutter eventually, 'but we—'

'Exorcized me?' says Livvy with a faintly devilish smile. 'That was really very unkind.'

'You shouldn't have tried to hurt Emily,' I say.

'Oh Adam!' she says impatiently. 'I was just trying to frighten her and get your attention. What do you think I am?'

'I don't know,' I say. 'Dead, actually.'

'Please,' she shudders, 'don't remind me.'

She looks like Livvy. She sounds like Livvy. It *is* Livvy. And suddenly it seems incredible that she should be standing in front of me. I'm overcome with a weird kind of joy, that I can actually see her. That she is here, reminding me painfully of how lovely she is. I have no idea how or why. All I know is I finally have the opportunity to talk to her about everything that has happened. Maybe we can put the past behind us once and for all.

I walk towards her.

'Dead or not,' I say, 'Liv, it really is good to see you.'

It's as I put my arms around her that Emily chooses to walk in.

Emily

Emily was just coming downstairs, when she heard voices in the kitchen. Knowing that Joe was ensconced in his room, she wondered who Adam could be talking to. She hadn't heard the doorbell ring. When she entered the kitchen Emily got the shock of her life.

'Adam, what the—?' Adam was in the kitchen giving someone a hug. Not just someone – Livvy. Livvy who was supposed to be a ghost. Livvy who Emily thought they'd got rid of. *Livvy.* She was standing in Adam's kitchen, looking alive and well, as if she hadn't been dead for a whole year. Emily stood rooted to the spot, not able to take in what was happening. Livvy was dead. Emily had been to the funeral, visited her grave with Adam, been haunted by her! How could she possibly be here?

Adam leaped back looking guilty, and the paranoia and jealousy that Emily had felt the previous day returned in spades. Livvy looked like the cat that had got the cream. Emily was suddenly overcome with a burning hatred. Till that moment she hadn't known she hated Livvy at all. But she really did. Livvy had caused Adam endless misery when she was alive, and been nothing but grief as a ghost. Now she was clearly here to make trouble. Waves of anger

263

were spilling out of Emily. How could Livvy be alive? What did she want from them?'

'Hello Emily,' said Livvy, with a sweet smile that made Emily want to slap her. 'This is quite awkward. I don't expect you thought you'd see me again.'

'No I didn't,' said Emily. 'What do you want, Livvy?'

'What do you think I want?' said Livvy. 'I've come to get my husband and son back. What are you planning to do about it?'

Emily looked at Adam, who was looking awkward, as well he might, and then at Livvy. She was looking very superior, as if she had the upper hand. Emily wasn't going to let this go without a fight.

'I guess Adam has a choice in this,' she said.

Adam looked even more uncomfortable. Emily might have felt sorry for him, if she hadn't been so angry.

'Emily, this doesn't change anything,' he said.

'Yes it does,' she said. 'It changes *everything*.'

Chapter Twenty-Three

Emily

'Emily,' Adam said slowly, 'it really changes nothing. But right now, I need to talk to Livvy. Alone.'

Emily felt a shock of disappointment go through her. She sagged back against the door.

'You want me to go?' She was stunned. Apart from her wobble the previous night, she hadn't thought for a minute in the last year that Adam was sorry for what had happened between them. But right now he looked really sad, as if she was the last person he wanted to be around. Her previous paranoia returned in a rush. Dealing with Livvy as a ghost was one thing; Emily felt sure she could stand that kind of competition. But could Adam really resist the temptations of a living breathing Livvy? Adam was a decent and kind man; it wouldn't surprise Emily at all if Livvy could work on his guilt and manipulate her way back into his life.

'No. Yes. I don't know.' Adam clearly didn't know what to do or say.

'It's OK,' said Emily.

Livvy almost purred with triumph. Emily choked back her tears as she realized she was losing Adam, right now, in front of her eyes. The man she loved was making a choice, and all too clearly he wasn't choosing her.

Part of Emily wanted to shout and scream, but she was conscious that Joe was next door. Besides she didn't think it would help. The best she could do for now was retire gracefully, though inside she was fuming and, quite frankly, incredulous. How the hell had Livvy done it? They had exorcized her. Father Dave had told them there was no way Livvy could come back to the house. And yet she was here in the flesh. It didn't seem either fair or right. Wasn't there some kind of ghost council they could turn to and demand answers from? How did you get a ghost to stay dead, or bugger off back to where they belonged? Emily had never planned to be part of a ménage à trois, particularly not with a dead rival who'd inconveniently come back to life.

'So I'll go then.'

'Yes,' said Adam. 'I think it's best.'

He couldn't take his eyes off Livvy. It was as though Emily didn't exist.

Slowly she walked away.

'This isn't over, Livvy,' Emily hissed. 'Not by a long chalk.'

'We'll see,' said Livvy smugly. 'Let the best woman win.'

And then Emily fled the house. Adam didn't even seem to notice, which made her feel even worse. She walked home in the snow, tears blurring her vision. She had wronged Livvy, it was true, but it was no one's fault that Livvy had died. It didn't seem right that now Livvy had the chance to reclaim her husband. But Emily wasn't married to Adam. And Emily didn't own him. Livvy did.

Adam

Livvy smiles when Emily leaves, and I suddenly feel trapped.

'What the hell happens now?'

'Now we have a nice cup of tea, and a chat,' says Livvy.

'You can drink tea?' I say. 'Can ghosts normally drink tea?'

'I've got a body again, in case you hadn't noticed,' says Livvy. 'And ever since I died I've been desperate for a cuppa.'

In a fog I go and put the kettle on, and we sit down and face each other across the table. It seems utterly weird having her in our kitchen again, as if the past year hasn't happened. I feel slightly claustrophobic. I have got used to life without Livvy, used to not worrying about what state I'm going to find her in. What if all that starts again? And what about Joe? I know he'll be happy to have his mum back, but her behaviour affected him too. I don't want her to put him through it all again.

'What do you want?' I say eventually.

'You,' says Livvy simply.

'Livvy,' I say. 'It's been a year. So much has happened. I don't know how you're back, but everyone thinks you're dead! Besides, don't you remember? How bad it was?'

I think back to the last couple of years of our marriage. We were barely speaking, and Livvy was scarcely ever sober. I was constantly on tenterhooks at work, waiting for another phone call from Joe to tell me that he'd got home from school and couldn't wake Livvy up, or that she'd been picked up drunk-driving. How she kept hold of her licence I'll never know, and I used to confiscate the car keys when I could, but somehow she was always one up on me and managed to find them again. It was a miracle she never had an accident. We had countless rows about it, and about the state she got herself into, but Livvy would never admit she had a problem. Our life together was hell.

'I know,' she says, and suddenly she looks vulnerable. 'And I'm sorry, I really am. I made a mess of things, but Adam –'

she reaches over and takes my hand. Hers feels warm, human, *alive*, I have a sudden flash to a memory of days when just to touch her was a thrill, just to be with her made my heart overflow with love – 'remember the good times? We had something special once. Surely we can find it again.'

'Livvy, I'm sorry I hurt you. I'm sorry we never got to say goodbye. But we can't turn the clock back, pretend none of the bad stuff happened,' I say. 'I don't see how this can work. I mean, I know you're here right now, and I don't think I'm hallucinating. I identified your body. I buried you and cried for weeks. You're dead, Livvy. Even apart from the fact I love Emily, you're dead. How the hell do we tell everyone you're alive again?'

'We'll find a way. Adam please,' she says. 'I just want to put things right.'

'So do I,' I say, and mean it. 'But that doesn't mean I want to be married to you. You do know that, don't you?'

Livvy

There's a long pause. That's not exactly what I want to hear, but it's early days. He's still in shock. I have to work my magic on him, that's all.

'Well this is bloody maudlin,' I say. 'Why don't we do something fun instead?'

'Like what?' says Adam, looking suspicious.

'Let's get Joe, and go sledging on the hill.'

Joe . . . I suddenly get a stab of worry. I've assumed he'll be happy to see me; I couldn't bear it if he reacts the way Adam has.

'I'm not sure that's a good idea, I've got to go to work for starters,' begins Adam, but I ignore him. It's time to show him the old Livvy. The one he fell in love with, who was full of fun and hare-brained schemes. We had such good times together in the early days of our relationship. Adam has a tendency to be strait-laced, and I loosened him up. I made him go rock climbing and bungee jumping; he always said I brought out the best in him, and I know he brought out the best in me. He needs to be reminded of how good it was, how good it could still be.

'Joe,' I call, 'Joe, where are you?'

I am not quite sure what reaction I will get, but my heart is bursting with love as he walks in the room.

And there he is, my lovely son, properly near me for the first time in a year. His face is wreathed with smiles, and unlike Adam and Emily he takes my presence entirely in his stride.

'I knew you weren't gone,' Joe says, his smile growing even wider. I haven't seen that smile on his face for a very long time. It makes me feel immensely glad to be alive again. Even if Adam isn't on board yet, Joe is thrilled I'm here. That's a good start: if I work on Joe, I'm sure he can work on Adam.

'Mum's back, Dad,' he says happily. 'I told you.'

'Yes, Joe, you did,' says Adam.

'Shall we go sledging, Joe?' I say.

'OK,' says Joe, as if it's perfectly normal for your dead mother to turn up at breakfast and demand you go out in the snow. I love him more in that one moment than I ever have done.

Adam looks like he's been hit over the head by a blunt instrument, but Joe's totally onside. Adam reluctantly fetches me a huge scarf and an odd hat – it's almost like he doesn't want anyone to recognise me, while Joe rushes out to the garage and finds the sledge where it's been stored for several years. Last time it snowed, Adam was at work, and I wasn't up to taking Joe out. It was my own fault. I'd gone for lunch with Miranda before he came home from school. I wasn't going to drink, because I knew Joe wanted

269

me to take him sledging, but Miranda persuaded me to have a spritzer. And when I got home it just seemed so easy to help myself to another glass of wine. The afternoon had disappeared after that, and I was vaguely aware that at some point Joe had come in and gone out again. It wasn't till I was woken by a knock on the door, and a bedraggled-looking Joe was standing there looking cold and hungry, that I realized he'd walked five miles on his own to go sledging, because I couldn't be bothered to take him. It was one of the worst moments of my life. No wonder Adam looked elsewhere. I can see now what a nightmare I was.

But this time, it's going to be different. I've got the chance to prove to them both I'm the wife and mother they deserve, and I am determined to embrace it fully.

Despite Adam's misgivings, we have a great time sledging. I've persuaded him to go into work late, 'After all it's not every day your wife comes back from the dead is it?' I say and Adam just nods. I think he has surprised himself and had a good time. The hill is full of families having fun. The snow has been so heavy, hardly anyone has gone to work today. And there are dads pulling little ones on toboggans and teenagers in onesies making massive snowballs and rolling them down the hill.

I insist on going on the sledge with Joe, who only winces a little when I put my arms around him. I feel full of zest and enthusiasm, it is great to be alive, and I am having the best time.

When Joe eventually has enough, we pile into a sweet little café and have hot chocolate and doughnuts. Even Adam is laughing. He hasn't laughed since I've been back on the scene. It makes me feel warm all over. I can do this, I know I can. Come Christmas Eve, Adam is going to be mine.

Chapter Twenty-Four

Adam

Despite my misgivings, I actually enjoy myself. For a brief moment I can see as I sit here in the café – with Joe and his hot chocolate and marshmallows just the way he likes it, looking deeply content, and Livvy, looking alive and beautiful just as she used to – that there could be a possibility that life could be good again.

I had forgotten how much we used to laugh together. I am reminded of the old Livvy, the one I fell in love with. But as I teeter on the brink, thinking maybe this is what I should do, all I can think of is Emily. I love her too, and I owe her everything. She kept me sane and stood by me when my life with Livvy was a nightmare. And when Livvy died, Emily listened and understood what I was going through. She has been my one bright spot in a hideously difficult year. How can I choose between them? How can I even be having to make a choice between a dead wife and a live girlfriend?

'So what happens now?' says Joe casually.

'Yes, Livvy, what are you planning?' I say. 'And how the hell are you even back in the first place?'

'That would be telling,' says Livvy, tapping her nose. 'Let's say there are people on the Other Side with the power to help, and one of them helped me.'

'So, is Mum going to stay?' Joe asks.

'That's up to Dad,' says Livvy. 'And you. Do you want me to stay, Joe?'

Oh, unfair, Livvy. What else is he going to say?

Joe looks at her thoughtfully.

'I like Emily,' he says, 'and so does Dad.'

'Yes, but I'm back now,' says Livvy. 'Emily doesn't have to be your new mum any more.'

'Will it be like it was?' says Joe. 'I didn't like it when you used to sleep in the daytime.' The way he says it, so matter-of-factly, breaks my heart. Livvy was so often drunk when he came home from school, he started to accept it as normal. But I hadn't appreciated till now how much he must have hated it.

'No, Joe,' says Livvy. 'I was very ill before. But now I'm better. I can come back and we can be a family again, if that's what you want.'

'Yes,' says Joe, 'that's what I want.'

At this I feel a knife twist in my heart. Livvy has manipulated the situation perfectly. I want to say to her that even if she is back, we don't have to stay married, we could get a divorce. But Livvy knows I can't resist Joe. I don't think I have a choice now. If Joe wants Livvy back, I have to take her. I don't know how I am going to tell Emily. It's going to break both our hearts.

Emily

Emily didn't hear from Adam all day. She should have gone into work, but she was far too agitated so rang in sick. As tempting as it was to find out what was happening, she was

272

determined not to crack and call Adam first. She felt desperate to talk to someone, but who on earth would believe her? Lucy, with her perfect family life, would be up to her ears in the pre-Christmas rush. Lucy was open-minded, and had been pretty understanding about the little Emily had shared with her so far but like anyone normal she would think it sounded completely insane for Emily to be worried her boyfriend was about to ditch her for his dead ex-wife. It *was* insane. No, she couldn't talk to Lucy.

There was Dad of course, but Emily didn't want him worrying about her, or thinking that she'd lost it entirely. She was on her own with this one.

Restless and unhappy, Emily threw on her warmest clothes and tried to walk out her frustration in the snow-filled streets, full of excited children throwing snowballs, or dragging their parents off to the local slopes to go sledging. She envied them their uncomplicated happiness, only wishing her life could be so simple.

For some reason Emily found herself drifting towards the nearest church. Somehow it seemed like the right place to be. A group of small children was rehearsing for the nativity on Christmas Eve. It was very sweet, and made Emily feel calmer. There was a tiny angel aged about five, who kept yawning, and two small boys dressed as sheep, who had to be separated for fighting. She marvelled at the patience of the organizers. There was an awful lot of stopping and starting, and children forgetting their lines.

But it was all worth it by the time they did their run through, and by the end of it, Emily had nearly forgotten her troubles as she was completely entranced. She had had the odd fantasy about having children with Adam: a boy and a girl would have been nice. She imagined what it would be like coming here, watching their children do this, seeing them play sheep and angels. It must be lovely to be a parent at Christmas. That seemed so unlikely now. By the time the children were singing 'Away in a Manger' Emily was sobbing loudly.

'It's always terribly moving, I find.' A woman in her sixties, who was sitting behind Emily wrapped up in scarves, leaned in to talk to her. Her voice sounded vaguely familiar, but her face was in the shadows and Emily couldn't quite make out her features.

'I don't even know why I'm crying,' Emily said.

'Oh but I think you do,' the woman said shrewdly. 'Why don't you tell me all about it?'

'I don't think you'd believe me,' said Emily.

'Try me,' her new friend said. 'I'm very broad-minded.'

So Emily told her. The whole thing about falling in love with Adam, though she hadn't meant to, and about Livvy dying and coming back to haunt them and now apparently being there for good.

'And I can't compete, can I?' Emily finished off bitterly. 'She holds all the cards. She's Joe's mother, Adam's wife, and they thought they'd lost her. I can't stand in the way of that.'

'Maybe you shouldn't think in terms of competing,' said the woman. 'It doesn't sound like Adam has stopped loving you. But he needs time. You should give it to him.'

'I should?' Emily said. 'But doesn't that let Livvy win?'

'Maybe, maybe not. But pushing Adam to choose isn't going to help either. You're just going to have to sweat it out.'

'Right,' Emily said, 'well thanks for the advice.'

She was a bit disappointed. For some reason she'd put her faith in her mysterious friend sorting all her problems out.

'I can't do that you know,' the woman said. 'It's not my job.'

'What do you mean?'

'My job is making you face the truth, even if it's unpleasant,' was the response. And then she got up and gave Emily a kiss on the forehead. Only when she'd gone did Emily realize the woman reminded her of her nan. But it wasn't Nan. With a profound shock, Emily understood she'd just spent the previous half-hour talking to her dead mother.

Livvy

'So what about Emily?' Joe says conversationally, as he drains his hot chocolate to the dregs.

Adam looks awkward and says nothing.

'What about Emily?' I say. I wasn't expecting this. I'd got the idea that Joe quite liked Emily, but surely now I was back, he'd see she didn't need to be around?

'Is she still coming for Christmas?' asks Joe. 'I bought her a present.'

'You can still give it to her,' I say. Let's be magnanimous about this.

'I bought you a present too,' says Joe. 'I knew I'd see you again.'

'That's lovely, Joe,' I say. I need to tread carefully here. Joe is so logical. He'll want to know that Emily is OK with all of this, which quite clearly she isn't. And I really don't want to upset Joe.

'Emily is still coming for Christmas,' says Adam firmly.

Yeah, right. Over my no-longer-dead body. I want Christmas with my family, the way it's meant to be. I most definitely do not want to share it with my husband's mistress. But I also don't want to have an argument about it in front of Joe. He's been through enough, and though he appears to be taking everything in his stride I know from experience that sometimes he can have a left-field response.

'We'll see,' I say.

'Only it's a bit confusing,' says Joe. 'Dad and Emily are going to move in together. Mum, did you know?'

'I did,' I say, 'but that was before.'

'When you were dead?' says Joe helpfully. 'But now you're not dead. So what happens?'

'I think that's up to Dad,' I say and leave it at that.

And me, I think. It's up to me, to prove to Adam I've changed and that we can wipe out the past and start again. That there's a possibility for us to find love again.

Adam looks stricken as if he doesn't know what to do. I think it's best I leave him alone for a while to let him get used to the idea that I'm here to stay.

So I say, 'Look you two, I'm going out for a walk, maybe do some shopping. You get on home, I'll join you later.'

I kiss them both on the tops of their heads and breeze out, but it doesn't escape my notice that Adam flinches slightly away from me. Bugger, this might be tougher than I thought.

I wander through the shops, marvelling for the first time since I've escaped from the car park that I can feel sensations and see clearly all the things going on around me. Before it was like I was in a fog, but now everything is bright and jangly and new again. I breathe in the fresh crisp air in delight. Imagine! Being able to breathe again. How fantastic is that?

At the bridge end of the river, there's a Christmas market. Gorgeous smells of cinnamon and roasting chestnuts hit you as you walk past, and heat pours out from braziers. As I walk among the crowds in a daze, drinking in the wonder of being alive, I fumble in my pockets and find a tenner there, from the day I died. Brilliant. I buy a gluhwein and stand looking at the river flowing, and the snow falling on the ducks.

The gluhwein has warmed me up, and given me confidence. So I boldly go to the shops to buy Adam and Joe a present each. I still have my purse in my fleece, and I choose Adam a jacket I know he'll like, and Joe a scarf and gloves. I've noticed his are looking ratty. But when I go to pay there's a problem.

'This card's been cancelled,' says the lady behind the counter. And she looks at me apologetically. 'It says here you don't exist.'

Joe's Notebook

This is the best day of my life.

We went sledging with Mum.

And then we had hot chocolate, just like we used to.

I like having Mum back.

I don't have to look at her star any more.

I knew she'd find her way home.

This is going to be the best Christmas ever.

Christmas Present

'Running into a few teething difficulties?' Malachi is waiting for me outside the shop.

'Go away,' I say. I was shocked by the card incident. I had thought I would slot back into my old life again, but clearly it's not going to be quite as simple as that.

'Not so easy coming back from the dead, is it?' says Malachi. 'All that red tape. Tsk, tsk. You should have thought about that.'

'Will you just leave me alone,' I say.

'No can do,' says Malachi. 'You're my responsibility for better or for worse, and I have to show you the error of your ways.'

'I've learned from the error of my ways,' I say. 'And I intend to prove it to Joe and Adam. Everything will be fine. We're going to be a family again.'

'So you keep telling me,' says Malachi. 'But let me show you this, and see if you're still so sure everything's going your way.'

It's nearly Christmas in my alternative present, and Adam and I are pretending very hard for Joe that everything between us is normal. A year since my accident, and where I should be feeling happy that I'm still here, and Adam is still with me, I'm not. I'm miserable as sin. Ever since Marigold had that chat with me, all I can think of is that Adam is back with Emily. I know it's her, because (though I am ashamed to have done it) I sneaked into his phone and found his text messages to her. I don't know what to do, but I'm too frightened to confront him again. Our relationship feels even more fragile than it did this time last year, and though I know it does no good, I can't help drinking more than I should. I try to cover it up when Joe is around, but I know he knows. What makes me feel worse is that Adam doesn't even bother to say anything any more if he finds me drunk. I am losing him, and it is all my own fault.

But the day we put the Christmas tree up it all comes to a head. I try my best for Joe's sake not to have a drink, though I am itching to open a bottle of wine. And we have a lovely afternoon, taking the decorations down from the attic and putting them up in the special order in which Joe likes to do things. He has the day marked down in the calendar every year. It is our special time, and I feel lucky that at least I have had the chance to do this again. Adam is supposed to be joining us, but he cries off saying he has to go into work. It's a Saturday, and his busiest time of year, but I can't help suspecting that he is lying to me.

When the decorations are done, without any preamble Joe announces he's going to Caroline's. I had been planning to take him for a hot chocolate but swallow my disappointment and drop him off there. He seems so happy, I can't let my misery intrude on that.

I get back to the house, and the Christmas tree is twinkling at me, full of its sparkly promise. But I am alone in

280

my house, and there is still no sign of Adam. I sigh and pour myself a drink, staring out into the garden at a blotchy grey sky.

It is dark before I know it, and I sit in the kitchen cradling my drink, wondering how things can possibly be worse now than they were a year ago, when I hear the key in the lock.

'What are you doing in the dark?' says Adam, coming into the kitchen and turning the light on. 'Where's Joe?'

'Out,' I say. 'How was work?'

'Oh busy,' says Adam, but I can tell he is lying, and suddenly I am sick of it.

'You haven't been to work, have you?' I say. 'You've been with her.'

To his credit, Adam doesn't lie. He sits down opposite me, his head in his hands.

'I'm so sorry, Liv,' he says, 'I wanted this to work, but I just can't carry on.'

'What are you saying?' I ask in a small voice, terrified by what I've unleashed.

'It's over, Livvy,' he says. 'I'm so sorry, but after Christmas I'm going to move in with Emily.'

Part Three

Christmas Future

Christmas Future

I'm back in the present again and Malachi is still with me. I don't know why he has to keep showing me all this depressing stuff.

'You're still not getting it, are you?' he says.

'What am I not getting?' I say. 'It's inevitable that Emily will get together with Adam whatever I do? I just don't believe that. I've this one opportunity to sort my life out properly and you're not going to stop me.'

'Livvy,' Malachi says, 'you could do this and hurt everyone in the process.'

'What about me?' I say. 'I was hurt. I didn't deserve to die.'

'I know,' says Malachi. 'But sometimes, things are just as they are. Your time is up here.'

'Why does it have to be?' I argue.

'Because that's just how it is,' says Malachi. 'Let me show you how the future is meant to be, if you stop interfering.'

'No, I don't want to see it,' I say stubbornly, but already I find myself standing outside a church.

'Why are we here?' I hiss to Malachi as he takes me up

to the church door. 'Is it a funeral?' It's a freezing cold day, so it's just right for one.

'Shh,' says Malachi. 'Just go in and watch.'

I enter the packed church. I can see people Adam works with looking happy and excited – even sodding Marigold – and on the other side of the church, lots of people I don't know. There is an air of happy expectation. Near the altar I spot Adam's mum and dad, and Joe standing with Adam. They're both smiling, looking very smart in morning suits and button holes.

No. No, this mustn't happen. I have to stop it.

The organ voluntary starts and everyone turns to look up the aisle. I want to scream as I see Emily, a winter bride in ermine and satin, blushing as she walks up the aisle with her dad. I swear he winks at Mum as he walks past her. Even Mum is here – how could she?

So *this* is the future Malachi is offering me? Emily and Adam getting married? I let out a howl of anguish, and drop down at the back of the church sobbing my heart out. No one can hear me of course, which makes it worse. In this future, I am dead, and my husband is marrying someone else, and no one else cares but me.

Adam is going to marry Evil Emily?

I don't think so.

Chapter Twenty-Five

Three Days till Christmas

Adam

After Livvy leaves us, Joe and I go home.

'What are you going to do, Dad?' Joe keeps asking me and I have no idea of the answer. My thoughts are churning and muddled. I wanted to see Livvy again to have the chance to talk about the past; and make up for the way I hurt her. I'm glad for the opportunity to tell her how I feel. But I don't want her back in my life. I loved her once, and this afternoon reminded me of that, but it was a long time ago and we were very different people. Besides, how on earth do you go around telling people that the wife who's been dead for a year, and whose funeral they all attended, has come back to life and moved in again? This isn't some corny soap opera where everyone wakes up and it's all been a dream.

I love Emily.

I want to live with Emily.

The thought of a life without her is impossible. I want my future to be with her, but how can I do that to Joe? I play the argument back and forth, and can find no easy answers. It's an impossible conundrum.

In the end, I call Felicity and ask her to come over. She needs to know what's going on.

'Mum's back,' says Joe cheerfully, when Felicity comes in. 'She's back properly.'

Stupidly I hadn't prepared Joe to be more tactful. Although how *do* you break such news to your mother-in-law about her dead daughter?

'Sorry?' Felicity looks stunned, and I don't blame her. I still haven't taken it in, and poor Felicity didn't even know till now that the exorcism hasn't worked. 'Joe's right,' I say. 'Livvy's managed to return from the dead somehow, and she wants us to be a family again.'

'Slow down,' says Felicity. 'What do you mean, Livvy's back? How? Where is she? Can I see her?'

'As in properly alive again.'

'But – the exorcism—' stutters Felicity. She looks pale and I make her sit down, and pour her a drink of whisky.

'Didn't work, apparently,' I say.

'But how can she be alive again?' Felicity is understandably struggling with this. Who wouldn't be?

'I don't know,' I say. 'All I know is she's not a ghost any longer.'

Felicity takes a deep breath.

'Where is she now?' she asks, shock still written over her face.

'Shopping,' I say. 'She wanted to go Christmas shopping.' And the absurdity of it hits me. My wife has come back from the dead and gone shopping. Two weeks ago, my life was complicated but beginning to settle. Now it's an entangled mess, and I can see no way out.

'I need to see her,' says Felicity. 'I need to talk to her. Find out what she thinks she's playing at.'

'Would you?' I say. 'I don't think she's listening to me.'

'Can't you, me, Emily and Mum all live together?' Joe looks puzzled.

'I don't think that will work, darling,' says Felicity. 'Where is Emily?'

'She went home,' I say.

'Why don't you go and spend some time with her?' says Felicity. 'I'll deal with Livvy.'

Livvy

I leave Malachi by the river, and march home. I'm freezing cold. I'd forgotten how cold actually feels. I've been wafting about through snowy streets without batting an eyelid, and now my feet are soaking wet, and I'm chilled to the bone. And I haven't bought any Christmas presents, because officially I don't exist. I wonder how easy it is to be declared undead. I haven't thought this through properly. Everyone thinks I'm buried six feet under; it's not like I can jump out of a giant Christmas cake and say, 'Ta-da! Surprise!'

Malachi is wrong. He has to be. This opportunity has to have some purpose, and if it's not to reunite me with my family, what could it be?

When I arrive home, I take the key I find in my fleece and unlock the door. It doesn't fit. Bloody cheek. Adam's changed the locks. I'm still an outsider in my own home. I have to change this, I have to. I ring on the doorbell, and the door opens. I'm expecting Adam, but—

'Mum?' I say in surprise. I'm not sure I'm up to seeing Mum yet. I've a feeling she won't be entirely on my side.

'Livvy,' she says. She gives me an awkward hug. We were never very touchy-feely when I was alive. Neither of us is quite sure of the etiquette, now I'm miraculously back from the dead. But she's my mum, and for the first time in a year I can properly touch her. I hug her more warmly, a lump building in my throat. And she responds.

'I can't believe it,' she says, her voice thick with pain.

'Hello Mum.' Joe is pleased to see me. 'Granny's going to sort you out.'

Oh is she? We'll see about that.

'Hush, Joe,' says Mum. 'Are you OK for a bit on your PlayStation? Your mum and I need to have a little chat.'

'OK,' says Joe. 'It's good Mum's back isn't it?'

'Yes,' says my mum, 'I suppose it is.'

But she doesn't sound too sure.

We go and sit in the kitchen.

'Tea?' says Mum.

'If I'm getting a lecture, I'd prefer something stronger,' I say. In the last few years of my old life, it often felt as though Mum only came over to tell me about where I was going wrong with my life.

'What makes you think you're getting a lecture?' asks Mum.

'The look on your face?'

'I don't want to give you a lecture,' says Mum, and I realize she's nervous, which surprises me. She paces up and down the kitchen. 'You know I'm not good at the emotional stuff, but you're my only daughter and I lost you. You have no idea how that feels. God knows there've been times in the last year when all I've wanted was for you to walk through my front door, and for none of this to have happened. I'm thrilled to see you, really, but I'm worried too.'

'There's no need to be worried,' I say.

'No?' says Mum. 'Livvy, what do you think you're doing here?'

'Trying to put things right,' I tell her. 'Please, Mum, I

need you to understand. I know it was horrible for Adam. I know I was horrible, but I'm here now and things will be different.'

'Oh Livvy,' says Mum, and there are tears in her eyes. 'It wasn't all your fault. I should have seen what was happening instead of hiding my head in the sand, and got you help sooner. Sometimes I feel I really let you down.'

'You didn't let me down,' I say, feeling choked. Although we've had our differences, I've always known she was there for me, even if I never admitted it.

'I could have done more,' says Mum. 'I'm sorry.'

We stand awkwardly contemplating a shared past of missed opportunities.

'I'm not sure you could have helped,' I say sadly, 'I can see now I wasn't ready to listen.'

'Well listen now,' Mum says. 'I don't want to be cruel, but what you and Adam had is over. He's with Emily now. You should let him go.'

Emily

Emily walked slowly back home, feeling more miserable than ever. The snow was turning to slush as a grey sleet fell. She felt cold, wet and hungry, and utterly confused. If she had just met her mum's ghost, she hadn't been given any helpful advice, even though it was a strangely comforting experience. Surely they must have some answers on the Other Side?

The one certainty Emily had clung on to for the past year was that she and Adam loved one another. She didn't think Livvy's reappearance would change that. But Emily also knew how decent, kind and responsible Adam was. What had happened to Livvy was so terrible, Emily knew

291

he'd want to do the right thing even if that meant his future with Emily slipping away.

To her surprise, Adam was waiting on her front doorstep when she got home.

'Adam?' She approached him warily, not sure what this meant. Had he come to tell her he was going back to Livvy? Emily felt sick at the thought.

'Emily,' he said. 'Can I come in?'

'Of course,' said Emily, the sick feeling not abating. 'Where's Livvy?'

'I left her behind with Felicity,' he said.

'What are we going to do?' Emily said as she led Adam into her cosy little lounge. 'If Livvy really is back, I can hardly move in now.'

'That's what I came over to say,' said Adam. He looked utterly wretched, and it was all Emily could do to resist pulling him into her arms. 'Whatever happens next, I want you with me. I don't love Livvy any more. Seeing her again has completely clarified it for me. I want to be with you.'

'Really? You looked pretty cosy in the kitchen.'

It was bitchy and a bit unnecessary, but Emily had to lash out at someone.

'Emily,' said Adam, 'don't be daft. I gave Livvy a hug because I was genuinely pleased to see her, but honestly, I'm over her. It's you I love.'

Emily felt a weak pulse of relief. She had been so sure Adam was going to tell her the opposite.

He pulled her towards him and she sank gratefully into his arms. 'I know this is a mess and a weird situation.'

'Define weird,' said Emily with a grimace. 'I've just met my dead mother in church.'

'What?' said Adam. 'How many more bloody ghosts are going to pop up? Can't anyone stay dead any more?'

'I have no idea,' laughed Emily, relief making her giddy. 'She wanted to help I think. She told me to give you space and time. And I can do that if you need it.'

'I don't need it,' said Adam. 'I know Joe wants me to take Livvy back. Of course he does. But I can't do it, not even for him. It's not the right thing for any of us.'

'I don't want to cause problems with you and Joe,' said Emily.

'I know,' said Adam. 'I'll try and explain it to him. If I can. I don't want to hurt him more than he's been hurt already, but my living with Livvy again won't make things better. He'll see that eventually. I'm going to tell her it's over. Like I would have done a year ago but for the accident.'

Emily leaned happily on Adam's shoulder, back where she belonged. She hadn't a clue how they were going to work this mess out, but as long as she still had Adam, she knew she could cope with anything.

Chapter Twenty-Six

Livvy

'Gee, thanks Mum,' I say. 'I thought you were on my team.'

'I'm always on your team,' says Mum. 'That's why I'm telling you this. Adam's had a rough time this year.'

'It's not been a bundle of laughs for me,' I say.

'And before that. Come on, Livvy, you know things weren't good between you.' Mum is remorseless and at this precise moment I want to throw something at her. The memories of what I was like keep returning and I don't care to think about the vile things I did. I want to remember how good Adam and I once were together. I know that we could be as good again.

'You don't have to remind me,' I snap. I stare out of the window. So many missed opportunities; things unsaid, or done wrong. Why can't Mum see this is the perfect moment to make things right?

'But this time I can make it better,' I say. 'I've been given a second chance. Who gets that chance? I can't waste it.'

Mum looks at me. 'But what about Emily?' she asks. 'You made life really difficult for Adam but he stood by you for more years than many men would have done. And now he's found a lovely girl. I think it's time for you to step back and let him live his life. I'd still be saying this if you hadn't had the accident.'

'But you didn't, did you?' I say. 'You never told me I was being unfair to Adam. You never said anything.'

'Oh I tried,' said Mum sadly. 'Don't you remember? The summer before your accident, I warned you that Adam was losing patience with you, but you ignored me. You weren't prepared to listen then, any more than you are now. What do you want from Adam, Livvy? If you really loved him, you'd let him go.'

'Mum!' I am incandescent with rage now. 'How can you say that? After what he did to me?'

'What did he do to you, Livvy? Apart from being incredibly supportive of your problems, with precious little understanding from you, about what you were putting him through?'

'He had an affair,' I say.

The words are out of my mouth before I've thought them through. Mum stares at me in incomprehension.

'Adam had an affair,' she says.

'So he hasn't come clean then?' I say bitterly. 'That figures.'

'Who did he have an affair with?' Mum asks faintly, although I'm sure it must be obvious.

'Who do you think? It was Emily. Adam had an affair with Emily. I found out the day I died.'

Emily

Emily and Adam sat cuddling on the sofa for what seemed like hours. She felt safe and secure, but horribly aware this was only temporary. Adam would eventually have to go home, though both of them were reluctant for him to leave. It wasn't often they got time alone. But Emily knew it would be selfish to keep him here, much as she wanted it, so she said nothing.

Adam looked at his watch guiltily, reminding Emily of before, when Livvy was properly alive, and they had snatched precious moments together. Adam had planned to tell Livvy after Christmas, but then someone she knew spotted him with Emily and the cat was well and truly out of the bag. And then of course, the accident had happened.

'Bloody hell, if Livvy's back for good, we have to go through this charade all over again,' said Emily. 'I'm not sure I can stand it.'

'We don't,' said Adam.

'What?'

'Have to live like we did. It's in the open now. We've been together for a year. If this really bizarre situation continues I'll get a divorce. Though I have no idea how you even go about divorcing a dead spouse.'

Emily laughed though she didn't really find it funny.

After some while Adam said reluctantly, 'I should go. I don't want to . . .'

'I know,' Emily said. It was what they used to say back then too, on those frantic nights when they had grabbed precious time together.

'It's been so nice being able to be together without complications,' Emily sighed. 'How can this be happening?'

'We'll get through it,' said Adam, kissing her.

They held each other tight.

'I'm very afraid of what the next few days will bring,' whispered Emily.

'I'll ring you,' said Adam, but offered no assurance beyond, 'and we'll sort something out.'

But as Emily saw him to the door, she felt doubtful it

would be that easy. Livvy was a malevolent witch who would stop at nothing.

Adam

Livvy won't want to hear what I've got to say, but I have to say it. We had a good time today, a reminder of how things once were, but none of that stops me wanting to be with Emily, or makes me forget the misery of the years between. I'm flattered – who wouldn't be? – that my wife apparently loves me and our son so much she's literally come back from the dead. That is pretty impressive. But we can't go back to the way things were.

I want a future with Emily. I want to marry her, and move into a different house, one without bad memories; a house where we can build a future, maybe even have some kids. I know it will be hard for Joe to accept it, and of course that worries me. But he's very logical, and in time I am sure he will understand.

When I arrive home, I detect a weird atmosphere. Joe is in the lounge on his PlayStation and barely looks up when I come in. Not totally unusual, but he doesn't even acknowledge me.

'Where's Mum?' I say, thinking how strange it is to be asking that question again.

'Kitchen,' mumbles Joe and goes back to his PlayStation.

When I go into the kitchen, it's to find Felicity sitting in there with Livvy with a face like thunder.

'To think I felt sorry for you,' she spits out.

'Come again?' I am confused. Felicity has been amazing in the last year, and even before that, always offering me quiet support when things were difficult. And then I see Livvy looking smug, and my heart sinks. Oh no, what has she said?

'Were you ever planning to tell me?' asks Felicity. 'Or was I supposed to be kept in the dark forever?'

'About what?' I say weakly.

'About your affair with Emily?' says Felicity, and Livvy looks on, triumphant.

Chapter Twenty-Seven

Adam

I was not expecting this. I've walked into a veritable shit storm with both Livvy and Felicity ranged against me. It's a pretty fearsome sight.

'Felicity,' I say. 'I have no excuses. Apart from the fact that when I met Emily, my home life was rotten. You know that. And—'

'Emily was there. I get it,' says Felicity. She's furious with me. 'But you let me believe that you only met her after Livvy died. How could you? I thought better of you than that.'

I feel like I've been hit in the stomach. I love Felicity dearly and her good opinion is vital to me.

'I didn't tell you, because there didn't seem much point,' I say. 'I wasn't trying to keep anything from you. It was such a difficult time and . . .' My voice trails off; Felicity's not really listening to me. She's gone pink in the face and is very agitated.

'It was a shock for me, thinking you'd found someone so soon, but I was genuinely happy for you. I thought some good had come from all this heartache. And the whole time you must have been laughing at my stupidity.'

'I wasn't,' I protest. 'I'd never do that, I just didn't want to tell you stuff that would only upset you.'

'Too right, it's upset me,' says Felicity. 'I'll see myself out.

'And Joe?' she says, pausing at the door. 'What about Joe? How are you going to explain it to him? What a mess.'

Felicity's gone in a whirl of indignation and self-righteousness. I've never seen her like this. She'd always been on my side, when Livvy and I were going through bad times. I honestly wasn't expecting her to turn on me. And now she has, and by the looks of things I'm not going to be forgiven in a hurry.

'Thanks for that, Livvy,' I say. I'm beyond angry with her. 'That was helpful.'

Livvy just smiles and says, 'She had a right to know. And let's face it, you are the bad guy here, not me, for once.'

'Livvy, what do you hope to gain from this? Just because you've come back, it doesn't mean I'm going to start again with you. I love Emily and intend to stay with her.'

'Oh, please!' Livvy looks at me in disbelief. 'You can't mean that.'

'I can and do,' I say.

'I thought you wanted to sort things out,' she says. 'That's all I've heard from you since I first started to see you again. I've been in your thoughts, remember.'

'Yes,' I say. 'I wanted to have the opportunity to say sorry for hurting you. It was horrendous knowing that the last words I heard from you were angry ones. But whatever you and your mum think, I'm not going to change my mind.'

'We'll see about that,' says Livvy. 'Shall we ask Joe what he thinks?'

'Livvy, you wouldn't,' I gasp.

'Oh wouldn't I?' says Livvy. 'You try and stop me.'

OK, so I wasn't expecting Adam to still be quite so on board with Emily. I'd been bargaining on Joe being enough of a reason for him to accept me back. Seems I was wrong about that. But I'm sure I can work on him. I've managed to get him in a flap about Joe, which is the ace up my sleeve. I'm sure Adam doesn't want our son to know he's been a naughty boy. So to wind him up I go into the lounge to pretend I'm about to tell Joe. Only he's not there.

'Joe,' I call up the stairs. He must have gone to his room. There's no answer. So I call again. Still no response. Upstairs, there's no sign of him. I suddenly get a bad feeling about this. When he was younger, Joe used to have a habit of disappearing when he was upset but I don't think he's done it recently.

Back in the kitchen, I find Adam with his head in his hands.

'Adam? Did Joe say he was going out?'

Adam looks up alarmed.

'No. Why? Isn't he in his room?'

'No, and his mobile is on the lounge table.'

I am starting to feel a sliver of panic, which I try to suppress.

We search the house again, but Joe is nowhere to be found. It's snowing outside, and he's left his jacket hanging on the peg.

'Shit,' says Adam, 'he's gone walkabout.'

It's something Joe does periodically, if he's upset.

'What if he overheard our conversation?' asks Adam.

'He can't have!' I blanch, though the thought has occurred to me too. I'd got carried away in the heat of the moment,

I hadn't meant for Joe to hear us. 'Maybe he's gone to see this Caroline girl.'

'And more likely he's done a runner,' says Adam. 'This is your fault.'

'Hello,' I say, 'I'm not the one who had an affair.'

'No, you're not responsible for any of this are you?' says Adam and I'm taken aback by his bitterness. 'Didn't you learn anything being dead?'

Adam tries Caroline's number, but she hasn't heard from Joe today.

'He can't have gone far,' I say. The panic is beginning to bubble up now, but I don't want to let Adam see it. 'Let's look for him.'

We leave the house barely speaking. The snow is falling thick and fast, but we can see Joe's footsteps on the path, heading left into town. Not knowing what else to do, we follow them.

We walk through the streets, which are quiet. People have finished late-night shopping and are on their way home. Any revellers are in the pub, or getting geared up for Christmas, like most normal people at this time of the year. More than anything I want us to be normal people again. And from having felt triumphant, now I'm feeling sick with apprehension. If something has happened to Joe and it's my fault, I shall never forgive myself.

After half an hour of fruitlessly wandering the streets, we both stop, and Adam says, 'Now what?'

We consider the pool, Joe likes to swim to de-stress, but he hasn't taken his swimming stuff. And then Adam's phone rings.

'Emily?' he says. 'This isn't a good time.' Followed by, 'Joe's with you, oh thank God.'

Emily had just been considering getting into the bath when there was a ring at the door. It had gone 8 p.m. Who could be coming to see her at this time? Her heart leaped. Could it possibly be Adam?

But it wasn't Adam. It was Joe. He wasn't wearing a coat and he looked bedraggled and freezing.

'Joe? What are you doing here?'

'I want to ask you a question,' Joe said.

'Does your dad know you're here?' Emily said, knowing how worried Adam would be.

'No, please don't tell him,' said Joe. 'I only want to ask this one thing and then I'll go.'

'All right, fire away. But don't you want to come in? You're soaking wet.' The least Emily felt she could do was try and look after Joe. Maybe if she got him inside she could persuade him to ring Adam.

'Oh.' Joe looked surprised, as if he hadn't noticed. 'I don't want to come in.'

'Please,' Emily said, worried now. Joe was shifting anxiously from one leg to another, and his lips were looking blue. 'I could make you hot chocolate.'

'Hot chocolate is good,' agreed Joe, and came in. He allowed Emily to give him a towel, and a fleece belonging to Adam that he'd left behind months ago, though Joe muttered something about it being the wrong colour.

But he refused to sit down and kept pacing up and down the kitchen in agitation.

'What's this all about, Joe?' Emily asked. 'Is it to do with your mum?'

'Yes, and about what I want for Christmas,' he said.

'OK,' Emily said cautiously. 'So what do you want for Christmas?'

Joe ignored her.

'Mum's come back. That's good isn't it?'

'Yes, I suppose so,' Emily said.

'When I was little Mum always asked me to make a Christmas wish on a star,' said Joe, 'and I've made mine tonight.'

'Oh,' Emily said, having a feeling she knew what that would be.

'My Christmas wish is for Mum to live with us,' he said. 'You have to go now. I don't need a new mum any more.'

'I was never going to take the place of your mum,' Emily said.

'You and Dad had an affair. Granny said so.' Joe came out with it starkly. 'That's bad.'

'Yes and no,' said Emily. Shades of grey were something Joe struggled with.

'But you make Dad happy,' he continued, 'and that's good.'

'Yes, it is.'

'People shouldn't have affairs,' said Joe. 'Mum was upset. That's why she had her accident.'

'I know, Joe, and I'm sorry. I really am. But your mum and dad weren't happy together for a very long time.'

'Mum wasn't well,' said Joe stubbornly.

'I know,' Emily said carefully. 'And it was very hard for your dad.'

'But everything's different now,' said Joe. 'Mum is back and she's well. Dad can love her again and you can leave now. We don't need you any more. That's what I want for Christmas.'

Emily suddenly saw that Joe had been having a logical

argument with himself. He hadn't actually needed her there to have it.

'Oh Joe,' said Emily, 'I'm sorry, I don't know if I can leave. I love your dad.'

'But you have to,' Joe said, and there were tears in his eyes. 'Mum needs Dad. And I can't have two mums.'

Bloody hell. How on earth to deal with this?

'Joe, I think we should ring your dad now,' Emily said. She had no idea what else to do.

'I don't want to,' said Joe.

'He'll be worried,' said Emily. 'And so will your mum, and I don't think you want to worry them, do you, Joe?'

'No,' he agreed reluctantly.

'I'll get him to come and pick you up. And then you and your mum and dad can go home and have a chat about everything.'

It was the last thing Emily wanted to happen, but Joe needed the support more than she did.

'And Mum will stay and you'll leave?' said Joe. 'Because if you don't, Mum will be gone for good.'

'What do you mean?'

'She's only got until Christmas Eve to get Dad back,' said Joe. 'She told me when we were out today. If you don't leave, Mum will be gone again. And this time forever.'

Joe's Notebook

This is bad.

Dad and Emily had an affair.

Mum found out then she died.

This is very bad.

But I like Emily.

She isn't bad.

She's nice. Dad likes her.

And Mum is back.

This is good.

I can't have two mums.

Emily has to leave.

Christmas Future

Livvy

'That was clever,' says Malachi as Adam, Joe and I make our way up the garden path.

'Shh! They'll hear you.' I am feeling rotten about what happened with Joe, and I don't want Malachi saying I told you so.

'Nah, they won't,' says Malachi. 'Haven't you noticed how well I can manipulate time?'

And then I'm back in another of his visions. Malachi's nothing if not persistent.

'Why are you doing this?' I say. 'Do you believe in torture?'

'I'm trying to get you to understand. If you were quicker and less self-obsessed we'd be there by now,' he says impatiently.

This time we're in a large house, different from the one I share with Adam. It's Christmas Day and Adam is there in a shiny new kitchen, cooking a turkey. His parents are sitting at the enormous kitchen table, chatting to Joe and Caroline. Joe looks older, and they both look very happy. Caroline's proudly showing off an engagement ring. Joe's going to get married? That at least is something I can celebrate. I never thought that would happen for Joe. I wish I knew her to tell her how grateful I am for the joy she's brought him.

But then Emily walks in, holding a wriggling toddler in her arms. 'Look who's just woken up,' she says. She's heavily pregnant, and Adam puts a protective hand on her stomach. She kisses Adam, and he ruffles the head of the little boy she's holding. A shot of hot jealousy streaks through me. I can remember Adam doing that to Joe. We were going to have the big family together and that never happened. I will *not* allow him to have this future with Emily.

I jerk away.

'No,' I say to Malachi. 'This is *not* how it's meant to be.'

Chapter Twenty-Eight

Two Days till Christmas

Emily

After Joe, Livvy and Adam had left, Emily poured herself a stiff drink and stared at the Christmas tree, whose sparkling white lights seemed to be mocking her. She had looked forward to this Christmas as an opportunity to put the past behind them; for her and Adam to take their first steps together in their new life. To think that a short few weeks ago, she had imagined she and Adam would be living together. Now their plans lay in ruins.

Emily took herself to bed sadly, but sleep wouldn't come. She tossed and turned all night trying to decide what she should do.

If it was just a question of Livvy having Adam, Emily would tell her to piss off. But because of Joe she couldn't. Emily had never seen him act the way he had tonight. Even when Livvy died, he had barely shed a tear.

Emily stared into the darkness, knowing that it wasn't personal. Joe liked her, she was sure of that, but to him she'd been a new mum, welcome while the old one was dead. Now his actual mum was miraculously alive again,

Joe had no need for Emily. For him, it was a perfectly sensible conclusion.

She loved Adam with all her heart and wanted to spend the rest of her life with him. But if Joe didn't want her there, she knew Adam could never be happy. Joe had to come first.

Emily was awake so long, she ended up watching a steely dawn break over the snowy rooftops. The world looked cold and lonely as she stared out at it; she felt more alone than she ever had in her entire life. But as a pale sun rose in the sky she'd made her decision. With a heavy heart, she picked up the phone to her dad. It was early but she knew he'd be up.

'Dad?' she said, a catch in her voice – how did she begin to tell him this particular story? 'There's been a change of plan. Can I come and spend Christmas with you?'

'Is everything all right?' He was instantly solicitous.

'Not really,' she said. 'I'll explain when I get to you. Are you sure it's OK for me to come?'

'Of course it is,' Dad said.

'And I won't be cramping your style?' Emily had lost track of which of his lady friends Dad would be seeing on the day.

'Ah, actually, you have me there.' Dad sounded a bit crestfallen. 'I've been blown out, can you believe it?'

Emily laughed. 'So we can be miserable together then,' she said.

'I won't be miserable if you're there, sweetheart,' said Dad, which nearly made her howl.

Once she had put the phone down she spent a couple of fruitless hours on the internet looking for a cheap train ticket. This late in the day, it was going to be damned difficult. Ideally she'd have liked to buy a ticket for today, but there weren't any to be had. It would cost her a fortune, but at least Dad would be glad she was there.

After Emily had booked her ticket, she felt a bit better. Even if it wasn't what she'd wanted, at least she'd made her decision.

Then, knowing it was his last day in the office, Emily texted Adam.

Lunch? she suggested. She had to talk to Adam and she wanted it to be somewhere neutral away from Joe and Livvy.

12.30? The text came pinging back. No kisses. Adam always sent kisses in his texts. Joe must have told him what he was after.

Followed by a *You OK?*

No, Emily wasn't. Her heart was breaking. She was planning to walk away from the love of her life, and she didn't think she'd ever be OK again.

Livvy

Adam is still not speaking to me after last night. According to him, it is my fault that Joe went off like that. It is on the tip of my tongue to say if Adam had only behaved himself, then Joe wouldn't have learned his dad was a cheat. But I don't think there's any point having a row about it.

Joe is monosyllabic on the way home. He just mutters something about needing to talk to Caroline, and then goes to shower off. Adam and I look at one another in concern. How on earth is all this affecting him?

But when he comes down to say goodnight, he gives me an awkward hug, and says, 'I like you being back, Mum.'

'I like being back,' I say.

'You will stay now won't you?' he says. And my heart lurches. I want to say yes, but I'm anxious that Adam is

311

never going to agree to it, and I've only got two days left to persuade him.

'If I can,' I say lightly. 'It's up to your dad.'

'Dad?' says Joe, and the look of hope in his eyes makes my heart contract. For the first time, I wonder about the wisdom of what I'm doing. I was so sure that I would find a way of making it work. But what happens if Adam doesn't give us both what we want? Where will that leave Joe then? Will I have made things worse for him? I kill the thought; I can't let it take hold of me, or I won't be able to do this.

Adam gives me a look, which I interpret as, Thanks for nothing, but just says, 'We'll see,' which seems to be enough for now.

When we're alone, he says, 'I hope you're satisfied.'

'Not really,' I say, and I mean it. That wasn't what I had intended at all. 'I didn't mean for tonight to happen. I'm sorry.'

'I know,' says Adam sadly. 'You usually are. You can sleep in the spare room tonight. I'll find you a towel and toothbrush.'

He doesn't even give me a kiss goodnight, but just leaves me to it.

And that's it. Our first night together under the same roof, and we're further apart than ever.

Adam

I'm having a manic last morning at work, which to be honest is a relief. It means I can stop thinking about the godawful mess my life is in, or the ominous text that Emily has sent me. There is only one thing to talk about. And I don't know how to resolve it and keep us all happy.

Joe clearly wants Livvy and me to get back together. Livvy

clearly wants the same. And I . . . don't. If I stay with Emily, Joe gets hurt. If I stay with Livvy, Emily does. No one can come out of this completely happy, apart perhaps from Joe. How my sins have come back to haunt me.

Emily and I meet up in our favourite café, by the river, overlooking the Christmas market. There's still snow on the ground and the streets are bustling with cheerful shoppers. Inside the café, Christmas music is blaring out, and there's a light-heartedness among the clientele that we're not sharing. It's two days before Christmas and my life is turning to dust.

I kiss Emily as she comes to the table with a latte, and try not to notice that she slightly pulls away. Not a good start.

'So,' I say.

'So,' says Emily. She looks tired, and has clearly been crying. She twists a paper napkin in her hand, looking so sad it breaks my heart.

'We're in a pickle aren't we?' She gives a small taut smile.

'That's one way of putting it,' I say.

'Adam.' She rubs her eyes, which are red. I'd rather be anywhere than here right now, having this conversation. 'I've been up half the night worrying.'

'Me too,' I say.

There's an ominous pause.

'There is no good way out of this,' she says. 'But when Joe came to see me he asked me for one thing for Christmas.'

'Which is?' My heart is sinking. Please don't say it, I think, please.

'I have to go, Adam.' Her voice cracks, but she waves away my attempt to hold her hand. 'Joe wants you to be a family again, and we owe it to him to give him that chance.'

'Oh Emily,' I say. She's made the decision for me, one I

am too cowardly to make myself. And yet I know she's right.

'So,' Emily says, wiping her eyes and pulling herself together. 'I've booked a train for Christmas Eve to Dad's. Don't try to stop me or I won't be able to do this.'

And she gets up and walks out of my life. I feel like my world has shattered into pieces.

Chapter Twenty-Nine

Livvy

Adam has gone to work, and Joe is seeing Caroline, so I'm alone in the house for the first time. It's nice being back here properly, with a body to wander around the house in, and remind myself of why I love it so much. It was my haven while I recovered from the miscarriages that nearly broke me before Joe came along. And in the early days of our marriage, the place I felt happiest. But oh, dear God, the mess two men living alone make. I decide I will clean up for Adam. It's clear Emily hasn't bothered.

Having cleaned the kitchen floor, and cupboards, I move on to the bathroom where I spend ages scrubbing the bath. Has Adam even cleaned it once in the last year? It doesn't look like it. After a couple of hours, I am bored rigid. I had forgotten how mind-numbingly tedious housework could be. No wonder I turned to drink. In desperate need of something interesting to do, I wander back downstairs to make a cup of tea and admire my handiwork in the kitchen, wondering what to do next.

A drawback of not being a ghost any more, one I hadn't considered, is that I can't follow Adam to work. I know he's meeting Emily because I quickly filched a look at his phone when he was in the shower. But I can't turn up and find out what they are talking about. Bummer. Who knew there were advantages to being dead? Even so, the tone of Emily's message and Adam's miserable-looking response have given me hope. Maybe she's going to do the right thing.

'And what might that be?' says a voice in my ear.

'Jeez, Malachi, how did you get in? And get off that work surface, I've just cleaned it.'

'Through the cat flap.'

'We don't have a cat flap,' I say.

Malachi shrugs. 'You have a cat flap, and I came through it.'

'Why are you here?' I ask. I'm not up for a nagging, but I'm bound to get one.

And sure enough, it starts.

'So how's it going for you, then?' says Malachi. 'You succeeded in driving Emily away yet?'

'That's not what I'm doing,' I say. 'I'm just reminding Adam he should be with me.'

'Ah, is that it,' says Malachi. 'You've got everything the wrong way round, but that's not why you haven't passed over yet.'

'Isn't it? So why am I still here then?'

'Because you cheated and broke the rules,' says Malachi.

'I've got a second chance and I'm taking it,' I say.

'So you keep saying,' says Malachi. 'Did it ever occur to you to ask Letitia how often this kind of thing has worked out, hmm?'

I ignore him. And he jumps off the table, and vanishes through a cat flap in our back door, which I swear wasn't there before.

He's left me with an uncomfortable feeling. Basically I took Letitia's potion without questioning anything too hard.

And now, with Adam not exactly playing ball, I'm wondering if that was wise. Maybe I should have paid more attention. Perhaps I should pay her another visit . . .

Adam

I come home to an empty house. Livvy has mysteriously gone out, leaving a note to say she'll be back later. Joe is also out, at Caroline's. It's not quite the last day at work before Christmas I was anticipating. I had planned to come home, maybe go down the pub with Emily, or sit indoors wrapping my presents. The turkey Emily bought is defrosting in the fridge, and I still have to buy vegetables for Christmas Day. I have never felt less like celebrating.

The heating is off, and the house looks different. Livvy seems to have gone into manic mode, rearranged the furniture and cleaned everything. It reminds me painfully of the days when she'd be trying to atone for a lapse and she'd have a cleaning spree to make amends. I'd come home and she'd have cooked me a lovely meal, to say sorry for all the nights when she just bought takeaways. The very thought of those meals makes me feel immensely sad.

I turn the Christmas tree lights on. But whereas before it had cheered me up with its sparkle, now it seems to have lost its shine, reminding me instead of everything that I've lost. There are presents for Joe, me and Felicity from Emily under the tree. Hers from me are still sitting in my bedroom cupboard waiting to be wrapped up. They include the ring I had been planning to give her on Christmas Eve. I was so excited when I bought it for her, a month ago, and now she's gone. How has it come to this?

Suddenly I'm furious with Livvy. She made my life hell when she was alive and then she died and I felt terrible, but I also welcomed the chance to be happy again. And she's taken that chance from me. Whatever happens now, I'm not sure I'll ever be able to forgive her. And how can our marriage work with that between us?

Emily

Emily left Adam and walked through the hordes of cheerful last-minute Christmas shoppers feeling overwhelmed with misery. But she knew she'd done the right thing. Joe needed his mum, and Emily couldn't and didn't want to take her place. She hoped that somehow Livvy and Adam could find happiness again.

Emily wasn't paying any attention to where she was going, but she found herself wandering to the green. Her feet seemed to have taken themselves there of their own accord. Before she knew it, she was standing outside Felicity's front door.

She might as well face the music and try to see if Felicity would let her in. Emily liked Felicity. She felt as though they had something in common, and it had comforted Emily to have a mother figure back in her life, particularly one who'd got on so well with Dad.

Felicity opened the door, before Emily could ring the bell.

'I saw you from the living-room window,' she said.

'Can I come in?'

Felicity sniffed, and then said, 'I suppose.'

Emily nearly laughed at her haughty demeanour. It really didn't suit her.

'I won't stay long,' said Emily. 'I've just come to say, I'm sorry that you had to find out about Adam and me the way you did, and also to say goodbye.'

'Goodbye?' Felicity looked genuinely startled.

'Yes, I'm going to my dad's tomorrow, to spend Christmas with him. I thought it was best.'

'What about Adam and Joe?'

'Joe needs his mum. So I've told Adam it's over.'

Felicity looked quite shocked now. 'I wasn't expecting that,' she said.

'Me neither,' Emily said. 'But I think it's for the best.'

To her surprise, Felicity said, 'I'm sorry it's ended like this.'

'I am too,' Emily said. 'And I'm sorry we weren't honest with you before. We just didn't know how to tell you. If it hadn't been for the accident, Adam would have left Livvy you know. We're not proud of what we did. But it happened, and I'm not sorry that it did, because being with Adam made me really happy. But I can't stand in the way of what Joe needs. I hope you can understand.'

Felicity listened in silence, and then sighed.

'It's not what you want to hear, that the son-in-law you love has cheated on your daughter, but I do understand. Livvy wasn't easy to live with, and you can't help who you fall in love with. I don't blame you, Emily. It's rough luck, all of it.'

She gave Emily a hug. Emily hugged her back, and then left. There was nothing more to say.

'Take care, Emily,' Felicity said, 'it's been lovely having you as a surrogate daughter. Even for this short time.'

As Emily walked sadly down the path, Felicity suddenly came running after her.

'I almost forgot,' she said, thrusting a parcel in Emily's hand. 'Happy Christmas, Emily. I'll miss you.'

319

Chapter Thirty

Emily

Emily was thinking hard and furiously as she packed to go to Dad's. She didn't think she could possibly live here now. It was going to be too hard seeing Adam and Joe. In order for her to do this properly, she needed to move right away.

Emily loved her flat. She'd had good times living here in the gap between Graham and Adam. It was where she had come to salvage the pieces and pick herself up after her marriage went wrong, and she had loved the independence and sense of freedom it gave her. But since Emily had met Adam, it had just been a place to tread water. At this moment the flat meant nothing to her if Adam was out of her life. After Christmas, Emily decided, she was going to put it on the market and move somewhere new. She still had time to go on her current IT contract, so at least she didn't have to change jobs as well. Maybe she'd be able to commute in from Dad's for a bit, though the journey would be hideous. It was the only thing she could reasonably think to do.

At least Dad was pleased Emily was coming home. He hadn't planned to let her know that he was going to be alone at Christmas, but was delighted she would be there instead. He hadn't asked too many questions, for which Emily was grateful, although thanks to the fact that he had apparently been skyping Felicity – which would have amused Emily immensely at any other time – he knew that it was something to do with Livvy. Emily had got the impression during their last chat that Dad thought she was making a mistake. Maybe he was right, but Emily didn't see what else she could do.

Emily's phone pinged. A text from Adam, asking how she was. He'd been texting her all day and she'd been ignoring him. She couldn't afford to talk to him. If she cracked now, she didn't think she'd be able to leave.

So Emily carried on packing, and trying to ignore the fact that her world was imploding, she'd lost the man she wanted to marry, and didn't feel like she'd ever be happy again.

Livvy

I realize as I approach the theatre that I have no idea how to get into Underworld, now I have my body again. But luckily I still seem able to see my ghostly friends, and there's my pal Robert of the dressing gown and slippers, nipping in for a quick snifter.

'How are things?' I say.

'Well look at you all alive and everything,' he says.

'Oh, you can tell?'

'Of course I can tell. You're solid,' he says. 'I expect you want me to let you into Underworld?'

'That would be great,' I say.

'Just follow me,' he says. 'You'll be wanting Letitia I expect.'

'How did you know?'

He looks me up and down.

'Everyone does, eventually,' he says, 'who does what you've done. They all come back to Letitia.'

Ouch. That doesn't sound good.

'I went to Zandra's latest reading,' he says as I follow him into the theatre, 'I think she's losing her touch. What on earth did you do to her? My son was there and had no idea I was, and Zandra didn't dare talk to any of us.'

'Me? Nothing,' I protest. Robert raises an eyebrow. 'Well maybe a little something. She held a seance, and it didn't quite go as planned.'

'Thanks for nothing,' he says grumpily. 'Good luck with Letitia, by the way.'

'What do you mean?' I'm suspicious now. Why does he keep talking about Letitia?

'There are lots of us who've been there, love,' he says. 'It never bloody works.'

My heart sinks.

'What do you mean?'

'Those of us who had the balls to try her potion and got the you-only-have twenty-four-hours-to-save-the-universe spiel.'

'Well, yes,' I say, feeling pretty stupid.

'Thing is, Letitia's selling an impossible dream. We only get to hang around to sort stuff out with our loved ones. And just going back to your old life and carrying on as normal doesn't work. But like everyone else you've probably gone and tried to do just that as if nothing's happened. Can't be done, I'm afraid.'

That's so exactly on the nail I feel sick. He can't be right. I don't want him to be. It's Christmas, surely I can make this work?

He stands by the broom cupboard.

'Are you coming with me, or what?' he says. 'You need me to get through the door.'

Robert grasps hold of me impatiently. His touch is cold and goes right through me. I feel a rather uncomfortable rush, and this time instead of a sensation of being pulled through water, it's like I'm being attacked by sharp shards of ice. I'm relieved when I'm out the other side.

Underworld seems incredibly busy. A few people wave, but most of them ignore me. I go up to the bar, to find DJ Steve, but he's not there. Lenny looks at me and whistles. 'Letitia really worked her magic on you,' he says. As I'm standing there, I'm aware of silent whispers all around me.

'Ouch, another idiot who's been had by Letitia.'

'Mistake, big mistake.'

'Someone should have told her . . .'

'Someone should have told me what?' I ask.

I have a horrible feeling in the pit of my stomach. Maybe I have made an error of judgement. God, I'll be cross if Malachi turns out to be right.

'It'll end in tears, dearie,' says a friendly-looking granny.

'What should I know?' I say.

'Letitia didn't mention it then?' says Robert, popping up beside me again. 'If it doesn't work, you're stuck in limbo forever, like this. Why do you think so many of us come here?'

Adam

The door slams and Joe comes in. He looks happy.

'Where's Mum?'

'I don't know. Out.'

'Oh,' Joe looks disappointed. 'I'd like to go sledging again.'

'We could still go,' I say, though I don't feel much like it.

'Nah, it's OK,' says Joe. 'Let's wait for Mum.'

He goes to turn the TV on, and I am left staring out of the kitchen window, thinking about Emily.

I can't believe I've lost her. I should have fought harder for Emily, tried to persuade her there was another way to solve this. But I keep coming back to the fact that Emily has done the right thing. For Joe's sake, there is no other way. And I will do anything for my son.

I keep checking my phone, but Emily hasn't called. I really want to call her, but she asked me very specifically not to, before she left. Instead I go and join Joe on the sofa. He's watching *Come Dine with Me*.

'Emily should go on this,' he says. 'She likes cooking.'

'Yes, she does,' I say sadly.

'She's a much better cook than Mum,' Joe continues. 'Maybe she could come back and give Mum some lessons.'

'I don't think that will work, Joe,' I say, trying to picture a scenario with Livvy and Emily in the kitchen that doesn't involve sharp knives.

'I didn't give Emily my present,' says Joe.

'I didn't give her mine,' I say.

'She should have presents, shouldn't she?' Joe says. 'Otherwise she might be sad. I wouldn't want Emily to be sad.'

'I think Emily probably is sad, Joe,' I say.

'Because she's not going to be my new mum?' Joe looks interested.

'That – and because of me,' I say.

'She'll find someone,' says Joe. 'She's pretty. Pretty girls always have boyfriends.'

Of course Joe has no idea what has actually happened with me and Emily.

'I'm sure you're right, Joe,' I say.

'But you're not sad are you, Dad?' he continues. 'Because you've got Mum back.'

324

'It's a bit more complicated than that,' I say.

'Why is it complicated?' Joe looks curious. 'You and Emily are still friends.'

'We can't really be friends now, though, Joe. Not with Mum here too.'

'Why not?' Joe still seems puzzled.

Because I'm in love with Emily, and not your mum, I want to say, but I actually say, 'Mum might not like it.'

'Oh,' says Joe. 'But she wanted to come back home, and now she's here I thought everything would go back to the way it was.'

I wish it was that simple. Life can never go back to the way it was; but for Joe's sake I will try.

My phone pings. There's a text from Emily, and when I read it, I feel a blow to my soul.

'We should take Emily our presents,' says Joe.

'I don't think that's a good idea,' I say. 'Best leave it.'

'We can give them to her after Christmas,' says Joe. 'When we see her at swimming.'

'No Joe, we won't,' I tell him. 'If Mum and I are to be together, we can't see Emily any more. Besides,' I reread my phone message, just to make sure I'm right, 'Emily's going away, and she's never coming back.'

Joe's Notebook

Emily is going away.

Dad says forever.

That is bad.

Mum is happy.

Dad is sad.

Emily is sad.

I wish everyone could be happy.

I wish I could have two mums.

But I can't.

Now I will look at Libra and think of Emily.

I wish she didn't have to go away.

Christmas Future

'May I borrow you for a moment?' Malachi appears strolling across the bar. The other ghosts in Underworld part in hushed awe as he wanders between them. He looks out of place here, but I get the feeling everyone is just a tiny bit frightened of him. This is just what I don't need right now. I've never seen him at Underworld before; what is he doing here?

'Why?' I'm scanning the bar for Letitia, but I can't see her anywhere.

'Letitia can wait,' says Malachi. 'I need to show you something.'

With that I am transported to my mother's house, I am guessing in the future, as it appears to have had a makeover and the lounge has been redecorated. The calendar is showing it's Christmas Eve and she is singing carols at the piano, with – a man? Mum has a man? Mum always said she couldn't marry again after Dad. No one would match up to him, she said. But with a jolt, I realize that she's still young enough to find love if she wants it. And with another, I notice she's not with just any old man. I look closer. She's with Emily's dad.

His fine baritone contrasts with her lovely soprano. I sit and listen; they sound good together. They look good together. I think about how lonely Mum must have been since Dad died. Perhaps she needs to be with someone again. I wish it wasn't Kenneth, but . . .

Mum makes a mistake on 'O Come All Ye Faithful', and Kenneth gets it wrong too. They stop and giggle over it.

'I'm so happy,' says Mum, leaning against him.

'Me too,' says Kenneth massaging her neck – ew! – 'To think that we both thought that life and love had passed us by.'

'We've been so lucky to find it again,' Mum says. Her eyes fill with tears. 'You're the best thing to come out of losing Livvy. If Adam hadn't married Emily, I might never have known you.'

Pass the sick bucket. Mum and Emily's dad are together because *I'm* dead? That's just fantastic.

'So the point of this is?' I ask Malachi, who's looking abominably cheerful.

'To show you the world keeps turning without you,' says Malachi. 'It's not all about *you*, you know.'

And he wafts off in that annoying way he has, flicking his tail. And I'm back in Underworld again, wondering if I'm really on the right track.

Chapter Thirty-One

Emily

Two days before Christmas, and Emily was at the loosest of loose ends.

There was a text from Lucy: *You still on for drinks tonight?*

Oh shit, Emily had completely forgotten Lucy's annual Christmas drinks party. There'd been many a year Emily had stumbled out of Lucy's house worse for wear after a rollicking good evening. In pre-Adam, post-Graham days, Emily would have been the first one knocking on the door. But this year she certainly didn't feel like going.

Emily still hadn't told Lucy exactly what had been going on; it sounded way too nuts – it *was* way too nuts. Besides, Emily knew she wouldn't be able to talk to Lucy about Adam without blubbing, and she needed to hold herself together till she left. Emily looked at the text again. She really didn't want to spend the evening in a happy house, full of bonhomie and good cheer, but she sure as hell didn't want to stay here staring at four walls and feeling damned sorry for herself either. So she texted back, *Sure, looking forward to it.*

She roused herself from her misery, and got glammed up

to go out. And temporarily, the putting on of warpaint and sparkly nail polish did make her feel a bit better. Oh well, Emily thought as she tried on a succession of outfits, I may as well get ratted tonight. Maybe it was even time to start project Get Adam Out of her Head and attempt to pull.

In truth that was unlikely to happen at Lucy's drinks party, where most of the men were taken and those that weren't were desperate. And really, she knew as she applied bright scarlet lipstick to give her courage, she was no more likely to attempt to pull than fly to the moon. She just wanted Adam – the one person she couldn't have.

Still, it was good to get out of the flat and better than sitting round moping for the evening. For about half an hour it even felt fun to go and have drinks with semi-strangers, and smile and sparkle, and say, 'Yes, really looking forward to Christmas, and you?' pretending her life was brilliant and happy, and not the hideous parallel universe she had been inhabiting since Livvy arrived home.

Luckily Lucy didn't have time to chat, or she'd have noticed something wrong. But much to Emily's relief she was too busy playing the cheerful hostess to ask awkward questions. Even so, the longer Emily stayed, the worse she felt. She envied her friend her happy home life. An unwelcome stab of jealousy overcame her and she decided she had to leave. She didn't want to become bitter like Livvy.

So with a flurry of air kisses and 'Merry Christmases' and a slightly disappointed, 'Oh can't you stay longer?' from Lucy, Emily fled into the night. She'd drunk more than she'd intended to and the effects hit her as soon as she walked into the cold. Knowing it was foolish, but unable to stop herself, she felt she had to go to Adam's house one last time. Emily had no intention of knocking on the door, but she just wanted to stand there quietly saying goodbye to the man and the place she loved.

When she arrived, the temptation to ring on the doorbell was overwhelming, but Emily knew she had to resist it. If she saw Adam now all her resolve would melt away. Instead she stood in the snow, looking at the pretty little house she had thought was going to be her home, tears streaming down her cheeks.

The front door opened – shit, that was the last thing Emily wanted – she couldn't face Adam now. But it wasn't Adam, it was Joe putting the rubbish out, and despite Emily's attempt to shrink back into the shadows, he spotted her.

'Emily,' said Joe as if he'd been expecting to see her. 'Dad says you'd gone away.'

'Tomorrow,' Emily said. 'I'm going tomorrow.'

'But you will be back?' Joe said.

'No, Joe, I don't think I will,' Emily said.

'Can't we be friends any more?' He looked crestfallen.

'I will always be your friend, Joe, but I have to go away, and it's better for everyone if I don't come back.'

'Oh,' said Joe. 'Is this because of Mum?'

'Yes,' Emily said, 'I'm afraid it is.'

'You look sad,' said Joe.

'I am sad,' said Emily, 'but I'll get over it.'

'Shall I get Dad?' Joe said. 'He's sad too.'

'Better not,' Emily said. ''Bye Joe. Have a lovely Christmas.'

'Thank you for my Christmas present,' said Joe, and that finished Emily off. She stumbled into the night before she could change her mind.

Livvy

I am picking my way through the crowd to find Letitia. It's weird being in here, now I'm solid again. Everyone else seems ethereal, and when they pass me, I get a shock of cold. Is this what it was like for Adam and Joe when I came close to them? I find it slightly unnerving. There are so many people here tonight, the cold shocks keep coming, and after a while they make me feel faintly sick. I'm also starting to panic. No one seems to have seen Letitia tonight. What if she's vanished completely? How will I get any answers then?

I finally track her down in another back room – this place is a warren, and much bigger than I had realized. She's sitting at a table, drinking rum. I suddenly feel a bit stupid. I've taken her potion without asking any obvious questions, so focused on getting back to Adam I didn't think about anything else.

'Hey girl, look at you!' she says in a drawl. 'Looking good, girl, looking good.'

'Thanks,' I say. 'You too.'

'So what can I do for you?' she asks, giving me a shrewd look. 'You have the air of a lady looking for answers.'

'I am rather,' I say. I sit down. 'It's just . . . well, I didn't really ask. What actually happens if I don't succeed, and Adam doesn't fall back in love me by Christmas Eve?'

'You should have asked that first.'

'I know, I'm an idiot,' I say. 'Well?'

She shrugs. 'You get to stay here, with us.'

'What, forever?'

'Pretty much,' she says. 'You've got one shot to sort your life and death out. You fail, that's your problem.'

'But that's outrageous!' I say. 'You should have warned me. I might not have done it.'

'If you remember, I did warn you. But did you listen?' I don't answer, and she smiles silkily.

She has me there. I'd have probably glossed over that bit

and gone ahead anyway. Letitia shrugs her shoulders. 'No one ever does.'

'So what do I do?' I say. 'Adam doesn't seem too happy to have me back.'

'You'd better go and win him over then,' is Letitia's unhelpful response. 'You've got till midnight tomorrow night.'

She dismisses me as if I'm of no concern, and I walk away from her in a daze. Bugger, bugger, bugger. I am seriously rattled and in strong need of a drink.

'Can I still drink your shots, like this?' I ask DJ Steve, who I find propping up the bar.

'Technically, you're still dead,' says Steve, 'so I guess so. You're welcome to try.'

I have a vodka and Coke to see how it goes. It doesn't feel as if I've drunk anything, but there's a burning sensation in my throat and I get a heady rush. That'll do.

'I'll have another, please.'

'Being alive that good, huh?'

'Better,' I say, thinking of how unhappy I've made Adam. 'Why didn't you tell me I could get stuck here?'

'You never asked.' Steve shrugs. 'Another?'

I know I shouldn't, but I'm not ready to face Adam just yet. One more drink can't do any harm.

Adam

'I've just seen Emily,' Joe tells me, when he comes in from putting the bins out, as if it is only of passing consequence. 'She said Happy Christmas.'

'What?' I leap up. 'Where is she now?'

'Gone,' says Joe.

I run to the front door, but there's no sign of her. Just

an empty street and softly falling snow. I could cry from frustration. If I'd had a chance to speak to her, I wouldn't have been able to let her go. Sod the consequences.

'What did she say?' I ask.

'That she's going away. I think she's sad.'

'I know she is,' I say.

'You're sad too aren't you?'

'Yes, Joe, I am.' To put it mildly.

'Emily says we won't see her any more.' He looks thoughtful, as if he is trying to puzzle something out.

'No, we won't,' I say.

'That makes me sad,' says Joe. 'It's because of Mum, isn't it?'

'What's because of Mum?' Suddenly a whirlwind pours into the room, in the shape of Livvy, but I get the impression she isn't alone. Someone I can't see bumps into me, and a lamp goes crashing to the floor.

'It's Christmas,' Livvy hiccups, 'so I brought some friends home.'

'Dead friends?' I say. Dead friends who've just ramped the volume on the CD up high and are playing Mariah Carey at a thousand decibels.

'They might be.' Livvy squints at me. ''S that a problem?'

'You're drunk,' I say flatly.

'Oh come on, Adam, live a little. I am, ha, that's funny.' She staggers about the place. 'I used to be dead and now I'm not, I'm celebrating.'

She puts her arms around me, though I try to pull away.

'All I want for Christmas is you,' she purrs. 'Don't be such a spoilsport. Everyone gets a little drunk at Christmas.'

'You always do,' says Joe.

'Joe, that's unkind,' says Livvy, peering drunkenly at him.

'It's true, Mum. You always drink. And then you get drunk. And then you fall asleep, and forget about me.'

'I don't,' she says. 'Don't be silly. There's nothing wrong with enjoying yourself.'

'Except the way you do it,' says Joe. He looks so upset to see his mum like this, I'm furious. She's only been back a day and already she's reverting to type.

'You really are the most selfish person I know, Livvy,' I spit out. 'Why the hell did you come back and ruin our lives?'

'But, darlings,' she says. 'I'm so happy to see you both.'

She bursts into tears and Joe allows himself to be hugged by her, but he looks so uncomfortable, I could throttle her.

'Right, I want your friends out of here, now!' I say, as the chandelier starts swaying ominously and doors bang randomly round the house. Lights keep flashing on and off, and there's clearly an argument going on about the music as someone has switched to the Stone Roses. How on earth am I going to get them all out of here?

'OK, folks, you heard the man, party's over,' Livvy says. 'Happy Christmas.'

To my surprise they take notice, the front door blows open, there's a whirl of activity, and then it slams shut and Livvy is the only one left.

'All alone with my two lovely boys.' Livvy grins beatifically, her earlier tears forgotten. 'It's going to be the best Christmas ever.'

Then she slides gracelessly and drunkenly to the floor.

Chapter Thirty-Two

Emily

Emily was booked on the 7 p.m. train that evening to Rugby. Dad lived in a village not too far away, and had promised to pick her up from the station. It was the cheapest train Emily could get at short notice, and she was deeply regretting her choice. It meant she had the whole day sitting staring at her empty flat. She didn't think she could stand it.

Or the fact that Adam kept ringing her even though he'd promised not to.

In the end Emily switched her phone off.

She had to get out of the flat, where the walls were pressing in too much, so she went for a walk and wandered the streets, going to favourite spots that Adam and she had been to together. One of their favourite places had been the river; Emily walked down to the towpath which led to a park where they often had picnic lunches in the summer.

It was freezing today and there weren't many people about; most normal people would be out celebrating or getting ready for tomorrow. There were still patches of snow on the ground, and the greyness of the sky was threatening more. Emily tried hard to summon up a picture of what it looked like here on a sunny day and failed miserably: a metaphor for her life.

She even went to the leisure centre. If she hadn't taken up swimming she'd never have met Adam. Was she sorry that she had? Right now, Emily was so heartsick, she wasn't sure whether it had been worth the pain. All she knew was that she was never, ever going to get over Adam.

As she walked back to town she spotted a black cat following her. She felt sure she'd seen it before. There were lots of strays around here, but this one was behaving oddly. It kept running across Emily's path, as if it was trying to tell her something.

It seemed to want to lead Emily to one of the many riverside cafés – typical that it would be one she and Adam were particularly fond of as it had a lovely view of the bend in the river, and in the summer you could watch the rowers going past. Part of her didn't want to go in and be reminded of such good times. But Emily was cold and miserable, and the cat seemed incredibly persistent. Suddenly it seemed like a good idea. She bought herself an Americano and went towards the table she and Adam had always used to sit at.

When she got to the table there was someone sitting there already, the last person she wanted to see.

'I don't believe this,' she said. Her final day here, and someone was playing a huge joke on her.

'Livvy, what the hell are you doing here?' Emily said.

Livvy

I had to leave the house this morning. I'm in disgrace and Adam and Joe aren't speaking to me. Why do I always do this to myself? It's like I've got a self-destruct button. Here

I am with my lucky break second chance, and I'm stuffing it all up again.

'Aha, at last, the penny drops,' Malachi leaps up on the fence next to me, looking smug as ever.

Just what I want.

'There's no need to crow,' I say.

'I have to get my kicks somehow,' says Malachi.

'What do you want now?' I say wearily, I'm fed up of him following me around and telling me what to do.

'Go to the river café and find out,' he says, jumping off the fence and vanishing. I'm still disconcerted by him doing that.

I look around me. I've got no money, I'm wearing Adam's borrowed clothes. Apparently he took all mine to the charity shop. You don't imagine that when you come back from the dead – that you won't have any clothes to wear. In fact there's a lot about coming back to life again that I hadn't factored in: I was here with no identity, since officially I'm still dead. If I did manage to get Adam back how on earth would we work that out? Knowing my luck I'd end up in jail for fraud like that canoe man.

Rooting around in his pockets, I scrabble together a fiver in coins. I've got nothing else to do, so I go to the café, get myself a latte and sit at a table by the window.

I've been there for about five minutes when I hear a voice I recognize instantly say, 'Livvy?', and Emily is standing before me. She looks gorgeous and young and vibrant. I haven't really twigged it till this moment. I'm nearly forty and she can only be in her early thirties. She can offer Adam so much more than I can, no wonder Adam chose her over me. My dreams of a happy reunion are all slipping away.

'Oh, it's you,' I say. Thanks a bunch, Malachi.

'Can I sit down?' she says.

I nod ungraciously.

'I wanted you to know I'm going away,' she tells me.

'I know, to see your dad for Christmas.'

'No, I'm moving for good,' says Emily. 'I'm going to sell my flat and go and live somewhere else.'

'Really?' I say, thinking, *result*. 'Can I ask why?' I'm surprised, I thought she'd fight harder for Adam. I would if I were her.

'Why do you think?' Emily says. 'For Joe of course. He wants you back, I can't stand in your way.'

Oh, that's not what I'm expecting. She's putting Joe before her own needs. I feel a prickle of guilt. That's what I should be doing, I'm his mother. Have I though? I've been so caught up in what I want, I've assumed Joe wants the same. Suppose he doesn't?

Emily sits and toys with her coffee.

'So you got what you want,' she says. 'You won. And I lost. You get to keep Adam after all.'

Right now, it doesn't feel much like a victory. I have a gnawing sense of guilt that my success has come at a huge personal price for Emily. She looks so unhappy and lost. Have I really done this to her? She doesn't deserve this, any more than I deserved to die. I try to dismiss the feeling, and remind myself she's the enemy.

'Thanks,' I say, 'I hope you have a lovely Christmas.'

'Yeah,' says Emily, 'I bet you do.'

She gets up to go. 'Try and deserve them, won't you?' she says. And then she leaves. I try to tell myself I've got what I want, that I've finally succeeded, but it feels hollow and empty.

'Got it in one.' The dark-haired woman who took my place at the seance has appeared from nowhere.

339

'Sorry?' I say. It's creepy having someone read your thoughts. I feel a bit of a pang as I think how often I did it to Adam when he was a ghost.

'You've been looking at this upside down,' says the ghost. 'But I think you know that now, don't you?'

'Who are you?' I ask.

'Can't you guess?' she says. 'I've been hanging around too, but I needed to make sure my husband and daughter were settled. That's what we do for the people we love. It's a sacrifice, and it takes courage, but it's what we must do in the end.'

'You're Emily's mum,' I say, feeling more than a little awkward.

'I am,' she says. 'And if you do the right thing, I can finally let her go.'

I take a deep breath. 'Thank you,' I say. 'You're right, and I'm sorry.'

'We all make mistakes,' says Emily's mum, 'it's what we do about them that counts.'

And with that she's gone, and I sit mulling it over for a while, staring out of the window, and then it hits me with sudden clarity. She's right. And Malachi's been right all along. I've been looking at this the wrong way round. I need to get back to Adam *now*.

Adam

Livvy has gone out again. God knows where. I managed to get out of her there's some underground bar for ghosts underneath the local theatre, where she had one too many vodkas. Apparently it's where all the ghosts at the seance came from, which seems no more unlikely than anything else happening right now. Even having ghosts partying in my house seemed normal.

Joe and I are trying to sort Christmas dinner out for tomorrow. I'm tackling the potatoes and Joe is peeling carrots. I don't think either of our hearts are in it.

'Is Emily ever coming back?' It's the hundredth time Joe's asked me that.

'No, I'm pretty sure she isn't,' I say, feeling leaden. I'm not sure I can bear it. Over and over again, it's like a litany in my head: Emily's gone.

'I didn't mean that to happen,' Joe says.

He gives me an awkward pat on the shoulder. How times change. This time last year, I was comforting him. Now it's the other way round.

'I know, Joe. It doesn't matter.'

Of course it matters hugely, but I don't want him blaming himself. In Joe's world it seems entirely reasonable that Emily and I could still be friends. I know I couldn't stand to be in the same room as her, and not be with her. Besides, Livvy wouldn't put up with it.

Joe looks very thoughtful.

'How can we get Emily to come back?' he asks.

'We can't, Joe,' I say.

'Oh, yes we can.' I start. Livvy is standing in the doorway.

'I've got it all wrong,' she says. 'All this time I thought I had been given a second chance to put things right with you two, by being back as a family again. But now I know I was barking up the wrong tree. I've had my chance. It's time to let you go.'

Joe looks perplexed.

'What do you mean, Mum?'

'I mean,' she says, 'my time with you was up a year ago. I've been kidding myself.'

'But Mum . . .' Tears rise in Joe's eyes. 'I want you here.'

'Oh Joe,' Livvy goes over to our son and holds his face

in her hands, 'you are the most precious thing in my life. I love you and I don't want to let you go, but I have to. It's the right thing to do.'

She kisses him on the top of the head, and says, 'But I will always be with you. Remember our special star? Every day and every evening, you look for that star, Joe, and know that I am looking out for you and always will.'

'Mum,' says Joe, 'oh Mum.' And he lets her hold him as he sobs his heart out.

I am staggered; I wasn't expecting this. And I'm touched; I know the sacrifice Livvy is making.

'Now dry your eyes, Joe,' she says eventually. 'You don't want Emily to go, do you?'

'No,' he says.

'Then we have to stop her leaving,' says Livvy.

Joe's Notebook

Mum says she's got things wrong.

She says she wants Dad to be with Emily.

And she has to go back.

To wherever she's been.

I am happy and sad at the same time.

I love my mum.

I miss my mum.

I wanted her back.

But then bad stuff happened.

It has been confusing.

But Mum says this is what she has come back to do.

So that's good.

Christmas Future

'So, finally she understands.' Malachi has just popped through the non-existent cat flap, while Adam frantically tries to text Emily. He doesn't seem to have noticed we have a black cat in our kitchen.

'There's no need to say I told you so,' I say. 'At least you got what you want.'

I think about the enormity of what I'm doing. I've taken Letitia's potion and now I'm going to be stuck in limbo forever, which is not something that is filling me with joy. But I know I've finally worked out the reason why I couldn't pass on in the first place, and at last I'm doing the right thing.

'Let me show you the benefit of your actions,' Malachi says, ignoring me.

We're back in the other house, the one that's bigger than this one. Emily is tucking two excited children into bed, a boy and a girl. They must be about two and four. The little boy looks a lot like Adam, and the girl like Emily. They're laughing as they put their stockings out.

'Are Granny Felicity, Grandad, Joe and Caroline coming tomorrow?' they ask as Emily tucks them in.

345

'Of course,' says Emily. 'It wouldn't be Christmas without them, would it? Now lights out.'

'Will Santa come soon?' they say.

'Sssh,' says Emily. 'Go to sleep. Santa only comes to good children.'

She carefully closes the bedroom door, where Adam is waiting for her. They smile conspiratorially at one another as they tiptoe down the stairs and start gathering presents to go in stockings.

Emily fetches some flour and puts it by the fireplace and makes footprints on the carpet. Adam eats the mince pie that the children have left for Santa and sips the sherry. With a pang I notice a picture of me with Joe on the fireplace. It feels good to know I won't be forgotten.

'It's silly but I'm so excited,' says Emily. 'Olivia was too little to join in the fun last year.'

Wait, they've named their daughter after me? I enjoy a small glow of warmth. It reassures me that somehow I'll be remembered. And I'm touched.

'Me too,' says Adam, and kisses her. 'It's going to be a perfect Christmas.'

Emily squeezes him.

'I love you so much,' she says.

'I love you too,' says Adam.

The scene fades and I find I am crying. For the first time I'm not jealous of Emily.

This is the way it has to be.

Chapter Thirty-Three

Christmas Eve

Adam

'This isn't some kind of sick joke, is it?' I say warily. I wouldn't put it past Livvy to say, 'Surprise! Just kidding.'

But she stares at me looking really unhappy.

'Do you think so little of me?' she says. She looks defeated and sad, the way she did when Joe was little and she was battling to get help for him against an often indifferent system.

'No, of course I don't.'

'But you don't love me any more, do you?'

I take a deep breath.

'Livvy, you're the mother of my child . . .'

I trail off, not quite knowing how to say what I must.

'But?'

'Oh Livvy,' I say, 'I know at the end everything got really messed up, but it wasn't all bad. We had such good times before it went wrong. And once upon a time, we were madly, foolishly in love and I'll always be grateful for that. It's just as much my fault as yours. If I'd been able to see you weren't coping, if I'd reached out more, maybe things would have turned out differently.'

'But they didn't, did they?' says Livvy sadly. 'I know I didn't make it easy, but I've never stopped loving you.'

'I know,' I say, 'and I will always love you too, Livvy. You gave me Joe. How can I ever be sorry about that? You're part of my life and always will be. But no, I'm not in love with you any more.'

Livvy exhales a shaky breath.

'I'm sorry,' she says. 'I'm sorry I didn't do the decent thing and die properly. I'm sorry I've come back and caused you all this trouble. I wanted to make things right between us, but all I've succeeded in doing is making things worse.'

She gives me a watery grin.

'I can't even get being dead right,' she continues. 'I should never have tried to find you again.'

'Oh Livvy, don't say that.' I take her into my arms and hold her tight. Really hold her, remembering the times we just used to hug and comfort each other on the tough days with Joe. 'I'm sorry too. I never meant to fall in love with Emily and hurt you. It just happened. I felt terrible about it, and then when you died, and you had sent me that text . . .' My voice trails off.

'That must have been really hard for you,' she says.

I nod. I feel choked up.

'I wanted so much to say sorry for all the pain I caused you. And I couldn't. And I felt like I'd let Joe down.'

'But if I hadn't died, you wouldn't have come back to me, would you?'

'No,' I say, 'I wouldn't.'

She pulls away from me, and dries her eyes.

'I think that's what I needed to hear,' she says. 'I pushed you away, Adam. My behaviour to you was appalling at times. It's more my fault than yours.' She takes a deep breath and goes on, 'So now we have to sort this out. I've one thing to do, and maybe this time I'll get it right.'

'Joe, have you any idea what time Emily's train is leaving?' I ask.

Joe shrugs his shoulders.

'Emily's dad might know,' I say, and give him a ring.

'Adam.' Kenneth sounds surprised to hear from me. 'Is everything all right?'

'I hope so,' I say. 'Emily's not answering her phone and I need to get hold of her. Do you know what time train she's getting.'

'I think she said she's getting a train at seven,' he says. 'She said she'll call me when she's on it. Do I take it from this that Emily might not be coming to me for Christmas after all?'

'With any luck,' I say. 'And if I manage to get her back here, you could come and join us.'

'And meet the delightful Felicity again? I wouldn't miss it for the world,' says Kenneth. 'I'm glad you two youngsters are trying to sort it out. I knew Emily was making a mistake.'

I check my watch; it's 5 p.m.

'We might just catch her before she leaves,' I say. She's still not answering her phone, but perhaps if we race round to her flat we'll make it in time. My heart is singing.

It's time to go and get the girl.

Emily

Emily arrived at the station in plenty of time. The meeting with Livvy had really shaken her up, and she decided she couldn't stay around a minute longer. The station was busy, and judging by the backpacks and suitcases most people were heading home for Christmas like she was. Emily pressed her Oyster card on the ticket barrier, but it didn't seem to be working.

'You're sure?' she asked the man at the gate.

'Sorry,' he said. 'You haven't got enough money on it.'

That was weird, Emily could have sworn she'd topped it up the other day.

Just as well she'd left early. Emily needed cash anyway, so she went out to the high street and drew some out. By the time she'd queued up behind four drunk lads on a Christmas pub crawl, Emily had missed her train to London. She stood waiting in the freezing cold for the next one, feeling very sorry for herself.

When the train finally pulled in, it was packed solid. Emily stood uncomfortably in a corner, leaning on her backpack. Everyone seemed cheerful, clutching bags of presents for the great Christmas exodus. Normally she'd have felt the same, but not today. In fact, Emily felt tempted to kill anyone who wished her a Happy Christmas, something plenty of them did.

The train was painfully slow, getting stuck at every red light between stations. At a couple of stops it waited with the doors open for no reason known to man. The guard apologized profusely, and the cheery people didn't care, but Emily was screaming with frustration. All she wanted to do was get away. Every mile away from Adam meant she couldn't change her mind.

Emily got off at Vauxhall, to change on to the Victoria underground line for Euston. But when she arrived on the platform it was to discover the Victoria line was suspended, and no one had thought to mention it till now. Now what?

'Should I get the bus or train?' she asked the man at the ticket barrier, who just shrugged his shoulders unhelpfully.

As it turned out Emily's ticket wouldn't let her through the barrier, so she had no choice but to get the bus.

She glanced at her watch: nearly 5.30. She still had an hour and a half. Barring any more mishaps, that should be enough time. The pavements had turned to grey slush, unlike the white sparkling snow at home, and Emily had to be careful not to slip as she ran for the first bus going into town and sank gratefully back into her seat. It seemed grossly unfair to be having such a rotten journey on top of everything else. Anyone would think someone didn't want her to get on that train . . .

Livvy

We arrive en masse at Emily's flat, and Adam marches up to the front door. The house looks dark and empty. She must have gone already, but Adam bangs on the door anyway.

'Emily, are you still there?' he calls. 'It's me, Adam. Can I come in?'

Poor Adam. As if I needed proof of how wrong I'd been, this would be enough to sway me. He's besotted by that girl, in a way he hasn't been by me for years. I was too blind to see it before.

'Glad you're finally getting your act together.' Malachi hops up on the garden wall beside me.

'You weren't a whole lot of help,' I say.

'And you didn't listen,' sniffs Malachi. 'You'd better get your skates on. She's not here. She'll be halfway to Euston by now.'

Adam is still banging fruitlessly on the door, as if he can't believe that Emily's gone.

'Adam, she's not here,' I say. 'We have to go to the station.'

It's an icy walk down there, and I'm seriously regretting getting my body back. Not only am I freezing, but I'm unglamorously dressed in Adam's T-shirt, hoody and Joe's trackies. I've had to borrow a pair of pumps Emily left behind and my feet are sopping wet. I'm likely to slip over any minute. At this rate I might end up heading back gravewards quicker than I thought.

We get to the station, puffed out and panicky. The next train is due any moment, and the one after isn't for half an hour. We have a nervous wait in the ticket queue, but miraculously the train comes in two minutes late, allowing us enough time to get our tickets, and leap on board, just as the whistle blows.

Adam attempts to ring Emily again, but her phone is switched off.

I'm beginning to get a gnawing ache of worry in my stomach. What if we don't succeed? Then I still don't get to stay with Adam, he doesn't get Emily and I shall be drinking in Underworld for eternity. I've had some laughs there, but I'm not sure I want that.

'Mum, thank you for doing this,' Joe says suddenly. 'I thought we could have you and Emily. But I was wrong.'

'We both were,' I say, 'but I'm glad I've got to spend more time with you. And I'm very proud of everything you're doing.'

'Are you?' Joe's eyes light up and he's off telling me about some astronomy programme he's been watching.

Whatever happens next, I've had some unexpected time with my son and I shall always be grateful for that.

Chapter Thirty-Four

Livvy

We none of us say much on the train. We're all clock-watching and worrying about getting to the station on time.

'Five forty-five,' says Joe helpfully as the train pulls out of the station. 'One hour and fifteen minutes to get to Euston.'

He keeps this up in a steady stream which gets more irksome as the train takes its time to speed up. When it does, I start to relax a bit more.

Even though I am worrying about the time, and about what happens next, if we find Emily, I also feel like a huge weight has been lifted off my shoulders.

For the whole of this past year, I thought I'd been given a fantastic opportunity to start my old life afresh. But now I know that's not why I'm here. Instead I've been given a chance to make amends with the people I love. It's not a chance everyone gets and I'm grateful. For once I have to do the decent thing and give Adam and Emily my blessing. I have to let go of everything that bound me to this earth, even Joe. And I know, looking at Adam and Joe together, seeing how well they understand one another now, they will be all right. And knowing the sacrifice Emily was prepared to make for Joe, I know that giving the man I love up to her is actually the best thing I can do.

'Are you sure you're OK with this?' Adam asks suddenly. And I smile reassuringly.

'Yes,' I say. 'I thought I wouldn't be, but I am.'

Because, although I wish it could be different, though I want to live my life again and differently, I can't. My time was up a year ago. It came to an abrupt end in a Lidl car park. It was horrendously bad luck, but it isn't Adam's fault or Emily's. And I can't condemn them to a life of unhappiness because I'm not here. I don't get to dictate from the grave how they live their lives. I thought I could, but that's not the way it works.

'Five fifty-nine,' says Joe as we reach Clapham Junction. We have sixty-one minutes to reach Emily.

'Come on train,' I say, as I used to when Joe was little and impatient on journeys. And I offer up a silent prayer: Malachi, if you're out there anywhere, please help us get there on time.

Emily

The bus turned out to be a massive mistake. Emily didn't have a clue where it was going, and the traffic was horrendous. In the end, she leapt off at Westminster, and raced through bright sparkling lights and crowds of shiny happy people to Charing Cross. She could get the Northern line from there. It was only six; she should still have time.

But somehow Emily managed to take a wrong turn, and ended up getting to Charing Cross at nearly 6.30. Her feet were damp and cold, the crowds were still huge, and there were more drunks about now. Could this journey get any worse? And didn't any of these smiley cheerful Christmas crowds have homes to go to? Emily had always imagined London was deserted on Christmas Eve.

She forced her way through the seething hordes, and did something she'd never done before, pushing her way on to the Tube past people who had been waiting longer than her. All sense of propriety was gone; Emily simply had to get on that train. She squeezed herself in beside three City types who were singing raucously and two office girls, sporting Santa hats and talking loudly about the party they were going to. Emily felt that she was in hell.

The Tube at least was quick, and spat her out at Euston at a quarter to seven. It was tight but she could still make it. Emily bowled her way up the escalators, but when she got to the ticket barrier, her ticket stubbornly refused to work. Emily stood and queued by the gate where a ticket inspector was standing. He was taking forever and Emily was frantic by the time he finally let her pass on to the teeming concourse where a group of carol singers stood in front of a brightly lit Christmas tree.

Her train was up on the board, and they were calling for passengers. She had five minutes, but the train was on platform 4, halfway across the station.

Emily started to run.

Adam

After a slow start our train seems to speed through most of the stops and we get to Vauxhall really quickly. We're intending to change there, but there's a problem on the Victoria line, so we stay on till Waterloo.

Emily still isn't answering my calls or texts. And the time is ticking away. It's gone 6.15 by the time we get to Waterloo. There's time, but only just, as Joe keeps reminding me, telling me precisely how many minutes to our train.

The three of us plough down the escalators to the Underground, frustrated by the number of gormless people standing in our way, singing and shouting. It's hot and crowded and nightmarish, and I can feel Joe struggling. Crowds make him claustrophobic.

We get on the platform and it's heaving. I stupidly hadn't twigged there'd be so many tourists in London for Christmas. I'd also thought most of the people heading out of town for the holidays would have gone already, but judging by the suitcases I am wrong. We have to let two trains go and there are so many people piling on the next one, the train is stuck in the station for ages.

'Twenty-five minutes,' says Joe. 'And it takes sixteen minutes on the Underground and five minutes to walk to the station.'

'Thanks, Joe,' I say, though that isn't helping. Only four minutes to spare.

Livvy squeezes my arm. 'It will be fine,' she says, 'we can still make it.'

I flash her a grateful smile, relieved she's on my side, and feeling weirdly comforted that for the first time in years we're actually working together. It reminds me that not everything about our relationship was bad, and I'm glad to have the opportunity to see her at her best.

'Six fifty,' Joe announces as we pull into Warren Street. 'Two minutes to Euston, five minutes to the station, we still have three minutes spare.'

'Not helping now, Joe,' I say between gritted teeth. My heart is pounding in my chest.

Joe looks puzzled.

'It's helpful to know,' I try to explain, 'not so good for my stress levels.'

We reach Euston and pour off in relief. I feel like I've got the wind at my back, and my feet are flying. Livvy and Joe are clearly struggling to keep up as I force my way through the frustratingly slow crowds. Don't any of them have trains to catch?

'Just go!' says Livvy. 'We'll catch up with you.'

And I am haring off, shoving my way up the escalators. Three sodding lots of escalators. And one of them's broken. Why do there have to be so many? I'm out of breath by the time I make it to the station concourse. I've probably pissed a lot of people off. But I don't care. All I know is the clock is ticking and I have to stop Emily getting on that train.

Chapter Thirty-Five

Emily

Emily was racing to the platform, out of breath, her chest tight and her legs aching, but she could see the train was there. Three minutes to go. She should just make it. The ticket inspector was slow, and took an age to look at her ticket – what was it with all these inspectors today? – before eventually clipping it and letting her through. Emily ran on to the platform at the exact minute the whistle blew. No, this couldn't be happening. The train wasn't due to leave for another two minutes. Emily legged it towards the doors but they shut in her face. She pounded furiously on them to try and get the guard to open them again but it was too late. The train was already pulling out of the station. She stood there frozen in disbelief. She couldn't have missed the damned thing, she couldn't.

Now what the hell was she going to do? She stood for about ten minutes, completely irresolute. Emily had no idea when the next train to Rugby was, but it was probably booked up. The ticket she'd bought was for a very specific time, and she probably wouldn't be allowed to use it on another train. She burst out into angry tears. At this rate it would be midnight before she got home, and God knew how much she would have to spend on a new ticket.

The barrier was opening up again. Emily marched up to give the ticket inspector a piece of her mind. If it hadn't been for him, she'd have got that train. But he seemed to have vanished. Great. Emily could have hit something in frustration. She could see from the boards that the next train was delayed, and when she got back to the concourse the queue at the ticket office was so crazy she couldn't quite face it. So instead she went to buy herself a coffee and stood disconsolately listening to the carol singers to consider her options.

She'd have to ring Dad at some point, to tell him she'd missed the train. Emily delved into the bottom of her backpack to get her phone. She'd shoved it down there so she wouldn't be tempted to ring Adam. Oh bloody hell. The battery had died. Did they even have public phones any more? Emily had no idea. She felt lost and lonely and wished she could be anywhere but here. The station was heaving and people were getting in her way as they had done all evening. After grumpily queueing up for her coffee, she then bit the bullet and made her way back towards the ticket office. Perhaps she could find some kind soul who'd let her borrow their phone. After all, even if Emily didn't feel the vibe, it *was* Christmas . . .

Adam

I scan the departure boards frantically. There it is, going from platform 4. I race towards the right, across the concourse, not caring who I mow down on my way. I speed down the gangway to the platform, I'm going to make it . . . there are still people going through. My lungs are bursting and my heart is hammering, but as I reach the ticket barrier the ticket inspector stops me short. I hear a whistle blow, and the train draws slowly out of the station.

I bend over, panting. My whole body hurts. Emily's gone. I've lost her.

I bang my fist against the railing in frustration. I was so close, but now it's too late. Livvy and Joe come racing up behind me, catching their breath.

'I didn't get there in time,' I say bleakly. 'I missed her.'

'Oh Adam,' says Livvy, and gives me a hug. It feels warm and comforting, the hug of a friend, not a wife.

'So that's it, I've lost her,' I say. I don't know what to do now. I have spent all my energy getting here, and now she's gone. I have never felt so bleak in my entire life.

'Come on,' says Livvy. 'Don't give up. Maybe you could drive up tomorrow instead.'

Weather permitting – they're predicting snow tonight – that's a good point, but it doesn't stop me feeling as if I've let Emily slip through my fingers.

'No point hanging round here anyway,' I say, and we head up to the main concourse. There are still hordes of people fighting to get on their trains, but it's hard to feel sympathy for them at this precise moment. I wish they'd all just bugger off out of my way.

We walk disconsolately back towards the Underground. I think Joe and Livvy feel just as let down as I am. I am so wrapped in misery, I don't notice at first that Livvy is tugging on my arm.

'Adam,' she says, with a catch in her voice.

'What?' I say irritably.

'Look,' she says.

And then the crowds part before us and miraculously Emily is standing there in front of me. She says, 'Oh,' as she takes in that I'm with Joe and Livvy. 'What are you doing here?'

360

'I thought I'd lost you,' I say, and then everything else is forgotten as we run into each other's arms.

Livvy

'So you did it,' a voice next to me says. 'Well done.'

It's a ticket inspector.

'I'm sorry, do I know you?' Who is this random stranger talking to me?

'Oh, sorry, I forgot.' The ticket inspector dissolves and Malachi is winding his way round my legs. 'As I was saying, well done. You did it.'

'Thank you. So, what happens now?' I say. 'Am I still stuck here for eternity? After all, I've clearly missed the boat with Adam.'

It feels good to have helped Emily and Adam, who are clinging to each other like limpets, but I'm not looking forward to spending the rest of eternity in Underworld. I mean I had some fun times and I enjoy flirting with Steve, but do I really want to spend the afterlife in Robert's company?

'Not exactly,' says Malachi. 'You sacrificed your needs for theirs, which negates the effect of Letitia's potion' – *now* he tells me – 'and now you have twenty-four hours' grace. You need to say your goodbyes. I'd start with Joe if I were you.'

'Mum, were you talking to a cat?' asks Joe.

'It's a long story,' I say.

'You have to go away now, don't you?' says Joe.

'Yes, I'm sorry but I do.'

'That makes me sad,' he says.

'Me too,' I say. 'And I'm sorry I don't get to see you all grown up, but I know you are going to be a fine young man one day, and you'll have Dad and Emily helping you all the way. Much better than your rubbish mum.'

'You're not a rubbish mum,' says Joe. 'You're my mum and you're brilliant. I'm glad I got to tell you. It's been bothering me.'

'I'm glad too,' I say, tears streaming down my face.

'I love you, Joe,' I say. 'I always will. Merry Christmas, Joe.'

'I love you too, Mum,' says Joe, words I never thought I'd hear my son say.

And then he hugs me, properly hugs me for the first time in my whole life. And we stand for a while and I cry for everything I've lost and all the things we're never going to do together. But thanks to Malachi, I've had a glimpse of the future and I know Joe will be OK.

And now I'm fading, and Joe feels insubstantial to me again. 'I'm so proud of what you will be,' I whisper, and then Euston fades away, and I'm back in the car park with Malachi again.

'Now what?' I say.

'You go on your next journey,' says Malachi. 'I can't help you with that bit.'

'I'd like to see them one last time,' I say.

'You will,' says Malachi, 'you will.'

And then he vanishes and, for once, I'm sorry to see him go.

Epilogue

Christmas Night

They're sitting around the table, all of them: Mum, Adam, Joe, Emily and even Emily's dad who came down by car this morning, at Adam's insistence. I've been watching them all day, though none of them are aware of me. I saw Adam and Mum making up, Mum in tears, when she finds out what happened. I've watched them drink champagne, and eat turkey. I've seen them pull crackers, and unwrap presents, and laugh together. Emily has put on a Christmas carols CD, and I love standing in the kitchen listening to the carols playing, it reminds me of being a little girl with Mum and Dad and Gran on Christmas Day. I don't mind not being part of it. I'm content to see them like this. And now my eyes are clearer, I can see how well suited Emily and Adam are. They look good together, and I'm glad.

Malachi appears through the cat flap.

'It's time,' he says. I am ready. Malachi has shown me what the future will be, and I'm happy for Adam. All my anger and pain have gone, and I feel at peace. I've come back and done what I had to do, and now I have to go.

The door blows open and everyone jumps. I follow

Malachi out into the snowy garden. It's a really starry night. I know, but can't feel any more, that it is very cold.

'How did that cat get in here?' says Adam.

'I think it wants us to follow it,' says Emily.

'It's Mum's friend,' says Joe.

They all follow Malachi into the garden. And then Joe says, 'It's Mum,' and I know they can all see me.

'Livvy,' says Adam.

'It's all right, Adam, I'm going now,' I say. 'I'll always always love you. Please don't forget that. I'm glad of what we had together, and I'm happy for you. Try to think kindly of me sometimes.'

Emily leans into him a little. 'Livvy, thanks for what you did,' she says. 'I'm sorry it has to be like this.'

'Don't be,' I tell her. 'It's just the way it is. Look after them for me, won't you?'

'I will,' she says, tears in her eyes.

And then I turn to Kenneth, and say, 'And you'd better look after my mum, or I'll be back to haunt you.'

'Oh, I intend to,' says Kenneth, who seems to be completely unfazed to be talking to a ghost. I decide I like him. I'm glad Mum's not going to be alone.

Mum stands there a little apart, and I go to her, and hug her. I can feel her warmth, but I don't know if she can feel me.

'Thanks for everything, Mum,' I say. 'I'm sorry I didn't make it easy for you, and was such a disappointment.'

'Oh my darling girl,' says Mum, 'you could never be that.'

And finally I turn to Joe, my beloved son, and say, 'Remember to be happy, and remember I will always look after you. You watch for Venus in the morning and evening. When you see that, remember me, and know that I am always thinking of you.'

''Bye Mum,' says Joe, and he smiles such a smile, it makes my heart expand with joy. I've done my job well after all.

And then everything starts to fade.

'Time to go,' says Malachi.

'Thanks for everything,' I say, 'and for putting up with me.'

'Oh get away with you,' he says gruffly. 'You're a walk in the park compared to the one I have to deal with next.'

The stars are shining very bright now, and our garden is fading to blackness, and I feel a sense of peace and contentment as I walk away and leave my life for the very last time.

Joe's Notebook

A mum is many things.

Sometimes she is kind and nice.

Sometimes she makes mistakes.

It was good to get my mum back.

But I know she had to go away again.

Even though it makes me sad.

I like it that my dad is happy with Emily.

I like it that Granny has found Kenneth.

And my mum did that.

And every year at Christmas I will look up at the stars, and make my Christmas wish.

And my mum will make it come true.

Because my mum is a star in the sky.

Acknowledgements

As usual there are many many people who supported me during the writing of this book.

I'd like to thank Etta Saunders Bingham for generously sharing her experiences of having an autistic son. I hope I've got it right, Etta!

I'd also like to thank all the many friends on Facebook who responded to an appeal to name my spirit guide cat – who knew there were so many great names to choose from? But particular thanks go to Lisa Lacourarie who came up with Malachi, which is just perfect!

My agent Oli Munson has provided enthusiastic and helpful support throughout the writing of *Make a Christmas Wish* – I hope you like the end result!

The team at Avon as usual have worked really hard on my behalf, but especial thanks go to Eli Dryden, my amazing editor. Without your acute and brilliant insights, this book wouldn't be what it is. You made me work extremely hard, but I think the end result is worth it!

And finally I'd like to say a massive thank you to you, the reader. Without you, my ideas would be nothing, condemned forever to whirl crazily round my head while my husband questions my sanity. Thank you for taking the time to pick this up, and thank you those of you who tweet me or email me. It really means a lot!

With apologies to both Dickens and Noel Coward, I'd like to also thank them for the inspiration. Livvy appeared in my head as a very angry ghost some years ago. It's been great fun finally telling her story. I hope you have as much fun reading it!

Julia